# A Stranger's Guide

# A Stranger's Guide

by

Charlotte Platt

SILVER SHAMROCK

PUBLISHING

# Chapter 1

*15 October, 1885*

    *Glasgow is a city alive with Others. Entire families of creatures live among the people, hiding in the scrum of life that has amassed around industry here. Worship of the Other is carried out next to the Sunday services and no one seems to question this. It is fascinating. I plan to document as much of the undercurrent as I can while I pursue my studies.*

    *I have managed to ascertain there are various families of flesh eaters, vampires, incubus, and a variety of spirits, all of which can be found with far less effort than one would anticipate. This city environment offers them a level of protection that is lacking in the villages, numbers flourishing with discretion. This is useful; though I am yet to decide what to do with this information. I shall record it as I am able.*

*27 October, 2017*

    October in Glasgow was much like October in Manchester—wet and edging into cold. I woke in the guesthouse to the drum of rain hitting the skylight. It was still dark out and a check of my phone showed it was just before 6:00 a.m. Growling low in my throat, I rolled over. I wouldn't have complained about a bit more sleep after the coach trip yesterday. I'd dreamt of dark spaces, pacing through blackness in the cold echo of high chasms, and I'd just get more of the same if I put my head back down.

    Grumbling as I got out of the bed, I switched on my laptop, watching it boot up while I stretched out my spine. The bed was fine, but I'm tall and a good stretch is a guilty pleasure. If I checked for work early, I had the rest of the day for tracking people down.

I mused over the bones of my plan: find people, talk to them about Sarah, find the next person. It wasn't a sophisticated way to find her, but it could work, and after three weeks I was getting desperate. I had a base here, and I could stay for longer if needed. Depended on what I got from Sarah's friends. The owner would probably be happy to extend my stay so long as I kept paying the bill.

There were two maintenance requests for small business clients, and I completed them before dressing and running over my plan again. It felt good to trace out the steps, grounding.

I really needed to see Sarah's flat share. Her things were still there, her roommates not yet scavenging the room for rent money. Not that they would hold off long; student budgeting was always tight. Maybe Dad could see to that, pay to keep the place. I only really needed to find her diary and speak to her flatmates, see if I could get details for any friends we didn't know about, or boyfriends. She never told me about her boyfriends. She'd always been talking about one of her flatmates, Alex, and I was keen to speak to her too. I had a meeting with Sarah's head of department at elevenish, so I could look about before that.

I checked the directions on my phone. It was still too early to head over to the flat. Probably no one up much before nine. The university should be first then, see if there were any tutors in. I didn't hold much hope. Not that Sarah was irresponsible with her course. She loved it almost as she loved the city, but I didn't see her sharing much with a tutor. They could be observant though, and could point out friends. Or boyfriends. It was worth a shot.

I dressed light, jeans and a shirt, sliding my jacket on top. I could always buy an umbrella if need be. I didn't usually bother with one; they just blew away in Manchester. I skipped the offered breakfast and left, joining the commuters on the street. I sought out a Costa, coffee and sugar necessary for the start of the day.

Ordering the biggest cup they had, I sat down, letting the barrier of my energy slip away as I watched people milling around me. I dislike crowds, that's why shielding myself from them with energy was my usual state of being, and the rush of it was like steel wool down my spine. Everyone moved through quickly, though, and it was intense without intent; no one was too stressed out about their coffee.

Once I was comfortable with the feel of the place, I downed my drink and left, heading up Sauchiehall Street and towards the West End. The quickest way was to cut through one of the parks, Kelvingrove. It looked large from what I saw online and there was a river I was looking forward to. Rivers are good, have an energy that's smooth and regular, even when they swell and tumble. Much better than people. There was a reason I kept my guard up around them.

This side of Sauchiehall Street seemed pedestrian, dotted with large houses and converted shops instead of the pubs and clubs I'd passed on the way to my guesthouse last night. It looked expensive in the way the houses sat back and separate, old money that paid for privacy and convenience. I couldn't say it was a bad thing, you could just feel the difference in the area. Glasgow seemed to be a city for that, mismatched parts sitting beside each other—conservatism and clubs, cathedrals and a necropolis. I could appreciate the contrast, but it'd take a while to come to grips with it. I didn't want to end up in a bad area without warning. No reason to draw the attention of the boys in blue.

Approaching tall railings, I found an entrance to the park and slipped through the iron gate onto a broad tarmac path. It was part of a network leading through the place, some branching off up a hill and others threading into wooded areas. There was a lot of people about, joggers and students and what I assumed to be people going to work from the suit trousers and trainers combo, office shoes bagged up for later. I had a clear view of most people; the park was a sweeping open space, the trees mostly bare and grasping up into the sky. There was a lot of them, trees, the grass dotted with copses here and there. Wide flower beds, bare for the winter, sat along the pathways like open graves, dark rectangles waiting to burst up.

I spotted what I thought was part of the university, a tall tower with ornate Gothic carvings at the peak, and headed towards it. The middle of the park held an impressive fountain, all fine old glamour and gold gild. The water was frigid in the October air, littered with rubbish, but it would be impressive in the summer. I threw five pence in and wished for luck before carrying on towards the looming building. Couldn't hurt.

The energy was nice, organic. It might just have been the trees or the river that ran through it in a rushing blue thread, but this was a good start to going without my usual protection. There was even some wildlife—bold little squirrels zipped between trees and peered out with more curiosity than fear. Must be used to the people by now. Probably got fed too. I managed to find my way to another gate which led to a pub, then a road, and then a reasonably clear path to the university itself.

The main building reminded me of Manchester University. It was the same monument to the value placed on learning, imposing and designed to be visible all over the city. I knew the campus was spread over various buildings—Sarah had talked about that when she was choosing it—with the jewel being that tower I was heading towards. I spotted the student union early on, a more modern building with posters and a crowd already thrumming about. Could be a good place to go looking for those flatmates, if I didn't find them at home.

I saw a campus map and made a line for it, checking over my options. It was too early for the office hours and I didn't want to be the dickhead who interrupted classes. I could mill around the university for an hour until the first set was finished or scout the flat out. I watched the students file into buildings around me and chewed my lower lip, undecided. The crackle of energy from people was starting to kick in, a hiss of white noise at the back of my skull, making my skin itch. No, better to go to the flat, sod their lie in, let the numbers settle down then come back when this was less distracting.

The map showed a path to the local subway, close to Sarah's flat. Easy enough to get a coffee somewhere and take a wander past. I could always try the door and see what I found. I was going to do it anyway but may as well pretend I was thinking about it first. Sensible, Carter.

I hefted my backpack and started looking for Byres Road through somewhere called Ashton Lane. This was an interesting little spot, full of expensive restaurants and pubs that looked trendy but not too hipster. Yet. There was a little cinema advertising retro movies and live shows, including a sing along of *The Rocky Horror Picture Show*. Well that would be fun. Sarah would like being taken to that. I felt an aching in my chest for a stretching moment as I slowed to a stop in front of the poster but pushed it aside. I needed more coffee. Sod all these feelings.

I found Byres Road and was immediately beside a subway station and a Starbucks—salvation.

Ducking inside, I tried to get my bearings a little, shake off the edges. The shop was narrow but stretched back, full of mums with prams and suits who looked like they should be elsewhere. The poor lot behind the counter was stressed enough for the rest of us, so I got in line and tried to be pleasant. Ordering something large and strong, I took the mug as close to the back of the shop as possible, hunkering down at a single table.

The university had been worse than I'd expected. I was tired and a headache was pushing forward behind my eyes, sharp as a needle. I hadn't factored for the throng of people between classes, out of practice from shielding. It had been years since I was out around crowds with no cover at all, the way Sarah walked around daily. The coffee might help with that, get me pumped enough that I would be able to ignore it. I could always buy some pain killers if it didn't.

I'd had to learn to scrutinize my emotions, make sure they were my own rather than picking up something new. So, what had brought the anxiety back, other than the being in a city I didn't know looking for my missing sister? It could be the university, the sudden contrast from the peace of the park. Or it could be the city itself, new and strange and rippling with power quite apart from the rest.

Sarah's love of the place was always clear. I could see her fitting right in. I should have practiced this before I came up here, but the police had been so unhelpful and we needed to find her. They thought she was just some daft lass run off with a new man, or that she had gotten in a 'predicament' and was unable to face the family. Like any of us would care about that, for fuck's sake.

I could feel someone watching me and looked up to meet an older man's gaze. He held my stare and gave a little nod. He was in his early fifties, I guessed, pale, with wide blue eyes and a lazy grin to match. Nice lips in a pouty sort of way, strong jaw line that could pull it off. I dragged my eyes away and checked him over.

He sat easily at a table across from me, long legs folded neatly to one side. The hair was on the long side for a professional, which I presumed he was from the suit, but it was swept back and styled neat enough. He was attractive, in that silver fox kind of way. Expensive looking clothes, black suit, and a green shirt that must have been chosen to highlight the eyes. His eyes were back to looking at mine curiously. It was an easy trick, but it gave him a quiet sense of power, electricity meeting water. Quiet in the everyday sense, the spiritual power was huge. He'd have been spotted a mile off if he wasn't shielding, but I could tell he was—not as good as mine, the edges showed through. It didn't feel the same. Interesting. But not what I needed to be dealing with now. I wasn't here to spot attractive magic users.

I gave him a nod and gulped the last of the coffee down, heading back outside.

Sarah's flat was in one of the large tenements that lined the streets, three or four stories packed on top of shops and pubs and whatever else could pay for a street front. It was a bloody busy street, and the ghost of my headache was still unfurling as I stood trying to orientate myself. I hovered close to the edge of the shop window, pressing back as the pavement became a sea of people suddenly expelled from the subway entrance.

A few places dotted around me tugged at my senses, the dull throbbing pulse of worship but not quite the same. There were certainly churches around but one felt tangled, messy. I put my head back against the wall and closed my eyes, trying to focus on what was snagging my attention. I had to trust my gut with these things.

It felt rougher than a church; the energy was raw and untamed by devotion. I wanted to see what that was—I hadn't felt anything like it before. Not that I went out unguarded much in Manchester, but I'm sure I would have noticed something standing out so much. Sarah certainly would have.

I shook my head, coming back to myself as I felt a light drizzle begin. It felt good, cool and grounding. I could go and see whatever that thing was later. The flat and her diary were more important. I pulled my guard back up in part, pushing down my energy levels so I could just sense things. Hopefully I wouldn't need to feel too much around the flat and the protection would stop the spike pushing at the base of my skull.

# Chapter 2

*5 December, 1885*

*The Collector's shop is a curiosity of the city. The gentleman himself, for it has been a gentleman I have met while investigating, seems to be well versed with Glasgow and Edinburgh. Where else, one wonders?*

*But to the point, The Collector is an individual who presents as a shop owner and sells the curiosities of magic. He is based in the west of the city with an innocuous sign that would give no indication of being anything other than a pawnbroker. He will give no name other than The Collector and that is sufficient to find him when necessary.*

*He has a variety of items in his shop which seem quite normal to those unaccustomed to the practice, but within these lay a variety of valuable pieces. The currency is not coin, but artefacts or intrigue. Intrigue is by far the preferred payment, but it is damned hard to tell what level of knowledge the man already possesses. He knew quite heartily, for example, of the incubi who sell their wares at the river, but was most pleased to learn of the skin crawlers who make their home in the city and counted that as an expensive point. For this he allowed me access to some of his more unusual items which I have listed below. I am unsure what he is and plan to return to the shop when possible. It would be most interesting to see what else I can gather. I do not have many artefacts to trade with, but my note taking in this journal should prove invaluable.*

The crowd changed a little here and there, growing thicker as the trains arrived and then waning as people milled about their lives. It was nice, sort of. Felt friendly. I thought about this as I went along the road, looking for the side alleys with access doors. Spotting the one I needed, I checked the buzzers and found names scribbled over repeatedly. Typical of student places. I pressed Sarah's for a full minute, just in case they were still asleep, then stepped back. I waited, bobbing on my feet, then pushed again.

A clattering noise came out of the speaker and then a very confused voice coughed out, "Hello?"

"Hi, it's Carter. Carter Brooks. I'm—"

"Sarah's brother, right?" came the response, a bit clearer.

"Yeah, that would be me. Can I come in?"

A click and I was left in silence. Then a loud buzzer went off, shrieking static over the speaker and the door unlocked with a thud. I went through and was welcomed by a dingy hallway. It had two doors leading off in either direction and a large stone staircase leading up into the chill air. I knew Sarah's flat was two stories up so jogged up the steps, surprised how little noise echoed around me. I came to the door and gave it a firm knock. A woman appeared as it opened, eyes narrowed at me.

"Carter?" she asked, giving me a look over.

"The very same. May I come in?"

"Sure," she said, opening it wider. She was dark skinned and had a wary face, eyeing me as I entered. The flat was decent, a cramped hallway that led to a large living room, and I could see what I assumed to be a kitchen further along.

"And you would be?" I asked since I was still being watched.

"I'm Alex. Sarah's told me a lot about you," she said, nodding to a sofa for me to sit on. They were huge and sagging and had probably seen a lot of things I didn't want to think about just now.

Alex perched on the arm of the other sofa, pushed back against one wall, and surveyed me. She was shorter than me, not hard given I'm six foot, and she was curvy but not overly so. Most of her hair was pulled up into a large topknot, thickly curled and bouncing as she moved. It gave her an air of continuous motion, energy. Snags of short strands pooled down the nape of her neck, stroking against the blazer she had layered over some magenta top underneath. Overall, it was a good look on her, nicely put together.

She was watching me like I was a live wire.

"I hope it was good. Sarah's told me a lot about you too. You're who she speaks about the most."

"Yeah, we're close. You here looking for trouble, Carter?" She asked it with a wholly sociable tone and an easy smile, but I could see real concern in her eyes. They were nice eyes, a hazel that showed the brown very strongly. I wondered just how much Sarah had told her.

"No, I'm here looking for Sarah. Figured her room was a good place to start and thought you guys might have some idea of who else I could speak to."

"Why not speak to us?" Her chin came up in defiance, daring me to dismiss her.

"I got some details from the police about the last few places Sarah was; none of you where there. Figured that's where I'd start," I said, my hands coming up to show no offence meant.

"And you didn't think we could help with that?" Her eyebrow was up now, less hostility than a strained kind of amusement that was rapidly getting under my skin.

"Given that her last known whereabouts were on her own, walking, not really. I wanted to get a look at her room, get her diary to see if there was anyone she was seeing, things like that."

"Ho boy, I sure couldn't tell you anything like who my best friend was stepping out with, definitely not," Alex began. I leaned forward and tried to cut off her steam.

"Look, Alex. I don't know why you're pissed off. But if it hadn't escaped your notice, your flatmate, my sister, has been missing for weeks and no one seems all that bothered about it. I don't know why, but I would like to change that." I grinned, too many teeth showing. I always flashed my teeth when I was starting to get my hackles raised, getting close to anger. "I just want to see if I can find anyone who might give a fuck and currently Sarah's diary seems like the best place to start."

Alex was quiet for a while, staring at me hard. She must have reached some sort of conclusion because she nodded, standing up and motioning for me to do the same.

"I'd be a crap best friend if I just gave you her diary. She'll kill me if she thinks that's what happened. I'll let you into her room and I'll let you dig around for whatever you need, and I'll tell you that she's not actually kept a diary that she's told me about for at least two years. She wasn't seeing anyone exclusively, but there were a few guys you might want to meet. I can get in touch with them for you."

Alright then. "You want to tell me what that was about in the living room?" I asked as I followed her upstairs.

"I don't know you from Adam and frankly, Sarah's described you as a bit of a dick. An unstable dick. One with his heart in the right place, but a dick," she said with a shrug. "Plus, you're right. No one seems to be asking enough questions. No one seems to care. I figure I can help you be useful."

"You figure you can help me?" It was my turn to raise an eyebrow now.

"It may have escaped your notice under that chip you are evidently shouldering, but I've lived with your sister for the past two years and I know our friends. I can get hold of people and set up a meeting with our group."

"Your group?" We were moving along a corridor upstairs and my head was starting to crowd a little again. The flat had a relaxing energy and Alex was giving off a pleasant vibe, sort of, but this was a lot more than I had expected from my flying visit.

"Yeah, our group. Some people'd call it a coven, but we're not really like that. It's more of a self-improvement class, long running. Different people with talents come to it and discuss what their gift is, how they want to develop it." She smiled as she explained, very proud of what sounded distinctly unappetising. We stopped outside an open door.

"And you've both been going to this?"

"Yes. Sarah wanted to get more from her gift, see if she could use it to heal or to help somehow. Mine's, well, different."

"Care to share or are you going to keep that one for after another staring session?" I sighed, looking around Alex into Sarah's room. Decent size for a student flat.

"You really are a jerk, huh?" Alex rounded on me, something short of a glare being sent my way.

"Blunt. It's always been an issue I've had. It isn't often appreciated," I said, seeing if there was anything I could feel out in the first instance. Nope. "It's just how I came out. And while I do try to keep a lid on it when I'm around people, I'm afraid I'm likely to be blunt for the duration of our association. At least until I can see Sarah."

Alex burst out laughing. "'The duration of our association?' What are you, a nineteen-thirties PI?" That image made me laugh too, a choked thing but a laugh nonetheless.

"Sorry. I tend to be short and Sarah being gone stresses me. It's kinda my default. I'll try to keep it polite and pleasant, but I can't guarantee how well that'll hold out. Do you want to tell me about your skills while I have a look at the room or would you prefer to wait downstairs?"

"Well, at least you'll try. How very good of you," she said, turning her back on me but staying in place. I let the silence hang as I went into Sarah's room.

It was distinctly hers, a decent sized bed covered with enough cushions to nest in with bits and splashes of colour mismatched all over. The carpet was a hopscotch of various rugs splayed over each other to coat the wooden floor and the window had a large printed wrap over it, giving diffused sprinkles of light. The posters were old classic advertisements: Chat Noire and Paris in the twenties, bright eyed young things staring out and challenging you not to seize your opportunities. It smelled of old incense and I smiled, her memory looming up.

I started examining the bookshelves as I waited for Alex to decide if she was in a sharing mood.

Sarah had kept her love of reading, a host of titles forming a mosaic wherever they would fit. There were some of the classics. She'd always had a soft spot for Bronte and Shakespeare. Then there were some on the history of art and what looked like books she would use for her studies, research material. A section towards the end of the case was geared towards the occult, which left a sinking feeling.

"My stuff isn't like your family," Alex said, "It's not as on the surface."

I paused, confused. "What do you mean?" I asked, peering over my shoulder at her. She was fidgeting a bit, to and fro like a kid in trouble.

"You know how Sarah and your mum can see? They can just tell if someone is gifted or a bit different, or if there's a spirit," she said, rolling fingers off her hand with the list. "Mine's different. I can feel if someone has a gift, and I can tell if someone is strong with it, but it's just a knowledge in me. I have old blood so my instincts are good, and if I focus hard, I can see the right decision, usually." She kept separating Sarah and Mum from me. Why?

"Usually?" I couldn't help the question. I turned back to the books lest another glare should be coming my way.

"Yeah, usually. Nothing's foolproof, you know, and sometimes you get the wrong read on someone. Or they're hiding it. Or they're just plain weird and they throw things off."

I was trying to pin down why she was so antsy about telling me this when something caught my eye in the books. Wedged on top of the occult section was a smaller volume, about the size of those Ladybird books you got in school and about twice as thick. It looked a bit battered and the dust cover was exactly that, coated in grime. The spine looked bare, but I couldn't tell if that was just because it was covered in whatever the hell was all over the rest of it. I pulled it gingerly, unsure how well it would hold together. It was really crammed in there. It came free with enough of a tug but fell to the floor. I bent to nab it and felt Alex step into the room, her vigil at the door abandoned.

"You found something?" she asked, peering over my shoulder.

"Don't know. Seems like it," I murmured, trying to wipe some of the grime off the front. It was like it was covered in ash, thick and gritty. There was a title just visible: *A Guide to the City*. Concise. I opened it and saw 'Glasgow' written in a precise hand on the first page.

"That's not Sarah's writing," Alex said, and I could feel the question in her voice.

"I know," I said, toying with reading on. It could just be a quirky book Sarah found at a second-hand shop. Or a prop. It didn't feel like one though. The book was filled three quarters full on each page, with space to add notes and scribbles in the margin. The writer used these to expand on points, rewritten areas and side narratives all over. The script was very formal, a neatness like school notes. Flicking through I could see the whole book looked to be filled, a curiosity in itself for handwritten notes. Someone had taken a lot of care with it, at least until it ended up coated in ash and stuffed into a bookshelf. Almost hidden.

The entries were all dated, the earliest being October 15, 1885. Shit. I glanced back to the first page and read what served as an introduction.

*Glasgow is a city alive with Others. Entire families of creatures live among the people, hiding in the scrum of life that has amassed around industry here. Worship of the Other is carried out next to the Sunday services and no one seems to question this. It is fascinating. I plan to document as much of the undercurrent as I can while I pursue my studies.*

Another eager student then. It didn't improve my mood.

"What the fuck is this?" Alex finally spat out, stalking away.

"Someone started writing about their time here?" I ventured. I slipped the book into the back of my jeans. Might be drivel, but there was no harm in reading it.

"I can see that. Thank you, Mr. Obvious. I meant, why the hell does Sarah have a book of some creep's ramblings on Glasgow? That's not exactly course material."

She'd started to pace, going from the bed to the window and back again as though someone would appear in the fifteen steps between.

"Alex, what is giving you a problem here?" I asked, watching her and feeling my anxiety rack up with hers.

"Something just occurred to me," she said, a hand going to her face and a nail being bitten, various emotions flashing. "It's maybe nothing."

"Spit it out, would you?" Her head snapped up to me and the flash in her eyes said I was being blunt again. I had to watch for that. "It might be helpful, even if it's just to rule it out?" I tried, hoping that would come off less confrontational.

"Sarah mentioned getting to know the city better, with her gift. She'd been all over already, of course—we all do that in freshers week getting used to the place. And when we're practicing." She waved a hand as if this was a normal occurrence. "But Sarah's been talking about going back around to places or getting into new ones we hadn't seen before."

"New places?" This was like pulling teeth.

"Yeah, like urban exploration? Getting into closed buildings or old subways, locked off spaces. Places people weren't often in, so they weren't disturbed."

I thought that one through. Great.

"Why couldn't she just like fucking and partying like a normal student?"

"Carter!"

"What? It'd be a damn sight easier to show up and shake down a few idiots in a bar than it is standing in her room, wondering if she's broken her neck falling down an underground shaft."

Alex's head turned to me like I'd slapped her.

"She's not dead," was all that came out. She said it with a finality that caught my curiosity.

"What makes you sure?"

"I'd know. I'd feel her. I might not see things in the same way Sarah does, but if she'd gone over to the other side, I would feel her there. Or my guides would tell me. I'd know one way or the other." Her voice trailed off.

"It's hard not knowing," I started, but didn't have anywhere else to go. That was it.

"Yes, it is. I love Sarah dearly and not being able to feel her, anywhere, is agonising," Alex smiled, a grim stretch of her mouth.

"Have you guys been checking, that way?" I asked.

"Of course we have, you twat. We tried that before reporting it to the police. Luke got our whole group together to see if we could find her, but we got nothing. Even if she'd been dead, we would have seen something."

"Luke?" I was getting tired of repeating her words.

"Luke Miller. He's our unofficial leader. Not that we have a leader, because it's just self-work, but he was the person to start the group off. He's good at getting people together and keeps the mood up. He thought if we all pooled together, we'd be able to find her."

"That's really helpful of him." My lips pursed, but I thought I'd kept the tone level. Alex's laugh disagreed.

"It was. He likes Sarah. Not that way," she said to my scowl, "Sarah's been going to the group for a bit under three years, her and Luke are close." Sarah hadn't mentioned a group like this in our chats, never mind a mentor. "She knew you didn't like it," Alex supplied, looking away from me. "The gift, her using it, she knew you didn't think it was 'appropriate.' " She air-quoted around appropriate. I shut my eyes to stop them rolling.

"We have different views on it."

"You have antiquated views on women and power if you ask me, but whatever," Alex said.

The fuck? "Alex, I don't know which of my views Sarah's shared, or if you just have a stereotypical view of northern guys, but can we safely assume you don't know shit about my perspective and work from there?"

"Sarah told me what you were like with your mum, resenting Sarah because she was closer to her," Alex ventured then stopped as I looked at her. A flicker of confusion showed for a marvellous second but vanished back into the fire behind her gaze.

Oh well. I took a good breath in and held it for five counts before I let it out again, trying to choose my words.

"My relationship with my mum and my views on the gift or whatever you label it, aren't relevant right now. Never mind the fact that you are totally off the mark or how exactly I'd come out with those views while growing up with my mum and Sarah. My mum uses hers for her fucking job, Jesus Christ," I said, shaking my head. "All that matters right now is that you know I want to find my sister, as we covered already downstairs, and I'm willing to do as much as I can with every lead I find. I really don't give a fuck what you do with, or think of, me so long as it is working towards getting Sarah back. Deal?"

"Deal," she said after staring me down again.

"Good. Is the staring part of your gift?" I asked, tired of it. Her eyes were nice enough but when someone stared at me this much, I was either getting kissed or punched. Those options were preferable, frankly.

"It is. It lets me dig in a bit. Like I say, I don't work the same way," she trailed off again, frowning then looking back up to my eyes. "Basically, I can focus in on someone's energy and feel my way forward. It can get a bit intense."

"Fine by me, so long as I know what you're doing and that you're not just looking for a soft spot. Can you think of anything else that could be useful here? Where's Sarah's laptop?"

"I have that—the police gave it back a few days ago, and I didn't feel right leaving it out in the open. Just in case."

"Sensible. Can I get sight of it?"

"It's not charged up. Came back from them flat."

"I have some cables back at the place I'm staying. I could charge it up overnight and see what I can find." I rubbed the nape of my neck while I glanced around. I could see parts of Sarah's work dotted around; the rest would be at her studio. I still needed to check there. I didn't know if it'd help. I just wanted to get a feel for her. I could drop my guard and see what I could feel here, but that would tip Alex off. She was clearly of the view I was unskilled and untrustworthy, and I could run with that.

"Where is it that you're staying?" Alex called as she walked to a room further down the hall. She padded back in with the laptop, a little notebook designed for carrying about.

"I'm at Renfrew Street, not too far off."

"You could stay here, if you needed. It's close to the uni and most of Sarah's favourite spots. We have another flatmate, but he's on tour with his band pretty much all the time. You'd have to use Sarah's room." The idea made me feel sick, but the thought was nice of her.

"Thanks. I might take you up on that. Depends on where we get leads."

"That's sounding a bit better at least," she said, more to herself, as she handed the computer over. I tucked it into my bag and pondered my next steps.

"Was there any particular piece of jewellery Sarah was working on?" I asked, settling on one train of thought.

"Well, she had a few commissions, but the rest of her things would be at her workshop, so you'd need to check there."

"Does she have a key here?"

"Yeah, on the table. She shares it with a few other students," Alex said, pointing to a small table beside the bookshelf. I saw a Yale key amongst a bunch of receipts, hair bobbles, and jewellery parts. That would be a good next step.

"I'll go to have a look now. Can you give me a call once you've been able to speak to those lads she was seeing?"

"Sure. Do you want me to see if I can set you up with Luke this afternoon? He'll be in the shop by then," she offered, not quite meeting my eyes this time.

"He runs a shop?"

"Oh no, he's a lawyer or something. The group meets in the back room of a shop."

"What, like a gang?" I laughed.

"For fuck's sake, Carter, it's a group meeting. We rent a room!" she snapped. "Not everything in Glasgow is crime related."

I was less and less enamoured with this group. "You remember we're from Manchester, right? We tend to keep an eye out for that shit."

She laughed a little at that, turning on her heel and walking out of the room. I went after her and down the stairs, trying to think of anything else I could get from her just now. I had the key for the workshop and that might give me some leads. I had the strange book and the knowledge that Sarah had been creeping around the city trying to find new and interesting places to screw herself up in. I had meetings with her paramours and the mysterious Luke being set up by Alex. That was the best I could do for now.

"Carter," Alex called, staring at me. She'd probably said my name more than once, by the look on her face. "Are you alright? You left the planet for a minute there."

"Sorry, just a busy head." I smiled, trying to pass it off. It wasn't a direct lie. She shrugged and nodded, putting a hand on my shoulder.

"I get you. It's stressful being here. You never have visited Sarah." I had to give her points for trying to keep the judgement out of her voice even if she didn't quite manage it. She seemed like a really annoying best friend.

"It's an interesting city," I said, neutral as I could manage. It wasn't awful from what I'd seen, but I was only about sixteen hours in and increasingly pissed off.

"Well done. You almost sounded like you meant that. Seriously, though." She turned me so we were facing each other, and met my gaze. "I want to help you find Sarah. I don't like that no one is asking questions, and I don't like that no one seems to be able to find her. I'm on the team." She said the last part very earnestly and was staring again. This had to be off putting for others too.

"Thanks for that, Alex. I appreciate it."

We exchanged numbers and I left the flat, something about her behaviour still unsettling. Alex was using her powers a lot if the staring was anything to go by, but I hadn't really felt anything coming off of her. She seemed to think only Sarah and my mum had the gift, as she insisted in calling it. I should probably have told her I had it too, but my skills were rusty. It would be more hassle than help.

Right now, I needed to find the workshop and charge up Sarah's laptop, see if she had anything on there about this urban exploration. I didn't know if the police had been told about that, but it wouldn't have helped. If the group had been looking for Sarah and hadn't found her haunting one of those spots then the police damn sure wouldn't manage it.

# Chapter 3

_I have met with a most unusual woman, of most interesting circumstance. She is a dancer at the Imperial School of Ballet in St. Petersburg, visiting Glasgow to establish whether a tour of her troop would be welcome and viable for the artistic community. In the current climate, I think not. The Italian workers have difficulty enough with their accent, and they are assisting with the development of the city. Never mind how a lad from Southside would go on understanding a visiting opera like_ I Vespri Siciliani.

_The Collector warned me that Ms. Marina, as she is known, was a most unique creature and upon my meeting with her I can confirm unique is correct._

_She travels in luxury with two large fellows, also dancers. She is a statuesque thing of the palest skin, an angular face with height in the cheekbones and a thin, straight nose. Her accent is not obvious, slipping through the conversation at times without creating difficulty, and while she is of average height for a woman, she commands a room immediately. Her behaviour carries the discipline of a soldier, though the dance schools are infamous for their training. Most intriguing, however, are her storm pale eyes. To be specific, her tears. When Ms. Marina weeps the tears formed begin to harden immediately, creating gems. These appear to be of the highest quality; she invited me to have them evaluated if I was concerned as to their nature._

_The reason for this most profitable weeping is beyond The Collector. I believe I have managed to discern it though. I have reviewed texts previously thought lost, found with The Collector, and only one other creature appears to have some similar trait. The Djinn are able to transmute physical items out of nothing visible to us on this Earth when granting wishes. If the teachings of the history of the Djinn_ *are true and they are made of fire as we are made of earth, then I would suggest Ms. Marina is one made of air.*

*When I spoke to her of this, in the politest way one can broach such a topic, she laughed with a heartiness that shocked her companions. Once calmed, she confirmed she may have been considered such once, but she now remained within our 'plane' and would not be returning to the air. It is therefore my hypothesis that she is what would commonly be called an angel and one which has been cast from the heavenly host. These are frequently painted as licentious figures that would tempt and corrupt this Earth. She, however, was of no such care. She was beautiful, but her focus of beauty was that of her dance and her travels. She cared little for those of us around her. It may be that she harbours some affection for those she trains and dances with, but I was left with no impression of this. How curious that we should see the fallen painted as wicked when they appear at best indifferent.*

*I wish to explore this matter further with her; I should hate such an opportunity to slip through my fingers. She has assured me she will be in Glasgow for the foreseeable months and would be happy to have further discussions. I will, of course, note these talks as they occur.*

I let my shield down as I walked towards the university. The streets were full of bodies and it would do me good to build a tolerance; the classrooms would only be worse. Groups of folks in a smaller space, all focused on one thing and noisy. No good.

My vacuum of knowledge about Sarah's life sat heavy in my stomach. We'd talked, monthly or so, but I didn't know anything about this group or Luke, the unofficial head. She knew I was less connected with this stuff, but it hurt that she didn't feel she could share. My experience with it had been a bit traumatic. I had tried to top myself to make the magic stop, but I wouldn't begrudge her connection with it.

We could discuss feelings and all that once I found her. Alex was right that Sarah wasn't dead. Mum or I would have felt that, even with my shielding. Her group would have felt that, too. So where the fuck was she?

Having no bearings in the city wasn't helping. Glasgow was nice to look at, the mix of old tenements and new developments rolling along with each other. A lot less red brick than I was used to, this place was all pale stone and big windows. The shops being handy was also good. This part of the city was littered with little bakeries and gastro pubs. All the better to catch students in a rush. I liked it.

As I approached the side lane leading to the university, I felt the pull of the powerful spot further up the road again. It would only take a little time to check it out. I hovered at the street for a beat, curiosity gnawing at me. No, the workshop might have an actual clue about Sarah. I set my shoulders and went into the thrum of people.

The art department had dedicated houses—actual houses the university owned—that had been converted into large studio spaces. There were wide windows in each gable end which filled the rooms with dim autumn light. Three work stations stood in the room Sarah shared, one per wall, and there was a scrum of materials dotted throughout. Mannequins and heavy tools lurked in one corner and works in progress sat awaiting completion. It felt intrusive, like I was in someone's bedroom while they were in the shower.

I could spot which work station was Sarah's straight away. It had pictures of Angel from *Buffy the Vampire Slayer* and city views I'd bet were her own, pinned to the wall. Growing up, she'd adored watching the cheesy American show, and I'd been roped into marathoning it with her. There was a spare laptop charger there at least, so I plugged the notebook in while I snooped.

She was tidier here than at home, the desk space clear. I pulled a couple of drawers open and was met with a host of tools and supplies in regimented lines. After opening and closing half the damned drawers, I stumbled upon an order book.

It was a jumble of sketched ideas and names in no real order, with phone numbers attached to the projects. There was nothing screaming out as unusual though. Some of them were a bit quirky. There was a set of what looked like thimbles with claws on the end of them, a broad leather dog collar with a D ring through it, a large cage like necklace which had a real Victorian feel. They were expensive too, if the figures scribbled beside the sketches were anything to go by. Not pricey enough to make someone disappear for though.

I shoved the book into my bag and glanced about for anything else. I closed my eyes, dropping my shield to feel out with my gift, when the door behind me opened. Yelping, I turned to see a young man entering the room, looking almost as confused as I felt.

"Who are you?" he asked, eyes hard. Charming. He was about my age from the looks of him, tall with hair bleached an off-white that was approaching violet. He had broad shoulders, but in the way rowers or boxers got, muscles used rather than grown at the gym.

"I'm Carter." I put a hand out, trying to be friendly. I probably didn't look all that friendly, to be fair.

"Carter who?" The chin went up now, his head tilting a little to look me over. He had sharp features, a thin nose matched with cheekbones like mine, quick brown eyes.

"Carter Brooks, Sarah's brother. I have her key." I held it up.

"Oh shit, right! She mentioned you before. Sorry, man. I'm Marc." His hand came to mine in a strong shake, and I got a sudden rush of feeling from him. There was guilt and fear and confusion along with a whole host of others smashing together like a bloody storm.

I looked the lad over again and saw no hint of this on his smiling face. His hair was long but up in ponytail, and he was dressed for the season in a shaggy fur coat, dark jeans, and boots. Altogether, he looked like he'd stand out in a crowd and had no problem with it. Was that eyeliner?

"You need me to clear out of the space, Marc?" I asked, letting his hand go. I could be reading too much into it. He might just feel bad for the rough looking dude with the missing sister.

"No, it's cool. I just wasn't expecting anyone to be in. Sarah and I share with another girl, but she's barely ever here and, well, Sarah's not around." He trailed off at that point and glanced about anywhere but my face.

"That's why I'm here," I said, aiming to keep it light. I couldn't discern anything unusual. He was human enough.

"I guess so. I'm sorry about that," he said. Then, looking at me properly, "Sarah and I go to some of the same parties. If you need to be touch with anyone, I can usually get a hold of 'em."

"Thanks. Alex offered to help me meet some folk, but it would be great to have someone in her class who can do the same." I smiled, surprised. Most folks wanted to stay away from trouble like this.

"I'm not from her class. I rent the space from the uni privately. It's no problem—I'd like to help. Sarah's cool. Alex is too, though she's a bit more strait-laced than Sarah, you know."

The shrug and easy grin didn't have the calming effect I'm sure it did on other people. Smiles like that were predatory. I didn't like predatory around my sister. Not that she was defenceless. She had a good head on her shoulders, but I knew what men usually meant with smiles like that.

"I take it no one's seen her since she's been reported missing then?" I asked.

"No, God, we would have said something." He shook his head.

"Just asking. There are lots of reasons people want to lay low. Friends keep that stuff quiet." I shrugged, mimicking his from moments earlier. He relaxed at that, some sort of common ground established between us.

"I know what you mean." He nodded, sucking in his lower lip as he looked me over. "Nah, Sarah didn't have anything like that going on. She was into a few scenes but nothing that would require her to hide from the police or anything like that. She liked some of the heavy stuff, aye, but she was never one for risks. She played it safe."

"Glad to hear it." I smiled again, trying to decide which version of 'the heavy stuff' would be less traumatic to hear about. Please be drugs.

"Luke always makes sure that it's all in a controlled environment. The stuff I bring in is all good quality." He smiled, lighting up like a bulb. His face was nice when he looked like that, more alive.

"Oh yeah?" I sounded like a parrot. "I didn't realise you supplied. Might ask you to hook me up depending on how long I'm here."

"Yeah, man, no problem." Marc's eyes flicked over me again, that lazy smirk pulling back through. "I'm sure lots of people'd love to help you out with that. They'd just eat you up. Sarah never mentioned you were into the scene."

"I'm her brother. She wouldn't want anyone getting crossed wires."

"Yeah, that could be weird. Who wants their brother to see them in an orgy, right?" He laughed. At least he felt like he could laugh. I felt a strong urge to punch him but laughed instead.

"Exactly. That's not her thing." Please, God, let it not be her thing. Please let me escape this fresh hell of a situation.

"We do have a party coming up. If I clear you with Luke, maybe you could see about coming? Sometimes we all wear masks, and sometimes we chill and mingle, see who floats whose boat, so to speak." He pulled his hair loose and retied it, twisting it into a low bun.

"I'd love to," I lied, feeling the kick of adrenaline flooding my blood. How had I gotten myself invited to an orgy? Why had I gotten myself invited to an orgy? "Luke being Luke Miller?" I tried vainly to pin down some parameters.

"Yeah, that's the guy. Hey, it won't be too weird for you, with it being folk who know Sarah?" he asked, tilting his head as he did.

I should get a label, *'lost sister, seeking clues.'*

"Everyone's new to me up here; it'd be weirder if it was people I knew." I shrugged again, feigning indifference. Why was I still having this conversation?

"You're still living South, aren't you? Sarah mentioned there was a good scene down there. Didn't really go there though; liked the privacy of up here."

"Manchester's a big city but scenes can be small, too much overlap. I'll be cool. No asking about Sarah unless someone says they want to speak," I said, turning to unplug the laptop. It would be nowhere near charged, but I wanted to be out of this space more than anything else right now. Too much information in too short a time. My brain was screaming.

"That's chill of you, dude, thanks," Marc said, patting my arm, and I could practically feel him purr. He was pleased about something in this situation, and I doubted it was the chance of seeing me naked. That warranted further questions, but I wanted to check what Alex knew about Marc before I shoved myself any deeper down this rabbit hole.

"No worries, mate." I pulled my bag open and loaded the laptop and charger as casually as I could.

"Let me get your number," he said, pulling out his phone.

"Sure." I smiled, a little too hard. I really wanted to be out of here. We swapped numbers, and I made for the door.

"Has Luke met you yet?" he asked, and my heart sunk.

"No, Alex was going to set us up."

"That's a good plan. Luke's chill with Alex. It's a good way to meet him," he said with a nod.

"I'm going to head off and see if I can get any more info. Hit me up when you can."

"Will do, Carter," Marc called as I managed to escape. What the fuck was I going to do about an orgy invite?

I got outside and into the rain. I loved it suddenly, the clean, fresh feeling of a physical pull away from the blaring chatter of my brain. I wanted to be somewhere that wasn't here and found the nearest university map. There was a park nearby. Not the one I'd come through this morning but a botanical garden. Perfect. There was a route that didn't take me through the uni—wonderful, I'd had enough of people. My shield should be down in case of anyone interesting but sod it, it could stay until I got to the park.

I left the campus, emerging onto a main road—Great Western Road, according to the map. I set off towards where the gardens should be, rolling the tension out of my shoulders. The area was decent. Sandstone was obviously popular here. Most of the buildings were made of it. It didn't feel all that different from home—a bit more pretentious, maybe. There was certainly a crowd of hipsters at every coffee shop I passed, being most street corners. There were a few artsy shops that would be expensive and unsatisfying, if what I could see in the windows was right. Not as many pubs as I'd expected.

As I approached the gardens, I saw a large church spire on my left, right around the spot of the old energy. It certainly looked like a church. Getting closer to the notice board, I saw it was a bar—a fancy one at that. It was called Òran Mór and looked like it was long converted. I'd have taken it for a church still if I wasn't pressing my face up to the railings to read the board though. It was posh, hosted a night where you could get a meal and a pint while a live play was performed, and it boasted a whisky bar. Of course there was a whisky bar. I don't hate whisky, but I don't love it either. Had my fill of people telling me how great it was when I worked behind a bar. Give me vodka or tequila.

The place held my curiosity though. The pull of something old and wild seemed mismatched to a bar and theatre. I toyed with the idea of slipping inside but exhaustion won out. A clear head would give me a better view. At least it had stopped raining now.

Turning, I spotted two squat red brick buildings with Tudor style black timber, wattle and daub on the upper story. They stood like little guards to the park entrance, proud and totally out of place among the iron railings. A large glass and metal structure rose up further back, dull from the drizzle. I crossed the road and entered, headphones in to dissuade any friendly advances. There were diverging paths, one leading up to what I took to be a hot house and the other out along more trees. I took the tree route and wandered up the sloping hill, cracking my neck.

There were people sitting throughout the park, on benches and under the trees on the grass, so I settled against a well-established horse chestnut with a broad trunk. Nature made it easier. I could feel the pull of a river nearby too, which was wonderful.

I lowered my bubble, the green space mercifully quiet. I could feel the river better now and the Òran Mór bloomed out like a briar rose, tangled and wild. That was something that needed looking at, nagging and snagging at me.

I felt around a little more. There was the water, and there was the flicker of something underground, a vague feeling of something large and elemental that vanished when I tried to focus on it. Well that was different. It had either put up a shield or it hadn't really been there and I was going crazy. Crazy was reasonable given the morning.

Setting it aside as another thing to look at later, I pulled out the book from Sarah's room. If I was going to get used to keeping my guard down it would be better for me to practice. Reading here was as good a way as any.

The diarist had certainly been busy given the number of entries. These varied between observational notes to detailed descriptions of creatures and people encountered, detached reports on the life around them. I found one from early 1886 that described Glasgow University and the ornate steeple I'd seen at the campus. The writer agreed it was *'ostentatious but to be expected from a university that bragged of its money in every way but openly.'* Quite the little critic.

I couldn't decipher if the writer was male or female, though by the timeframe was more likely to be a male. It read like someone on a scientific expedition, noting everything down but separate from the things they observed. He didn't want to be connected. There was an element of pride in the isolation. Not clinical, but something like that.

He'd been exploring the city and documenting what he found, the 'Other' as he called it. Some of the descriptions were brief, *'coven of witches, mostly harmless but some with talent,'* and some went into scientific detail, observations of habits and routines over weeks.

I read through the first few pages: people and the city itself, notes about vanishing statues, and disappearances along the rivers. The writer was aware he risked being ejected from the university for his practices and discussed attending church every Sunday, keeping up appearances. There was even mention of Lodge meetings, but I wasn't getting into that.

Not yet, at least.

My phone rang, dragging me out of the diarists' musings. I grabbed it out of my pocket and answered automatically, a bad habit from freelancing.

"Hello, how can I help?"

"Carter?" It was Alex, thank goodness.

"Yes, speaking" I said, leaning my head back against the trunk and closing my eyes. I could feel the steady beat of nature coming through and slumped into it, enjoying the sensation. The wood was pleasant against my scalp, cool from the rain.

"I've spoken to Luke. He wants to meet you."

My eyes opened in surprise. "That's good," I said, neutral as I could manage.

"He wants to see if you can help with Sarah, as soon as possible," she said in a rush, sounding pleased as punch. "I have classes until three, but he said he'd meet us at the shop any time after that."

"I don't know where that is."

"I can meet you when I'm done and take you there?"

"That'd be great, thank you." I smiled, trying to put it into my voice.

"Cool, meet me at the subway station and we can make it from there. Bye."

I was getting to meet the mysterious Luke. He seemed interested in finding Sarah which had to be good, right? Some of the other things I'd heard made me a little dubious, but I wasn't going to judge the guy if he liked swinging or whatever. Each to their own and all that. As long as he was helping me find her, I didn't care.

What to do 'til then? I could stay in the gardens until I could face people, then go back to Renfrew Street—charge her notebook, and read more of this little exploration of crazy in the 1800s.

I put my head back against the tree again, slipping one headphone back towards my ear, when I sensed something come up beside me. As if it had stepped out of the ground. Oh, fuck me.

It felt curious, so I cracked one eye open to look. An old woman stood there, smoking and wispy at the edges, with a smile on her face. She wasn't tall, maybe a head above me from my seat, and appeared content to watch me for the moment. This was new.

"You're here looking for someone," a rich voice whispered close in my ear.

"My sister," I said, opening the other eye and glancing around. No one else nearby to share this weirdness with. Joy.

"Blood always calls to blood." Her lips moved but the words still came from close by my ear, wind stirring my hair.

My spine tingled and I held myself still, fighting panic. Don't freak out over a tree, Carter.

"You're not the usual that comes in here," she said.

"What would the usual be? Do you see people often? Or do people see you often?"

She laughed, smiling again. "Sharp for a young one."

"I try," I said. Words didn't want to leave my throat. I was stamping furiously down on the panic sparking along the edges of my brain, my fingertips, snaking down the long muscles of my legs as my heart jumped in my chest. She was most certainly not human, and I looked to be talking to myself. Or a voice in my head.

This was why I didn't deal with this shit.

"We see a lot here in this green," she continued, watching me with dark eyes, like rich earth. "We see people come and go and come again. Much like we do in a ring."

"You're a tree spirit?" I asked, turning my head to look at her properly. She was immaterial still, but I could see her face clearer now. Her eyes were almost black and her skin was a deep tan, like someone who worked outside all the time. Guess she did.

I did not like this.

"Well done. There's a few of us here now. We've grown into the place."

"That's very interesting. If you don't mind my asking, why are you talking to me?" I tried to be polite but the anxiety was pushing. Sweat started to seep down the back of my neck, chilled by the breeze.

"It's not often we get one who can see us," she said, pushing out her lower lip. "It's nice to speak to those who can. There were one or two who used to come regularly, but none for some time."

"I can understand," I said, surprised by her sadness. I hadn't expected anything to miss me while I was burying my gift. It left me with a vague feeling of guilt perched between my ribs.

"I reckon I know the one you're seeking," she whispered, close to me again.

"What?"

"A girl, this blood you're seeking. Been here a while. Used to come and do the same thing you're doing now. Not as talkative as you but a bonny one, and good with what she did. Not here anymore though. Not seen her."

"Do you know how I can find her?" I asked, twisting around to face her.

"No. I'm sorry." She shook her head and sounded like she meant it. "But we can ask others to look."

"Others?"

"Ones like us, other branches. Some of us are fixed, some of us not. Some can go between. We can look, if asked."

"That would be good, if we find anything to say where she is," I said.

"Or where she's not," the tree spirit said with a solemn nod.

"That too," I said, feeling like something was being talked around. "If I can ask, why would you help me?"

"We like her. She was nice when she came. Polite. Got a bit upset when one of us first came forward, and didn't talk like you do, but nice. We don't like seeing young ones lost. Maybe we can't help, truly, but the offer is there."

"Thank you. I think I understand." I didn't. "Do you have a name, should I call out to you?"

"None of that sort of thing for us. We are as we are." She waved away the question with the shape of a hand. "Come and sit by me and ask. If we can answer, we will."

"You keep saying we. Are there many of you?"

"A handful of us here, a handful there. We are enough."

"Thank you. Can I ask one more question?" She nodded. "How on earth do you know English?"

She laughed again, shaking her head "I'm not speaking to your ears, dearie. I'm speaking to your spirit. No language there."

"Oh, okay. I'm going to go now. Thank you."

"Take care," she said and then was gone, like a bubble popping.

I was so done with this place.

I stood up and grabbed my bag, wiping dirt off my jeans. I pulled my bubble solid around me as I left. I felt chased by the spirit, the sound of her voice. My anxiety flooded out as I went, sweat and the twitches of adrenaline clashing as I tried to settle myself.

What the fuck was I meant to do when a tree started talking to me? That's not what happens in normal situations. That's not what you do in the normal world. You'd look like you were high, or crazy, or in the middle of a breakdown when a tree starts talking to you. I didn't want to get labelled as being crazy. It was hard enough to focus on finding Sarah without worrying I'd get sectioned.

I stared down Byres Road, back to the train station. I was meant to be walking around with my guard down, but I could barely stomach it. Three hours was a long time to be around people. Fuck that. I could look at the laptop—I did that for a living. I knew how to do that backwards.

# Chapter 4

I have been discussing the nature of rituals with The Collector. We deliberated the principles of transubstantiation and the envelopment of the pagan traditions within the church, the basic control of the masses. The Collector also expounded on the modern use of ritual, not for social advantage but individual development.

There are rituals an individual can undertake to contact ancient things, which the pagans worshiped, to bargain. He told me of wishes granted, not dissimilar to those talked about in tales of djinn, but with vastly greater power. These sound comparable to traditional demonic exchanges though without the sale of a soul. Some form of exchange must occur, either through worship or sacrifice.

He allowed me to read the details of such transactions, covering all the base desires of love, beauty, and riches. What struck my attention was a trade offered by one such being, a boon of your own description in exchange for the sacrifice of time. This being can be appeased by rituals that take a significant undertaking, years in some instances. This allows it to collate the energy invested as well as the sacrificial items. It requires total dedication but the rewards are both tangible and far in excess of those found elsewhere. I asked The Collector if he has undertaken such rituals and he advised he had not, though he was aware of others that allowed symposium with such beings. I am tempted to develop this further.

I find myself wondering if my friend inherited his title. If he is just one of a number of Collectors who have carried this knowledge forward. It would explain his depth of understanding for such a fellow, barely beyond his thirtieth year in appearance but well read and with a knowledge most of my professors could only hope to attain. I remain uncertain if I should discuss this with him or retain *the theory until I discover further evidence. I will ruminate on the issue. I must seek out some other matters for him meantime.*

The subway back was uneventful, and I wandered towards the guesthouse dragging my heels. This was not what I liked my life to be like. I liked the order and structure I could create with my business. I liked not knowing things people didn't want to share. I liked not having trees accost me in the park while I was trying to calm down. This gift dragged you in and shoved you against things you weren't meant to know, and I hated being exposed to it again.

But it was working. I had potential leads on Sarah since this morning; I wouldn't have those without it.

"Fuck it, Carter," I muttered, hefting my bag higher up my shoulder. "Charge the laptop, read the book, meet Alex." It was a plan, though a vague one. I would keep my head busy and not think about a tree spirit speaking to me.

The laptop would only take about an hour to get active from a totally flat battery—I could read while it charged. I could keep doing things 'til the panic sank further down my chest, less likely to spill. I reached the door and went straight upstairs, keeping my headphones in.

I chucked my bag on the bed and followed it, flipping onto my back and glaring at the window.

I knew I was being a brat but the churning in my gut wouldn't stop. I was ruffled down to my bones. Sitting up I put the laptop on charge then went down again, checking my emails on my phone. Once they were answered I fished the book out of my bag. It smelled old, the musty fug you got in shops where stock hadn't moved in a long time. I ran one finger along the grime and balked, wiping it off on my jeans. Ash, maybe, or very fine dust.

I'd reached my fill of weird stuff for the day. I hadn't even met the legendary Luke or the rest of this group yet. Did I want to read the ramblings of another enthusiast of this gift? I shrugged, thumbing through the entries and looking for something normal. Even our guide writer must grumble about people, or shops, or something.

I found a section discussing a dubious shop run by The Collector, a chap who sounded part scam and part charlatan. The guy's writing sounded grounded at least, more than I had expected, if a little... I wasn't sure. He was ambitious. I was still presuming it was a man. Felt like a guy, and one who wanted to get his hands on more powerful things than he could do himself. That got messy too easily; dangerous. It read like he was thorough though.

A flick through the rest of the book showed continued investigations over years. Determined guy, this one. Sarah had thumbed through this more than once if the dog-eared pages were anything to go by. She was obviously interested. It would let me get a feel for what else to expect in the city, I supposed.

I left the book on the bed and went to the laptop, jabbing the power button. The screen lit up but faded again, too low. Alright then, that would need a while longer.

I weighed my options, balancing on one foot and wrapping my arms round my chest. I could read more of the interesting, if not unsettling, guide while the laptop charged. I could email my mum and update her. I could catch an hour's sleep, make up for the early start and the creeping exhaustion from having my guard down. It would get easier, but sleep might rub off the edges of the adrenaline hangover too.

I settled to the idea and stripped to my boxers, closing the curtains before slipping under the covers. The book was tucked under my pillow so I could read if sleep evaded me, and I set an alarm on my phone for an hour.

I was surrounded by blackness, as if I was staring up into the sky on a clear night. Except I wasn't laying on anything. I was just there in the middle of a void.

This was new.

I'd had a few dreams associated with the gift, October being the worst, but not like this.

Turning my head to glance to either side, but there was more nothing. I tried to walk forward and found I could do so, but I couldn't see myself moving anywhere. I swung my arms out and touched nothingness all around. Fuck this. I put my hands to my face, patting down to my neck and shoulders. I was here at least. With nothing else to do, I began to walk forward again.

"Hello?" I called out, hoping for an echo. I was answered with a deep chuckle.

"It speaks," said a voice that belonged to something immense. I stopped, closing my eyes for all the good it did. It was almost human sounding but moved through my whole body like the ripple of an earthquake. Old then, as well as big. "I wanted to see who was here to cause difficulties and I find a scared pup," it continued.

"Do I know you? I usually know people before they're this rude to me." I opened my eyes again. Still black.

"You don't know me, but you will. And I will come to you whenever I wish, and you will not be able to stop me," the voice promised, cool and pleased.

"I suppose there's not a huge amount to be gained from asking your name?"

A further chuckle, "I have none. However, you may call me Dex, if you wish."

"I'm not sure I want to talk to you at all, but it's polite to ask. Is there a reason you're speaking to me?"

"I know why you are here."

"Here being a massive black void I can't see out of?" I regretted the words as I said them. Antagonising the thing was probably a bad plan. I had no point of reference for this shit. Fuck.

"Here in this city. Here hunting." It rumbled the last word in a way I felt along my bones.

"Wasn't aware that's what I was doing," I said, glancing around again. I could faintly make out the shape of something moving under me, vast enough that it was like watching an ice sheet creep in.

"Aware or not, you hunt. For a girl. Or for those who harmed her."

"Is there any point in my asking why you think she was harmed?"

"Ones such as I do not think, they know."

"Ones such as you?"

"Old things. Old enough to know your needs and intentions long before you do." Something in the tone of that last part made my stomach jolt, tense and quivering. My heart kicked against me, railing out of my ribs. This was not a good meeting or a good situation.

"Needs and intentions, huh. So how old are we talking?"

"Old enough to recognise a human stalling for something to say."

"Great, so a sassy ancient being decided to fuck with my sleep pattern." I was grateful for the chuckle that came after that.

"You are panicked because you do not know my intentions and wonder how I brought you here."

"As far as psychic readings go, you're getting warmer."

"I could assist you."

"You kinda of skipped a few steps there, mate. How could I trust you to help when you jump into my dreams without warning?"

"I did not come into your dreams, Carter, I brought you where I wanted you." Ah, it knew my name. Fuck. That wasn't good in any of the traditional senses. Names had power.

"My apologies. You can see where my confusion may have come from?" I asked, still watching the shape moving in the blackness.

"Indeed. You are still stalling."

"I'm wondering why you'd want to do what you're offering. And why you're talking to me. And who or what you are. Lots of things, really."

"A curious mind can be a good thing. Do you think you could understand the answers?"

"I think I could try," I shot back at the smugness behind the mystery voice. What sort of a name was Dex, anyway?

"A shortened one," came the answer.

"I didn't ask that out loud."

"You didn't need to."

"That's creepy. Why are you offering to help me?" There was a silence and I felt a shift in the darkness, like a cat shaking itself off.

"I like the hunger of your mind. I could use it. If you let me, I would help you with your hunt." I felt a large eye watching me from far off. I could feel it was just the one, somehow, in this void place. Fuck me.

"Yeah, I'm still not sure 'hunt' is the right word."

"You set out with vengeance in your heart. You think she is dead and plan to avenge her."

"She's not dead." I said, too quick.

"No, she is not," it agreed, and I hated myself for the arc of hope that flew up my chest. "But she will be if she is not found."

"That sounds like a threat." I stepped forward and was knocked to my arse by a rumble through the void.

"If I wished to kill your sister, I could do so without you. I do not wish to do so. I care little of her fate and my offer is simple. You do what I need, and I will assist you."

"What do you need?" I laughed, staying on my back. It didn't change the view; I wouldn't be changing anything here.

"Yes. Even ones such as I have desires and your physical body can help with that." There was a pause, full of potential, while my mind raced.

"Am I going to be given time to think about that? And are you going to answer any of my other questions?" I asked.

"You will have time. And I have given you all the answers you should need. Consider my offer."

"Sure thing."

"And I leave you with a question."

"Go on then," I said, shaking my head.

"Why have you not simply asked me where she is?"

# Chapter 5

_7 December, 1885_

The Collector has allowed me time with certain items to create records of them. He finds my curiosity an unusual but useful indulgence, with assistance within the shop being the only requirement for my continued study. I have noted my favourite discoveries so far below, but I continue to be confounded by how this gentleman has access to such a variety of items without substantial risk. Though the creatures of the Other I have discovered have so far been benign, the collection at his disposal is such to attract the avarice and malice of interested parties, and yet he remains free from harm.

One presumes he makes the usual payments to officials, within this city at least, to ensure protection from the usual criminal element, but what about that of the Other? I do not know with certainty yet how he protects himself, but I intend to detail any discoveries of interest below.

The first such one, as I was handling today, is a bone-handled knife. It is a jawbone, with the blade housing running the length of the bone. The teeth are intact and sharp, though from the number and variety one could think they were human. This knife will cut the wielder upon use and is not guaranteed to bleed clean, with notes of infection and known deaths from sickness of the blood. I am told a lack of use makes the knife hungry, and it is thought it may alter or enhance emotions of those around it to ensure bloodshed. The Collector tells me this is often gifted and frequently won as a spoil of battle. Within his shop it is offered for sale but not recommended for human possession.

I woke up soaked, swinging at a phantom perched on my chest. The dregs of the dream sloughed off me in a cold sweat and my chest shook with the rattle of my heart trying to stall, shaken out of its rhythm. I took a shuddering breath in and held it for a long count, breathing out slow as I could.

"Come on, Carter, you're in Glasgow. You're here" I said, threading my hands through my hair.

I tightened my grip and pulled 'til I could only focus on the sharp pain. It quelled something, my brain kicking in, and I kept breathing in counts until the pattern was a rhythm. I could do this.

I let go and ran a hand over my face, focusing on the feel of my skin. Rolling out of bed, forcing myself not to think, I pushed myself into the small bathroom, turning the shower on. I set it to hot and got in, drenching myself under the water until I was flush pink.

Sitting on the bed, towelling my hair, I went over what had happened. I could rationalise it as stress, or as my fears for Sarah manifesting. I could make myself believe it.

Wasn't true though.

Something slipped in while I slept and had taken me a wander to somewhere—fuck if I knew where—then taunted me about Sarah. Was taunted the right word? Felt like it. It had given me a name, but it likely wasn't a proper one. At least not enough to use in magic. Not like I would be able to do shit, anyway. Shit.

So, what was it, and how the hell did it know me? Was it honest in the offer? Fuck me, and fuck this place. I wanted to go back to the damned tree spirit. Tendrils of fear still crept close, crowding the room. I'd never encountered something like this. I'd never even heard of it. This was why I didn't deal with this shit.

I pulled on some clothes and checked the laptop again. Charged now, it powered up like a dream, right until it asked for a password. Fuck. I tried different variations of the usual poor choices, but Sarah had listened to my nagging and set a personal one. I stared at it for a hard second then closed the lid, shoving it back in my bag. Alex might know the password, or have an idea, so I could ask her.

I gave my room a once over again and stopped, nabbing the book from under my pillow. Might be an idea to get some food as well. My bones ached and it would be better to keep my blood sugar up and all that bollocks. I bumped down the stairs and left the guesthouse, heading back towards Cowcadens.

Alex was propped against the Starbucks sipping on something tall with a multi-scribbled label as I walked out of the station. I eyed it for a moment too long, and she snapped her fingers in front of me.

"Hey, Carter, you need this more than me?" she asked, glaring.

"Sorry. I might need to get one," I said, shrugging to shift some of the tension. "Do you know Sarah's password, by the way?"

"It's usually her birthday backwards. You want this? It's a mocha." I couldn't tell if she was taking the piss or not but shook my head. "You look like shit," she offered helpfully.

"Gee, thanks, and I'm the blunt dickhead?"

"You alright?"

"A bit shaken up. Long story."

"Tell me the short version while we walk," she said, pushing off the wall and heading towards the gardens. I followed her, glancing back at the coffee shop retreating in the distance. Alex pushed her cup into my hand as we came to the large junction.

"Drink then talk," she said.

"It's kinda hard to explain," I said, sipping the drink and revelling the heat it brought to my chest. "Probably better after our meeting."

"You think you'll have a clearer head then?" She snorted and I frowned, passing the cup back.

"Do I want to know what you mean?" I asked.

"I think you're going to find out some stuff about Sarah you might not like and now would be a good time to clear your mind." She shrugged.

I felt a dark little part of my brain twist in dislike and pushed it back. Alex obviously had some ideas about me and they'd have to be resolved. That was the nice thing to think, right? Nicer than telling her

I could dip in her mind and tell her secrets she didn't want to tell herself. We continued down the street in silence.

"Did you have any luck with those guys?" I asked.

"One of them. The other hasn't text back yet. I can get a hold of him tonight if needs be. I know where he works. Do you want to meet them both together?"

"Separately. Save them any embarrassment."

She snorted. "Your sister's missing and you're worried you'll hurt their feelings?"

"More like one will clam up if he doesn't want to tell the other how he likes to fuck, but yeah, feelings," I growled, glancing over at her. "That an issue?"

"No, no issue here. I just find it weird you're pussyfooting around."

"Says the woman who forgot to tell the police my sister was running around to all these abandoned buildings."

"That's some bullshit," she spat, stopping. I glanced at her hands, ready to push back on a heel if she swung for me.

"And yours wasn't?" I stepped closer as people moved past us on the footpath. "Where the hell is this coming from?"

"When were you going to mention you'd met Marc?" she asked, crossing her arms.

"I don't know, maybe when I was done speaking to the cult leader you set up a parley with. What's the issue?"

"He said you wanted to come to the party. Sarah never mentioned you being on the scene."

"I'm glad to know news travels so fucking fast. I said I'd attend the party because lots of people who know Sarah should be there. People who talk when disinhibited, which last time I checked tends to happen when an orgy goes well!"

"Shut up!" she hissed, glancing around like someone would be listening. "They're not orgies. They're parties. Open minded people coming together and enjoying themselves."

"Alex, I don't care who or what you fuck. So long as there's no kids or dead bodies involved, knock yourself out. I saw an opportunity to check out a crowd of people who know Sarah and took it. You worried I'll spoil your reputation?"

"Oh, fuck you, Carter. I'm here trying to help, and you're slipping around like a fox."

"What does that even mean?" I sighed, my hand going to my forehead and massaging my temples.

"It means I don't trust you poking around that area of Sarah's life," she said, mouth pulled off to the side and glaring at me again. Oh fuck this tantrum. I leaned in, eye level to her and glared back.

"I'm looking for my missing sister. I don't care what she's been doing. I want to know she's alive, safe, and can come back here, or home to my parents, if she wishes. Now stare at my soul or whatever the fuck it is your particular brand of this weird bullshit is and tell me what part of that was untrue."

She glowered back before turning away and huffing a growl.

"I know you're not telling me the truth about something," she said. "But none of that was a lie."

"Right. So now we've again agreed we're working on the same thing. Can we continue on to this infernal meeting?"

"Fine, but only because I don't want us to be late for Luke. After that you're telling me whatever it is you're hiding."

She started walking again and I followed, rolling my eyes.

"Not that I owe you any explanation but sure. If it'll stop you flipping between pleasant and psychopathic every half a conversation, we'll do that." Sanctimonious cow. I'd tried being nice. She could go stew in her own sense of entitlement. "Is there anything I should know about Luke?"

"Like what?"

"I don't know. Does he have a facial scar? Can I not mention The Beatles? Anything like that?"

"Well, he's a lawyer so don't crack any of those jokes, but other than that no. He's great."

We arrived outside a hippy looking shop, the store front painted a deep teal and the window full of fairy statues and crystals. It looked nice, if nothing special; you'd see similar in any other city. We stepped through the door, Alex first, and I felt the change as the door closed.

There was a man sitting across from the entrance in a low sofa, arms outstretched along the back. Oh, coffee shop guy. Still in the nice green shirt too. Alex moved forward to make the introductions, but he beat her to it.

"Carter, I assume?" He smiled, standing and holding out a hand. His accent wasn't Glasgow, a bit softer and lilting, but it was Scottish.

"That would be me. You're Luke," I said, needlessly. His hand was warm and dry and I spotted a silver bangle lurking under one of the cuffs. Something about the easy smile was setting me on edge, and it felt like I had a crackle of energy down my spine when he took my hand. No, not felt like. He was testing if I had skills. How damn rude.

"I am, indeed. I'm so sorry about Sarah," he said with the air of someone who was used to saying it. A lot of bad news for clients then. "We're all distressed over her absence. Sarah was a huge benefit to our group. Such a joy for life, and so much curiosity."

"She was always a bit of a cat that way." I grinned, my smile stretching too tight as I pulled my hand free. Alex stepped in to save us both.

"Shall we go to the back room, so we can speak?" she asked, nodding to a door covered with a sheer curtain.

"Lead the way," I said, hands twisting the strap of my bag.

It was Luke who moved forward, nodding to the shop keeper as we went past. She was an interesting lady, bright red hair up in a bun to reveal tattoos along her neck and collar bone, swirling in a knotted pattern. She looked like she didn't miss a lot.

The room had a large circle marked on the floor and smatterings of throw cushions, bean bags, and mismatched chairs scattered around the periphery. I glanced about trying to keep my brows down.

"This room is for group activities," Luke said. They had everything lying about: crystals and ritual items on tables, singing bowls and an athame out in plain view. "We undertake activities together here with other rooms for one on one or smaller gatherings," he continued, watching for my reaction.

"That's great to hear. Can we speak about Sarah now?"

He raised an eyebrow briefly but nodded, sitting on one of the chairs and motioning to an ancient, overstuffed love seat for me and Alex to share.

"Sarah's been working with our group to explore her powers for some time. We're multi faith in so much as we all have some connection to the above but no set allegiance."

"Not Wiccans or mystics or whatever," Alex said, raising an eyebrow at me.

"Noted," I said, looking again to Luke. He was watching me as if he was trying to puzzle something out. "Yes, Luke?"

"You have a connection." No question in his tone.

"Bingo. How does that matter?"

"Sarah never spoke of you having it. She mentioned your mother, and her own. She was excelling. Sarah's very talented, but she was inexperienced outside of group work. That could lead to her being reckless. I'm concerned you may share those traits." Well, you had to give him points for bluntness, didn't you? Got to admire the bare face of that comment.

"We share a lot of traits. Sarah uses her connection more than me, and we have differing views on that."

"You don't enjoy your gift?" Something like a smile was on Luke's face as he said it, though he moved it away quickly. Curiouser and curiouser.

"I found it less than helpful. More of a concern than a gift." I smiled, batting my lashes to diffuse the glare coming from Alex. Luke noticed and tilted his head a fraction.

"You hadn't told Alex? She's talented and shared a lot of practices with Sarah." Alex flashed him a smile but came back to glaring at me shortly thereafter.

"I'm sorry, okay? I keep it under wraps. And it isn't like you broadcast yourself as my biggest fan."

"Why can't I sense you?" She frowned, looking back to Luke like a child looking to a parent. His face changed into a broad smile before he looked back to her again.

"Because Carter here is very good at shielding, I would wager. Were you concerned we were a group of eccentric theatricals?"

"Something like that." A bunch of idiots dressing up and playing Halloween was more the phrase I would use. "Though you're not dissuading me with that handshake trick." Luke laughed at that, a warm sound in the cold room.

"My apologies. I had assumed some things as well. Sarah didn't speak of you having any knowledge of these matters. I worried you were here looking for someone to blame for her disappearance."

"I'm just trying to find out where she is," I said, watching Luke as he considered my words. He wasn't entirely wrong. "You said Sarah was studying here?"

"Yes, she's been coming to the group since she came to the university, or shortly thereafter. She's worked with a variety of different magic types, stretching her skills. We allow a mixture of group and personal work and this lets people learn to see the other side more clearly."

"Sarah wouldn't really need that..." The rest of the sentence died in my throat. "Sarah was more comfortable in her skills than me, and she had more practice with Mum, so she wouldn't have any difficulty there."

"She felt she did," he said. "Between her studies and personal, issues, shall we say, she felt she was losing touch with her gift." His comments tugged at a concern in the back of my mind.

"She didn't mention any extra studying to me," I said in the least accusatory way I could manage.

"As you say, she knew your views on the topic. I imagine that's why she never mentioned you to me when we worked together," he said.

"You worked together a lot?"

"Sarah's invaluable," Alex chipped in, grinning in a way that didn't reach her eyes. "She's a natural. Could work energy well with the group. Luke was helping her get used to working with other people's energy." I raised an eyebrow at the older man and he nodded.

"She wanted to explore her powers. That's what we help people achieve." He leaned forward, opening his palms to me. "We all want to see her back home safe. If there's anything we can do to help, all our resources are at your disposal."

"Thank you for that," I said and meant it. It was nice to feel someone else, with a bit of clout, was serious about Sarah being missing. The guy was obviously well put together and confident enough for me to bet he had a reason for that. "You mentioned she'd been working with the group a while?"

"Yes, she had been pursuing skill development with my assistance, testing her gift in different situations. If you don't have a lot of experience with your powers, then it may be too dangerous for you to replicate."

"Worried I'll draw too much attention?" It was out before I could help myself, and I felt the chill of the look they gave me.

"I was more concerned you might not be able to protect yourself, but I see your plan is to disarm any potential threat with sarcasm," Luke said, clicking his tongue. "I would feel better if you'd allow me to gauge your level of power. I can ask someone to assist you with the search if necessary and—"

"I'm doing that already," Alex said, frowning between the two of us. "Or do I not get a say in finding my friend?"

"I'm sorry, Alex. I didn't mean to dismiss your role." Luke smiled, settling her. "I simply intended to see if we need ask anyone else to assist. Carter, would you allow me?"

He stood, beckoning for me to do the same. I got up from my perch and stepped closer, waiting for whatever it was he intended to do. He held his hands up, shoulder height and palms facing me again.

"If you'd be so kind." He nodded to my hands. I stepped closer and placed my palms against his, glancing away so we weren't staring. This wasn't awkward and space invading at all.

"Carter, what I'm going to do next is feel your level of energy. This usually shows how well connected someone is," Luke said, breath tickling my cheek.

"Usually?" I glanced back to him, cocking a brow.

"Some people don't have a good connection despite having a lot of power; others the opposite. It's a general tool rather than an in-depth test."

"I could always just drop my guard," I said and was met by a sardonic flash behind his eyes.

"While I'm always in favour of guards being dropped around me, if it's your intention to stay hidden while you look for Sarah it would be best to test this way."

"I'm willing to go unshielded, it's just easier for me to keep it up while I'm around people," I said, trying to hold eye contact without it being weird. It was weird, anyway. This guy was so self-assured it should have been off putting.

"Then by all means," he said with a smirk, closing his eyes.

I felt the shiver of his energy pressing close and decided to slap him in the face with mine, dropping my shield fully. He moved back as a result, twitching an eyebrow in turn. Served him right, smug git. He pushed closer after the initial shock, chest almost touching mine which was unexpected, but I wasn't about to step away. He was the one asking for a show. I heard Alex shifting behind us somewhere, but I was too busy watching Luke to check on her. His face was moving, little quirks of lips and eyebrows. He looked thoroughly pleased with himself.

"You okay there?" I asked after a minute of blaring silence. I wasn't one to be bashful, but he was close enough to count my freckles. As if on cue, his gaze met mine from under his lashes, pupils blown and that bright blue crackling in amusement.

"I'm fine, as are you, it appears." I raised an eyebrow, glancing over at Alex to check if she had heard the same thing, but she wasn't there. Shit. "She left to let me get a better read on you," Luke supplied.

"Nice of her. You happy? And can we separate?"

"If you're in a hurry, of course."

I took a merciful step back, my hands falling to my sides while he kept his place. He was easy enough to look at, but I liked my space and he was very friendly now that Alex was gone. Wasn't rushing to get her back in either. I watched him for a beat.

"Satisfied?" I asked.

"Yes, I think you'll be fine. Sarah was certainly attuned very differently to you, but I know she had training with your mother. You can handle yourself. However, I would prefer Alex were with you if you intend to go looking for anything involving our group."

"Reassuring to know," I said, surprised by the smile it brought back to Luke's face. "Have I said something funny?"

"Not amusing, but it's heartening to see Sarah and you share a sense of humour." He turned away, busying himself with his briefcase. "Sarah found it equally annoying to be tested and was as full of comments when she realised the type of powers I practice with."

"And those would be?"

"I use natural energy," he said in a matter of fact tone. "That includes energy from meditation, drawing it from the Earth, from freely given blood and in some instances sexual energy. Sarah found this worthy of many muttered comments and jokes about grateful clients."

I could see Sarah having a lot of fun with that if she trusted the guy. Sex magic was old school and every hippy colony through the ages had tried to use it. Badly. But those who could use it were usually respectful and treated those participating decently. Sarah must have thought Luke was alright to joke with him about it.

"Let me guess, she'd say you could get paid twice if someone was really pleased?" I ventured. It wasn't his fault I was wound up. He chuckled, eyeing me.

"Something along those lines."

"Is that where the sex parties come in?" I asked, innocent as I could muster. He hesitated, turning to watch me again.

"Am I to assume you've made the acquaintance of Marcus?"

"You know I have. There's no way he's having that chat with me and not telling you."

He chuckled, stepping closer again. I stepped back and found myself bumping into the loveseat.

"I suppose that was passive aggressive. You'll have to excuse me, habit of the profession."

"You don't say. Did you and Sarah ever…." I trailed off, hoping the implication was enough.

"We practiced together in a variety of forms but never shared sexual energy. Sarah assisted with some of the rituals, but I never joined with her."

"You could have just said no." I groaned, that mental image now seared somewhere in my brain. "I didn't know Sarah was practicing that."

"As I said, she knew your views. Perhaps that's why she didn't share you with any of us."

"Eh, that probably has more to do with me slitting my wrists when I was younger," I said, flashing one arm up to show the scar. "Wanted to cut it out when I couldn't stop the noise."

"That's a most direct approach. I can see why she would be concerned. You are more…settled with it now?" he asked, a hand going to cup my wrist. He traced the white line of one scar and I hissed air through my teeth, shaking my head.

"Not really, but it's the only thing that's going to find her. She's not here and she's not dead, so I've got to think outside the box. This shit lets you look in all sorts of boxes."

"That's a heavy undertaking, Carter," he said, still holding my wrist. "You must have felt very strongly to take such drastic steps."

"The way this works for me isn't the same as Sarah's, or my mum's even. I get things dropped in my head or seen by a glance or just because someone touched me. It was a bombardment, constant noise and information, when I was younger. I've gotten significantly better at shielding, as you've seen. Sarah channelled hers differently, used it for art and making things. Better that way."

"She certainly has an impressive set of skills in her jewellery making," he said.

"That why she was designing kinky shit for you?" Again, it was out of my mouth before I could catch it and I froze. He laughed, looking me up and down.

"Not everyone is as opposed to their connection with the gift as you are. The items Sarah made for me assist with that," Luke said, amusement dripping in his voice. "Perhaps having some more connections would make it easier on you?"

"Are you hitting on me when I'm here trying to find my sister?" I tried to make the question sound incredulous, but it came out surprised. Smooth, Carter.

"Merely offering guidance. And a shoulder, should you need one," Luke said. Perfectly polite and a hint of a raise to his eyebrows. I should have been insulted, or annoyed, rather than impressed at the balls of the guy. I shrugged it, and him, off and grabbed my bag.

"I should get Alex and go." I took a couple of steps then looked back to him, meeting an impassive look on his face. "Thanks for your offers. I'll keep them in mind."

"Do let me know if you need any assistance. I've been in Glasgow some time."

"There's one thing." I shook my head, toying with the flash of an idea. "It might be a wild goose chase."

"Please, Carter, anything that helps."

I pulled the book out of my bag, tossing it between my hands.

"I found this in Sarah's room. It's a hand-written diary, I guess, of someone in Glasgow. Someone who was practicing." I held the book up for him, and he brushed his fingers against mine as he took it. "I don't know if there's anything to it, but Alex mentioned Sarah was exploring places and it calls itself a guide. Has she ever mentioned it to you?"

He was captivated by the book, his eyes some mix of confusion and curiosity. He opened the first page and read over it slowly, slower than I expected a lawyer to read.

"I must confess she hasn't, though I'm not surprised she was hoping to discover more. She's keen to build her power. The city offers many opportunities." He thumbed through the pages, eyebrows quirking at some entries.

"Did she ever mention the name Dex?" He made a good job of not reacting, but I saw his eyes change, a flash going through them. Was that fear?

"I've heard the name though not in my own practice." He lied, looking at me closely. "Why do you ask?"

"I may have met them," I said, watching that news settle over him. He drew up straight, turning his full focus on me.

"Met them?" he repeated.

"Them. It. Not sure what pronoun you would use. Through a dream, after reading the book." I nodded to the slim volume in his hand. I didn't know why I'd offered it up, except to reassure myself that I wasn't going crazy.

"I imagine that would be most distressing. That name is attached to a very old being. It would be powerful."

"Sounds about right. Sarcastic too."

"You spoke with it?" his voice pitched up in shock. That wasn't reassuring.

"I more listened, which was unusual for me as I'm sure you can tell." I paused, feeling sick. "It told me it knew where she was."

"Have you spoken to anyone else about this?" Luke asked, passing a hand over his mouth and chin.

"Not really had the chance. It's been a busy day."

"I would urge caution in sharing this. There were those associated with its worship throughout Glasgow, in areas I would hope Sarah wasn't dealing with." He stopped, the frown coming back.

"Do you know any reason it'd be interested in her? Or the people you mentioned, that worship it?"

"I'd have to check my records. There are other names it goes by which may be useful. I could research further, and we can discuss this over dinner?"

"Okay, if you let me have your address later on, I'd like that." I nodded, unsure of where this was going.

"I'll look forward to it. But you must take your leave, and I will have to investigate." He still had the book, and I held my hand out for it. He quirked an eyebrow. "I can examine this further as well if you wish?" he asked, tapping the spine.

"It's okay. I'll keep reading. If Sarah was using it then maybe I can trace her steps."

He handed the book back and reached for me, gripping my shoulder, "I can see you're dedicated to finding her, Carter. I intend to do whatever I can to assist."

"That's very kind of you." I smiled, half way meaning it, and then went for the door before it got any weirder.

# Chapter 6

*14 May, 1887*

*The Blantyre Free Church, with its unfortunate end and new beginning, may hold a clue to the areas I have been discussing with The Collector. I knew of the different planes already, of the links between this world and others. I did not know of the potential to connect the worlds, to travel between them.*

*The Collector speaks of this as if it were normal conduct for him, and I can only hypothesise that he has found some safe method. I do not know what level of protection one would need for this, but given the implications, I must imagine it is some higher magic than that which I have access to.*

*With Parish records I have been able to ascertain that the fire of 1864 was started through unknown causes and that the rebuilding of the church commenced in 1872. Reasons for the delay vary with accounts. I feel it prudent to examine the site. If the fire was to allow a physical space for a portal there will be evidence.*

*My reasons are thus: We know the appearance of these portals varies between which planes are connecting, and that the connection fosters a large sum of energy, the level dependent on the planes. This energy is unfocused and unpredictable, hence the unfortunates who are lost through them sometimes to fairy lands and missing ships. What if a portal could be stabilised?*

Alex was curled up in the same plush seat Luke had been in earlier, tapping away on her phone. She unfurled when she heard the door close.

"We good?" she asked, raising an eyebrow.

"What's that look for?"

"Not telling me you were already hooked up was a shitty move."

"I'm sorry. I didn't know how real this place would be, and I don't go around shouting it from the rooftops. Can we head back to the flat?" An ache was pushing at the back of my skull. I could feel the shop's energy pouring off in sheets. It was intense, and I didn't want to exhaust myself keeping out the continuous white noise.

Alex watched me for a beat then nodded, leading the way out of the building. She gave the owner a wave, calling out to her as she walked, "See you next time."

"Safe travels," the woman replied, not raising her eyes from whatever it was on her counter. I thought she might have been blessing things, but we were out of the shop before I got a better look. Once we were on to the bustle of the street the energy of the shop dropped off suddenly, leaving a dizzying vacuum.

"Must be some pretty strong shielding on that place," I said, breathing through my nose to settle my stomach.

"Well, you'd know." Alex replied.

"If you want to ride me about trying to make sure I'm safe while in a strange place by using an ability I spent most of my life avoiding then can you at least wait 'til we have either tea or vodka?" I asked, turning around to face her. Vodka would not help the headache, but at least the hangover would feel worth it.

She looked at me for a second before bursting into giggles. This wasn't helping my mood. Or the promised headache. She had an annoying laugh.

"Ride you?" she asked, brows high and a wicked twinkle in her eyes. "Is that an invitation?"

"You know what? I can see why my sister got on with you—you both have the humour of a five year old," I said, shaking my head.

"I'm sorry, Mr. 'secret and mysterious', I didn't realise I was meant to kill my sense of fun along with my attendance record." That one at least made me smile. "Anyway, I think someone else had eyes on you."

"What?" My head snapped over to her, the comment catching me off guard.

"Oh please, Luke was so busy eyeing you up that I barely got a look in."

"He'll be more interested in my 'gift' than me."

"I don't know, wasn't your gift he was checking out in the shop front. He's pansexual and he's not afraid to act on an attraction." She grinned. I couldn't decide if the grin was from experience or vicarious enjoyment of my suffering.

"That's flattering, but I have one or two things to focus on."

"If you needed to let off some stress, I'm sure he'd help." She shrugged, bringing her palms up in the motion. "Just because you're focused on the task at hand doesn't mean you can't look after yourself too. If you're into that. No issues with me if you are ace."

"I'm not an asexual, I'm bi, but I'm also cold, far from home, worried about Sarah, and in need of liquid sustenance." I looked about, checking my bearings to see if we were nearly back.

"Okay, no pressure. Just wanted you to know we're cool. And if you're into that with Luke, that's cool too. He's a good guy." She slowed a little and glanced around. "You want to grab something to eat or are you about to race off?"

"Food would be nice. I've not eaten much today."

"There's a trait you two share," she said with a half grin. "Sarah's terrible for getting into the flow of a thing and ignoring everything else."

"Where's good?" I asked to distract her from the frown I could see growing.

"Do you do sushi?"

"Hell yes," I grinned. "Love the stuff."

"Okay, then we'll Ichi Ban it. This way."

She led me to a small restaurant tucked between an off license and a take away. We were seated towards the back and brought menus the size of my forearm, water set on the table before our waitress vanished. I blinked a couple of times and checked over the selection, the joy in Alex's stare boring into the top of my head.

"Impressed?" she asked, eyes gleaming.

"Yeah, this is great. It's a right little gem."

"We have a few of those. Sarah always thought you didn't visit because you thought Glasgow was all stabbings and drug dealers."

"You did have the busiest court in Europe for a while. I would've loved to visit, but she wasn't too keen."

Alex opened her mouth to say something but our waitress reappeared and we ordered. Alex turned back to me as the waitress disappeared into the kitchen.

"What do you mean, wasn't keen? She was always talking about missing you."

"You can miss someone without wanting them around you, especially in our family." I sighed, rubbing a hand over my face. "Do you think she'd want to risk me bumping into her friends from those parties, or seeing her commissions?" Alex's face flashed through four grimaces before she opened her mouth, which was quickly shut again. "Alex, I don't care. Whatever Sarah does is Sarah's business and none of mine if she didn't want to share it."

"I can see what you're saying," she agreed after chewing it over.

"Great. Not to kill the mood, but can I ask why you're suddenly being nice? I'm not complaining, but you've been blowing hot and cold all day, and now we're doing sushi."

"First, I knew you were lying to me, and I hate that." She started counting off on her fingers. "Second, you're a bit of a dick. Third, you were hiding something. I could see that with my gift, but I was still getting told to help you, which makes me grumpy. And fourth, you are really fucking with my schedule which is not what I like." She fell silent as the food arrived and eyed my selection before digging into her own. "But, it's all for Sarah, and I felt you when you were back at the shop. You're not like her, but you have it. Plus, my lot says you're good news, so I've got to go with it."

"Your lot?" I asked, soaking a roll in soy sauce.

"Yeah, my… I guess you would maybe call them guides? Like spirit guides. I wouldn't call them that. They're my ancestors. They help me find my path and grow. They approve of you, so I've got to help. I don't have to like it when you're a pain in my ass, but helping you helps Sarah, so that'll have to be tolerated."

"I'm glad to know I inspire such tolerance." I bit into another roll and chewed for a while until I could form my question. "Right, this is going to come out all wrong, but, if you have someone on the other side talking to you, is that how you know Sarah's not dead?"

Alex nodded, continuing to make her way through her sashimi.

"And you didn't mention this during our chat this morning because?"

"Because you looked like a lying sack of shit stood on my doorstep, and I didn't feel like telling you everything."

"That's fair. Anything else you feel like telling me now?"

Alex pushed a slice of tuna around her plate for a moment, her jaw working. "Sarah said you hated this stuff. She said you hated your mum for passing it to Sarah, and you didn't speak about it with her." She ate the slice before she continued, "She talked like you knew about it but didn't have it. Why'd she do that?"

"Because I do hate it. My gift lets me see what's going on with people. It also means I sometimes know stuff, suddenly; no warning. Or I might fuck up and blow a light out when I'm stressed. It's not something I got used to like Sarah did. I'm not sure if it's because we experience it differently or if she's better at it, but I did resent it and pushed mine away. If Sarah wasn't missing, I'd still be doing that." I set my chopsticks down and took a deep drink of water. "I didn't resent Mum for passing it to either of us, but I probably did resent how it made Mum and her closer. And I don't think Mum ever really forgave me for pushing it off."

"If I can ask, why isn't your mum up here looking for her?"

"She couldn't make it. She's got work commitments that won't go away. And someone needs to be there for the police to mollycoddle."

"Not a fan of the boys in blue?"

"I have a pretty face and a tendency to get hit by pissed off boyfriends." I shrugged, cheeks heating up.

"You're a stealer?" She leaned forward, scandalised, and stole one of my nigri in the process.

"No, but I get the occasional drink bought for me and the occasional boyfriend doesn't like that." I stole a slice of avocado in retaliation and paired it with one of the remaining rolls on my plate.

"Sounds nice," Alex said, watching for a reaction.

"Oh yeah, I love getting smacked in the face by drunken idiots." I scoffed, rolling my eyes. "I think Sarah was protecting me. She knew my views as everyone keeps pointing out, and she'd know I would worry about who she was around. People can try to take advantage."

Alex snorted as she drank, looking at me incredulously. "You think anyone would stand a chance against Sarah?"

"I think people can look at you like a resource rather than a person when you have something they want. And Sarah used to be cruel with her power sometimes. If she was in the wrong mood."

"What d'you mean? I've seen her be a bitch sometimes but never cruel."

I rested my chin on one hand, pushing a salmon roll round my plate. "I saw her do it once. There was this girl, Tara. We were only young really. Sarah would be early teens. Tara had taken to picking on one of Sarah's friends. Turned out Tara's parents were getting a divorce and it was messy, fights at home all the time, and this was her acting out. No one at the school knew that. No one knew about the divorce except the parents, Tara, and the lawyers. Except Sarah knew, because sometimes we know. So after a particularly bad day of Tara going at this friend, Sarah started poking her about the divorce. Nasty, direct questions, like when her dad had started sleeping with the babysitter and had her mum really gone through his wardrobe and cut all his suits to bits. Questions kids aren't meant to know about. Tara lost it. She was inconsolable. They had to send her home. She came back the next day miserable and was like that 'til the end of the year. Sarah shouldn't have done that, but she thought it was fair because Tara was a bully."

"She was a kid though." Alex said it, but her face was pinched in discomfort.

"She was, and when I found out, I made sure she didn't do it again. But if she's under pressure or in danger, she can lash out. We all can."

"What happens when you lash out?"

"Depends on why it is," I answered.

"Go on?" she prompted, not taking my hint.

"Sometimes lights fuse out. Sometimes things move. Sometimes I tell people things they don't want to hear."

"Things move about? Like Carrie?"

"Bloody hell, no. I mean like, this one time I saw a guy who was abusing his wife. It wasn't obvious, but I could see it. The way she was scared about strange things. The way he would watch her do things and then take credit for them. The way he would make comments about her coming home to their kid dead."

"What the fuck?"

"Yeah, he was a real nice guy. This one time I was at their house and I'm watching him do this, and I just thought how much I wanted to see him get a taste of his own medicine. And as I focus on that the Welsh dresser behind him comes tipping forward, knocks him on the head, and smashes his collection of plates."

"You tipped a dresser on him?"

"I was sitting on the other side of the room. I didn't mean for it to happen, but I intended for him to pay for what he was doing. We're not a great family for self-control."

"He does sound like a bit of a dickhead, though. I'd want something like that to happen."

"Would you set something in motion to make it happen?" I asked.

"No, I'd speak to the woman," she said after a pause, her mouth pulling down.

"Which is what a sensible person would do. Mine wasn't a deliberate action, but I should've kept my shit in check, and I didn't.

He beat her after the hospital trip, said it must have been her doing. Despite her being in the kitchen."

"Okay, no, he really deserved it." Alex threw her napkin down, brows down low.

"That's not the point, though. Without the proper control our stuff gets messy. It spills over in places it shouldn't. Which is why I wasn't too upset that Sarah was working with a group. It's not a bad idea if you know they're safe."

"Is that approval I hear?" Alex asked, stealing the rolls that were left on my plate.

"I approve of what she's trying to do. She thought about going into psychiatry to help people, but she was worried she might say something she wasn't meant to know. Can you imagine how badly that could go with someone who was already unsure of what was real?"

"I guess so." Her smile dropped away.

"You alright?

"I've told Sarah she should get in and about people's heads. That probably didn't come off as good as I meant it."

"She'd get what you meant. We're not a soft lot. She was happy with her choices."

"You sound very sure about that."

"We did talk sometimes, you know."

"I know that," she snapped. "But it didn't seem like you guys were so close."

"Siblings need a bit of space, you know. I let her set the rules, didn't want to stomp on her groove. Shall we go?" I nodded to our empty plates.

"Sure. I'll get this."

"You don't have to," I said, tapping the wallet in my pocket.

"Call it an apology for this morning."

"Alright." I nodded, watching her go towards the till.

We stood outside the shop, breathing in the crisp air of the night. It was dark enough to see a few stars poking through the darkness.

"What's your plan this evening?" Alex asked as I looked up and down the broad road.

"I'm shattered. Plan to sleep."

She laughed a little at that, eyeing me up. "You know Sarah does something similar. She'll go all intense about something and then get tired."

"We're good at going hell for leather." I nodded, watching Alex check me over again. "You okay?"

"You want me to walk you back to the subway? I need to meet up with those guys and see if they'll talk to you, so I'm headed there."

"Sure," I said, falling in step with her. "You think they will?"

"I hope so. They're not bad guys, and I know they've not done anything to her."

"You sound very sure."

"I've checked."

"Course you have." I smiled despite myself.

We walked along towards the subway station in silence. My mind fell back to chewing over the meeting with Luke and the weirdness of the city.

"Alex, does Sarah like that park over there?" I pointed to the mock Tudor building we were passing by.

"The botanicals? Yes, she loves them. Used to say it was great to people watch, get a feel for the city."

"I can see what she'd mean, yeah." I nodded as we rounded the corner and passed the unusual bar, throbbing with energy.

"Why?" Alex pushed, watching me again.

"I met someone who said they'd seen her there, someone connected to this stuff. She's never mentioned them to me."

"Don't take that personally. She wanted to have a clean division between here and there. Lots of people want that when they come to uni." Alex shrugged, tucking her hands into her pockets.

"It's just a lot to take in." I chewed my lower lip, feeling out the words as we arrived at the station. "I came thinking I could find her, and all I'm getting is a picture of someone I don't know. It wears on me, you know?"

"I get it. You sure about the room? It'd save you travelling back and forth. Cheaper than where you're staying too."

"I'll think about it."

"Good. Cause that's kinda a sketchy place you're staying at, and I'd feel a bit better about it if you were here."

"Thanks. Once I'm less of a sleep zombie I'll come back to you."

She smiled and went off towards the flat. I shuffled into the subway station and got a ticket, lurking on the platform 'til the train arrived. The sway of the train and the near empty carriage was welcome, peace in the maelstrom of today. I reached the guesthouse without incident and threw myself into the bed, hoping for sleep.

# Chapter 7

<u>22 March, 1886</u>

I have returned to The Collector each opportunity I find for trading information. The Collector has a vast wealth of items which do not just inhabit his shop but his home, some of which I have been permitted to view. However, as previously denoted, his knowledge of the city and the workings within is far superior. We have begun a reasonable trade in such things, and it is my preferred currency. Time for my studies must be prioritised to ensure a good impression for my apprenticeship, but my study of the city must advance further too.

The Collector discussed undertakers within the city who are noted for their exemplar service and utter discretion. They ensure a body is interred within an entirely too swift timescale, impossible with the administrative requirements of reporting a death. The price charged, while not immodest, does not account for the level of workmanship required. The Collector made introductions to allow my visit to them, as I am told an unannounced appointment is ill-advised.

I was able to visit with the good Mr. Christie and his family to evaluate their unusual situation. Mr. Christie is part of a line of flesh eaters commonly referred to as ghouls, though that term is often misused. They have inhabited the area since the mid fourteenth century. The first of their line was one who lived amongst us natural folk, passing as a butcher, until he was forced to reveal his character during a famine. This brought about a glut of food for the fellow and he could not explain his continued health except for cannibalism or witchcraft. He was forced to flee.

He joined civil society some years later under an assumed name, and the family has worked under some trade involving either death or meat ever since. This has resulted in notable issues for them, such as the unfortunate incidents in Bennane Head and the public killing of *the Bean clan who had taken to open cannibalism. Mr. Christie notes the man Sawney Bean was indeed a cousin of his late relatives and attempts were made to reduce his brazen nature, but to no avail. The King then saw to that.*

<u>28 October 2017</u>

Something was touching me in the darkness. I was floating amongst several somethings if the sensation was anything to go by, lingering brushes on my back and legs.

"Do I want to ask what's going on?" I said aloud, keeping my eyes closed.

"That depends on whether you wish to know the answer." Dex sounded close to me, and much smaller.

"Are you doing that?"

"Touching you? Yes."

"Why?"

"Because I can reach you here, and I want to taste what you are like. You do not feel like she did."

I felt water, warm as blood, lap over my chest as I flinched. I opened my eyes to see an expanse of stars above me, the sky dotted throughout as far as I could see. There wasn't a moon, but they lit the tips of the waves pale silver. No tide that I could feel, just the lull to and fro.

"You've felt Sarah?" I kept my eyes on the stars and not on whatever was still moving over my body. The pressure gradually left and I was alone, floating in the dark water. I didn't recognise any of the constellations.

"Yes. She has been to visit me, in a way."

"What does that mean?"

"She may not have been aware it was me she was speaking to," it conceded, having the decency to sound contrite. Dex's voice still sounded like water over rocks, the rush of the tide on the beach.

"You've been stalking my sister and felt the need to tell me this?"

"I wanted to. Because you are new in this city, and I want to feel you." Oh, fucking joy. "And because I wanted to see if you had considered my offer."

"Why the ocean?" I asked, giving in and raising my head to glance about. The water stretched off forever, with a small island in whatever direction my feet were pointing. I pushed my legs down so I was treading water, facing the island. It seemed like where the voice was coming from. I could swim to it.

"I would not recommend you do so," it said. I felt the water around me move and glanced down, spotting a mass of seaweed like tendrils below me.

"Is that you?" I asked, looking between the seaweed and the island.

"Yes." The voice was coming from the island. It sounded smug again.

"Right. Why are you both an island and tentacles? Which are stroking me. 'Cause that's kind of not okay."

"In my space, I dictate what is okay. You have not answered my question."

"You didn't answer mine. Why the water?" I splashed some, petulant. This was only slightly better than the black void.

"I thought the water might be more appealing—you are fond of rivers. Now I have answered you. Have you considered my offer?"

"Why would you help me?" I countered, slipping onto my back again. I should have been more worried, but at this point there was fuck all I could do if it decided to pull me under.

"I've already told you. I like your mind."

"Nothing with this shit comes for free."

"I would expect a fair trade. If I assist you, I want something in return."

"Always a catch." I said, shaking my head. "What would you want? I'm not all that likely to have a first born to trade you."

"I don't need young lives, though they are more useful. I doubt you would have the stomach for giving children away with how closely you chase your sister."

"You know emotional manipulation only really works when the person isn't aware you're doing it?"

"I find it works just as well when they know it and cannot do anything about it." A seaweed strand stroked my leg then dropped back away. Subtlety was not anyone's strong point here, huh?

"What would you want from me?" I asked.

"I can offer you far more than finding your sister, Carter. I can teach you how to use your gifts to your advantage. You would not need be afraid of them anymore."

"I'm not afraid of them. I don't like them."

"You're a man who wishes to be in control of things and yet you choose to ignore such an advantage. That implies fear or arrogance, and fear is more likely. You would face your fear for Sarah."

"I really hate you saying her name," I said, moving my arms through the water.

"And I really do not have any reason to care about that." The voice from the island sounded warm and amused, but I could feel tension.

"You never finished, what do you want." I reminded it.

"For you to serve me."

"That could cover a lot of things. You have something particular envisaged?"

I felt the chuckle of the great thing through the water. "I have a variety of things that require assistance from your physical plane."

"You live on a different physical plane?"

"I do. Somewhere I can take you, but you could not reach without significant effort."

"Does it take you much to get me here?" I asked, shivering as one tendril lingered on my lower back.

"Not this way, no. If I were to assist with your search, I would desire your assistance with my endeavours."

"Still really vague there, Dex."

"Do you think it wise to be deliberately antagonistic when I am your only way out of here?" The water surged a little, rippling over my jaw.

"Do you think that'll scare me when I know there's nothing I can do to change that?" I asked with a laugh, wiping my lips with one hand.

"You are avoiding answering my question."

"You're not telling me anything."

"I would be remiss to give details until I knew I had your agreement." It made it sound reasonable.

"I wouldn't really agree until I knew what you wanted. And what you can do for me. I know you can't get Sarah, or you'd have dangled that over me. But you know where she is, so that implies she's somewhere you can't get her. Her group can't find her, so she's not on our plane. I know you're old and powerful, so that has to mean she's either on someone else's plane or one you don't have access to. But that's just what I've been picking up from our little visits. Am I the only one asking you about her?" I asked, twisting over to tread water again and watch the island. Squinting, I could see something like a body sat there, but the starlight didn't give me enough to make out details.

"You are," it said after a beat.

"And, am I correct?"

"In which assertion?"

"That she is somewhere you can't get her."

"Yes. I could tell you where but not assist you with returning her." It sounded smug still, the tendrils still feathering over me here and there.

"And do you know how long she has left?"

"Yes."

"Will you tell me?"

"What would you give me for that?"

"What would you want?" I asked, bobbing against the lap of the waves.

"I am uncertain. I could demand you return here so we can continue our discussion. I could demand a sacrifice. I could demand time from your life."

"You can get that?"

"Yes. I can take life essence." It left that hanging in the air for a moment and I bit the bait.

"Is that how you survive?"

"No, I am of much more than simply that. The essence is beneficial to me, but not essential."

"So why would you want mine?"

"Because your talent is intriguing, and I would enjoy savouring it."

"You're so creepy."

"I am certain you mean that in the most antagonistic way, but it would indeed be the case, yes."

"And if I asked you how long she has left now?"

"Then I would want something from you here," it said, smug.

"That sounds like it'd put me in a much worse situation."

"That depends on what you consider to be worse. We do not have to be enemies, Carter."

"We don't have to, no. And you've been very polite to me, even if you keep dragging my consciousness off to somewhere I don't know. But I'm not sure I want to give you that."

"Consider it and we will speak again. If you are happy to assume Sarah has that long left."

"You would have given me a time limit already if she didn't." I shrugged.

"Clever boy," it agreed.

I awoke coughing, the ghost of tendrils slipping over my skin. My stomach turned, dry heaving froth and spit, the water not there but the sensation clawing at me as I stumbled to the bathroom.

Sitting back from the bowl, I rested against the cool wall for a moment, my pulse thudding through my temples. I breathed through the last wave of the retching and went back to the bedroom, checking my phone.

"I'm at Renfrew Street in Glasgow. I'm very firmly here in this bedroom," I murmured, splaying my hands over the bedspread and breathing open mouthed in the dark as the last dregs of the dream died off. The shower called to me, but that might wake other guests, so I rolled onto my back and stared at my phone screen instead. My spine felt like it had a livewire attached to it, and I glanced around the room for something else to do, something to focus on. The lights of Sarah's laptop blinked, now charged.

Dragging some clothes on, I padded to the desk, turning the device on and logging in with Alex's suggestion. The artsy black and white nude of the background wallpaper stared at me, all sultry eyes and half shadowed breasts. Nice enough picture, I supposed. I started rooting around her desktop, checking apps and generic folders to see if anything jumped out.

Sarah had a spreadsheet to track her commissions, and I was impressed that the names were carefully coded. A calendar app notification popped up, reminding her of a party tomorrow night at an address I didn't recognise. Google brought up pictures of a townhouse looking back at me from the street view, all sandstone and high windows. It was detached with something like a fence of trees distancing it from the road. Nice for the city. Private. Could be the party Marc mentioned. I toyed with an idea for a few minutes then texted him.

*Hey mate, Luke's cool with me going to that party we spoke about. You still keen?*

I was fifteen minutes into her dissertation ideas when I got a text back, *I heard, pal! Do you need a lift?* I was just surrounded by helpful people.

*That'd be great, thanks. Wanna help me with the dress code?* It was obvious bait, but I was hoping for some time to press him a bit.

I closed the dissertation and started digging through Sarah's personal matters. She could shout at me once I could hear her speak again.

The comments from Dex went back through my mind, about her being on another plane. I'd never heard of that happening outside of fairy tales and astral projection. I'd investigated that a few years back, when a big B-movie made it a major plot point. It was a lot of hassle, your spirit off wandering while your body was left like a rag doll. Sarah wouldn't do that. And it'd mean her body was somewhere, which would have been found by now. I typed in a search on her hard drive for 'plane' and 'astral' to give me something to watch on the screen.

I glanced around again, passing a hand over my eyes. Blue sparks danced behind my eyelids and I dropped my head, tugging my hair up again. I knew Dex was trying to make me want its information. It was tempting. Was it all that unreasonable to trade parts of me for Sarah? It would make Mum happy, and that was rare enough. Sarah was the better child, so it'd be appreciated—even if Mum would call it madness. If I could get details of what Dex really wanted, it might be worth looking at. That could, of course, also just be 4:00 a.m. talking. I couldn't find a logical argument to deny it against the screaming anxiety in the back of my mind though. I stored it in my head for later, along with all the rest.

I looked back at the screen and saw a few hits on 'plane,' jewellery only. I plucked up my phone, checking work emails and looking up the news before throwing that on the bed too.

I stalked over and grabbed the book, perching on the edge of the mattress. Reading might be good, focus me. Turning on the lamp, I shuffled back against the headboard, flicking through the pages. I had been reading about The Collector, so I looked for other bits on him. It didn't take long. The enthusiast was enchanted with this shop.

The diary went on for years, at least three that I could see from skimming. Hooked, I started over from his introduction, racing through the entries.

The guy discussed meeting The Collector, finding cursed items, going around the city to visit fallen angels and flesh eaters and demons disguised within other workers. He narrated it like a damn safari, discussing the longer-term implications for the city, how close he had gotten to this Collector guy, his own descent into practicing magic and rituals. It went old school colonial at the end, his justification of the self-confessed wicked things all centred around him knowing better than the stupid masses he was surrounded by. Great. Fuck.

I put the book down, pushing it out of reach lest it jump up and bite me. Ghouls dressed as morticians and now Lucifer in Swan Lake? I started to giggle a little and had to bite into the meat of my hand to choke it off before it spilled out of my control. I let go when I tasted copper. This was insane.

It could be just that, a disturbed writer. That would be nicer, this book being some crazy man Sarah had been reading about to see what he'd said rather than a tour of the weirdest places in the city.

That idea pinged around the back of my head, and I looked between the book and the laptop again. I cancelled the searches and instead looked for guides. The idea was half formed and I couldn't place what I was after, but it was worth a shot. A few immediate hits came up with university orientation and the such, so I left it ticking over.

I grabbed for my phone again, smothering myself in the normality of web design and customer queries. I still felt tight as a piano string, my shoulders and neck stiff with the dream and the book, so I walked through to the bathroom, hopping into the shower. The water might at least relax my muscles.

I came back feeling like I could sleep again if I really put the effort in.

Dropping back down in front of the laptop to check the results, my heart yanked awkwardly at the sight of a file, 'A Guide to the City,' stored away with Sarah's accounting folders. I toyed with the idea of calling Alex. She'd be less than grateful for a wake-up with no evidence, so I opened it instead, holding my breath.

The screen went utterly white for a long moment and then a list started to populate. My breath went out of me as I saw dates start to appear beside addresses and question marks, page numbers, comments in short hand. This was something. It was pages of something in fact. She was cross referencing this book and parts of the city and noting the results. What the shit, Sarah?

She'd logged it all like an experiment, giving the date she visited, the page number in the guide, and what was there. It'd been going on for almost a year, if the dates were accurate, dotted here and there each month. The addresses were spread all over the city from what Google said. She hadn't named anything in her notes, just referenced the page number in the guide, so you'd need both.

I flicked between the list and the book. The entries were mostly in the city, though some wandered quite far out, one to a place called Blantyre that I'd never heard of. It looked about a half hour drive out of Glasgow, meaning she'd put some real effort into this on the word of a crazy man. A crazy man I didn't even know the name of. Neither did Sarah, but she'd believed his writing enough to track down the entries. Okay, I could run with that for now.

Sarah had a mixed success; some of the places no longer existed or had been built over. A few of the entries sounded a little more involved than others: *'visited, no response, try again,' 'visited, discussed with for some time, will return,' 'visited. Do not return.'* These were all more recent than the other entries, timed a day apart, some two a day. The visits had been constant before she vanished. Fuck.

I felt like I had lightning in my veins. My heart crawled up into my throat as I looked through the details. This was the closest I'd come to her. It wasn't enough to find her, but I could at least start tracking where she'd been.

I emailed her list to myself and sat back in the chair. My blood was thrumming through my head like a base line and I struggled against the falling sensation it created. I had to make some sort of plan, but my mind was still foggy from the early wake up.

So instead I set out what I had. Sarah had been using the guide as—well, as intended. Alex had mentioned urban exploration, so Sarah's notes should lead me to where she'd been. I considered the idea of telling the police, chewing on that like I could taste it. That would mean handing over the book, and I didn't want to do that. No police then.

Luke was willing to make introductions at his party, so I could see if anyone there wanted to speak about her. I was dubious, but between the commissions and the nature of the parties it would be worth seeing.

Something about Marc and Luke still pulled at the back of my mind, but I didn't have any solid reason to suspect them. There were the guys who were seeing Sarah. I was less worried about them now, seeing Sarah run around the city hunting magic. Instead, I was worried as hell she'd gotten into something bigger and scarier than she expected.

It was a start though, more than we'd had since the beginning. I stood up, shaking myself off and pacing around the room, trying to quell the anxiety in my bones. My head was starting to spark, ideas lancing about but not bringing anything up, no realisation lurking. I needed to sleep more. Decisions made in this state of mind were usually plain stupid.

*Let me know how you got on last night*, I texted Alex, flinging my phone onto the table and dragging my limbs back into bed. I pulled my bubble up around me and burrowed under the covers.

# Chapter 8

<u>31 October, 1887</u>

Tonight is the culmination of half a year's preparation to verify my theory.

It would be dishonest of me to say I was not enthralled with the principle as much as the potential of this experiment. To know what happens on the other side of such a connection, to be able to establish not only that it exists but what exists beyond the precipice, is tantalising. I have prepared a selection of items I think most fitting, a mixture of protection and aggression. I hope it will not be needed.

I shall attend the Cathedral before the connection is established and observe the formation, seeking action once I can substantiate the portal. If I can do so, I will then continue with my venture and access the other world. My friend assures me this connection is to a habitable, stable environment, so the affects should be minimised. I look forward to reporting on what these are.

The well of St. Mungo appeared an unusual site for such an occurrence, but it has been in use of some form of worship or another since the sixth century. It has been of such paramount importance to the city that the Privy Council of 1629 sought to outlaw pilgrimages to the same, calling them a 'great offence of God, scandall of the kirk, and disgrace of his majesties government.' The pomp of such an announcement coming from the Privy Council was of course lost on them, but not I.

I am pleased this opportunity allows me to develop my theory of the fire at Blanytre Church. I am excited for the discussions my friend and I shall have after this.

*Dude, you up?*

*Carter?*

*How can you still be asleep, I thought you worked for a living!*

*Carter, call me.*

*Call me damnit.*

*Dude, wtf, call me!*

I awoke to several missed calls and a series of texts from Alex. I groaned and checked the time, heart sinking that it was almost eleven. I dropped my head back onto the pillow and uttered a dark curse, pushing myself up and checking the mirror. Hair was a mess but that could be a look, I guess.

I dialled Alex as I jogged down the steps, heading for a café.

"Carter, I need to see you. I'm home after one, can you come past?" she asked in a rush.

"I'll see you there."

I grabbed food and tried to catch up with myself as my mind raced. There were so many threads available now, branches going off into the gloom of wherever Sarah had vanished. I settled on speaking to the shop keeper who watched more than she spoke.

I made my way over, the subway sticky with the stale smell of other people but not too cramped. The streets were still busy, bustling as the trains pulled in and draining off to the flow of pedestrian traffic. Sticking my head through the bright shop door, I looked around to see if anyone else was about.

"I wondered when you'd be coming back," came a voice from within, and I stepped inside. The woman looked me over for a moment then nodded to a seat in front of the counter. I could see her better now, her skin dewy and eyes a dark brown, hair still up in a bun. Her dress hid some of the tattoos, her three-quarter sleeves tight against the skin.

"Why'd you expect me back?" I asked, sitting to watch her work. She was blessing things again, a white linen square laid out beside a tray and a bowl she was signing over. Stones sat in the bottom of it.

"You looked too interested not to. Why are you shielding again?"

"Oh shit." I forced my guard down, grimacing. "Habit."

"I can appreciate that." She nodded, refocusing on the bowl and muttering. I felt a little fuse of energy and smiled, watching as she finished it off.

"D'you do this all day? You were blessing yesterday, too."

"Not all day, just when needed. These stones need it now." She smiled at me as she took each stone individually and set them at points in the tray beside her. "So, Carter, what did you want to ask me? I'm Lou, by the way."

"What makes you think I want to ask things, Lou?" I replied, watching her hands as they took a new set of stones up from below the glass. They were nice hands, thin fingered and nimble. She reached for a bundle of something green and lit it, allowing the smoke to build up around her. Smelled like weed.

"Because you're curious and looking for your sister. Questions usually follow in such circumstances." She wasn't accusatory. I liked that. She looked at me again and I spotted an absence.

"I don't know if Sarah's told you about me, but I don't do as much of this as she does. I wondered if she'd mentioned looking for things in the city?"

"Things?" Her tone raised a little, the question being stamped down on.

"Places. Alex mentioned Sarah was getting interested in urban exploration; I wondered if she'd spoken to you about it."

"She'd be more likely to speak to Luke. He's been in the city longer."

"But not around longer." She looked at my face, turning her body to me.

"And what makes you think that?" she asked, gaze flicking over my face like it might melt off.

"Because shielding makes a hole where your energy should be, and you're a chasm. But the rest of them don't notice."

"That could mean I prefer to protect myself. It's a busy shop."

"Did Sarah spot you?" I was watching the tension in her shoulders, the hard line of her jaw. She paused, sniffing once, then shrugged.

"No," she said, turning back to the stones and the smouldering bundle.

"What is that?" I asked, nodding to the green.

"Sage."

"For purification, cool. So, what are you?"

"That's awfully rude, you know." She said it with the tired sigh of many women I knew, and it stung to be on the wrong end of it.

"So was your pointing out my shield, but you did it, anyway." I shrugged, rolling my neck.

"That was forward. Though beneficial to you. You want to look for Sarah with your skill."

"I suppose. Why should I trust you, since Sarah didn't know what you were?"

"Because no one else in thirty years has managed to spot me, so take solace in how intrepid you seem to be."

"They must not have been looking closely." I smirked, watching her eye me through the corner of her lashes. She smiled and carried on with her stones.

"Few do." A silence sat between us while she continued to work and I felt about with my power. She didn't seem to mind.

"Would you let me see you without your shield?" I asked.

"Now why would I do that?" She laughed with it, shaking her head.

"Because I can't tell what you are unless you do."

"And why on earth would I let you know?"

"Curiosity. You're not angry that I can tell, you're surprised. Sarah and I are alike, and if she couldn't spot you then you must be very good. I bet you'd love it if I could guess. It's not like I could do anything about it."

"That's not entirely true now, is it?" she asked playfully, leaning on an elbow against the counter and staring me down. "You could cause all sorts of trouble if you wanted to."

"You sound like you'd enjoy that, but I was planning to be reasonably unnoticed. If that's possible."

"Well, you have done a marvellous job of that so far."

"I can't help it if someone rang a bell when I walked in the room. Not my call. I have no interest in screwing with what you've got here." I held my hands up to indicate there was no danger.

"If I were to let my shield down, what would you do?"

"I would look at you. Generally, I can see."

"Sarah couldn't," Lou said, grinning again.

"Sarah wasn't looking." Because she had a group fawning over her instead.

Lou hummed, considering. "And if you couldn't see it?"

"Then I would feel you with my skill."

"Like Luke does."

"Mine's different than his, but the idea's the same."

"Could I?" she asked, that grin starting to look a little feral now.

"As in could you feel me? Well, my shield's down, and since I'm asking, I suppose it would be rude not to reciprocate."

"Come over here."

I rounded the counter and she stood facing me, pulling the pins out of her bun. That was all it took. I saw her change in front of me, her hair floating up around her face and her skin taking on a tint of green around the extremities. Claws slipped out of her fingers, shiny and dark green, a wicked curve in them like a cat. Her eyes were still the same brown, but the whites had flecks of gold in them, like thin seams.

"Oh wow," I said, flinching as I said it.

"That's a nicer reaction that most. How do I look to you?"

"What?" I looked up at her face, trying to read the question.

"I know what I look like, but what do I look like to you?"

"You look like you're sprung out from the earth, all green and gold and brown. Your claws are a bit scary, but you're very beautiful."

"Impressive," she said, twisting her hair back into the bun and popping back to how she had looked before. My head spun a little from the change.

"Is that an enchantment on your hair?" I asked as my head struggled to catch up with my eyes. I'd seen some similar things when I was a kid, clothes that made you confident or pretty, but not that smooth.

"On the pins," she said, turning back to her sage and linen.

"I can see the appeal. So, given the green and gold I'm going to take a guess and say you're either a sprite or a fae. Not entirely sure which."

"Very perceptive for someone who doesn't practice."

"I'm a geek. I know some stuff by exposure. The rest I've picked up from Sarah. She has good notes."

"She was always curious." Lou nodded, pouring water into the bowl now and submerging the sage into it.

"Why didn't you feel me?" I asked, sitting back down with a thump.

"What are you stalling from asking me, Carter?" she replied, looking at me again. I could almost see the gold in her eyes still.

"Well, that was a question. And I wanted to ask if you've tried to find Sarah. But that might be rude."

"I didn't feel you because I didn't need to. I asked to see your response. Your powers are obvious when you're using them. And no, I haven't tried to look for Sarah. I checked if she had passed on to the other side and once I knew she hadn't, I let it be. There are many reasons someone could want to be lost, and it's not my business interfering."

"You are fae, aren't you?" I asked, watching the spark of her eyes.

"That is what you call us, yes. Though I dislike some of the representations you have come up for us, especially the pantomime ones."

"You dislike fairy godmothers?"

"We don't make it our business to intrude. Some of us may be fickle things, stealing pretty humans off, but the majority are more concerned with other matters."

"I feel like I've touched a nerve. Sorry."

"It's not your fault. I appreciate the need to find kith and kin. For what it's worth, Sarah has a sensible head on her shoulders, and I doubt she'd have gone off blind. Even if she were to have met something awful, I don't imagine she would have left herself without an exit. You need to find what that was."

"The awful thing or the exit?"

"I imagine both would be useful." She submerged the linen square into the water and spoke a few words aloud that I didn't understand. She wrung it out, folded it into a small triangle, and then passed it to me. "For your travels."

"What is it?" It sat light and bright in my palm, barely filling a quarter.

"It's protection, of a kind. When you're alone in the dark it will help keep the worst of the shadows at bay."

"Thanks. What do I owe you?"

"It's free."

"No offence but literally every fairytale says nothing is given freely." It was like rule number one in all of them. Come on.

"Then call it payment for your silence as to my nature. And get out of my shop before you manage to insult me again." She smiled as she said it, but I could feel a bristle to her words. So I put the triangle in my pocket and made for the exit.

"Thanks for all your help," I called at the door.

"You're welcome. It's for Sarah more than you." I frowned at that but left. I didn't want to antagonise the mystical being.

I stepped out of the shop and made a line for the botanical gardens, looking for a Wi-Fi connection. Something in there must have one. I settled at the garden's cafe, ordering lunch then getting connected.

I had an hour 'til I needed to meet with Alex and I wanted to get an idea for where Sarah had been most recently. The notes felt like she was aiming for something given the increased number of entries and all the comments about revisiting or pursuing further. I began my own list on my phone, noting the physical locations she'd been to and trying to map it out. There was nothing that jumped out, no pattern to the addresses, but it meant I had the details on hand.

Speaking to Luke about it appealed to me. He was already looking into Dex and this might help clarify if it was Dex or the acolytes she'd encountered. Neither option filled me with joy, but I would take all the 'not dead' options I could find. Dex's offer still clung to the back of my mind like mould. It would let me know how long she had. Dex said it could let me know where she was, and that would mean a world of trouble gone. All it wanted was a trade of something, life essence or doing shit for it in Glasgow. I assumed in Glasgow, at least. It could drag me to wherever it was we had our conversations, so it wasn't beyond the realms of reasonable thought that it could operate outside of Glasgow.

Too good to be true. It was never that easy. There was always a catch. I just had to figure out what it was. This was starting to give me a headache again.

I finished up my meal and headed to the flat, my head buzzing. I felt the prickling of the headache kissing the backs of my eyes and rolled my neck again, willing the tension away. Alex met me at the door again and let me in, her mouth set and face pinched.

"Sorry I'm late," I said, slipping into the living room and sinking into a sofa.

"It's fine, I was just back in, anyway," she dismissed. "Tea?"

"Always. How did last night go?"

"About that. You know how I said there were two or three guys I knew she was seeing?"

"Affirmative." I nodded, following her into the kitchen.

"My meeting with them was odd. I spoke to each on their own, like you said—"

"I think I actually said I should chat to them because they might be more comfortable speaking to a dude and not Sarah's best friend."

"That would take too long. Anyway, when I was speaking to them, they all told me they'd hooked up with Sarah now and again, but that she wasn't seeing any of them on the regular." She looked at me like this was a revelation.

"I was kind of taking that to be the case, given your comments about there being two or three of them?"

"No, Carter, I mean she wasn't dating them at all. Sarah's been out almost every night, for weeks, and I thought she was trying a few of them out before she settled on one, but she wasn't. She's been seeing them maybe once a week each, if that, enough to keep them interested but nothing more."

"Okay, so she's been keeping it casual. What's your point?"

"What's she been doing the rest of the time? She's not been in the workshop that much. Marc would've mentioned something. And if she's only been seeing these guys one day a week then it leaves her with a lot of free time."

"You're assuming they're telling the truth." I knew her answer before it came.

"I checked. They are. It explains why the police were so disinterested with them. The guys were barely seeing her enough to be considered by the investigation. I mean everyone knows it's always the boyfriend, but none of these guys are that."

"Alright, so they're telling the truth. Where she going instead?"

"I don't know. And I don't know why she would lie to me about it." She frowned, lips pulling to the side.

"I thought you were excited about this from the texts." I said, taking the mug of tea she passed to me.

"I was excited about having new information. But the more I've thought about it, and now that we've spoken about it, the more worried it's making me. I know everyone keeps some things quiet, but Sarah didn't lie to me. She knew I could tell."

"If you looked."

"If I looked," she repeated, pinning me with a long stare.

"Maybe she knew you wouldn't."

"Don't say shit like that, Carter." Alex shook her head, going back through to the living room and sitting down hard.

"Seriously, maybe she didn't want you knowing what she was doing," I said, joining her.

"Why would she keep something from me? We're best friends. She told me more than she told you. She had no reason to lie to me."

"Or me, but she still did." I shrugged, sipping my brew.

"We all know why she lied to you. I'm not the same," she said, waving a hand at me.

"I know I'm going to regret asking this, but care to share just what you mean by that, Alex?" In no universe would this be good.

"You know, your feelings about the gift. That judgement."

"I thought we were getting pretty friendly and you come out with that? That's pretty fucked up." Why was she being like this? I felt my face flush as I tried to divert the anger sparking off into something else.

"I didn't mean it that way. Don't be a dick."

"And what did you mean?" I pushed the words out, willing my pulse down.

"I meant that she didn't want to put you in a position where you'd feel the need to try and interfere with her life."

"You mean like now? I highly doubt worries about interfering were what made Sarah keep this from me. Worries about me telling her what a shit idea it was to advertise herself, maybe, but that's not the same thing."

"Well, fine, if that helps you sleep at night. But why would she lie to me?"

"Probably to either keep your nose out or keep your neck safe." I sighed, drinking my tea.

"What's that meant to mean?"

"It means that maybe she was doing something you'd disapprove of, and she didn't want you to know. She has a track record for doing that. Or maybe she wanted to keep you safe from something dangerous. Either way, she was out doing something and was making sure you didn't know what it was. Have you spoken to Luke about it?"

"Why would I?" She bristled, putting her cup down.

"Maybe it has to do with his stuff. You said they'd been working together. Could be they were doing stuff together." Her face blanched. "I mean, maybe he's working on something himself, and she's been helping him."

"She wouldn't need to lie about that." Alex crossed her arms, huffing at the idea. Was that some jealousy?

"She would if Luke asked her to. Maybe it was personal stuff. Maybe it wasn't him at all, but it'd be worth checking. That I'll do next time I see him. We can look at what else there is."

"There isn't anything else!" Alex shouted, eyes blazing at me like I was an idiot. "I thought this would give us a clue about what she was doing all the time, but if she wasn't with them then there's nothing else to go on."

"I found some stuff on her laptop," I said, knocking the rest of my brew back.

"What? Why didn't you tell me?"

"Why did you think I was texting you at 5:00 a.m.?"

"Right." She deflated a little. "What is it?"

"It's a list of places Sarah's been to and made notes about. Did you ever go with her doing that urban exploration stuff?"

"Did it with a boyfriend for a while. Didn't like it. Why put yourself in danger with weird old houses?"

"I heartily agree, but Sarah has been doing just that. I wanted to have a look over them, in case, you know."

"That sounds good. I'm sorry those guys were a strike out. I really thought we were on to something there." She cracked her knuckles and fixed me with a look again. "You think this will help?"

"It lets us make sure she's not trapped somewhere licking moss off the walls," I said flatly, and she shot me a glare.

"Don't say that shit!"

"Hey, she's alive and well enough to find moss in that one. Take the silver lining." I shrugged.

"You're a strange man. Sometimes I can't decide if you're distraught or inconvenienced by her disappearance."

"I find that focusing on what I need to do helps me not think about that too much. It's better that way. I need to speak to Luke at some point before that party, and I should speak to Marc, too."

"Why Marc?" she asked with an arched brow.

"Because he's my lift, and since my only clues about it are sex and some very interesting commissions I found in Sarah's work space, I need help."

"I could help with that." My head tilted as I heard that.

"I thought you'd find that weird."

"Weirder than you attending the sex parties your sister went to, while you're trying to trace why she's missing?"

"When you put it like that." I shrugged, "Okay, what's the dress code and what system do you use?"

"Dress code is formal or kink, depending on your preference, and what sort of system do you mean?"

"I mean, do we show up in a green shirt if we're ready to party and a red one if we're watching, or...?"

"We chat and see how people are feeling. You're making it sound predatory. It's a relaxed thing. Though, if you are totally not wanting anything to happen there are ways of showing that. Might make people a bit wary of speaking to you."

"Right, so I need to find a suit."

"A Topman suit would do."

"I can afford better than that," I said.

"I don't doubt it, but where are you going to get a nicer one in that time?"

"Surely there are tailors in Glasgow."

"And they're going to be busy because it's the October holidays, so there's seasonal balls and parties to plan for," she said, as if it were the most normal thing in the world.

"I wasn't aware that seasonal balls were still a thing. Right. Could you help me with that?"

"I can take you to Topman."

"Sure." I gave in, shaking my head. She was so much like Sarah.

"Okay, so we need to hook you up with a suit and start looking at these places you mentioned."

"I have a list of them on my phone. Can we get to any today?" I asked, passing my phone to her.

"I know some of these. Others are a bit weirder. Like this one here. That's a shop," she said, pointing to an earlier entry. "This one is part of the botanical gardens, this one is a club. This one I've never heard of though." She passed the phone back to me, thumb highlighting another.

"Thornwood, you mean?"

"Yeah. I know there's a primary school named that over in Partick, but why'd she be looking at a school?"

"Can we go see?" She scrunched her face up but nodded, taking the phone back and scribbling on a notepad she'd produced from somewhere.

"If we go to them in this order, that gets three looked at and then we can take you shopping as well."

"Alright, Mum." I laughed, shaking my head. Alex flinched. "You okay?"

"Sarah says that when I nag at her." She picked up a few things and shooed me towards the door.

"I can imagine." A pang ran through my chest as I grabbed my bag. "Come on, if we head off now you can get me dressed up for the party. Will you be showing me off on your arm or would I cramp your style?"

"Showing you off? Your confidence is amazing."

"I'm a pretty man. It's got me more than one drink before." I shrugged, preening a hand through my har.

"And you think I need help from a pretty man?" I could hear a smile in her voice.

"I think I could make good bait," I offered.

"Bait?"

"Throw me out into the social waters and see what comes to take a bite."

"How far are you intending to take this fishing metaphor?" she asked with a laugh.

"I was aiming to work in something about tackle, but I feel it's going to be a reach."

"Flattered as I am that you'd be willing to act as bait, I think I'm quite skilled enough, thank you." She sniffed as we made our way onto the street.

"No doubt about it. I only offer as I'll need you to make introductions. You may as well get something out of it."

"Ah, this is for my benefit. I see." Alex raised an eyebrow and elbowed me in the ribs.

"I was thinking more that it would be a thank you since I'm going to either have to cling to your arm or drink my way through it."

"Why not both?" she asked with such honesty I turned to look at her. "Seriously, the place is an open bar. If you're worried about it, I don't mind acting as cover, but feel free to go for Dutch courage. Just don't cramp my style if I tell you I'm going off to be with someone and we're all good."

"Alright," I said, following her along the road. "So, where are we going?"

"The one I said was a shop is close to your new suit, so I thought we could do that last. Which leaves us the one at the botanical gardens and that school. Since it's October holidays, the school will be closed. We can scope it out then head back to the gardens."

"Lead the way."

# Chapter 9

*9 December, 1885*

*Further to my earlier notes, I have come upon a book of longing within The Collector's stash. The book catalogues details of the wishes or coveted items of previous owners, some struck through. There are specks of blood on some pages and a warning for the cost of wishes scrawled in a frantic hand over some of the older entries. Most of the writing within is erratic or unclear. This may be due to what appears to be water damage. I am surprised the book remains whole given the level of use and wear it evidences.*

*One page speaks of the ability to trade wishes with a dire warning of the cost but no details as to what that cost may be. From some of the more coherent notes it appears certain previous owners have attempted to trade wishes with other contemporary owners, but it is unclear how this has developed. It is unclear how this communication has been facilitated between the owners. I am unaware of what magics would allow one to write into antiquity, or to the vaulted future. Lastly, it is also unclear if all the references to trading relate only to other owners of the book or with greater beings mentioned within. The only matter clear is that there was some level of success. Warrants further study if more items are unavailable.*

The school was decent looking, a large red brick building surrounded by a playground and a playing field with a smattering of trees. Nothing unusual. Something was snagging on my gift though, a hum I could feel through the air.

"What else is around here, Alex?" I asked, failing to spot anything.

"Not much. There's the park over the road, but that's tiny."

"Can we check it out?"

"Sure." She nodded, crossing the road to a small green space.

There was a kid's play area stuffed with climbing frames and a full line of trees around the boundaries. I liked it, a natural curtain separating you from the bustle of the city. A blackened sandstone wall ran along one side which reminded me of the cathedral.

"Is all the sandstone marked like that?" I asked with a nod.

"Pollution," she said.

"You're quiet," I said, as we walked aimlessly.

"Just watching you work. Sarah's different in her methods." She stepped hard on some of the leaves on the grass, a firm crunch beneath her foot.

"That doesn't surprise me. Mine's pretty basic. Mostly I just see things, sometimes feel them."

"What do you feel here?"

"It feels like there's a bruise on the energy," I said, looking around. It was empty except us. There was the promise of rain in the air. I could smell it.

"Come again?"

"It's like the energy of the place is all normal until you reach one point which is just throbbing. I don't know what that is."

"You mean, like a portal?"

"I don't think so. That would be like a door, I think. This is more like a thin bit. Like a sore tooth that you push your tongue against."

"Someone's sealed something up?"

"I guess so." I nodded, drifting towards the wall again. There was something about it that didn't fit. We walked most of the length of the park before we spotted a pair of arches, one behind the other, in the same dark stone.

"What's that?" I asked as we got nearer. This was where the tug pulled. As we got closer, I could see some heavy fencing in place to block entry, proper security gates, and barbed wire.

"Someone doesn't want us getting in, whatever it is. Kinda looks like a railway tunnel." Alex hummed, giving one of the railings a firm shake. Nothing happened.

I looked over the arch, the air around it almost crackling. It felt electric, like the wind before it snows, little slips of light and colour leaping here and there.

A carving at the bottom of the second arch tugged at me. It was about a foot high and roughly done, depicting a five-pointed star with what looked like it was meant to be an eye in the middle of it. The eye looked shabby, the ellipse of it shot through with a ragged line, but it was jolting to the senses. I felt it ripple against me when I pushed with my powers. There was a flash of blood and yearning, predatory hunger, pushing up and curling its arms out before it snapped back to the rough carving. Oh no. Nope.

"What did you do?" Alex snapped around to look at me.

"I felt to see what that weird street art was. That's the bruise."

"Why did it glow?"

"I felt it push back, but I wasn't looking, to be honest."

"Carter, it flashed up with a yellow glow. Like a cat's eye or something. What the fuck?"

"I'd say we'd best leave this alone. Feels like it's been dealt with already."

"What?"

"I mean, we're done. We shouldn't poke it again. Or talk about it. Next stop?" I stepped away, pacing off over the grass and back to the tree line.

"This is wholly unsatisfactory, you know?" Alex called as she caught up.

"It's not exactly what I was expecting either," I said, glancing back as we went. "The carving's not a bad thing, I think, but it might be keeping a bad thing in place. It was active enough to push against me when I was feeling it."

"Is that normal?"

"I don't know. I'm not in the habit of doing this. But it feels like it's meant to be there, and it has enough power to respond. That's a little terrifying, and I fully plan to leave it alone."

"Like a coward."

"Like someone who doesn't fancy finding out why a person felt the urge to carve an arcane symbol that leaks bad energy into a stone arch. You know, a sane person."

"I don't enjoy feeling like we're running away from something when we don't know it's a threat."

"When you see a fire door shut in a burning building, do you open it to see if the room's on fire or do you feel the handle?"

"Check the handle."

"That thing feels like a handle. And if it was glowing then I'd say we're best leaving it be, right?" I asked, shoulders hunching up about my ears.

"I guess. Where to next, the park or the shop?"

"You said the park before."

"It would make sense," she said, "but we can always check the park out on the way back."

"Won't it be closed?"

"Sure, but there are ways in. Why, you scared of the dark?" She elbowed me in the ribs, and I rolled my eyes at her.

"No, just unwise to go into something we don't know when it's dark out."

"You've been in the gardens. It's cool. Plus, I want to see you in a suit, check if you polish up as well as you threaten to."

"To the shop it is then."

We took the subway to the city centre, bustled up the steps by the flow of people rushing between doors. They tugged us out into a paved square, hemmed on two sides by large buildings. The open space was dotted with benches and the bare bones of trees, linked up in a semi-circle around the underground entrance. The shopping centre on one side was shining and flashy against the sandstone and brick flanking them. It opened out to something I recognised though.

"We're on Buchanan Street!" I said, nodding up to the sloping hill ahead of us.

"We are. Why are you excited about this?"

"It's nice to recognise somewhere. The river's down there, and the cathedral is over that way, and there's a big railway station in the opposite direction."

"Okay, Google Maps." Alex laughed with a shake of her head. "Did you look it up or have you been here before?"

"I came down here my first night in Glasgow. Wanted to be near the river."

"Thinking about throwing yourself in?"

"Fucking hell, will you lay off it with that?" I hissed, glaring at her.

"Just saying. You're like the highest risk group for suicide."

"And I have to find Sarah before I can even think of such fun things," I said, tilting my jaw at her.

"Fine, I'll stop, but if you do start feeling like that then talk to someone. Doesn't have to be me, just someone. Come on, the shop's under Central."

"What's started all this off? You weren't so worried about my health yesterday." I shoved my hands in my pockets and fell in step with her, passing through a gaggle of children making for the station.

"It was brought to my attention I may have been a bit of a bitch to you."

"I thought our sushi date was perfectly pleasant."

"Before that, in the shop, I wasn't being sympathetic. And much as I think you should get the hell on with life and use your gift, Luke pointed out I was being unreasonable given everything else going on."

"Thank you, I think." What the hell? She was more mercurial than a thermometer. "Did Luke say anything else?"

"Like what, if he liked you?" she teased.

"I don't know, anything. He's the closest person to Sarah aside from you. He have any ideas?"

"No. He told me back you up, not like you need it given that trick at the park."

"But you know the city and I don't, so that's a huge help." And you're being used to keep tabs on me by Luke, but whatever.

"We're nearly there. It's this newsagent."

We stopped a few paces from the door. Looked like any other 24-hour shop: neon sign flashing away, the large front window partly coated in posters. It shone bright against the dimness underneath the tunnel, but that was the signs rather than any divine intervention. I closed my eyes and felt about with my gift. There was some energy moving around inside the shop but not like the thing in the park.

"Nothing obvious on the outside. May as well check inside," I said, glancing to Alex. She was already going towards the door, so I jogged after her.

The electronic jingle of a door sensor chimed as we stepped in, and I checked the place over. There was the usual long counter by the door with a selection of cigarettes behind it and rows of well stocked shelves on either side of the floor space. It wasn't a huge place, longer than it was wide, but they made good use of the space. It had bright, strip lights and the door sign flooded it with colour. A stockroom door was open at the far end, and I heard a thump of boxes being put down.

"Sorry to keep you waiting," we heard as a man came through the door towards us. He was an older East Indian gent, probably in his sixties and a bit taller than me. And he was on fire. Literally on fire. I could see it licking up the side of his face, over the slicked hair shot through with silver, and on his shoes.

"Holy shit! Are you alright?" I shouted, lunging towards him.

"Carter, what the fuck?" Alex grabbed me as I went forward, wrenching my shoulder back. "What are you shouting about?"

"He's on fire! Do you not see that he's on fire?"

"If you would keep your voice down please, good sir," the man said in an unreasonably calm voice for someone who was alight. He walked forward, looking between us and the door, and stopped in front of the counter.

"How are you being so composed?" I asked Alex. "Why aren't you freaking out?" A horrible vein of hot metal crept through my guts.

I'd snapped, gone mental. My head had gotten used to not dealing with this crazy shit because of shielding, and given it up for a bad job when I dove back in. I was going to have to trade whatever Dex wanted, get Sarah back, and hope that didn't get me killed. My chest shrank as I panicked, anxieties clawing at my ribcage and coiling about me. I knew I was tipping into a problem and clasped my hands together, squeezing until the knuckles shone white under the lights.

"Carter, the man's fine. He's not on fire." Alex was looking at me wide eyed. Then she stepped back, like I might take a swing for her. Or infect her.

"But." I gulped, trying to pull back from a full panic attack. "I can see him. He's covered in it." My voice was weak, straining even to me. He was though, head to toe. He wore a long smock like top with loose trousers in matching shades of brown. The flames were rippling over him like he was covered in petrol. Rippling over him but not burning him, I noted somewhere away from the cold sweat and thudding in my chest. I made my mouth shut, breathing through my nose and clenching a fist against my lower ribs to kill the fluttering in my diaphragm.

"He is not quite wrong, miss," the man said, smiling at me and patting my shoulder as he stepped behind the counter. He began to restock one of the cigarette cases, still on fire. "I'm of fire rather than on fire, which is possibly what's causing your friend some distress. Would you like to pass him something from the fridge? I think he'll need it."

"You're what?" Alex asked. He stared at her until she moved to the drinks cooler.

"Djinn?" I managed to get out between stuttering breaths. It felt like my heart would stop it was beating so hard, my throat thick from the adrenaline pulsing around me. I hadn't had one in so long that my old coping mechanisms were rusty, so I forced myself to focus on the feel of my hands gripping each other, the smell of grease and traffic stale on the air.

"Yes, well done." The man seemed pleased with me for that one, eyes twinkling. "Though my name is Mr. Kardar, and I do prefer to be called that."

"You're a genie?" Alex asked, passing me a bottle of water. I began gulping it down, pressing it to the sides of my neck between mouthfuls.

"Djinn are a race, not just spirits in lamps." I grabbed my elbows in opposite hands, gripping and making myself relax in increments. The urge to put my bubble up was an agonising nag in the bottom of my chest, sanity so close. "Sorry, Mr. Kardar, that was rude of me."

"Shouting at me or explaining me away?" he asked with a small smile. It was entirely disconcerting. He was still on fire. I was having difficulty with this.

"Both. Sorry about that."

"Am I to assume you've never encountered one like me before?" he asked with a look of patient frustration. This was going so well.

"Correct," I said, straightening up and fiddling with the bottle.

"I imagine it would be quite shocking. I understand. To most people, we don't appear to be burning, but seeing that would indeed be a concern. At least your friend knows you would be quick to put her out should she be set alight."

"You don't look like you're burning, actually, just on fire. Lots of flames." I waved a hand over my torso and head to show where I saw it.

"What is your name, sir?"

"I'm Carter Brooks. Just Carter is fine."

"A pleasure to meet you, Carter. And you, miss?"

"Alex is enough for now." She folded her arms and frowned back and forth between us.

"Charmed. Would it be prudent for us to continue this conversation somewhere we may not be so easily disturbed, or do you wish to carry on here at my counter?"

"Best chat somewhere else," I said, watching the lick of one flame up over his chest. I could almost feel the heat.

"I'll ask my wife to watch the shop, and we can speak in the back room."

"Mr. Kardar, is your wife also djinn?" I asked, tossing the water bottle between my hands. Would she look the same? Please look the same and not covered in fire.

"Yes, and she would take much worse to the threat of being patted out than I do, so I request you refrain from screaming at her." I nodded mutely. His smile was still perfectly polite, and he was far less angry than I expected. Maybe he worked all the anger off with the flames.

He picked up a phone from under the counter and said a few words in what I thought might be Urdu before we heard footsteps on stairs. A shorter hijabi lady emerged from the door, her flames far higher and brighter than her husband's and a solid glare aimed at Alex and I. She simply nodded as she took over his place at the counter.

"If you would follow me," Mr. Kardar said, leading us to the stockroom. It was a box room really, with a set of stairs at the far end. We went down to a basement that had a sofa at one end and a kettle by a sink at the other. A heavy table stood in the middle, where someone's meal sat abandoned.

"Tea? It may help with the effects of that shock," Mr. Kardar said, clicking the kettle on.

"That would be lovely. Two sugars, please," I said.

"Hot and sweet, just like the Red Cross advises," he said. "Alex?"

"I'm good," she said, shaking her head as she claimed one corner of the sofa. I plopped down next to her, tired from the fading adrenalin. He made the tea and passed it to me before looking over us again.

"May I ask why you have come to visit me?" he asked.

"I'm looking for my sister. She's missing," I said, sipping my tea. The mug was burning in my hands, but it wasn't on fire and I was so grateful for a heat source that made sense.

"Miss Sarah?" he asked, his face falling.

"You know her?" Alex said, rising from the sofa. It was my turn to grab her arm and pull her down, holding my cup out to one side for safety.

"Yes, we've been having discussions about some areas she was interested in. She has some excellent insights. I was aware she hadn't visited for some time, but I thought this was due to the pressure of her studies."

"She's been missing for about three weeks," I said, watching him. He was telling the truth as far as I could tell.

"You're her brother?" he asked, looking me over again.

"By blood and raising."

"She did not shout that I was on fire." He said it with a smile, but I could feel the accusation. He was leaning against the table, licks of flames dying back as they tumbled over the metal.

"Our skills are different. Sarah feels more than sees. I see more, have to shut my eyes to get a proper feel."

"How curious. She had mentioned you but nothing about you being skilled."

"He tries not to be," Alex interjected, and I shot her a look.

"You reject your nature?" he asked, crossing one ankle over the other and leaning in a little.

"I saw ghosts and vampires at a young age. You saw how well that went just now." I shrugged, hating this conversation. "Sarah's much more in touch with her gift."

"And yet yours offers more clarity. How unfortunate for you it manifested that way."

"Thanks. You're the first person to get that," I muttered, looking back at Alex. "Do you know what Sarah was doing?"

"She was speaking to various other people in the city. There were a lot of questions about past groups, the evolution of our presence in the city. How and where we hid our true natures. She wanted to know details of how we cloak our presence."

"Like, she wanted you to hide her?" Alex asked, back to frowning.

"No, she wanted to know our historical ways. We haven't had to hide ourselves as much. Not many can tell what we are. Our religion has made more people upset than our manifestation."

"Do you know who else she was talking to?" I asked, an itch starting up under my skin. This was good, it gave us an idea at what she was looking for.

"Not with enough certainty to say," he said, his smile sad. "I would be happy to assist with your search—I am very fond of Sarah—but I can't help in that regard." He took a cigarette pack out of his pocket and held it up. "Do you mind?" he asked. We both shook our heads, me still sipping my tea. He lit one off his finger, and I felt Alex jolt next to me.

"Did you do that to spook her?" I asked with a laugh.

"Just to show her you were being genuine in your concerns, Carter. She thought you mad."

"He looked like he was having a breakdown, to be fair," Alex said, crossing her arms and sinking back into the sofa.

"You want him to." He raised a brow at her, blowing smoke up towards the ceiling.

"That's ridiculous." Alex bristled, glancing over at me.

"But true, if your intent is anything. You like Sarah but not him. Why is that?"

"It's not true! I feel he's too precious about his powers, but I don't want him to get hurt."

"You wish to prove yourself to someone. How unfortunate." Mr. Kardar took a drag and looked to me again. "I don't think she would hurt you, but she would let you endanger yourself and then save you. We can see these things."

"I don't have to listen to this," Alex shouted, shouldering her bag and making to stand up.

"You don't have to listen at all, Miss Alex, but you could use your very old blood to look at me and know I was telling the truth." The challenge sat heavy in the room, and she slumped back into the sofa.

"I wouldn't let you get hurt," she said as she chewed a nail. "Sarah'll kill me if that happens. I hated how Luke looked at you like you were a new toy. Then he said you could go off looking, like you'd be able to find something we couldn't. And then you did, which was sickening." Oh, that jealousy. So that was why she was hot and cold today.

"I'm only doing this to find Sarah. I don't care about your group, or Luke, or any of that. I don't even care about this bloody city. No offence, Mr. Kardar." I nodded to him. He shrugged and nodded back.

"I know. I get it. I thought if you got a fright you'd go back to Manchester and we could focus on finding her."

"She's my sister. You think a fright would make me go back? For fuck's sake, Alex, I used to take beatings for her in school. Someone would have to kill me to make me stop looking for her. I even believed that crap about you being less of a bitch."

"Well, you lied to me first," she said, sullen.

"I might actually hate you." I sighed, downing the rest of my tea. It burned, but it was good, matching my mood. "Mr. Kardar, thank you for the tea and for what you've been able to tell us. I think it would be a good idea if we left now. I promise that if I come in again, I'll not shout about you being on fire. Could you apologise to your wife for us disturbing her meal? I don't think she approved of us."

"No, she felt we should take you down here and burn you to death. I thought that might be a touch aggressive."

"I'm very glad you took that view," I said, eyeing him again. He could do it. "Come on, Alex, let's go."

We shambled up the stairs and out towards the door, nodding to Mrs. Kardar on the way out. We got an angry frown in response, but her flames were smaller.

Once we were out of the shop and walking away, I looked back at Alex. The silence stretched on until we left the railway bridge, and it was scraping down my nerves by the time we reached the square.

"So, what the fuck?"

"I wasn't setting out to hurt you." She huffed, crossing her arms again. "And I did listen to what Luke said. I just thought that maybe if I let you go mess up, you'd back off, and he could focus on her rather than you."

"The only thing he's looking at me for is to get her back. You must know that," I said, the urge to pull my hair out rising.

"I don't think so. But I'm sorry. It was a shitty thing to do. If you get hurt looking for her, she'll still kill me. We okay?"

"You're such a bloody brat, you know that? I wouldn't have much choice but to be okay, would I? Sarah's still missing, so we're stuck as it is. I'd prefer it if you spoke to me rather than taking pot shots at my psyche, but we can work towards that. Now, I believe you were going to take me suit shopping?"

"You still want to go?" For a woman with old blood she was like a fucking child sometimes.

"I still need to go to the party, and you're still my social wingman, so yeah. Let's get me dressed up. Have you told Marc you'll be joining us for a lift?"

"I messaged him but haven't heard back. The shop's that way." She pointed to the large glass and steel shopping centre. Great, crowds, my favourite.

"Yay." I groaned, squaring my shoulders and following her.

"Carter, when he lit that cigarette it was like there was a flame just...on his finger. Like it just came out of his skin." I nodded at her curiously. "Did he look like that all over?"

"More like he was covered in it. I could still see him, but under a layer of fire."

"That's normal for you?" she asked, turning to stare at me as the escalator took us up a level.

"No, as I think my shouting and flailing proved."

"Alright, idiot. I meant, is it normal for you to see others like that?"

"It depends on what I'm looking at, but yeah. I'll see whatever there is. Sarah can do it too, but she has to try harder. She gets the feelings easier. Her intuition's great."

"I wonder why she was speaking to him," Alex frowned again, worrying her bottom lip. "She never mentioned any of this."

"Maybe she thought she shouldn't out folk. Most people want others to think they're what they present as. Safer."

"That's unfair. People with the gift wouldn't discriminate against them."

"Maybe they don't agree. Mr. Kardar didn't like me explaining what he was. I shouldn't have done it. Just because you're happy to know about them doesn't mean they're happy for you to know."

"You make it sound like we're going to go after them."

"Some people would."

"You can't think we'd do that?" she asked as she led me to the shop.

"No, but just because your intentions are good, that doesn't mean everyone's are. I know you trust your group, but Sarah was obviously trying to protect people's privacy."

"I suppose she did that with you. I'm mad at her for that, a bit, but it's understandable given your views."

"So, what sort of suit are we looking for?" I asked, aiming for literally any other subject.

"Can you tell me more about the djinn while we shop?"

"I don't know a huge amount about them, just the basics. They're made of fire in the way we're made of clay."

"What do you mean made of clay? Here, hold this up." She passed me a deep teal shirt, not at all my colour, and I held it against me for her review.

"You know how some creation myths talk about man being built out of clay and then having life put into him? So, we're crafted out of that and djinn were crafted out of fire."

She shook her head, taking the shirt back and passing me a dark green one instead. "And you believe that?" She fished around for a tie.

"I don't have a bloody clue, but that man's made of fire, so I'll take it as partially true if nothing else." I took the tie she offered and held it up as well, watching for her reaction. She nodded and went towards the suits.

"What else is there?"

"They know more about the world than we do, 'cause they can see more. Some people think they're invisible—that's where part of the genie myth comes from."

"Invisible?"

"Yeah, they're on a different system to us with the whole fire thing, so why wouldn't they be able to do that? I've not heard of it happening, but no one would exactly see it."

"Alright, I'll go with that."

"The genie idea comes from people using magic to trap djinn in exchange for magic on demand. It's a terrible idea and generally ends up in the human dying," I said, watching her flick between some patterned monstrosities.

"Be careful what you wish for and all that. Are you more a straight cut or tailored kind of guy?"

"More like once the djinn gets free, they're going to kill you for having the audacity. Trapping someone and using them as a magic slave is very much not okay. Straight cut."

"Yeah, I'd do some hard shit if someone tried to pull that with me."

"That's why people don't shout it from the rooftops. There's always someone wanting to take advantage."

She looked at me with her head tilted to the side. "You're such a cynic. Here, try these on." She handed me a bundle and pushed me towards the changing room.

I took in the ensemble she'd given me once I was safely behind the curtain. It was a black suit with matte lapels and that deep green shirt. Might bring out my eyes. The tie was a silk monstrosity with a deep green and black paisley pattern, accents of dark blue. It'd do. I scrambled into it and came out for Alex to give me the once over.

"So?" I asked.

"Damn, you do polish up nice. We could try you with a blue shirt, but I think you'll be fine in that."

"If this gets your approval then I'll stick with it." I retreated into the cubicle, happy she was so pleased.

"What do you want to do now?" I asked Alex, threading the suit bag over my wrist.

"Honestly, I feel like crap and want to go home. But that may be my own fault. We could look at the gardens. They'll still be open. Let me see that list again?" She held her hand out, and I passed my phone over. "If you're up for it, there is another place Sarah went to nearby. We could check that out and do the gardens tomorrow. I could take a real look over the list tonight and match what's near the flat or around the city?"

"That sounds good." I was tired too, and my head was spinning with the promise of a headache yet to bloom. "How close are we?"

"About a block away. We've walked past it twice." She frowned, a crinkle popping up between her brows. "It's up an alleyway."

I followed her back towards the railway bridge, but we took a hard right up the dodgiest looking street I had seen since I arrived. "Really?"

"I told you there was an alley. It's just ahead." She nodded to a pink neon sign outside an industrial looking building that read 'Golden Globes' with little worlds where the Os would be. A strip club, fabulous.

"You've got to be kidding me."

"This is the place. I've never been in it myself, but I've heard good things. They have a real fancy champagne lounge, apparently." She must have felt my stare on her. "One of my friends dances. She told me about it."

"I've no issue with the stripping, Alex. I'm more wondering why Sarah would come here."

"Me too. Not her scene. It's closed. The girls won't get here 'til about eight, so we're not having any luck before then." She shrugged, leaning against the bricks.

I looked around the alley and back to Alex, hissing air out through my teeth. Pulling out my phone again, I scrolled through the list, checking the date Sarah visited. It was clumped together with the more recent visits, so that was likely a someone rather than a something if Mr. Kardar was anything to go by.

"We can leave it for now. I'll come back later tonight. It'll raise less questions if I go in alone."

"You want to come back to the flat for food or you going to head back?" she asked, pushing off the wall.

"I'm going to go get some sleep for a few hours."

"Sensible. You look like shit again. The group is meeting tonight. We usually do one before a party so we can all connect. I'm sure Luke would be okay with your coming along if you wanted to meet people."

"When?"

"Starts at seven. Usually lasts a couple of hours."

"Okay. I should be able to make it. Can I walk you to the subway?" I asked, eyeing the shadows in the alley.

"Sounds good."

# Chapter 10

*9 December, 1885*

*I have discovered a memento mori carved into a rosary. The rosary is otherwise plain, though well crafted. The underside of the cross shows a face with flowing hair and a skull visage. This is a fine necklace and bears the mark of heavy use. It also bears the screams of a desperate death when the cross is placed against the skin. The beads do not show the same vision, but when using this in prayer and kissing the cross, one is presented with the murder of a young woman.*

*She appears to be in a cold country, running through a forest in the snow. It is daytime, and she is utterly alone, with the exception of her pursuer. She flees to a church, seeking sanctuary, but it is closed and she is instead set upon. She is beaten about the head until she falls still, and then her body is lifted over the shoulder of the assailant. The vision ends here, but the impression of the cold of the forest and the fear experienced by the woman lingers.*

*An interesting thing to note is the fear she feels is not only that of the chase, but that she knows her attacker. It is worth further consideration to assess whether this is a haunting or simply an attachment to the jewellery.*

I made it to the guesthouse and hung up my purchases, scowling at them. They'd do. Plugging my phone in to charge, I flopped onto the bed, not bothering to change except toeing my shoes off before I tugged the covers over me.

I knew I was dreaming when I felt grass underneath me. There was the sound of waves again and looking up, I was met with the same wrong stars. Something in my gut wrenched as I looked at them.

"You wanted me today," called the inhuman rumbling of Dex, tugging me back. I glanced around and saw I was now on a clifftop, a stony beach down below. The starlight was bright enough to watch the waves crash, but there was still no moon. The voice sounded close, almost right beside me, but I couldn't see anything in the grass. No tentacles either, so a good start.

"I thought I'd gone mad. Seemed like a reasonable thing to do," I said, turning onto my back.

"You met one of the djinn," it said, savouring the last word. "And brushed up against the old, hungry things in the tunnels."

"You watching me? That's a bit rude."

"You knew I was."

"You could at least resist gloating." I sighed, pulling my head up to glance about the darkness. I could almost make out the shape of something further along the cliff, like the shadow of a person that was bleeding out at the edges, blurring the starlight around it. It wasn't far off. I could walk to it.

"I know about them already. I have been here a long time."

"In this place we chat in or here in Glasgow?" I asked, settling back into the grass.

"Both. You fear I will use them?"

"The thought had occurred to me. If you're busy offering me a deal then you've probably offered deals to others."

"I have, to many who caught my attention. But I have told you why you present a uniquely interesting proposition, Carter," it crooned, and I felt the shadow turn to look at me.

"I doubt I'm the first person like this that you've found," I said, too tired for this banter.

"Not the first, but you are here. I could help you. We could work together. You know that, you know my offer, and today you wanted it."

"I did. And then I figured out that I wasn't insane, so I didn't anymore."

"You think my help should be a last resort. Why not take it now and preserve the days you would spend chasing magic around a city you barely know?"

"If you're going to keep saying how special I am then you should stop insulting my investigative skills." It laughed at that, and I felt the rumble through the ground beneath me. The word days stuck in my mind, ringing like a siren.

"Perhaps. If you were working with me, I could give you so much more. No stumbling around in the dark, no fear of what is on the other side of the shadows. No worry about the gift being stronger than you are." The voice was creeping closer as it spoke, honey sweet, the shadow looming larger.

"You can't give her to me."

"No, but you could lessen her suffering. And she is suffering, Carter. Three weeks is a long time to be on the wrong plane."

I sucked air through my teeth, hating it. "I don't doubt you're telling the truth," I said, trying my words slowly. "And I was tempted to give myself to you when I thought I'd lost it. But you can't get her back; even if we strike a deal, I have to do that."

"I will keep bringing you here so you can discuss your progress, then." I could hear pride in its voice. "Do you wish to stay here now? It is peaceful, and I will not encroach further."

"I think I'd rather sleep," I said, rolling my head to look back at the stars. The backs of my eyes burned with the view.

"As you wish," it agreed, and I felt the world fade.

I awoke feeling fine this time, no panic and no lingering feeling of monstrosities touching my skin. It could play nice, then. The orange of the street lights glowed through my window, and I groped around for my phone. Tugging it free of the charger cable, the screen flared into life and told me it was after seven. The group meeting would be going on by now. I could show up late. There would be more people then. And I had shit to do first.

I needed to go back to that strip club. I didn't relish the thought.

After washing my face, I plodded in front of the wardrobe, squinting. I would have to look respectable to get past the doors, which meant a shave at least. I could bluff respectability with a shirt and some black slacks, given that I only wanted to speak to the girls. I shaved and dressed, then yanked on my leather jacket. Sarah was my phone's background, in case the bouncers recognised her. I reviewed the list of Sarah's comments. '*Visited—worrying. May need to see her again.*' Not ominous at all. What type of weirdness could there be at a strip club, aside from the usual human excesses?

I swung past a noodle shop I had found on my first night and ambled down Sauchiehall Street, slipping between the throng of bodies. The pubs were full and people spilled about between open doorways, the take-aways spouting light and the smell of cooking grease. A drizzle came on as I started down Buchanan Street, and I was slick by the time I made it back to the Golden Globes. It was still too early for it to be open, so I pressed on the intercom.

I got no answer to my first two buzzes, so I leaned on the button until someone came to the doors.

"Clubs not open yet," growled the slab of muscle who opened it. He was a decent looking guy, square jawed and no-nonsense brown eyes, currently glaring at me.

"I know. My sister was around here a while ago, speaking to one of the dancers. She's gone missing, and I don't know if anyone spoke to your lady here."

He looked me over and glanced at his watch. "Do you know who she spoke to?"

"No, just that she was here. It's written in her diary."

"You got a picture of her?" I pulled out my phone and showed him, her smiling face lighting him in the gloom. "Why're you here? That accent's not local."

"Because it's been three weeks and no one knows where she is."

"You spoken to the police?"

"They've been no use. Probably think she's dead. I'll be five minutes. I just want to see if the woman she spoke to is in and check what they spoke about. I'll be away before opening."

He stepped away from the door, leaving me in the rain and dark. The alleyway didn't get any better at night. Sounds of traffic came up from the road, mixing with the white noise of a crowd. Muffled words pushed out from the door, the hiss of a walkie talkie scratching against the gloom.

It opened again.

"I'm going to frisk you first, then I'll accompany you to the changing room. Anything funny and you'll be sat in the cells," Muscle Man said.

I nodded, holding my arms up and spreading my ankles so he could pat me down. I'd done it at enough airports, so what was a back alley in Glasgow? He looked through my bag too, quirking an eyebrow at the old book. "Reading material. I spend a lot of time waiting for people." He nodded, leading me in.

It was a modern place, the bar running the length of the far wall with booths scattered around and three poles along the performance catwalk. With all the lights it looked like a normal club, minus the obvious. We passed an industrial looking staircase led up to the champagne lounge, all polished metal and studded leather.

Muscle Man led me to a black painted door beside the stage, knocking a staccato pattern. I saw the door open but couldn't see much else from behind his massive shoulders, so I busied myself finding other photos of Sarah on my phone. There was an exchange of words in a language I didn't know, and then he walked through the door with me following in his wake.

The changing room was basic: a large mirror lined with bulbs and a low bench covered in make-up, costume bits and sequins. There were five women, some in robes, and some still dressed in their street clothes, one walking back to join them by the lights.

"This man is looking for his sister," said Muscle Man. "She was here a month ago, speaking to someone, and she's missing. He isn't with the police, and he won't stay long. I can stay here if you want." He looked back at me. "Show them the picture."

I stepped forward and held the screen up. "I appreciate the fact that it's been a month, but if anyone remembers who she was speaking to that would be a big help."

"I think it was Elisha," said a small blonde in heels that made me wince. "She's giving Dave her playlist. Should be back in a minute."

"I can wait at the bar if you'd prefer," I said, looking over to Muscle Man.

"No skin off our backs," said the one who had opened the door. She was gorgeous, tall and strong framed with a plump smirk to her lips. She wore it well, a level challenge in her eyes.

"The bar would be better," said Muscle Man. I nodded and followed him out the door. "I'll ask her to come to you." He nodded to a seat.

"Thank you." I smiled and hopped on one of the barstools. I kept my phone out, alternating between Sarah's list and her photo while I waited. I twisted about on the bar stool, jogging one leg on the footrest.

"I hear you're looking for me," said a slightly accented voice behind me.

"Elisha?" I asked, spinning round and almost falling off the seat. "Oh shit!" I managed to keep my voice down but couldn't hide the look on my face.

"You have the sight. It's been a long time since I met one like you. Your sister didn't have this," the thing that was pretending to be a woman said, stepping closer. "I would prefer you didn't scream. I'd hate to cause a scene and have Darius remove you."

"No scene. Promise," I said, looking her over. She shone like she was made of smoke and light. The shadow of wings that weren't quite there hung huge over her shoulders. Her face was beautiful if a little hard, a quickness to her eyes that spoke of mistrust. She kept shimmering between looking normal and this glowing, amazing thing. My head was trying to process it. Her hair was alternately a neat black waterfall down her back and a storm cloud floating about her. Her eyes, stunning and outlined in dark kohl then pouring out purple light between one blink and the next. She looked to be in her mid- twenties, but I could feel her age in the energy pouring off of her, cascading down and spilling to the floor before melting away. It was like standing next to a waterfall. "You're the fallen, aren't you?" I whispered, my voice constricted low in my throat.

"That's what some people call me. Others are a bit more certain I'm demonic. I don't care. You are looking for your sister; show me her picture so they do not become concerned." I handed my phone over. Her skin was mesmerising, dusted pale but swirling and glimmering. It was like mother of pearl brought to life, and I tried to stop my eyes chasing any particular glint as it passed.

"She spoke to you, about a month ago?" I asked, watching the shadows of the wings again. They were flitting in and out of being there at all, scraping out along the back of the booths.

"Yes, Sarah was not happy. If you shield yourself I'll be less distracting." She grinned at me as she handed the phone back. "She wanted to ask me questions about my being. Why I was hidden, why I work here." She circled her hand to encompass the club.

"You dance. You like having their attention."

"A bold statement for someone struggling to speak." She smirked, shrugging. "But not untrue." She shook her hair and her wings rippled.

"Do you still teach dance?"

"When did I?" She asked, all innocence. Her skin sparked gold and silver and soft pinks, then back to pale flesh. I felt like throwing up.

"When you were a ballerina, the way he described you…" I trailed off, shaking my head, "Sorry. I'm being rude. Sarah was asking why you dance?"

"She asked why here rather than some professional stage. I told her dancing is dancing. The ballets are too famous now, your face recorded. It lasts. I work where I like for as long as I like then move on. She thought I could do more."

"Sounds a bit judgmental for Sarah," I said, scratching the back of my neck with one hand. If I scratched hard enough it would distract me from the nausea. That worked, right?

"She may have had an argument with Dave."

"The DJ?"

"Yes. She was asking for me by my stage name, and he thought she might be a jealous girlfriend. It happens."

"And Dave thought you needed protection because?" I laughed, shaking my head. Even when she looked human you could see the smooth muscles in her arms, the taut line to her shoulders.

"Because not everyone can see my wings, little searching boy."

"Less of the boy," I grumbled, eyes back to the floor.

"You're all children to me. She was asking questions about the other side."

"Death? Or other planes?"

"One is a variant of the other, but the latter. She wanted to know more about them, how they interacted with here. She talked about that as much as the guide."

"You know about the book?" I asked, tensing my arm so not to reach for it.

"Of course. All of us knew he was keeping notes. Not everyone's still here, but those who are enjoy it. We never thought anyone but The Collector would end up with it. To see a little girl running around trying to solve it like a puzzle was entertaining."

"Well, she's missing now, so I'd say she fucked that up."

"Or solved it. You don't know what her questions were for." She glanced behind her, to the staircase, then back to me. "I must ask you to leave now. Darius will be back shortly. If you wish to speak with me again, summon me."

"How do I do that?" Because apparently fallen angel summoning was the first thing you learned in magic, naturally.

"You don't know the arts?"

"Try to avoid them. Just here for my sister."

"An interesting approach. In that case there is a dance studio on Bath Street. I teach during the day. I will not interrupt a class for you, but you can wait until one finishes."

"Thank you for your help," I said, and meant it.

"Hey Faith, I need you up here to check the play order," came a shout from the top of the stairs. She sighed, then rolled her eyes.

"In a moment, Dave," she called.

"Faith?" I asked with a laugh. She flickered again, light and normal and glowing like the sun through a pinhole camera.

"A girl has to have some jokes." She smiled, her accent coming out a little stronger. "Go, now."

"Right, going, thank you." I hopped off the stool and made for the outside door, nodding to Darius the Muscle Man as I went.

I walked a little off from the door then put my back to the bricks, gulping air into my lungs with my eyes screwed shut. The night was cold, and I could feel the blunt chill of the wall through my jacket. The rain had stopped, and a few deep breathes helped shake off the adrenaline. Talking to a fallen angel felt like having a conversation with a small sun. I stretched the tension from my neck and started towards the train station—I was tired enough to sleep and my eyes burned like when I looked at the stars in Dex's world.

The subway was busy, and I was grateful for the damp blast of warm air as I trotted down the steps. It was grounding, distinct, and filthily human. Three nonhumans in one day was a personal record for me. It was progress, had to be, but it hadn't gotten me any closer to finding Sarah. My brain fizzed from seeing Faith and I leaned back into the sway of the train, letting it rock me. It was nice to have the cocoon of grime on the floors, the stale scent of the trapped air.

I emerged into the night with a clearer head and worry nagging my gut. Scoping the group out was a good idea. However, I had a visceral repulsion to being stuck in a room full of people who thought they knew what they were doing. I made it to the shop just after half past eight and found it mostly empty; Luke, Alex, and Marc left tidying up.

"Sorry I'm late," I said as I came in.

"I didn't know you were coming, Carter, or I would have asked the group to stay back," Luke said with a grin and moved to give me a hug. I tried to dodge it, but he pulled me close and clapped me on the back. I froze, giving in and hugging him back when it was clear he wasn't letting go.

"Sorry. Got distracted," I said into his shoulder. Goddamnit.

"By a strip club," Marc said, waggling his brows at me.

"Kind of," I said, flashing a look at Alex.

"Alex told us you were meeting a friend of Sarah's. It's good you've been able to reach people we couldn't." Luke smiled as he eventually let me go. Clingy.

"She was helpful." I smiled, unsure how much Alex had said.

"I'm pleased to hear it. Could you join me in the practice room? I have something I want to show you. Alex, Marc, do you mind?"

"It's fine. We're nearly done here. Carter, you wanna meet me back at the flat and give me the details?" she asked, stacking cushions into a corner.

"Sounds good." I nodded to her, nerves coming to my chest again. Luke was fine but being alone with him in the shop didn't really appeal to me. I'd only known the dude a day. I didn't like people enough for this.

"Great, see you there," she called as I followed Luke into the dim room. He flicked on some lights and led me to a set of large throw pillows, sitting across from me and folding his legs.

"Are you finding it difficult to keep your shield down?" he asked, fixing me with a look I'd bet he used on clients. The room felt clear and empty after their use—it was nice to sit in peace.

"It's tiring, but I'm noticing it less. I forgot this morning but managed to keep it down the rest of the day."

"I'm glad to hear it. I wanted to speak to you about Dex."

"Go on," I said.

"I didn't wish to worry you unduly at our first meeting, but I've researched further and can only find direct contact leading to disaster."

"I'd kind of picked up on that. It keeps offering to tell me where Sarah is if I buy into indentured servitude. It's also really fucking with my sleep pattern which is no good." He did a good job of trying to keep his face blank.

"It offered you Sarah?" His tone was as neutral as his face. Definitely a work voice.

"No. It offered to tell me where she is. It can't get to her. I don't really know why, but it would've used that directly if it could. All it could say was where she is. And it'll only do that if I promised to help it."

He was quiet for a beat, staring at his hands before looking back up to me. "Has it offered anything else?"

"It offered to tell me how long she had left. If I traded."

"How long she has left?"

"It's words. Said she was in a hard place and running out of time," I said, leaning back and resting my weight on my palms. Some of the tension pulled out of my back, and I rolled my head to either side.

"That sounds as if she's trapped somewhere. This must be so hard on you. If you'd like assistance keeping it away, I could ask some from the group to—"

"To what, exactly?" I snapped my head up, frowning at him. "It keeps grabbing me while I sleep. Not a lot you can do about that."

"I'm concerned it will attempt to influence you into doing something untoward. It's already offered to trade with you."

"Yeah, I got around that," I said, offhanded, watching for his reaction. There was a distinct twitch before he found his voice.

"Got around it?"

"It was being smug and let the information slip. I didn't make a big deal, and it didn't notice. Even said it wanted to keep having me back."

"What do you mean by 'having you back?'" He was physically paler now. That had to be a bad sign.

"When we speak, I'm in it's place. It takes me to there to talk." I squirmed on the cushion as Luke stared at me.

"You mean, it takes you to it's residence?" he asked, his frown deeper. His wrinkles weren't deep, especially for a lawyer, but they were getting clearer the longer we spoke.

"Yes, that's exactly what I mean. That's why having someone come and put up a circle or something wouldn't be any use. It's not haunting me. It's taking me off on a jaunt."

"That's both fascinating and vastly troubling. Do you know how difficult it is to do what you are describing?"

"I think we both know the answer to that is a no." I raised my eyebrows at him, sitting back up.

"Apologies. I forget you're not as well practiced. Your natural gift is impressive for one so untrained."

"I keep hearing that."

"Oh?" He tilted his head, watching me. "Go on." He put a hand to my knee.

"That's why Dex likes me, I'm an oddity. A useful oddity."

"Has it said that?"

"It was telling me how useful I would be while it was offering Sarah's location. It's always about what someone can get when people are praising this stuff," I spat, my anger roiling up against my tiredness. He stiffened, his face going blank again.

"Some of us wish to help those struggling with their gift."

"Most of the time it's to help them get whatever the teacher wants," I said, standing from the cushion and stalking to the other side of the room. I stopped in front of an altar on one wall and toyed with some crystals, the white noise pushing back at my mind.

"I'm sorry you feel that way," Luke said. "I assure you, I only want Sarah to be found safe and as well as she can be." He sounded honest and turning to look at him, he looked pained. He had followed me, was almost close enough to touch.

"I believe you," I said, forcing my anger back down. "I'm trying to piece together Sarah's last actions, see what I can stir up from friends."

"Hence attending the party." Luke smiled, edging a step closer. "I'm looking forward to seeing you there."

"Not scared I'll frighten the guests?"

"I've told the group you'll be present. They're happy to help. Should something suspicious occur our members will report back."

"Like a neighbourhood watch." I stepped back from him and bumped into the altar. "You like caging me in Luke."

"Do I?" he asked, moving forward ever so slightly.

"You do. Why is that?"

"Perhaps I'm curious. Why you rail against your gift. Why Sarah didn't mention you when she was happy to discuss your mother. Why you insist on working alone."

"I'm working with Alex.".

"Reluctantly," he replied, stepping so he was in front of me.

"It may have escaped your notice, but Alex can be a bit volatile."

"She's passionate. Almost as passionate as Sarah."

"And as vocal about her issues. She wanted me gone so you could look for Sarah."

"I'm aware." His eyes were flicking over my face as if it would change.

"She was willing to endanger me to scare me off."

"That is regretful, but her intentions were good," he said with a small pout.

"Why do you want her with me?"

"For your assistance."

"Not for yours?" I asked, tilting my head to look at him.

"Carter." He smiled despite the shock in his voice. "You think I'd have someone watching you for any reason other than to help?"

"Yes."

"And what other reasons would I have?" he asked, head tilting to match mine. It was bird-like on him.

"To keep an eye on me and see if you could learn anything from what I find. Alex is devoted to you."

"Almost as much as Sarah," he said. "They joined the group together and have both worked hard. Alex feels a loyalty, for my helping with her gift. Her experiences were difficult. She can empathize with your position."

"You put two broken birds together?"

"Are you a broken bird? I certainly don't think Alex would call herself that. Or you. She's been impressed with what you've shown her."

"Maybe not. But you still want her on me to make sure I don't screw up," I said.

"My intention is to assist you. Any additional benefits, while helpful, are secondary." He was telling the truth again. I could feel it. Confusing man.

"We can play nice, so I'm sure you'll be getting plenty of those."

"I'm glad to hear it." He smiled and gripped my shoulder, holding on for longer than necessary. "This must be a great strain on you."

"What else can I do? Can't leave her lost. No one else has managed, so I've got to try."

"I'm sure you'll succeed. There was one other point I wished to discuss." His hand was still on me. I fought the urge to shrug it off, enjoying the contact now that it had happened. The loneliness of the city and the chill of rain had caught up with me, and I felt drained.

"What was it?" I asked, wanting to sit down again.

"The practitioners involved with Dex," he began, and I had a flash of a thought.

"Yeah, were any of them collectors?" I blurted, wanting to get the idea out before it left me.

"What do you mean?" Luke raised an eyebrow.

"That book I told you about, the guide? It talks about a collector, or The Collector, I should say. He's this character who stashed items and information about the others around Glasgow."

"Others?"

"Non humans who lived here."

"You know some?"

"They're described in the guide," I not-quite lied. "This guy details meeting them, and he keeps talking about The Collector. I wondered if the position got handed down, like a title?"

Luke nodded as he thought. "I understand your meaning. That would tie in with what I planned to share. There is a resurgence of practitioners seeking to work with Dex. This may explain why it's able to contact you. Usually these sorts of communions require ritual and sacrifice."

"So Sarah might have bumped into them, and that's how it knows where she is?"

"That's my concern, yes," he said, a grim pull to his mouth.

"That's kind of a relief."

"How so?" Luke asked, brows low together.

"It said Sarah had been speaking to it, though she may not have known who she was speaking to. Made me worry she was getting dragged into something she didn't understand. But if they've got sights on her then they're seeking her out."

"You feel that's better?" Luke looked unconvinced.

"It's better that someone's looking for her rather than her being led blindly. She'd hate that, and not just because it would prove me right." I chuckled against something tight twisting around my ribcage.

"You'd prefer she were targeted rather than tricked, because it would distress her otherwise?"

"She's my sister. I don't want her hurt. She's never going to be able to stomach this city again. She loves it here, and now it'll be tainted by this." The wave of pain that had been behind my anger crested and poured down, a flood of ache in my chest. "I want to know she's safe, you know? I can't do much for her, but I can do that."

"We're all going to assist with that as much as we can," Luke said, pulling me into another hug. I let him, appreciating the heat of his chest against mine. I was so tired, and it felt good to have contact.

"It told me she only had a few days left," I said.

"We'll find her." He put a hand to the back of my head, stroking through my hair. "We'll make this happen, Carter." The surety of his voice was more comforting than it should have been. It felt so good to have someone say it out loud.

"Thanks," I said, pulling away.

"It's quite alright. I must depart now, but I'll see you at the party tomorrow. I'm here should you need anything. Try to rest." He punctuated the point with another shoulder squeeze. "We'll all do whatever we can."

"I'm going to speak to Alex then head back to sleep." He was still close, enough for the heat of his body to warm me. He lingered for a moment longer then stepped back, going to the cushions.

"I'm glad to hear it. She'll appreciate the news. She misses Sarah dearly." I nodded and moved towards the shop. "Carter?" he asked, as I opened the door

"What?" I glanced back at him.

"I do look forward to seeing you tomorrow. Alex told us about your outfit. It sounds delightful."

"We'll see when it's on." I shrugged, smiling at him.

"I shall, indeed."

"Night, Luke."

"Until tomorrow." He nodded, framed in the light.

It was still cold out but the rain was holding off, and I felt my tiredness lifting as the chill air filled my lungs. I tugged my jacket up against it and hurried towards the flat. I hit the buzzer and was met by Alex at the door.

"Thanks for abandoning me with Luke," I said as I came in.

"Oh, hush. He's a little sweet on you. Did he have anything useful to discuss? He never told Marc or me anything good."

"He's worried about me wandering around the city poking things to see what they do," I said.

"But I'm with you." Alex bristled in her seat.

"Which is what I pointed out. I think he's really worried I'd drag you into trouble."

She softened at that, settling her shoulders a little. "I suppose it's nice of him to worry. Nothing else?" She went through to the kitchen and put the kettle on.

"He offered to have someone bless my room, protect me while I'm lost and lonely." I sighed theatrically and leaned against the counter. "Did you tell him about the djinn?"

"No," she said after a beat, "I didn't. I should have, because he could maybe help them. But like you said, they might not want everyone to know. It'd be rude to do that without speaking to them. Did you tell him?"

"No. For the same reasons. I don't think we should without their explicit permission. We can speak to them about it if we think it would help."

"I hope you're right," she said, passing me a cup of tea.

"We'll have to see. The dancer wouldn't tell me much at her work, but she's given me an address if I want to speak to her some more."

"Do you?" Alex asked through the steam of her brew.

"She mentioned Sarah looking for new places, like Mr. Kardar. I feel like I didn't get everything out of her. There's also someone else from that list I want to see if we can find."

"We were lucky with the ones we found today," she said, sipping her tea and stretching her neck. "You planning to kick over every can in the city?"

"Pretty much. I'd like to check out the botanical gardens tomorrow."

"I've tutorials all morning but should be free come lunchtime. You okay to wait for me?" she asked.

"Sure. Where will I meet you?"

"The campus would be good; we can plan our route for the other places."

"Great. Do I need to do any other prep for this party?" I asked, setting my cup down. I leaned back against the counter, rolling my neck too.

"No. Luke's set the ground work. I'll be your plus one as long as you need me. If anything comes up, we'll know."

"That's helpful."

"He's trying. He's gotten more worried about her."

"Oh?" I looked at her, seeing the frown again.

"I don't know what you said, but he's more stressed since you arrived. At first I thought it was 'cause you'd mess up, but now I think it's Sarah not being here."

"Is he this close with everyone?" My tone was mostly non-confrontational.

"No, but he's been working with Sarah for a long time. He feels a duty to care for those he's teaching."

"Like you?"

"Like me. Though Sarah had been more involved in his rituals."

"Why, if you don't mind my asking?"

"I'm not as into his type of magic."

"The sex stuff?"

"Not just that, but yes. I appreciate the usefulness of masculine and feminine magic, but I'd rather be part of a committed pairing than use the base energy."

"Married magic?"

"That is a massive over simplification of a culturally and spiritually respected joining, but yes, that's the idea." She rolled her eyes at me and drank her tea.

"But Sarah and he never joined that way."

"No. I'm sure Luke would have been happy to help her develop that style of magic, but Sarah didn't want to. Said it would blur lines."

"Ethically appropriate decisions are so rare," I murmured, grateful Sarah had been making some good choices in this cluster fuck of a situation.

"It'd all be consensual. We don't do anything funny."

"I know, but he's like your teacher. I get it that everyone in this situation is an adult and can make their own choices but still, could be kinda dicey."

"I wouldn't see it that way, but we've worked with him for a long time. I get how that might look. But it never happened, and she's been off making her own enquiries, which is worrying. Our group doesn't do that."

"Is Marc part of the group?" I asked, pushing the other train of thought out of my head.

"No. He provides some of the extras there."

"Like what, he's your supplier?"

"He gets the parties a little extra. He knows about the group but doesn't practice anything himself." She shrugged, finishing off her cup.

"An orgy with drugs. Hurray." My head dropped along with any enthusiasm that had been crawling into my brain.

"Don't be a prude. I'm not talking heroin. Just some edibles and a bit of molly to get people chilled out if they feel like it. The party's very relaxed, people like to unwind." She shrugged again to end the matter, and I didn't have the heart to argue. I should have expected this.

"I promise not to be a prude, but I won't be taking anything. I need a good look at who's there. I'm going to head back to the guesthouse. I'm shattered."

"You do look wiped out. Get some sleep and I'll text you where to meet tomorrow."

"Thanks, Alex." I smiled, going to give her a hug and leave.

"You're welcome. You okay?"

"Sure, why?" I asked as we parted.

"You're hugging me. You don't like me."

"I don't dislike you, though I am still pissed about that stunt earlier. It's a goodbye hug. Don't make it weird." It was weird, but it felt like the right thing to do.

# Chapter 11

*24 February, 1887*

*I have discovered the most unusual creature. It is formed of what I expect may be ectoplasm or some similar substance, for it can transubstantiate between solid and ethereal in a way I have only previously witnessed in a haunting.*

*This being is not dead though, or if it is then it is the most curious ghost I have ever found. The body is substantial, thick as a crocodile and broad as a mill worker. The face, if it can be attributed as such a thing, is hideous. Two eyes, dark as coal and round as pennies, sit atop a mouth shaped like a wish bone that is brimming with teeth. What teeth they are too, gnarled and snaggled with hooks upon them! I would not believe reports of the thing if I had not encountered it myself.*

*The elemental power associated with it is not insignificant, though I am yet to observe it undertaking any action that would indicate higher intelligence. I came upon it near the ship yard. Water seems to be its preferred medium given what behaviour I have been able to observe. I am not optimistic as to developing any sort of relationship with it as the creature flees when I approach. However, the method it deploys upon fleeing requires further study, as it seems not only to become insubstantial but vanish completely.*

I walked to the station, kicking thoughts around like empty cans. I was debating whether I should tell Alex about Dex. Luke hadn't told her either. Why not?

"You're getting yourself a lot of attention." The voice broke my thoughts, and I turned to see Marc standing beside me on the platform.

"Sorry, I never saw you."

"It's cool, I didn't want you to. But seriously, you're getting a name."

"With who?" I asked, huffing a laugh.

"In the group. Luke's been pretty vocal about it."

"Good things?"

"Some of them, yeah." He shrugged his fur clad shoulders. That coat must weigh a tonne when it was wet.

"And the others?"

"He's warning people to stay away because his sights 're on you. Maybe not as plain as that, but it's what he means."

"That's going to be counterproductive." What was the game here then?

"They'll tell Alex if they see anything, but Luke's marking you as his. Might want to watch your back."

"Why, you sweet on him?" I cocked my eyebrow to him.

"Too old for me. But he's shrewd. He'll have a reason for wanting you, even if it's to claim he planted a flag in that ass. So to speak." His eyes went back to the tracks, and he leaned against the wall.

"Why're you telling me?" I asked, joining him.

"'Cause I know he does some weird shit. This group is nice enough, but half of them are dotty or desperate. Luke isn't. His shit's real. So's Sarah's."

"She spook you with it?"

"Don't pull some shit, I know how to fight my way out of most things." A man after my own heart. "I'm not stupid enough to think my stuff is the only stuff Luke dabbles with. He's a control freak, likes to get his way."

"So Luke wants to fuck me, and he might not be as genial and magnanimous as he seems?"

"Your sister's right. You are an arsehole."

"Dude, I'm sorry, not meaning to be a dick. Just a bit confused as to why you're telling me this now." A push of warm air hit my face as the train pulled up. We stepped on board, sitting next to each other and hunching together.

"I see a lot of things. You have to in my line of work. I've seen Luke look at Sarah like she's a prize, and now he's looking at you the same way. If she's coming back from, wherever, I think you're the one to find her, and I'd rather see you do it."

It took me a minute to process what he was saying. "Are you sweet on her?"

"Sweet as anyone in supply and demand." He sniffed, swiping some unseen lint off his shaggy coat. "She's decent."

"Alright, thanks. Do you trust Luke?"

"As far as I trust anyone who's paying me."

"Is that a no?" I asked, my brain starting to lag.

"It's an 'I would be careful' but given the moon eyes you're getting, maybe you'll be safe."

"Has he hurt someone?"

"Not that I know of. He tends to just make things happen. He's good at it too. I'd take tips if my clients already weren't so keen to come back. But they are, and there's always more of them."

"Why you dealing?" I asked.

"A man's got to eat, and it's fun." There was an honesty to it.

"Bit dangerous, no?"

"Only if I get caught. I'm really good at blending in."

I looked him up and down. "Sure."

"This is my stop." He hopped up, heading to the doors. "See you tomorrow night."

I was left on the train to chew over that odd conversation. Marc wasn't exactly warning me off Luke, but he'd seen the same hunger I had. It could just be Luke imprinting on me because he'd not fucked Sarah. Alex wouldn't keep quiet about something like that though, and she was busy cackling about how cute it was that Luke liked me. Marc's comment about a prize was ringing in my head, but it could be my own suspicions rising again. I resolved to think about it in the morning and got off at Cowcaddens, restless and unsettled.

I pulled my jacket up to fend off the chill and wandered towards the guesthouse, listless at the idea of sitting in all evening. I could go to a bar and drink enough that I'd pass out; I hadn't done that in a few years. It'd guarantee a headache in the morning, and I didn't fancy trying to use my gift on top of a hangover. I stopped, reached in my bag to rescue the crumpled street map from underneath everything else. Finding my location, I looked for some sign of a green space. It was almost as good as a river, and it'd let me chill for a bit before going back. I spotted Garenthill Park a street or so up and made for it, finding it to be an odd mix of playground and coliseum.

The front part was a mix of grass and cobbled patches leading to a large square performance space, broad stone rows of seats and a central staircase rising up. It was dotted with stout cube lamps and tall iron streetlights, patchwork levels of illumination glowing in the dark. Two stone channels led down the sides of the steps and out past the front levels of seating to create little rivers streaming down. It was like a forest senate room, half nature and half theatre.

I went up the steps and through the scraggy bushes there to find a squat pyramid with a railed platform at the top, like a lookout point. There were a few children's play things smattered about, a set of swings and a slide, a rough wooden climbing frame. The real news up here was the huge mural that covered the boundary wall. It was an eclectic scramble of symbols and colours, lips and eyes and globes and a kaleidoscope of colour with '1978' at its centre. It looked like someone had a similar idea with the flats that bordered the park, a distressed quartet of geometric patterns dividing the gable wall.

I settled onto a bench beside a light and pulled out my phone, checking over Sarah's notes. She had a mix of items and people listed, details of a succubus here and a maybe vampire there, haunted trinkets and cursed spaces. Nothing tied together except that this guide's nameless narrator kept going back to The Collector.

He'd got increasingly fixated on finding more, flitting across the city for secrets like a magpie. A great critic of the status quo, he ranted politely about how he would order things if he had the power to do so. Wanting power became quite the pursuit, with more visits to The Collector and more trades as the book went on. And then it stopped, left incomplete, after he spoke about going to do a ritual to access a great power. That didn't sound good. Either it had gone so well for our plucky diarist that he didn't need to keep writing, or he'd died. Likely, there was no middle ground.

I flicked through the dates, trying to spot anything from Sarah's comments about rituals or The Collector. There were plenty of mentions in the guide, our narrator had become close with The Collector. The diarist had noted their talks about religion and philosophy, discussions on the imbalance between the wheels of action and those using them. Power and what it meant.

It was a very frank relationship, something between friend and mentor, and I could feel the writer's yearning to have what The Collector had. Was this who Sarah had caught the interest of? I went over the list on my phone again, checking if the shop was still there or if she spoke about him. The Collector was bound to know about the value of her powers.

That sparked a thought– if Sarah was valuable then I could be too. Dex was already offering me a deal. What about getting an agent? There had to be magical middle men. I could be good bait. I packed the book away and headed back towards the guest house.

"Mr. Brooks?" a younger gent at the front desk called. I hadn't met him before so I nodded, going over. "A package for you. Your colleague said you needed it ahead of tomorrow." He handed me a padded envelope—it only had my name on, no address. No return details on the back. Only Alex and my parents knew where I was staying.

"Brilliant, thanks very much for holding that for me," I said, nodding to the chap and jogging up the stairs. What the shit?

I got to my room and opened it, tipping the contents onto my palm. A braided leather bracelet slipped out, a flat silver charm shining up between the straps. It was a tree, branches reaching up and around to intertwine with the roots, the links between them looping and swirling in Celtic knots. It was pretty, like something you'd see at an arts fair, and I picked it up to examine the intricacy of the moulding.

As I touched the metal my jacket pocket seared like fire. I dropped the bracelet while I shook myself out of it. Once the burning abated I emptied my pocket out. The linen triangle Lou had given me shimmered, the scent of sage pouring off it.

I looked around the room and, confident I was alone, bent down to the bracelet again. I held the linen over the charm. No change. I picked up the bracelet and turned it around in my hands, feeling the linen starting to grow warm as I touched the tree. I had enough time to look at the back of the silver before the triangle burned again, ice going through my veins as I saw the makers mark. Two over styled initials sat on the trunk of the tree, 'SB' dead in the centre. The linen was glowing now, yellow light shining out.

I dropped the bracelet on the table and sat, trying to quell the fluttering in my throat. I knew her mark even if the style was different on this one. Someone had found it, cursed it if Lou's gift was right, and left it for me. It'd been after I was away too, so they knew where I was staying, and that I was out.

That was a lot of information to know about me given I'd only been here a few days. I was usually good at picking up if I was being watched. Low level paranoia was a staple of mine. Glasgow was a new city and my guard was deliberately down, so I couldn't be sure. Careless, Carter.

Alex wouldn't be stupid enough to use something of Sarah's, and I didn't think she'd stoop to cursing me. There'd been enough shame with her clumsy pushes. Plus, she was back to being reasonable. Hopefully.

Anger started to seep up. Hot rage prickled along my scalp at the idea of someone trying to fuck with me, using something from Sarah to rattle me. Someone knew I was digging and was trying to warn me off. Or maim me, depending on the curse. I could ask Luke to have a look at that.

I turned to the laptop. Sarah had kept good records of her commissions and this wasn't her usual style, so it must have been ordered. I searched her lists, looking for mentions of trees and charms. A recent design came up, male bracelet of entwined leather and a tree of life charm she had made from scratch. There was no price listed, but I spotted Luke's name on the details. He'd requested it made for Allhallowtide, whatever that was, and was precise about the types of knots to be shown. I could see a scan of these on the file, taken from stone carvings somewhere. I Googled Allhallowtide and discovered it covered from Halloween 'til the second of November, with a different title for each day. Maybe it was for this party.

No finish date or details of payment on file, which showed on all the other completed commissions. So she hadn't finished it before she vanished. Yet here it sat with me, complete and dubiously delivered. Someone was having a fucking laugh.

I put the bracelet back in the envelope and turned Sarah's laptop off. I would research The Collector tomorrow, when I couldn't taste my anger and fear mixing on my skin like oil.

I stripped and threw myself into bed, tossing onto my back and staring at the ceiling. I knew what would happen when I fell asleep—Dex. I could ask it about The Collector, or who had sent me that bracelet. But nothing came for free, and if I started giving it something now, it would push harder. It was confident I would trade, and I could see why. The city was amazing, but it thrummed with all of the Others here, jostling along under the surface. It left me cold, hopeless. So much all at once that my brain was struggling to process it. But I had to try.

I was back on the cliff, this time laid down into the heathery grass. Waves rushed against the shore below me by the scrunch and pull I could hear booming regularly. The stars were brighter than before, almost more so than the moonlight. They were still all wrong, none of the constellations what they should be. A stab of worry bloomed in my gut, but I pushed it away. I couldn't fix it, so there was no point in panicking. A fire crackled and I sat up, spotting a circle set back from the edge. Standing, I wandered over and sat at the cusp of the light, inside its warmth.

"You're quiet," I said after the silence went on too long.

"I thought you would want time to think," came a reply from the other side of the fire. I couldn't see Dex because it was outside the illumination, almost visible in the starlight. It was closer to human size now, tall and broad chested and flickering about the edges. I couldn't look too long at the shape.

"If I asked you some questions, would you answer them?"

"Yes," it said in the next breath.

"Would there be a catch?"

"That would depend on the question." Naturally.

"Would you tell me the price, if there was one, before you answered?"

"Of course. I don't trick people, Carter," it purred.

"Except when they don't know they're speaking to you," I said.

"Your sister was a special exception."

"Course she was. Why?"

"That one will cost."

"Let's start basic then. Do you have other people working for you in the city now?"

"Yes," it said.

"Would you tell me if I had met them?"

"No."

"Why not?"

"Because it pleases me to have them aware of you. You could be so much more if you'd let me help you, and that potential is a beautiful thing. Beauty can scare those unused to it."

I thought that one over and nodded, seeing its idea. "Well that's hardly fair, Dex," I ventured.

"How so?"

"If you're busy using me as a threat without my consent then you're already getting my service." I tilted my head at the shape flickering in the dark. "I've not even agreed to trade with you yet and you're using me as a scare tactic."

"You will," it promised, "But you have not yet. I suppose that should allow you some answers, to make all things fair." It said fair as if it tasted unpleasant. What was fair to a creature like this?

"Did you tell someone to send me that cursed bracelet?"

"I did not. That displeased me. I do not favour those who act beyond their sacrifice."

"Sacrifice?" A shot of cold went down my spine.

"All trades require sacrifice, Carter." I could feel the smile in its voice. "And for those who please me I am generous. Not so for others."

"That's nice to know. Do you mean literal sacrifice, or effort?"

"Both. I enjoy sweat as much as blood."

"That's good, I'm much better at one than the other."

"I doubt that. If you were given the right opportunity, I think you could spill blood beautifully."

"We're getting creepy and off topic." I cleared my throat. "Will you tell me who is working for you?"

"I could name a few dozen humans. Did you have anyone in particular in mind?"

"Do you have dealings with someone known as The Collector?"

"Yes."

"Have you done so recently?"

"Yes."

"Can you tell me precisely where Sarah is?" I pushed, eyes narrowing on the insubstantial phantom.

"Yes, and how to get there."

"How long does she have left?"

"Less than four days."

"Fuck!" The shout was out of me before I recognised my own voice. I stood and paced about the fire. "What would it cost to get her location?"

"Service for fifteen years."

"Fifteen years?" I stopped, looking at it.

"That is how long it would take for you to find her again, and by then it would be her bones, so that is what you would trade. It would be within your plane, and I would be willing to let you undertake matters further than Glasgow, subject to your return. If you did not return, I would take the time from you."

"You mean you could whack fifteen years off of my life?"

"If I wished to, yes. It would harm you, and given the frail nature of humans, I do not know if you would survive."

"But couldn't I just give you the fifteen years then?" I asked, curious as to the practicalities as well as the implications.

"I would not accept that. You are more useful to me when interacting with others."

"Alright. How many questions left?"

"As many as you like, but two more for free."

"You must have been using me a lot."

"You have no idea," it growled, and I felt the hunger in its stare. Fuck me. This was not okay.

"What was that curse meant to do?"

"To confound and confuse you. Make your investigation more difficult. Warn those you approached that you were an ill omen."

"How nice. That's not what the charm was intended for?"

"No. It has been deliberately changed. Your fairy friend does not know how much she has assisted you."

"Will I find The Collector in Glasgow?"

"Oh yes, he does not stray far from here. There are too many opportunities. That is your last free answer." I felt the heat from the fire surge, logs popping as it sparked up.

"What, no location?"

"You did not ask for one outside of Glasgow."

"Alright." Bloody bastard. "Do you have other names?"

"Yes."

"Would you tell me any of them?"

"At a price."

"All of them at a price?"

"I will tell you the Romans who came here called me Dis and were wrong, but they are all dead now, so that hardly matters."

"Are you a god?"

"Not in the way you understand that word, but something close."

"Fuck."

"That would not be one of the services. Your body could not withstand it."

"Really?" I asked, considering leaping off the cliff at that particular thought.

"Do you wish to test my advice?" It at least sounded amused.

"No!" My heart yanked in a panic. "You hear myths. Zeus as a bull and all that."

"Trust my word." It chuckled warmly.

I swallowed hard. "I do, I do. Have the people, and non-people, I have spoken to so far lied to me?"

"No," it said to my surprise.

"No price on that one?"

"You would know that answer yourself if you were not so worried."

"I think I should go now."

"You can sleep before the fire if you wish. Or at the cliff. I will not come nearer."

"Alright. The fire sounds good."

"Goodnight, Carter," it breathed, sounding close.

# Chapter 12

<u>2 June, 1886</u>

There is an irregular pattern of deaths emerging at the riverside. It began shortly after a young woman, Annie McCrory, was pulled from the water. No further investigation was made in relation to her autopsy, and it was accepted that she had drowned. There is little mention of the further injuries that painted the body, or the sheer amount blood that turned her clothing scarlet. The persuasion of money must be as strong as ever for that matter not to be referred to the Procurator's Office. It is known who committed the act, but given his father's position, it's unlikely any punishment will be forthcoming.

After her death, however, a pattern began to emerge. Young men have been found floating face down in the river shallows, thoroughly drowned rather than simply dumped. There is little similarity to the victims except for one concerning detail, the removal of their external reproductive organs. One hopes, truly, that this is done after the drowning. It is enough to make one cross their legs.

The reason for my interest in this matter is that the murders are being committed by a ghost. Poor Annie's ghost, it seems, if the rumours from the medical college of a certain injury, upon a certain learned Member's son, are correct. Why a parliamentarian was not wise enough to seek a private doctor is beyond my ken, but if she did to him what she wrought upon the others he may have had no choice. My sympathy for him is entirely absent. A brute cannot expect a lass to make no issue of an attack. Killing her in retaliation may come back in worse forms for the man yet.

29 October 2017

I woke up without the psychic hangover this time. That had to be a bad sign. I rolled out of bed and showered, scrubbing hard to make sure I felt real. I checked my emails, completing a couple of requests before trotting downstairs.

"Was there a note with that package I got yesterday?" I asked the man behind the desk, another new face with strong dark eyebrows and a warm smile.

"Nothing's been kept back. Is there an issue?"

"No, I wasn't sure which department sent it over is all— I'll check with them later."

I smiled and headed back to my room. It had been a long shot that they'd leave a note.

Plonking myself back onto the bed I dragged Sarah's laptop over and propped the guide open beside it, ready to find this guy. Maybe. Some entries connected, pieces about information traded with The Collector mostly. Not much about the man himself. Sarah's list mentioned an address on Great Western Road that was connected to him, a small pawn shop Sarah had marked up as '*Visited, need to go again.*'

I didn't have anything else to do this morning.

Grabbing my bag, I stuffed the guide inside and put my headphones on. Pausing at the door, I plucked up Lou's gift and slipped it in a trouser pocket, before shoving the cursed bracelet into my bag too.

Great Western Road was busy, lots of people milling around as I wandered around the side streets a little while. I was surrounded by vintage shops and health food supermarkets, all very Artisan. It was different from the path to the university, less commercial, fewer corner shops and restaurants. By the water, you'd think you were in a different city altogether.

The shop still had the traditional sign: three gold balls, shiny and well cared for. It was tucked into the edge of the river, a skinny set of steps leading down to the door from one winding street. The windows were thick with shelves, jewellery of all sorts and stones laid out to entice. It was a fine sight for a magpie. The lights were on and the sign said it was open, so I opened the door, ready to fake interest in a set of opal earrings.

A set of wind chimes jangled as I entered, and I heard shuffling from a door beside the till. No one appeared though, so I continued to browse the stones and metals on display. The cabinets were tall and well-lit underneath, so the stones glowed like embers. It was a bit too open for a shop expecting desperate people. 'Cause you usually were when pawning something, just a little.

"May I help you?" came a rich voice from behind me. I jumped, spinning to see a man now at the counter. He was shorter than me, with dirty blonde hair and unusual eyes. I walked towards him to get a better view at those eyes, their colour like worn sea glass. Or maybe they were the colour of ice. They appeared to change as I looked. I couldn't stop watching them, despite the slick thud of fear that rippled through my stomach.

He was scrawny, a faded band t-shirt covering slim arms and way too many rings on his fingers. Old rings too, bashed and grimed with wear. He wore bangles on his wrists, heavy aged silver. Too big to stay on those scrawny wrists. My pulse fluttered in my chest, screaming danger, and I couldn't tell why. I just wanted to work out what colour his eyes were. The two impulses clawed against each other as I stared at him.

"Sir?" he asked, looking at me askew, before shaking his head and glancing down. "I think I know who you are." A bright smile.

"And how would that be?" I asked, gazing at those ring covered hands. If I didn't make eye contact the impulse to look at them should go away. Count the rings, focus on something else, Carter.

"You're looking for someone. Word gets around. I'm surprised you haven't come sooner."

"I've only been here three days, mate," I said, glancing up at him. "You aren't easy to find."

"And your guide is missing, isn't she? A shame to lose a family member so carelessly. What do you wish to gain from me?"

"You're The Collector?"

"Yes." He tilted his head.

"You trade for information?"

"Amongst other things, as most of us do." He nodded, smiling again.

"I'm looking for my sister."

"I know."

"Do you know where she is?"

"No, though she has come to speak to me before."

"About?"

"That would depend on what you intend to do with that knowledge."

I was back to looking at his eyes, pine green now, and something in my gift was still screaming. "What are you?" I asked, unable to get the warring urges in my head to settle. Too much noise.

"Why do you ask?"

"You're not human. I thought you were, but nothing about this place is right. You're not right. Almost but the edges blur." I waved a hand at his form, watching those changing eyes.

"How observant you are." He grinned, all teeth. "You may want to look away for this." He pulled at the skin of his temples and it came away, from the hairline and down, off his skull and neck until a new man stood there, weather beaten and immense. The rings and bangles were still there, fitting now, and he was about a foot taller, eyes shining yellow as a cat's.

Power radiated off him like steam, roiling the surrounding air with a shimmer of dark promise. It was less disturbing than Mr. Kardar, but only because of the warning. I looked up at him in confusion.

"You would call me a demon, if you felt the need," he supplied.

"Well shit," I muttered, glancing round the shop. "That's why you don't need security."

"My clientele will generally not attempt to steal, but yes, this is why I don't need protection, in the traditional sense."

"Got it. You don't know where Sarah is," I said, looking at him again. "Do you know what she was doing?"

"She was trying to get to the bottom of that little guide." He pointed to my bag. "And before you ask, I don't want that cursed trinket you have. I'd only sell it to some poor idiot who'd gift it to a family member and wonder why they hated her."

"You can tell it's cursed? It didn't activate 'til I touched it."

"We have different talents, Mr. Brooks."

"Carter. The guide; you know anything about the writer?"

"I was close with the man for some time. He studied law at Glasgow University and held quite the controversial views. Ever so eager."

"You know his actual name? He didn't sign his diary."

"John Mercer. It wasn't safe to leave his details at the time. They'd only stopped killing witches a hundred years before. He wasn't an idiot."

"Thanks. That's something to go with."

"He didn't go by that name for long," The Collector said, as if this was entirely natural.

"He thought you were a title rather than a demon," I said. "He discuss that with you?"

"At length. We spoke of all kinds of thing. He had a keen mind for philosophy and a knack for people. Could have been a preacher if he wanted."

"Went into law instead," I said, trying to see any reaction. Those cat eyes blinked.

"Common wisdom said it paid better. It lied, but who wants to know the truth behind common wisdom?"

"His diary reads like he worked for you."

"He assisted me with matters in return for information. He was never in my employ. I don't trade souls or such complications. That's best saved for the elder things."

"Like Dex?"

"That's an awfully big name for a little human to be throwing around," he sneered, frowning. "How do you know that one? The guide doesn't speak of it."

"It's quite the chatter box. Been visiting me ever since I got here."

"It visits you?"

"Well, more like it takes me to it, but we end up having conversations. Like those you had with old John."

"You understand you're doing something others would literally kill for?" he asked after staring at me.

"Don't over sell it. I'm not a tourist," I said, passing a hand through my hair.

"People will sacrifice animals and more to commune with Dex. Some rituals call for humans to be killed for him."

"Oh right, all those ritual killings we hear about."

"Do you think there would be anything remaining after a being like that was sated? The sacrifice vanishes, no trace. Not unlike your sister, though there have been no rituals recently to explain that."

"You'd know?"

"Rituals like that are large energy events. It's akin to having a tornado come through town."

"Okay, yeah, you'd notice that." I nodded, relieved and pushing off the creeping fear railing against my mind. I was chatting to a demon about ritual magic. This had to be on the list of bad ideas. Poor life choices.

"What do you want, Mr. Brooks?"

"If I'm honest, I thought you were a human doing something dodgy that Sarah had stumbled on. But that's way off."

"While the majority of what I do is certainly 'dodgy,' all Sarah wanted from me was confirmation that I existed and information on the other side."

"People keep mentioning different 'other sides' to me. What do you mean?" I asked, mindful of Dex's comments that Sarah was somewhere it couldn't reach.

"The other side of the veil, the other planes outside your world."

"Sounds peachy."

"It's not as terrible as you no doubt imagine, but each is entirely its own. Cosmically so. Some are hospitable for humans, others hostile."

"People want to visit them?" I asked, the implication of that comment kicking me between the eyes.

"To commune with the beings living there, or to allow access to planes further afield by travelling through one to another. All of them connect to each other, but not all the time. Some have larger periods of time between connections, as with the orbit of planets."

"Yeah, I get that."

"Glad to be of service." The bright smile again. "Sarah wanted access to the details of such rotations, which I provided her with. At a price."

"What was the cost?"

"Information."

"Will you tell me what that information was about?" I asked. Why was dealing with demons like getting teeth pulled? I thought that was meant to be fairies.

"Details of the magical practitioners in the area."

"You tell her how to get out, and she tells you what she's leaving behind?"

"Something like that." He looked at me like I was a dog who had finally learned a trick.

"And if I could bring you information?"

"Then I would be happy to trade with you as I did her. My rates are much more generous than Dex offers."

"Can you tell me anything else about what Sarah was looking for?"

"She was looking for a way into somewhere not often present. It only rotates a handful of times in a human lifetime, and she wanted to access it before the next connection."

"Why?"

"That will cost you, as will the details." I stood in front of him, chewing the inside of my lip.

"What about me?" I asked.

"What about you, Mr. Brooks?"

"You've met Sarah, you know how she works. You don't know how I work. Or what I know. What if I gave you some of mine?"

"Given Dex has expressed an interest in you, I think that would be considered bad for business." He frowned, looking me over. "But if you wished to bring me new information about local practices, I would be receptive to that."

"Okay. I can work on that." I nodded, and in a blink The Collector was back to his thinner, compact self. My stomach gave a little jolt but quickly settled.

"Easier on the human eye," he said, looking me over again. "I look forward to seeing what you bring me."

"Thanks."

I was out of the door and up the steps, back into the dying warmth of autumn. Around the vintage shops, I started to breath normally again but couldn't shake the edge of fear. Walking along the river, dipping into the energy of the water, I made a line for a park bench. Sitting down I stared into the lapping current, willing myself still and peaceful. Or as peaceful as I could be after talking to a demon. Fuck.

My phone told me it was nearly eleven, far later than expected. Must have been the shop. How many fucking magic shops were there round here, anyway? No wonder it was such a popular area for practitioners. I let myself put up my guard for a few minutes, revelling in the quiet, then forced it back down and started off towards Great Western Road. I could get a drink at the student union and nurse it for a while until I met Alex. That would be sane and reasonable and not at all terrifying.

I perched in a corner booth with a large coffee and the guide on the table. The Collector's comments buzzed in my head, about places that weren't always there. Surely that would be mentioned in the guide. But what would they be called?

I didn't have the stomach to read the whole thing lest I learn some new terrible thing that poor diarist wound up involved in. Well, that

John got involved in. I knew he was a John now. And John had gone in eyes open, waxing philosophical with a demon. Not entirely innocent.

But his writing felt genuine, in his belief that he could change things. He wanted to do better than those in power, felt he could use his gift to do so. Brave, for the time. That was another thing I should have asked The Collector about. He said John had changed names. What was his new name?

I'd make a list next time so I couldn't get distracted by that person mask he wore. And I'd have a list of information to trade. There was Luke and the group; I didn't owe them anything and it was the most magic information I had. I didn't want to mention Alex.

I pushed that debate to the side and started looking through the guide again, skimming for talk of places and spaces. I came across one about halfway through, talk of a church.

It was built as a free church, The Blantyre Free Church, and had burned down in 1846 but was rebuilt shortly thereafter. John took the view that the fire had been no accident, but instead were preparations for a portal. He spoke at length on what this could be, references to the ideas of fairy circles versus a physical event that came and went. It sounded close to what The Collector had told me about, enough to warrant more reading.

I looked it up on my phone and saw it had burned down again in 1978, unlucky. Two fires didn't make a pattern, but they made a strong coincidence. I went back to the entry in the diary for it.

He went on for ages, describing what he thought would be involved if he tried to stabilise a portal, what he could get from it. Good old-fashioned colonial mindset then. I shook my head, making a few notes on my phone and finishing off my coffee. I skipped ahead through his different discussions with The Collector, which all sounded creepier now that I had met him.

I knew John survived whatever stupid idea this was. There were more entries past this, but I was wary of reading his descent into darker matters. He seemed so sure he would be able to handle whatever came his way, like there was nothing that could knock him off course. I couldn't tell if that was sheer arrogance or the innocence of discovery. Maybe not innocence given he was talking to a demon.

Still, reading about his slow corruption, what he became, sat ill in my stomach. I didn't know how many of these ancient things were kicking around the area, but if my dealings with Dex were any measure, the story couldn't end well. That was another question for The Collector, how many like Dex were there? I started a list on my phone.

*At the union café, let me know when you're free,* I texted Alex, hoping she'd come so we could plan the afternoon. I was antsy about the party already. I could feel it in the back of my head. That must be what was making me fidget. That and the demon I'd met, but we could look at that later. Thinking about that too long wouldn't be great for my sanity.

*Running late, will meet you there xx,* came her reply.

I sank back in my seat, more pleased than I should be. Sipping from a takeaway cup, lest she be early, I set out my plan for this evening. The group would be looking for suspicious people and give me or Alex the nod. Which really meant giving Alex the nod, given Marc's comments that everyone else would be scared off me by Luke.

Luke was nice enough, certainly keen on showing his interest, but that wasn't the main point of the party. It was to see who else was there. This was the only link I'd found between Sarah's work and her group, so it had the biggest overlap of people she knew. There had to be someone. Well, someone other than Dex.

Thinking of Dex, fifteen years was a long time, but at least I wouldn't be dead. I'd be permanently tainted by some horrible evil, but I was already permanently different anyway. Would it be much further along to work for this thing?

I was brought out of my plotting by Alex who flopped down opposite me. She was in a giant knitted cardigan, tied at the waist, and she fiddled with the oversized collar as she sat.

"Penny for your thoughts?" I said to the stormy look.

"Thinking about tonight. I don't like that we're spying on the group."

"We are, can't do much about that." I shrugged. "On the plus side we can cut down the pool of suspects. Is Luke ever going to share those names with me?"

"I thought he would've already." She toyed with the wool some more. "He might be trying to get the list whittled down first, see who we have that overlaps. The party group is pretty big."

"That would make sense."

"We can talk to him about that tomorrow, he won't want to speak about it tonight," she said, shaking her head. "What's the plan for today?"

"Fretting about this party and checking out some more places."

"Where did she find all this?" Alex asked, looking at the list on my phone.

"The dirty book we found in her room."

"That ratty thing?"

"It's a diary—from someone who practiced magic in Glasgow years back. It has entries about him going around, finding things. Sarah was seeing if they were real. Most of them are legit."

"Why would she even do that?" Alex sighed, folding her arms on the table and laying her head down.

"Curiosity, wanting to test her skills out, trying to find something. Her notes are pretty sparse, details of when she visited and if there was something or someone there. I think she was trying to keep it quiet."

"I can see that, yeah." She sat back up, her mouth curled down in a disapproving line. "I just wish she'd told me she was doing this."

"Me too. Best we can do is track her and see if we can dig anything up. Maybe it'll help, maybe not."

"I don't like that you're right."

"Welcome to being most people I know." I grinned, trying to get her to match it. "I was thinking we could check this place first." I pointed to one of the entries, close by.

"That'd be easy to get to. Are there any others you want to check in particular?"

"There's mention of a well in Glasgow Cathedral and something at Trongate. Might be worth looking at them."

"Anything in the necropolis? Sarah loved it there. Said it was like walking into the colour lavender."

"Energy of the dead is different to that of the living. Can be kind of relaxing if you need a break."

"I thought that was just mopey Goth kids." Alex laughed, no joy in it.

"Much as I was one of those, no, graveyards are peaceful. Usually." I hoped she would run with it.

"Usually?" Of course not.

"You get the occasional haunting. Or old school ghouls. But they're pretty uncommon."

"Like flesh eaters?"

"Yeah. Most of them don't lurk in graveyards anymore, but some like the tradition. Aesthetic."

"How do you even know this shit? You don't do anything with your gift."

"I've been around graveyards before."

"Anything else I should look out for?"

"Probably not. Vampires are usually more stylish than that."

"You're serious," she said after staring me down.

"A lot of them do night jobs. Porters, morticians, coroners. They have ages to get a skill, so why not?"

"The whole dying in sunlight thing?" she asked.

"It's more like they're super photo-sensitive, from what I remember."

She quirked an eyebrow at me. "Carter, explain."

"My parents knew one, and I could tell what he was."

"And you asked him about it?"

I nodded.

"He was cool with that?"

"He took it better than my parents did. They said it was terribly rude. But I didn't know, so I asked. He spoke to me about it for a bit, and I toddled off quite happy. I was like four."

"And you suppressed your gift later?"

"I couldn't control it when I was a kid. As I got older, I could stamp it down."

"Fair enough. Remember anything else?"

"Bits and pieces—they weren't all as bad as Stoker said, but some of them were, so to be careful. When they were desperate, they'd eat whatever they could, like most things do. They can live off animals, but humans are a better meal. The light sensitivity, night shift work, liking clean places."

"Clean places?"

"You know the old myth about vampires having a compulsion to count grains of sand or salt? It's based off them being clean freaks. I suppose super senses means you're able to notice everything that's dirty."

"That's a good point." She nodded, distracted. "Back to this afternoon. We'll need to be at the party around half past eight, so we'll need to get ready about seven. You're coming over to the flat, right?"

"To get ready?" What?

"Yes."

"Why would I?"

"So I can make sure you look right." She said it in such a matter of fact way that I didn't have the heart to argue.

"I'll have to go back to the guesthouse to pick up my suit but sure."

"Good, it's settled then. Do you want to stay over?"

"Get back to you on that depending on how the night goes?"

"No problem. Go get 'em, in fact," she said with a laugh, and I rolled me eyes at her

"I mean, in case I need to investigate something. For this afternoon, I was thinking we could check those places out and then go past that dancer I was speaking to last night."

"What's the story with her?" Alex asked.

"She told Sarah about getting to different places."

"No, like was she a djinn too?"

"Oh, shit, no. She's different. She's a fallen angel," I said.

"You're fucking with me."

"Have I ever yet?" I asked, my smile stretching a bit too tightly.

"No, but I keep hoping you've grown a sense of humour."

"Rather than the city being scary?"

"Something like that," she said, shaking her head. "That's bad shit."

"Not as bad as the demon I was chatting to earlier, but he's a whole other story."

"What?"

"I'm kidding!" I lied and hoped she wouldn't check.

"Not the sense of humour, I meant. I don't know how I feel about meeting one of those."

"I can go solo if you'd prefer. You can wait outside?"

"Sounds better. Whereabouts is she?"

"There's a dance studio on Bath Street. She said she was available there."

"We could go there then. Let's get on with the ones here. We've not got much time." She stood up, slipping out of the booth, and I followed.

# Chapter 13

<u>14 May, 1887</u>

I have been considering my research on ways between the worlds: theoretically, a portal could be made stable through the expenditure of energy. If one were to saturate the area in which it will appear, this could create an anchor allowing the portal to form a tether there. A fire would be one such way to do this, expending energy in the burning and transformation of the place, allowing that energy to remain by not harnessing it, not rebuilding, but allowing the charred scar to suffer openly. This has the additional benefit of creating a focal point for locals to pour the energy into, fretting and worrying about the consequences of such a disaster. This latter point is conjecture on my part, but it would be an easy way to harvest passive energy.

I do not know if this process would prolong the connection between the worlds or simply strengthen the existing connection, meaning this join could be explored. It is not that different to exploring the poles or the Northwest Passage; seeking out the safest route is paramount. Knowing the right time to make such endeavours will assist greatly, and my friend can aid with this. If such experiments could be undertaken then it would permit exploration and potentially the excavation of the world connected to us at that time.

Caution would be required. I doubt most worlds will be hospitable to a raiding party, no matter how cordial. The crux of the matter will be conducting myself in a way that will not draw attention from either the hand wringing masses or anything on the other side of such a joining point. I have no need to announce myself with pomp or ceremony. A simple visit would be enough.

We left the union and went towards the botanical gardens, stopping outside the Òran Mór.

"What's that place like?" I asked, nodding over my shoulder.

"Fancy. Big in the traditional music scene. Good parties," Alex said with a grin.

"There's a lot of power coming off of it."

"More so than most ex-churches that are now pubs?"

"Kinda." I nodded.

"Did Sarah check it out?"

"No."

"Do you want to?" she asked, leaning on the railing.

"Sort of, but it's not urgent."

"Let's go in. You can show them Sarah's picture, ask if they've seen her."

We rounded on ourselves and went up the broad stone steps, winding into a classy bar. It looked like a great place to have live music, with arching ceilings and long open space perfect for dancing. My glowing impression of it went plummeting down when I noticed the barmaid had the wizened, sullen skin and frame of a mummy but was smiling and chatting away with her regulars. Shit.

"Hi, how can I help you?" she asked as we came up to the bar. Her hair was wild and looked like it had been deliberately made as large as possible, tossed up and out in a dark mess about her face. Eyes the dark red of wine met mine, her teeth stained with it too. I stammered for a few second before falling silent, and Alex gave me a sideways look. She took over, pulling out her phone.

"We're asking around about my friend, his sister, who's missing. Her name's Sarah," she said, showing a photo of them together. "She's not come home and we're worried."

The barmaid looked at the photo and chewed on her lower lip, considering. The skin of the lip split and blood, thick and black, oozed down. I yanked my energy up before I said something stupid. The change was instant. A curvy young woman with a neat braid now stood behind the bar, staring at me.

"What did you just do?" she asked.

"I put a shield up," I replied, sheepish.

"Why?"

"Because I can see, and while I'm sure you're a lovely person, I wasn't expecting to see you?"

"Oh, you've got it! Well that's not happened in an age."

"I keep hearing that," I said.

"And do you know what we are, pretty lad?" came a husky voice from behind me. I turned to see a stout, middle aged woman with red hair and a coating of freckles. There was a challenge in her eyes, brows raised and a hand on her hip. She was immaculately dressed in a business suit and bristled.

"I have no idea, but it was a bit of a shock."

"You must have been able to feel it if you've got the sight," said the redhead.

"I could. Didn't know it was you. Thought it was the church."

"Carter, what is going on?" hissed Alex, glancing around to make sure we'd not caused a scene. Not yet at least.

"Your lad's had a fright is all. He's never met a maenad before," laughed the younger one, smiling. "He'll be over it soon."

"The myths say you're mad women and murderers, not barkeepers." I frowned, looking between them.

"Times change—people notice bodies torn up and ravaged." The smirk on redhead was equal parts pleased and predatory. "We don't need to do that anymore. The festivities can be done when we like."

"Art and alcohol in a house of worship. Nice setup. You didn't happen to see my sister?"

"Let me have a look." The younger one passed Alex's phone over and the redhead glowered at it. "I know the lass, but I've not seen her for a long while. If she comes around, I can say you were in."

"Thanks a lot, Mrs., um, what should I call you?" I asked, keen to keep them happy.

"Alala, no need for Mrs.," she said, handing the phone back.

"Noted. Thanks again. Alex?" I nodded towards the exit. She looped her arm in mine and tugged me towards the door.

We got outside and I made a line for the gardens, Alex jogging to keep up with me. I went to the area I'd found before, beside the tree, and let my shield down to get the feel of the park. Green was good. Nature was good.

"What was that about?" Alex asked, rubbing her arm.

"You never heard of a maenad?"

"Let's assume no." She rolled her eyes at me.

"They were the worshipers of the wine god, the god of dark enjoyment. Excess and party and that kind of stuff."

"Sounds fun."

"Aside from the bit where they tore people to pieces, literally speaking, yeah they were a hoot."

"How do you know this shit?" she asked, leaning against the railings.

"They're in a lot of ancient myths, as a bonus and a warning."

"What do you mean?"

"They're devoted and give their god a lot of power, but they're also crazy and tear people apart. Though they don't do that bit so much anymore."

"Right. Gonna skip their next pub crawl."

"I would support that decision," I said, wiping my hands over my face. Why that on top of a demon?

"Why'd they creep you out so much?"

"The barmaid looked like a B movie monster soaked in wine. I wasn't expecting it. I'd sensed something weird and primal, but I thought it was just with it being an old church. Though it's a smart move, I guess, build a pub in a church and worship the god of excess. It's like short circuiting the need for a congregation."

"I feel like it's cheating when the customers don't know," Alex mused, glancing at the line of trees between us and the pub.

"They're going into a pub in a church. It's not really hidden?"

"I suppose. I don't like it though." She crossed her arms and shook her head. Glad to know there was something solid we could agree on.

"Me neither. They're not hurting anyone though, so I'm just never going to go back there, if I can help it."

"Good plan. What's next?"

"This place in the gardens," I nodded towards the railings she was on.

"Oh, the old subway!"

"What now?"

"I know this place. It's part of the abandoned subway system."

"That's some Ghostbusters 2 shit. What are you talking about?" I asked.

"Some are stations built to extend the subway lines, but they were never opened. Others are ones that were used but closed off when the routes changes. They're all over bits of the city."

"So that place we were at yesterday, those arches with the sign?" I asked, thinking of the hungry thing waiting.

"I don't know if that's one of them, but it's in the right area."

"That didn't occur to you when you were telling me about her going urban exploring?" I asked, trying my best not to look at her. I could have been looking for those.

"I didn't even think about it. Everyone knows about them!"

"I'm very happy they do, but since I've been here literally days, it might have been worth mentioning?" I gave in and looked at her, trying not to scowl.

"Sorry, it's such a common thing I didn't even think she'd be looking at it."

"It's fine. Let's see what we can get from it."

"Do you need to get down into them?"

"Can we?" I asked, peering at the gap.

"Some of them are locked up, but I'm sure we can find a way around." She led me out of the gardens and down Great Western Road towards the river. I followed her, glancing down the side street that led to The Collector as we passed. We arrived at Kelvinbridge Station and Alex motioned me after her, trotting down the long line of steps.

This led to a large set of metal security doors, size of the ones you got on commercial garages.

"We raiding Fort Knox?" I asked with a laugh.

"We get in here. We can follow the tunnels right through to the station in the gardens."

"Do we need a flashlight?"

"No, there's plenty of daylight, mostly. The tunnel under the road is dark but not that bad. We can use our phones."

"How'd we get in?"

"That I will need a little bit of help with—any good at picking locks?"

"I can do a basic one. Why?"

"Great. Here's a hair clip. Carry on." She handed me a bobby pin and nodded to a padlock on the metal door.

"Alex?"

"Get on with it. We've a time limit." I took the pin off her, crouching at the door. To my surprise it only took a few minutes to get it open.

"We're good," I said, standing and pocketing the lock. "How'd you know I could do that?"

"Sarah can too. Figured it would be a family thing. In we go." She grinned, slipping through the door with me quick on her heels.

The inside was an awful mess, the cold concrete covered in graffiti and rubbish. It looked abandoned, maybe used for shelter when needed, the discarded items basic and practical.

"Alex, do I want to know why you know about this?"

"I told you, I dated a guy who was into it, got taken exploring. This way."

She led me past the remains of a platform and some heavily rotted steps, out towards a waiting tunnel. It was dim walking in but after a few minutes, we came to a turn which led into a long straight stretch, light filtering in from both entrances. We got our phones out so we could see the crunching gravel underfoot.

"Are we under Great Western Road now?" I asked, eyeing up a rusting street sign marking 'Bank Street' about half way up the brick wall.

"Yeah, all the way until the next turn, then we're in the gardens."

"It's quiet for having a main road on top of us," I said, flaring my gift out to search for activity. The tunnel rippled with energy, the after glare of something having been there. I couldn't place what it was, the dregs left like the salt mark from a high tide.

"They look after this one, because of the road above. It's dry, too. That helps," Alex said, pointing to modern looking plaster.

"This place doesn't feel weird to you?" I asked.

"No weirder than I expect a subterranean tunnel to feel. Why, you get something?"

"It's like the hangover of energy. It's faint. We'll be running alongside the river, right?"

"The Kelvin? Yeah, it runs by the railway station."

"Maybe it's something to do with that." I'd no plan to find either way if I could help it. The tunnels were interesting, but I didn't like the idea of being swarmed by something.

We reached the next turn and emerged into the disused station, light flooding in from above. Scrambling up onto one of the platforms we looked it over.

It was quite something to see, the path of where the tracks would be leading out towards a fully fenced exit and flanked with broad, stretching platforms. At the end, by the fence, there were hefty support brackets, new steel amongst the rust. Probably due to the traffic.

The staircases leading to what would have been the entrance in the gardens were still there, short sets of stairs with wide landings for each turn, sealed off at the top. You could clearly see where the pedestrian entrances would have been on both sides, the broad ironwork leading to the tiled expanses.

The ventilation gaps let in brilliant sunlight through the vegetation growing over them and gave the place a muddled luminosity, like looking through old glass. Nature was busy reclaiming it, huge swathes of green running along the track lines and graffiti coating the walls. It looked like birds had nested in the metal girders at some spots.

"Lots of paint," I said, nodding to the tiles.

"Artists do a lot of it in the city it's well respected," Alex sniffed.

"You ever been to Manchester, Alex?"

"No, why?"

"We have a lot of artists there too."

She scoffed but her frown left, so I took that to be approval.

"What was Sarah looking at down here?" she asked, glancing around the open space. "It's gorgeous, but I don't see anything obvious."

"Neither do I, and that's the point of my stuff. Give me a second, come stand here." I nodded to the spot by me and closed my eyes, stretching out with my gift. I could still feel the sensation from the tunnels, cobwebs of energy strewn around. Something was flickering at the edges of the space, like a weak signal on a radio, spurting forward and vanishing. "Is there anyone there?" I asked aloud, just in case.

I didn't expect the hissing response that came from the set of stairs behind us.

"Carter, what the fuck?" Alex tensed.

I could feel her crackling with nerves. "Step closer to me if you want, or hug me. I can get a shield up quick."

"I can take care of myself," she barked.

"I don't doubt it, but I'm more practiced at shielding than you and we make a smaller target if we're together," I said. "Are you willing to talk to us?" I asked louder, trying to figure out what I was speaking to.

Another hiss was followed by the slow clicking of something against metal. A figure came walking down the steps of the platform, ethereal but tall and broad. It was the white of things at the bottom of deep water, starved of sunlight and still strong, with huge black eyes and a coat hanger mouth.

It was bigger than me, walking upright but closer to a monolith of matter than a human. The arms had webbed ends and sharp talons. Something that could be a head, smooth and slight, raised from the rest of its body. It looked streamlined despite the bulk, no sharp edges or extraneous frills. It was like looking at a slab of water trapped between glass, undulating but solid. Energy rose off it in wisps, melting into the air. Alex moved in front of me and wrapped her arms around my waist, still watching it.

"Can you speak?" I asked it. It had responded to my first question. I didn't get a response but a flood of emotion, distrust and confusion and longing. I took that to be a no then. It pushed again as if to confirm, dipping its head as it did so and looking at me. "Can you understand what I'm saying?"

A growl of sorts came back to that, sharp teeth being shown in the curved hook of a mouth.

"Is it really there?" Alex whispered. It growled at that too.

"I think it likes that you can see it too. Is that right?" Almost a purr this time, which must be good? Please be good. "Okay, I can keep talking to you or I could do something like what you do. I think I could, at least. Would you like that?"

A low hiss came back so I shrugged and kept watching it. It was a bit closer now, staying in the shadows but watching us both.

"We're looking for someone, a girl like me. Have you seen her?"

It purred at us again, stretching forward a little. It reminded me of a cat, sort of. I felt a push of emotions again, happiness and warmth.

"You like her?"

A trill this time, a nod of what I took to be the head. Okay, that wasn't too awful then.

"Do you know where she is?" I asked.

A sad push, dropping head.

"Okay, thank you for that. I can tell you're sad she's not here. We're sad too. Did Sarah come and find you before?"

A purr and a cock of the head to one side. I felt a push of some half-formed thing, not a thought but an intention maybe.

"She found you, but she wasn't looking for you?" Alex said, looking between us. It nodded.

"Do you have a name?" I asked. We got a long stare. "Alright maybe a stupid question, sorry. Not sure what to call you."

"Blob?" Alex asked, "Like a blobfish?"

A soft noise came out at 'fish' so I nodded.

"If that's okay, we'll call you Blob? I don't think we can speak your language." I felt an amusement so took that as approval.

"Okay, Blob, we're trying to find Sarah, the girl. She found you here. Are you meant to be here?"

A cooing noise and sadness came across the space between us.

"Did you get stuck here?"

A nod and big blinking eyes. I chewed that information over a few times, thinking of the best question to ask next. "Did your place cross over with here?"

Another slow nod, the energy coming off it flowing and crackling out like lightning.

"Was Sarah trying to get you back there?"

It paused at that, staring again.

"Was she trying to find out how you got here?"

A strong nod.

"Did she say she'd help you get back?"

A further nod.

"Okay, so she was helping, but she had been looking for something else?"

A satisfied twitch of that mouth and approval radiating off it now.

"Did she tell you when she thought you could get back?"

A blank look came to Blob's eyes.

"Oh shit, like planets," I said. Both Blob and Alex looked at me in confusion. "Blob, did Sarah speak to you about our moon? That controls our water?"

Strong recognition of that, a firm nod.

"You like the water?"

Joy came over the link we had, so I took that as a yes.

"Do you go to the river?"

A strong yes to that too, eager bowing.

"Okay, that's good. Did Sarah say how many times the moon would pull strongly before you could go back?"

A sadness came again, a small bob of its head.

"If I hold up my fingers can you nod to the one she said?"

It looked over at me, eyes sharp. It nodded a little. I started with one finger up and worked my way up to five before it gestured.

"Five months?" Alex asked, and I nodded patting my pockets.

"Blob, I want to have a look at something in my pocket, is that okay?"

I pulled out my phone and it hissed, baring teeth and moving back a bit. I opened the list of Sarah's visits. The gardens had been close to the beginning of her physically going to places, almost five months ago. Her comments simply said 'Halloween?'

"Blob, did Sarah tell you how to get back?"

Disapproval rippled over me.

"You didn't need her to tell you how, just when?"

A curt nod.

"Sorry, wasn't sure," I said, face flushing red. That was a bit of dick question, I supposed.

It gave what I took to be a dismissal and pointed to the far end of the tunnel.

"That where the join comes up?"

It nodded.

"Was Sarah bringing you things to help?"

It nodded again, a soft curl of sadness coming over.

"You knew she was missing?"

I felt the agreement, the surety that she would not have left it there. Oh my heart, that hurt.

"I'm sorry about that Blob; that must have been hard. Is there anything we can do to help?"

It began to shake its head, then stopped. It nodded slowly, gesturing its head back over where a shoulder would have been.

"You want me to come to you?" I asked, confused.

It bobbed its head.

"Carter, you're not?"

"Let's try it," I said, letting go of Alex and walking forward, standing tall and looking up at how much taller it was.

Up close I could see feet of a sort, solid claws attached on them as well. It still looked immaterial despite the physical presence, and I tried not to think about that. Leaning in close, its mouth hovered over my hair. I felt the huff of breath move slowly down my face and over both sides, close to my neck. One huge eye came up to mine, my face reflected pale in the darkness, and I felt a roll of approval and familiarity come from it.

"Are you scenting me?" I asked, wondering if it had an idea of what that was.

It understood enough to nod and give a small purr, a little grey tongue, or what I thought was a tongue, licking where my jaw met my neck. I froze at the roughness of it, but there was no malice or hunger, so I smiled. This apparently please Blob, who gave a further nod then went back off towards the steps.

I watched it climb the first set then settle into the flat area of the initial landing, before fading out of sight to leave motes spinning in the light. I stood blinking for a few seconds before turning to look at Alex.

"That was not what I expected," I said.

"Can we leave, right now?" she asked, half shaking in the sunlight.

"Yes," I all but shouted, making for the tunnel we'd walked through.

We were about a third of the way into it when Alex cracked, "So what the fuck happened?"

"We met Blob," I said. I ducked past the swing of a fist I felt coming and sped up my pace a bit. She had to work it out and trying to sock me one wasn't unreasonable, but I didn't need a shiner before the party. After a few steps, I glanced back at her. She stood still, looking back at the tunnel and towards me over and over. She wasn't doing so well. It looked like she'd been crying. Possibly when I was being scented.

"What does that even mean?" she shouted, "What was that?" I padded back to her.

"I don't have the faintest idea," I said. "Female, I think, from a different plane than ours. Hence the leaving energy all over and melting into the steps."

"Melting into the steps." She laughed, and I could hear the thrill of panic in it. I grabbed her shoulder, pulling her to walk in line with me.

"I'm here. I don't melt." I smiled best I could. She reminded me so much of Sarah, furious and ready to swing at something and righteous.

"I've seen the stuff from practicing. I know what can be done. That was like having an alien in front of me."

"I don't think Blob is any more alien than the things we find in the bottom of the ocean, but I get what you mean."

"Is this what you feel like?" she asked sullenly as we reached the end of the tunnel.

"Pretty much, used to at least. It's a bit easier now. Except for Mr. Kardar. That really freaked me out too, as you saw."

"When it was speaking to us, or whatever that was, it was like having someone else inside my head."

"I got it a bit different, like emotions."

"I've never had that. I never want that. It's horrible. Not Blob, but the feeling of someone else pushing into you, overriding you." She shuddered, and I pulled her in to me, hugging her and rubbing her back.

"I'm sorry it was bad, and I'm sorry that it's so weird. I'm sure Sarah would've wanted to spare you if she knew it would hurt or upset you."

"That's a trait in your family," she grumbled into my chest.

"We try," I said, pulling her away. "You still up for looking at the rest or do you want to call it a day and head home? I'd get it if you want time to get back to normal before the party."

"That sounds amazing, but we have to look at the others. I'm not doing any more face to face shit though. If you think there's a sentient being coming, you do that on your own."

I nodded, heading for the large metal doors. We relocked them and set off for some hope of normality.

# Chapter 14

*23 March, 1886*

*While the presence of ghouls in the city is notable, what I hasten to transcribe is the nature of their living here. These beings have disguised themselves within our cities and towns while feeding from our very dead. This has led to a preference for becoming butchers and undertakers but has also induced them entering the medical profession by becoming physicians and pursuing morbid pathology. This has allowed them a ready knowledge of the dead and dying, and given them access to corpses.*

*In turn, this has greatly reduced the need for active hunting, which was common for the ghouls of folklore—see the discussion stemming from Galland's translation of* One Thousand and One Nights. *Mr. Christie confirmed that this allowed a level of interspecies interaction previously unheard of given the risks to and by humans. While we are their prey, we do of course have an aversion to their appetites and a preference to remain alive and animated.*

*Points to note for further study: While a ghoul may change its appearance through its arcane nature, this seems to be restricted to those they have eaten, limiting their potential for disguise. I saw no indication of their aging process; while Mr. Christie appeared to be a gentleman of forty or so years, there is no confirmation that the face I saw was in fact his. It may have been some previous morsel that felt it suitable to become an undertaker. I would like to discuss this further and see if there is any true form of the creature or if this is as fickle a thing as it appears to be.*

We took the subway to the city centre, emerging into the sunlight and bustle. It was a good feeling compared to the stillness of the tunnels.

"Coffee?" I asked, nodding to a converted ticket office now offering take away drinks. Alex hummed her agreement, and I got us both the largest they offered. We sipped them as we walked by the river, Alex showing me the undersides of the bridges that straddled the water.

"They turn the lights on at night, so you get these perfect tinted reflections. Sarah went through a stage of trying to get photos of it. She'd drag me down here with her so it'd be safer, and we'd see if we could break into those little parks." She pointed over the water to the grassy banks, lined with trees. "The court over there has some great views. It's next to the traffic bridge, and you can see the river going in both directions. Gorgeous at night."

"I came down here my first night in the city. Tested out letting my shield down. Water makes it easier," I said, sipping my drink.

"How come? I've heard of focusing on a candle, but water's a bit generic."

"I think it has to do with the energy of it. Water's simple. It can be powerful, but it's effortless. It just is. Like space, or magnets, or mountains. They can be huge and overwhelming to us, but they just exist."

"You went to the vodka of the energy cabinet and got hooked?" She quirked an eyebrow at me.

"I find it easier to start off with a big blank slate and then work in the more complicated things. People and places, they get complicated really quick. You see too much, not enough, notice a difference others can't see. It gets crowded." I tapped my temple. "Water, the woods, empty space, they're quieter. I needed that to get used to having my guard down again."

"Which you're doing well at. What happened to all the headaches?"

"I don't know." I shrugged. I hadn't thought about it beyond my near exhaustion. That was probably a bad sign.

"I'm impressed. It's hard to break a habit, and you're doing it for a good reason." She downed the rest of her coffee and nodded back towards the shopping centre, "Let's go get started. Dance studio?"

"No. Save that for last. She kinds of fries my nerves. It's like standing next to an explosion."

"Tell me about it while we walk up to the cathedral then." She smiled. It took effort, but she managed it.

We wound our way up towards the cathedral, and I described Faith the best I could—the strange shadows of her wings and the swirling mass of her skin. I couldn't remember her eyes. Alex wrapped herself tighter in her cardigan and sighed.

"Aren't you worried about some of this?" she asked.

"Loads of it, but what did you have in mind?" I replied, cocking my head to look at her.

"Fallen angels. Things from some other dimension. This is heavy. Sarah's been working with the group for a long time, and we've never been near this. Are you sure she wasn't doing something dangerous?"

"Like what?"

"Stop throwing questions back at me. What if she got pulled into the wrong thing? What if she thought she was helping and someone tricked her? You said it yourself, people with your type of powers can get targeted. What if she's been trafficked?"

"If she'd been kidnapped you guys would have spotted her when you looked. You didn't, so she's not here. Maybe she's where Blob should be, or somewhere like that. But she's not here, or else we'd have found her." And I wouldn't have an ancient being taunting me about her whereabouts and welfare.

"That's really not helping." Her voice was tight again, hands pushed deep in her pockets. "You mean she's in another dimension?"

"On another plane is how I'd put it."

"How long have you known that?" The anger was creeping back in too.

"I've suspected it for a day. Got it confirmed this morning," I said, mostly honest.

"And you didn't think to tell me?"

"I wanted to speak to the dancer first, to verify it."

"That's reasonable," she said after a beat. "But if you hold out on me about this, I'll find a way to get into that skull of yours and drag you down."

"Fucking hell. What's going on with you?" I turned to look at her again, feeling her glower burning the side of my face.

"Oh, I don't know. I went through a hostage situation with a creature I can't even name and you've told me my best friend is off in some other dimension. Why ever would I be upset?" She was up to a shout by the last part of it, throat hitching. She stopped walking, catching her breath.

"You wanna talk about Blob?" I asked, waiting for her to catch up.

"No, I do not," she snapped, starting off again, "Why do you think the fallen angel can tell us about the dimensions thing, anyway?"

"I'm pretty sure she can go between them. So if I was looking to get into one, she'd be the best place to get advice. Like a holiday, but full of terror and looking for Sarah."

"Cheery," she deadpanned.

"Gotta find the silver lining somewhere."

"Have you spoken to Luke about this?"

"No. I've not spoken to him since yesterday, and I wanted to check things before I started causing upset."

"That's one way of putting it. He's going to hit the roof."

"You think so?" He'd been calm, if concerned, so far.

"He's devastated about her being missing. He doesn't want to show you that because you're doing so much. It's more than we've been able to do." She looked down at the pavement. "You can tell him tonight, before the party. It'll keep him focused."

"Why wouldn't he be focused? It's his party."

"Never mind. Just trust me."

"Alright," I said, lost.

The cathedral was beautiful inside, an enormous open space studded with a ribcage of pillars and high, sparkling windows. It was emptier than the other cathedrals I'd been in, chairs dotted around the pillars but not lining the interior.

"They're in the northern wing," Alex said.

"Huh?"

"The benches you're looking for—they're in the northern wing. You can see them on the way out if you want."

"I'd like that," I said, distracted. I was caught up in the tall ceiling and the joyful feeling of the space. I'd been in churches and cathedrals that felt irregular before. Notre Dame had been like that, physically beautiful but soaked in violent history. It poured over you when you first went through the doors, blood and anger and so much death. The sensation didn't stay too long, and I'd enjoyed the cathedral, but I was wary.

"What are you doing?" Alex asked, standing beside me. I realised I'd been staring up at the ceiling and not responding to anything she said.

"Sorry. Got lost in my own head."

"Want to talk about it?"

"I've been to cathedral's where it's miserable. Holiday in France, ones in Manchester. Here feels good. Happy."

"That's good to hear. We're going to the Lower Church."

"As in a depressed church?"

"No, doofus, it's a church underneath the northern wing of the cathedral. You get there from the nave."

"Naturally, we're stacking churches now," I said, trailing after her.

She led me down to a vast, vaulted thing, well-lit with high set lights and thin windows slipped between the pillars. There was a cordoned off area in the middle, a raised platform with a quilted cover of blues and greens leading to an orange centre. It was obviously important—several prayer cushions lined up next to it and all the benches aligned to face it.

"St. Mungo's crypt. Or St. Kentigren, depending on which translation you prefer. Both the same guy," Alex said, stopping with me.

"Who was he?"

"He was the son of a princess, raised by a saint. He founded the original kirk, and the city, in the late sixth century. He got beatified after he performed four miracles, retired to Wales, came back to Glasgow after a pilgrimage to Rome and an invitation from a King. He was buried here, though the cathedral we're in was built later in the early eleven hundreds."

"How do you know this? I read the website, and I didn't know this." I laughed, nudging my arm into hers.

"I did tours for a summer. You get the speech down pretty quick." She grinned, leaning back on a pillar as I looked about.

The energy here was old and raw, pleasingly deeper than upstairs. The thrum of it pressed against me, like bright sunlight on my skin. I approached a wooden topped well tucked towards the back corner, past ancient stone coffins displayed on the walls. A pulse of white energy flickered from it before rippling out into the area.

"You see that?" I asked Alex, nodding to the lid.

"The well? Yeah, you lift the hatch to see it."

Alex came over and opened the hinged half, revealing a shaft down to the water. A metal grate stopped anyone from taking a dive, but you could hear the echo and feel the cool dampness seeping up. I peered over, ignoring Alex's raised eyebrow, curious at the energy shimmering off it. This was nothing like the blip from earlier, but it reeked of power.

"Anything weird happen with the well?" I asked, pulling my head back in case of another surge.

"Except the man with the four miracles?" Alex asked with a sardonic brow.

"Fair point. Anyone gone missing or stuff like that?"

"Not that I've heard about, though that's not what they'd tell tourists. Why?"

"The guide talks about ways to get between the planes. Mentioned this place in passing. And that's what Sarah was looking into."

"You think the well is one?"

"I don't know, but it might be a little example of it."

"What does that even mean?" Alex sounded exasperated, tugging at one side of her hair.

"The difference between a door and a window, I guess," I said, leaning down close to the grate, "You're meant to get through a door, but a window will do if you need it." There was no way this thing had moved in years, never mind weeks.

"She cat burgled into an another dimension?"

"I'm meant to be the literal and blunt one. Quit stealing my thunder." I smiled as I looked up at her, trying to lighten her mood.

"That's what you're saying though, that the well's one of those windows." She crossed her arms and frowned between me and the wooden top.

I stood back up lest she slam the lid. "I think so. I'd do a test, but it's not exactly the best spot."

"You'd what now?"

"Drop a microphone through, or something soft, see what they're like when we pulled them back up."

"Why do you even know to think to do that?"

"I work in IT, which is basically problem solving. Same here." It came out more defensive than I would've liked, and I went back to focusing on the well. No sign of more energy coming from it but there was that tremor of potential hanging in the air. "Anyway, can't test it in a public space. Too many people coming and going. Just an idea if we find any others."

"Windows or doors?"

"Windows. If we find a door, I'll go through it."

"You can't be serious." Her statement was backed up with a stare, and I contemplated lying for a moment too long, "You are, what the fuck dude?"

"Might get her back." I shrugged, straightening up.

"And it might kill you if you go through the wrong one. What will she do then?" Alex shook her head.

"I know how to check whether it's the right one," I said, dodging her eye contact.

"And how pray tell would that be?"

Bargain something with the ancient being that wants me to serve it. "Blood knows blood. I could feel it if she was there. I'd have to prep a bit. I'd need time to mediate. But I could do it." It wasn't entirely false.

"But you can't do that now?" she asked, head snapping to look at me.

"No. No more than you could track her down. I need something to aim at for it to work."

"Makes sense," she said, pushing off from her spot against the stones. "Can Sarah do the same?"

"If she needs to."

"You guys have genetic echolocation?"

"Something like that, sure," I said with a laugh.

"Your family is weird, man."

"We are. Can't do much about that."

"Guess not. You done here?"

"Think so. I wouldn't mind staying for another one of those little flashes, but I don't know when it'll come back."

"Little flashes?" she asked, glancing about.

"From the well."

"They said they got some orbs on the spirit photography a few years ago. That sort of thing?"

"It could be." I nodded, looking over again.

"Alright, where next?" she asked, heading for the steps. I fell in beside her, skimming through my phone.

"Glasgow Cross is the next one listed. What's that?"

"The old tollbooth, I'll bet, up near Trongate. They used to hang folk there, once they moved it away from Glasgow Green. Dead bodies spoiled the public park look."

"Oh, goody." Fuck.

"What, you don't like gallows?" she asked as we came out of the Lower Church.

"More like I don't like what's left over afterwards. All the death and the crowds of onlookers—it leaves a mark. Sometimes you can see it or feel and smell it."

"That must get complicated. We kept the death penalty for goddamn ages and had loads of killing sites. They're everywhere."

"Hence the shielding."

She started like she meant to say something then closed her mouth, shaking her head. "I'll lead the way," she settled on.

We walked towards the river again at a pace. The sun was low in the sky and bathed the cathedral in the ends of the day, oranges and pinks snagging on the exposed pale stones that hadn't been blackened with pollution.

"Should we go through the necropolis later on?" she asked, glancing at the footbridge across to it.

"Much as I would love it as a palate cleanser, not today. There's no real mention of it in the notes. We can come back tomorrow?"

"Not really my spot for hanging out and eating pizza." She shrugged, continuing past it and onto the main road.

"That's oddly specific."

"Long story. Do you want to go to the dance studio after the toll booth?"

"Yeah. I can go there solo if you want? It'd be easy to grab my suit and come over to the flat after."

"Do I look that bad?" she asked archly, slowing down so I could walk in line with her.

"It's been a weird afternoon. If you don't feel like lurking outside while I chat to a fallen heavenly host, I'm okay with that."

"That's nice of you to offer, but I'll take my chances. You're totally taking me to dinner afterwards, though."

"Isn't it a bit early?"

"It'll be past five by the time we're done, and you'll want food before the party, right?"

"Fair point." I nodded, my stomach constricting at the idea of the party. "What did you have in mind?"

"Pizza? There's a really good place under Central Station," she said.

"Okay, it's a plan. Where is this place we're heading to?"

"This way. It's about five minutes."

We were still in the city centre but this part felt more industrial, pubs and furniture shops instead of shopping precincts or clubs. It was like home. I shook the thought off as we went, looking at the odd antique spots and bars we passed. There were an increasing number of food places, and the coffee shops came many and often, mingled between the pubs.

"We near a stadium?" I asked after the fourth 'no shirts, no colours' sign we went past.

"Not far away. Up there." She pointed off to her left and carried on, unfazed. "There's an excellent market and music venue that way too."

"Sweet. I love a good market," I said and felt the stereotype flooding off me. Bugger it, that one was true.

I could see what I suspected was our destination rising in the skyline; a stark sandstone tower peaked with a steeple like roof. There were blue clock faces showing time on each side. I could almost house a princess in it if I could find a suitable dragon. It looked bizarre, surrounded by roads and modern office buildings, but it stood tall and proud on its own island, between the traffic. It'd obviously had repairs done to it. The different shades of stone blended as it rose up.

"It was the City Chambers once," Alex told me once we were in front of it. I craned my neck for a full view. "And a collection place before that, as the name gives away. Has been hit by fire and flood and still stands to watch the five main roads converge."

"More of the tour?"

"It sticks in your head."

"What's that behind us?" I nodded my head back to the road and the metal structure that came up from the pavement. It was like the body of some metal snake, all opaque glass and a rib cage of dark, semi-circular railings.

"That's what's left of Glasgow Cross. It's a ghost station now."

"Spooky. Can we get in?"

"Why would you want to go into another one of those places today?" she growled, bundling her cardigan about herself again.

"See if there's anyone else like Blob."

"Anything else you mean."

"Same difference at this point," I said, taking in the length of the structure, the low way it hugged the pavement.

"As far as I know, the tracks and station are still there, but the access is walled up."

"Damn. Would be nicer than this." I nodded to the impressive tower.

"Why?"

"Less blood leftover. Let me see if I can get a read on it." I sat down, legs crossed, at the base of the building.

"What are you doing?" Alex asked, moving to stand next to me.

"Seeing if anything is lingering. Sarah's entry doesn't go into detail."

I pressed my back into the stone, as much physical connection as I could get, and made myself relax in increments. It had been an age since I'd done this in such an active place. I reached out tentatively with my gift and met a wall of white noise, the images of crowds and betrayal and blood flooding over me. I retched, squaring my shoulders before pushing back into it again.

I saw a sparkle of energy coming from across the road, at what used to be the station, but it was faint and nothing as entrancing as the old stones I felt at my back, the sucking wound of age and expectation. Something else was moving ahead, an energy older than the station. A woman stepped forward, washed out but lovely looking.

She was soaked with water, her bloody dress weighed down. The dress was long and billowing, giving the impression of layers and heft. Her neckerchief was wrapped close around her but askew, like it had been tugged tight, and her hair hung loose and ragged. The feeling from her was distress, but she gave me a soft smile, pointing off towards the river. I wanted to ask her what was wrong, why she was here when she wanted to be by the water. She started to fade off and I panicked, moving to follow her.

I felt a hard shove jarring me off the stones and opened my eyes to a cursing Alex.

"Why?" I asked, rubbing my shoulder.

"You went white as yoghurt and started crying. Wasn't sure if I should slap you or not."

"Talking to me wasn't an option?"

"Tried that. You weren't there," she said, chewing on a thumb nail.

"Might have projected a bit there."

"You're not meant to do that without a safe circle and someone grounding you, dickhead. What if you got stuck?"

"Is that likely to be the biggest risk I take until we find Sarah?"

"No," she said, mouth pulling down in a line, "But you don't need to be reckless. Tell me next time and I'll help. I'm good at channeling. That'd be saner than you opening your head at an execution site."

"Alright, deal," I agreed as I stood up, dusting the back of my jeans off. My head swam for a moment, but the black spots faded with a few huffed breaths. "A woman's spirit came up from the river. Any history there?"

"The river's always been the heart of the city. Sometimes a drunk drowns in it, but otherwise it's normal. Why do you think she wanted you to look there?"

"She was pointing to the river before she faded off. I think we should check it."

"Nothing else? No message?"

"I can't talk to them when I do that. I just get the image and the interaction. Not much else."

"Weird."

"Yes, that's the weird part of this," I said.

We followed one of the main roads to a traffic bridge, peering over the edge once we reached the middle. The water churned away but was otherwise impassive.

"It's flood season now," Alex said, looking at the clay brown current. "The station we were talking about'll be flooded. The water gets high right until mid-November."

"Shit. Best not go for a paddle then."

"How do we find your ghost woman?"

"Give me a minute," I said, closing my eyes and reaching out again. This was so much better with the river. I felt the flicker of her on the bridge and then shooting away, over to one of the banks. She did the same a few times, coaxing me over. "Right hand bank, near those big glass pyramids."

"The shopping centre?"

"Something near it, yeah. She keeps going over to a spot there."

We followed the footpath onto the river walkway. The flickering woman popped up on the pathway as we reached another bridge. Alex stopped dead, looking over to me. "That her?"

"Yeah."

The ghost pointed towards an ornate church over the road beside us, the broad front plaza studded with the bones of the trees. I'd felt it when I was by the water the first night here, a pulse like the one coming from the mosque over the river.

It was a beautiful sandstone building, gothic arches on the door and windows with baroque towers and peaks fronting the main building. It reminded me of back in Manchester, the gothic village churches that had gold leaf and intricate moulding all the way through. At the very top sat a statue that looked out to the east, watching over the river and bridges.

"The church?" I asked.

"Cathedral," Alex interjected. I raised an eyebrow. "It's a cathedral, St. Andrews. Or The Metropolitan Cathedral Church of Saint Andrew, but St. Andrews is quicker. It's the primary Roman Catholic cathedral and the mother church in Scotland. It's popular for weddings too, hence the shops." She nodded to a dress shop sign.

The ghost quivered in front of us, smiling at Alex and pointing to the cathedral again.

"You want us to go there?" I asked. She shook her head, frowning. She pointed to Alex, then to me, then to the church again. Great, ghost charades. "This is where Ouija boards come in handy."

"Those things are rubbish. An invitation to get messed up," Alex said, face scrunched tight. "I could channel."

"You sure that's a good idea?"

"Do you have a better one?" she asked.

"I didn't think the board was that bad."

"I can do it without her taking over. Let's go sit on the steps, and I'll get connected. That okay with you, lady?"

The ghost remained where it was, so I took that as approval.

We perched on a set of steps, tucked behind bushes still green in the autumn. Alex shook her shoulders loose before dipping her head low and focusing on the ghost woman, still beside the river.

Alex stared hard for a few seconds before the woman flickered, reappearing in front of us and peering down at Alex. Her gaze turned to me and I nodded, watching the water drip down her hair and vanish before it landed on the walkway.

"What's your name?" Alex asked, and I watched the ghost reply to her. "Annie," she repeated to me.

"Why did you come to the toll booth?" I asked.

"Your sister needs you. You were close before. She needs you to find her," Alex said as she watched the ghost speak.

"What do you mean, close?"

"You found a door but didn't step through. She can't step back. Her door's gone. When it comes back, she'll be in danger. She needs you to find her before he does."

"He?"

"The old one."

I blanched, glaring at the ghost. "That's taken care of," I said, looking back at the cathedral.

"No, it isn't. You think you know what he wants, but you're too far away to see," Alex said, brows drawing close. "Carter, what's she talking about?"

"That demon I spoke to you about earlier."

It wasn't a lie to be exact. Safer to keep Alex out of the way of Dex. If it wanted me, it probably wanted her too. She had more practice than me. It'd been interested in Sarah. Too many risks, too many people to get hurt.

"Go back to the door and find her. You must find her before he does."

"How do you even know this?" I asked, hands coming up to tug my hair. This was worse than Blob, but at least I could talk to her. Kind of.

"She found me. Knew what I do. Didn't try to banish me. Told me her plan. She deserves to be found."

"Knew what you do?"

She began to speak, and I saw Alex's' eyes go wide, her head shaking a little. "I find the ones who are stumbling home along the river. I guide those who deserve to make it home, dance with them 'til they're safe. I take away the ones who don't deserve to be found."

"Take them away to where Sarah is?" I asked, hopefully. That was the best possible option right now.

"No, to the river." I couldn't tell who it had come from but the intent was clear.

"You drown them?"

"The water takes them. I just lead the way. They weren't meant to go home."

"And I'm never leaving the house again once I'm done finding Sarah," I said, as much to myself as to Alex. "Do you know how to reach her?"

"Through the door. All the doors come soon, but she'll be in danger from him then. You must find her before then. She's repeating that bit over and over now," Alex said, looking between Annie and me.

"Thank you for your help, Annie. We'll do our best to get to her. Can you speak to Sarah now?"

She shook her head, saying something to Alex.

"She says where Sarah is, she can't reach. Nor can most." I stood up, coming up taller than the spectre in front of me.

"We've got to go and speak to someone else who might be able to help us find Sarah, but you've done a lot," I said. The back of my brain whispered that most people would see me and think I was talking to thin air, because that's what this stuff did.

Annie nodded then blinked out of view.

"We're not doing that again," Alex said from behind me.

"Difficult?" I asked, turning to give her a hand up.

"I channelled a ghost killer. A ghost who kills people. Ghosts aren't meant to do that, Carter."

"Sounds like she doesn't do it directly, just tricks them."

"That doesn't make it better." She sighed, bone deep.

"I know. Come here," I tugged her closer into a hug, her head tucking under my chin. "It's been a shit day and that was intense. But we know what we suspected about Sarah was right. I couldn't have found that without you."

"Yes. She's somewhere in another dimension and can't get out of it. While a demon tries to hunt her down. Did she break a deal or something?"

"I don't know. I don't think so. She left in the middle of things, but I feel like she'd have mentioned that."

"Do we need to protect her from something?"

"We'll ask her that when we find her," I said, holding her for a long minute. She was warm against me and the fuzz of her hair tickled the skin under my jaw. "Shall we go past that dance studio then head to your place with pizza?"

"I think I'm going to skip out on the second bit. I need to take a salt water bath and cleanse myself after that," she said, disentangling.

"That's cool. I get it. Want me to come around half past six? I can be later if you want more time."

"That's fine. Walk me to the station?"

"Course." I smiled, starting towards the subway. She was reminding me a lot of Sarah again, the feistiness and the deflation. Sarah wasn't one for being down too long though, and I expected the same of Alex once she was removed from the weirdness a bit.

# Chapter 15

<u>23 October, 1886</u>

An accident has befallen Henry Barnes of the Merchants Guild. Henry is the most awful bore, always prevaricating from his membership duties and seeking to pick off the smaller businesses. He is also disinclined towards Tom Abdul, the Liverpool merchant sent to seek new trades with the river dock owners.

Henry despises those who have joined us from across the continent and Tom is clearly marked as such, with coarse dark hair and skin like rich clay. His accent is thoroughly English which did not endear him to many in the meetings, but his business and accounts are diligent and swiftly expanding.

He is also a djinn, as discovered by some minor investigation on my part. This is a matter that troubles me. I would betray my position within the administration if I broached this matter and he took ill to it. The opportunity to speak to such a being, however, is enticing.

But to return to Henry. He was drunk at the meeting. That in and of itself is not of note, but he was of a sufficiently belligerent disposition to anger Tom. A purse full of coin was thrown in Henry's face in challenge, unanswered. Then Henry was removed by one of the older administrators.

That evening, word reached us that Henry's prize ship was ablaze and likely to be sunk. Tom was accounted for, having been at the Guild office's all day and into the night, but I have little doubt he arranged this in some fashion. I must endeavour to discover how.

We parted at St. Enochs and I walked towards the studio. I found it after a few passes, below street level on a wicked hill. They looked about to close, a troupe of young dancers filing up the stairs with their parents.

"Are you still open?" I called as I stuck my head in the door. I was met by a man behind a desk who shone like Faith did, roiling with changing symbols and ripples of power. His skin was deep black and his hair cut close to his head. Did all angels look so beautiful?

"Not all of us, but thanks." He chuckled, beckoning me in.

"That's not a cool trick," I muttered, blushing. "I'm looking for Elisha."

"Faith? She said you'd be round. She's finishing up; I'll let her know you're here."

"You're also one of the fallen?" I asked as he stood up. He was tall, six foot five or six and looked awful relaxed for being crammed behind a desk.

"You not sure what to call us?" he asked with a lazy smile. His accent was almost American but not quite, the edges rubbed off.

"I don't have a clue, and the book I have just calls you the fallen, which is kinda blunt."

"I'm sure you're never blunt." He smirked, knocking hard on one of the doors beside the desk.

"Seems stupid to piss off someone who could make my head explode," I said, biting the inside of my cheek to keep from blurting more.

"You think we do that?"

"I think you could if you wanted. Angels always say 'don't be afraid' when they appear to humans. Figure there's a reason." I shrugged.

"A sensible approach. I'm Tobias." He held a hand out, and I stared at it for a second before taking it. I was greatly relieved not to be shot to the other side of the room.

"Carter. Are you hiding your power?"

"Yes."

"You weren't when I opened the door."

"You weren't worried about me then. Would you rather I didn't?"

"It's unfair to do that on my account is all," I said, looking him over. He wouldn't have been out of place modelling, those brown eyes lined with thick lashes. Had to be here by preference over necessity.

"Correct about the preference," he said, smiling again. "You have a very busy mind."

"Please stop doing that," I said as nicely as I could.

"He can't help it any more than I can," came a voice behind me.

"Fair enough. Can we talk?" I asked without looking over.

"Naturally. This way." She turned back into the room, and I trotted after her, nodding my thanks Tobias.

The sight of her was less traumatic now, her shadow wings being the biggest distraction. Power came off her in waves. The swirl of glyphs and colour over her skin was entrancing, but the gloom hanging over her was worse. She took a seat on a bench. I hovered a few steps away, unsure where best to go.

"Come sit by me. I don't bite."

"Promise?"

"Would you trust the promise of a fallen one?" she asked.

"Pretty much. Not got many other choices."

"A sad truth," she said, patting the bench. I sat a short distance from her, trying to keep the edge off by avoiding eye contact.

"Would you prefer I mask myself as Tobias did?" she asked.

"No. I can shield myself if it gets too bad."

"Thank you. What did you wish to discuss?"

"I spoke to The Collector today, and to a few others."

"Yes, you smell like Annie," she said with a laugh.

"You know the ghost?"

"She's been in Glasgow for some time. She is known."

"You know she kills people?" I asked, glancing at her. The wings had spread out, broad and dark like a bird of prey.

"Yes." She nodded and her skin flitted into sun kissed gold, then back to pale flesh.

"I expected more of a reaction," I said.

"It's not my business what she does. She has not tried to harm me or mine. Nor has The Collector. Why do you wish to speak about him?"

"Sarah was dealing with him before she disappeared. I thought she was trying to hide from him, but that's wrong. She's hiding from something, and I think I know what, but I need to be sure."

"You think she hides from the thing toying with your sleep."

"How do you know about that?" I asked, turning on the bench to look at her.

"It suits me to know about it, so I do."

"I hate this city," I said, head slumping down over my chest.

"It doesn't hate you. It's rather fond, if anything. It suits me to know what powerful things are doing in this city, and Dex is one of those. You are tempted by him." I glanced up to see a blank look on her face.

"It wants me for fifteen years in exchange for telling me how to get her."

"You wish to protect your sister, I understand. Dex is not a good creature. He's powerful and patient and excruciatingly old, even for my kind to measure. Any deal he makes will benefit him more than you."

"I got that. Is it a he? It's not really given me any gender when we've met."

"I know him as a he, but you're correct that he's beyond anything like that really." She nodded, smiling at me. It flickered between that and a stream of purple energy, leaking out into the room. "It is him she hides from. Do you think Sarah would be able to forgive herself if you stayed here in servitude?"

"I'd only be losing fifteen years. It's like going to prison but with a little more freedom."

"And a debt to a being more powerful than you."

"Banks are more powerful than me, and I could take a longer mortgage. They get to keep everything if I fuck up."

She looked at me for a beat before she began to laugh, giggling behind her hand after the first chuckle overtook her. "That is the most human way I have heard someone discuss such things," she said with a grin that looked almost normal. "Fine then, if you choose to take that path, Tobias and I will be here to share your time. We may be able to assist you in some ways. Though you may not be looking at all your options. If he will trade with you on this, he may be willing to trade other things. Was that all you wished to discuss?"

"One other thing. Annie kept pointing to the St. Andrews cathedral and talking about a door. Is there a portal there?"

"No. There is one at the larger cathedral, but you already smell of there. Did you connect with it?"

"Showed up a bit too late; it was closed."

"It is erratic. You can try again. Did Annie say Sarah was there?"

"No. She kept saying all the doors were coming, and we needed to find Sarah before then. That Sarah's door was hidden, but she was in danger when it came back."

"Sarah hid herself somewhere she could not be accessed until the barriers are weak. I would see who else is looking for her. If Annie thinks another is involved, I would believe it."

"She's that good?" I asked.

"She watches very closely for who she will take dancing along the river banks. I trust her judgement."

"Is she an elemental?"

"No, a ghost. Drowned by a rapist she unmanned," she said, and I felt an instinctive twitch at the wording. Couldn't blame the woman.

"That would explain the preference for drowning the bad ones," I said tightly.

"Indeed. She didn't share this with you?"

"Not that detail, no."

"She must have liked you."

"Good to know. I should head off. Need to go pick up a friend." I stood up, glancing over at her. She was still a writhing galaxy of power and light and the wings pulled out above her.

"Take care, Carter. You would do well to guard yourself from those who wish to influence you for their own ends. Consider all your options."

I left the room with her warning knocking around my brain and nodded to Tobias as I was leaving.

"Off so soon?" he asked, looking to the door.

"Got a party to go to," I said, hesitating by the desk. The dude felt decent.

"Oh yes, the sex party. Enjoy yourself." His eyes sparkled at the last part, and I shot out of the office.

I swung past a sushi place and took my order to go, eating as I walked along Buchanan Street with the swelling crowd. I wasn't in a rush to get back, or to go to the party, but Faith's words had stuck in my head.

Who else was looking for Sarah? I knew Luke and Alex were; I was with them. There was the mysterious Marc who swung between flirting with and terrifying me. He was out for himself though. There was the group Luke had mentioned, the Dex worshipers. I hadn't found any of them yet, but if Luke was right then they'd be looking for her. This party was my best bet at finding anyone else sniffing around, so I had to make an appearance. Would be a shame to waste the suit if nothing else.

I checked for any of malicious packages awaiting my return, but thankfully there were none. The cursed jewellery had been in my bag all day without incident and sat innocently there as I looked at it. I dropped the envelope on the bed and took a photo. I didn't want to take the item with me. If anyone was sensitive enough to feel it then they'd be spooked off.

I grabbed my suit and some primping stuff I wouldn't miss in the morning then set off, walking down to the subway with music blaring in my headphones. The train was busy, the crowd of people nudging against me as the carriage rocked. It wasn't overwhelming and as wonderful as that was, it should have been bad. Why had it become so easy, was Dex interfering somehow? I hadn't given it anything, so that wouldn't be a fair trade. Maybe it was sheer stress and anxiety that was helping, blocking everything else out.

Hurray.

The West End was bustling with people, the pavement lush with bodies milling around. I slipped between them and across the road, buzzing the door to the flat and trotting up the tenement steps.

The door swung open to reveal Marc. He was in full resplendent showmanship: a dark grey three piece, double breasted, suit with broad red check pattern, off white shirt, and a red and cream paisley tie. Between that and his hair, now up in a bun, he looked like an Edwardian gentleman who got lost in charity shop. And he looked pleased as punch with it too.

"Carter, you're late!" he chastised, ushering me in.

"I have to get in a suit and splash on some cologne. How am I late for that? I'll need like ten minutes."

"What about pre-gaming?" he asked, flashing me a wolfish grin.

"For fuck's sake, I'm not drinking. I need a clear head."

"Mate, you will need at least one drink in you to make it through the night, if not several. I have tequila and Alex is drinking wine. Which do you prefer?"

"Are you like this at every party?" I asked as I laid my suit down.

"Much worse." He winked. "I could help you with other stuff if you'd prefer?"

"No E before the orgy. That is not what I'm aiming for tonight."

"I have other stuff."

"Magic stuff?"

"Nah, but I have good weed and some coke, if you'd like it."

"Tequila will be fine, and you'd better bring it back with salt."

"Salt, as in...?"

"As in, if it tastes like anything less than the ocean, I'll deck you."

"A-OK." He grinned, vanishing into the kitchen.

"Alex?" I called and heard a yell from the bathroom. Alright then, not too late. I started to get changed in the living room and was halfway buttoned up when Marc came back in with a tray of shots, lemon wedges, and a shaker of salt.

"A tray?" I choked out.

"They're not all for you. We can share. Nice suit."

"Alex spotted it; the style is all hers. I'm sure I'll shine up nice enough though." I shrugged, finishing the buttons and taking the shot handed to me. A lemon segment followed.

"One before you do the tie, to pull off the style."

"Says the man in a red check number?"

"Hey, I'm gorgeous," Marc said with the same grin he had given me in the workshop.

"You are, but I'm nothing close to drunk enough yet to even start going there." I shook my head and held my fist out for the salt. He poured a line along the stretch of my thumb and raised his own shot in a toast. Both of us licked our salt, poured our shot back, and bit a lemon in unison. It was potent and smooth as it went down, but the citrus was sharp, fresh and welcome.

"Christ on a bike, where did you get that from?" I asked as I shook the kick off.

"That's a good old Fortaleza," he said.

"And assuming I don't know what that means?"

"Classic Mexican tequila."

"Old school, nice." I moved to the mirror in the hallway and slipped my tie on, dredging for the memory of tying one from school. I tried twice before giving in and ambling back into the living room. "Any idea how to tie a double Windsor?"

"You can't tie a tie?" he asked, reclining on a sofa like an oversized cat.

"I can do a single, but I thought a fancier knot would be needed for this evening."

"You know most people are going to want to take that off you rather than look at how nicely it's done?"

"Shut up. Can you do it?"

"If you take another shot."

"You trying to get me drunk?" Not that two shots would do it, but still.

"Just enough to make sure you have a good time. These things can be intense. You might try 'nd have fun." He stood up, bringing the tray with him.

"And the real reason?"

"Carter," He pouted as he passed me the glass, "Are you accusing me of having ulterior motives?"

"Yes."

"Such mistrust." He tutted, pouring salt for me and raising his eyebrows as he held out the lemon. "If I did, would you object to them?"

"Depends on what they were," I said, licking the line and taking the tequila back. I bit the slice and hummed my approval of the sour tang, passing the glass back to Marc. "Tie, now."

"If I did have other motives, they would be good ones," he said as he fiddled with the material. One finger brushed along my neck, careless.

"Such as?" I asked, tilting my jaw to dislodge the touch.

"Maybe I'd want to make sure someone was looking out for Alex. Or for me."

"You look like you can handle yourself pretty well."

"Just 'cause you can doesn't mean you want to," he said, pouting again.

"I'm your carte blanche to be reckless?"

"I don't need any back up for that. But if there was someone in the group who was targeting the young and able, Alex would be a prime target. That would be sad."

"If they can't get Sarah use Alex instead?" I asked, watching his hands move.

"Someone might think that, yeah."

"Hardly think she needs me to look after her," I said, scoffing.

"Absolutely not." He chuckled, tightening the knot and patting me down. "But you'll spot things she won't. That little trick of yours is awful useful."

"How do you know about any of my tricks?" I arched an eyebrow.

"Luke mentioned an incident with Dex."

"Doesn't everyone love talking about that."

"Sounds impressive," Marc said with a tilt of his head.

"Terrifying, more like. How do you know about things like Dex?"

"I know various folk into this stuff. It's an open secret that some have been trying to court that one."

"You couldn't have mentioned it last night when you were playing station stalker?" I asked, a spark of annoyance biting in my chest.

"I didn't know last night. Luke kept it quiet 'til I mentioned some weirdness going on. People getting antsy, asking for more than usual. That only happens when something big is going on, and even with Halloween it's excessive. Luke thought it might be because of Dex."

"Oh, they're high and worshipping a creepy ancient being. Hurray."

"Yeah, it's a jamboree of fuck ups. But you can see through it. So, look. And if you think any of them are going to be making a move on her, let me know. For old times' sake, I want to make sure she's okay."

"Sounds like there's a story there."

"Not one I plan to share. Now, don't you look fancy," he said, tucking a pocket square he'd produced from nowhere into my top pocket.

"Told you I scrub up nice. You gonna tell me the story?"

"I owe her. Would be sad to see her gone. There might be nothing, but I'd rather have a safety net."

"Not something I'm often associated with."

"No. Sarah kept you quite the little secret," he hummed. "But I'm sure she had her reasons."

"We can hope," I agreed, checking my hair in the mirror. I'd pass.

"Are you two playing nice?" I heard from behind me. I turned to see Alex standing in the doorway, slipping into her heels for the evening.

She looked stunning, a garnet dress that contrasted with her hair and eyes, so they shone. It had a deep vee-neck and skimmed along her waist and hips to a flowing skirt that split halfway down, showing a sliver of leg. Her hair was teased out to frame her face gently, leading my eyes to her plum colour lipstick. The heels looked small enough to last the evening. She seemed happy with the overall look as she checked herself out in the mirror, popping a hip to watch the skirt sway.

"Nice as lambs," Marc said, passing a shot over to her. "Salt and lemon?"

"No cinnamon?" she asked.

"Alex, why do you say these things when I give you good tequila?" Marc asked, shaking his head. She held her hand out and took the salt, not smudging her lips as she knocked the mix back and bit the wedge.

"That is good tequila," she said, brushing off any excess salt and grabbing a small red bag from one of the sofas. "Taxi?"

"I thought we were riding with Marc?" I asked, glancing between them. I had wondered with the tequila.

"Oh, no. I'll be having far too good a time to be the designated driver."

"I thought one of the rules was not to try your own stash?" I asked.

"All my sins will be alcohol or body based, I assure you." The smile came back with practiced ease.

"Taxi it is, then." I nodded, looking back to Alex.

"Fine, I'll get one booked and we can head off."

"What about after the party?" I asked Marc as Alex stepped into the kitchen on her phone.

"You'll see." He shrugged, checking himself over in the mirror again. "Would eyeliner be too much?"

"You know it would be. You just want a reaction out of me." I laughed, shaking my head.

"Spot on. You're good at that."

"And you're good at presenting." I smiled, teeth flashing.

"Both useful in the right circumstance." He winked, glancing to the kitchen door before continuing. "I mean it about Alex—if she goes home with someone that's fine, but make sure she's not a target."

"I'm the bait. You know that, right?" I asked, by brows coming together.

"I know that's your plan. Doesn't mean you're going to be."

"Surely my ignorance and charm will make me irresistible?" I batted my eyelashes at him.

"You're planning to play dumb?"

"More the brooding, soulful type who's torn apart by the loss of his sister. Far too concerned with my pain to notice anything other than the kindness of those helping me." I continued the look from under my lashes, pouting slightly.

"Make it a bit chattier, less lost puppy, and you might pull that off." He nodded. "Or, get drunk and see who tries to take advantage."

"Of me or her?"

"They're all going to want a piece of you, but I'd check for both."

"You make this sound so appealing. I thought these were fun gatherings?" I tried to keep a straight face but lost it at the end, the smirk pulling my lips up.

"They're whatever they choose to label them as," Marc shrugged again, hands slipping into his trouser pockets. "It's your best bet at spotting someone."

"Are you spooking Carter?" Alex bustled back in with an accusatory glare at Marc.

"Just reminding him how popular he's going to be—everyone loves fresh meat." He slapped a hand on my shoulder, and I tightened my jaw against the urge to shrug it off. I had my music if it got too bad.

"Marc, you're wicked! You'll be the topic of conversation, but they'll behave. Especially given the eyes Luke's been giving you," she said, grinning at the last part.

"Which I'm sure is more to do with my powers than anything else," I said, eyes going back to Marc.

"He's not looking for anything like that at the party. It's about having a good time, which I intend to have." Alex tutted.

Marc raised his brows at her then glanced at his tray. "There's a shot each left, for the road?"

"Sure, the taxi will be here soon," she said, holding a hand out for the salt.

"You guys usually show up to these things smashed?" I asked.

"If it only takes three tequilas to get you smashed then I am mightily misinformed about Manchester." Marc laughed as he passed me the glass.

"Motherfucker, I used to drink absinthe. This is nothing," I countered, standing tall. "I was more thinking there might be a rule about drinking and consent?"

"We'll not be anything close to that drunk, and we have designated chaperones to make sure everyone's safe," Alex assured me, passing the lemon slice over.

"Very sensible. I'm pleased to hear it," I said after I swallowed.

"I'm sure Carter won't be needing one. He looks like he could handle himself. Not that he'll need to at the party. There'll be a line of volunteers." Marc leaned in, shoulder to shoulder, and bounced off me.

"Marc! Stop it, you terror." Alex batted his arm with her bag, mock glaring at him. A horn sounded outside and saved me. Alex grabbed a red cloak with a fur trim that must have been fake judging by the colouring and shooed us out so she could lock the door. We poured into the taxi with Marc in the front, shotgun called for the music choices. He gave the driver an address that meant nothing to me and we took off into the traffic.

"We're going to be a little late, but it's fashionable," Alex said, leaning close to me. "I'll have to introduce you to the host when we get there."

"Luke isn't the host?"

"Oh no, he's the organiser, much more complicated."

"Right."

"Samuel can be a little odd. He's cool, but kinda formal. Just so you know."

"Anything else 'just so I know?'" I asked, stomach tightening.

"There's communal tables of supplies should you need anything. If Samuel likes you, he'll give you some wine. That's about it. Relax." She gave me a grin, and the echo of Sarah slapped me in the face, the same excitement and open enjoyment in her expression. It was painful in the quiet, quivering way, and I swallowed the hurt down with a nod to her.

# Chapter 16

I have begun a most unwise endeavour. There is a succubus who frequents some of the established practitioners within the city, sampling them at her leisure. She presents as nothing more than another intrigued young woman, curious as to the magical, but I have seen her marking—the stub of a tail flicking underneath her skirt. I am puzzled as to why other practitioners do not appear concerned with this, but that is another matter.

I approached her to test her recognition, seeking to establish whether she is able to perceive my magic in correspondence with the way I saw her nature. This lively discussion led into an evening's company and a dalliance I am certain is ill advised. And yet I find myself wishing to ensure a repeat of the events.

The Good Book warns that such creatures leech life, thus weakening their victims to the point of exhaustion and then death. Such was not the way with this encounter. I feel hale and heartier than I have since I began my studies. Equally, she seemed satisfied with our joining and left with an ambiguous promise to return. And after that promise, I yearn.

I hesitate to recount this to my friend, lest I am some foolish clod who has been beguiled by a baser demon. However, in failing to do so, I may leave myself exposed to development of a weakness I can sorely afford to bare.

We arrived at a detached property, the ground floor windows spilling light along the driveway and painting the ferns along it golden.

I was surprised to find such a secluded place in the city I knew there was a road just behind us, but the sound was well muffled by the green barrier. Purchasable privacy.

"Nice." I whistled as we scrambled out.

"Come on," Alex said, taking my arm and leading me to the door. She struck the brass knocker three times, glancing behind us to Marc. He stood off my side, face calm and the ghost of a smile lurking. The door swung open and a masked man bowed, sweeping an arm in welcome.

"Really?" I asked Alex with a look.

"Really," she said, leading me in and shrugging off her cloak.

"Your jacket, sir?" the man asked.

I shook my head with a smile, holding my arm out for Alex. The masked man glanced to Marc and away again.

"Where's his accent from?" I asked Alex, as she led me down a corridor. It was panelled in dark red wood and had a carpet plush enough to muffle our steps.

"Edinburgh. He's hired in," she said, smiling as we emerged into the main room.

It was long and crammed with people, the chatter of the crowd carrying over like waves. Ho boy. There was a selection of evening wear on show, formal suits and the odd tux mingled together with backless gowns and skimming black dresses that teased a bit of interest. It was clear people came here in little groups, darting back and forth like fish in the shallows as they exchanged glances and whispers. An expectant energy hung in the room like a mist, buffeted and swirled as people touched and looked and planned. It was a substantial place; several doors branched off the mushroom grey walls, some open and showing slivers of rooms.

"And you want to introduce me to which one?" I asked.

"Samuel. We'll find him in the kitchen."

"Where's that?"

"Just this way." She took my hand and threaded us through the crowd, making apologies and nodding as we passed through the scrum of people.

"Bit crowded isn't it?"

"Some of them'll be away before the real fun starts, and the side rooms hold a lot."

"Good to know."

"Try not to sound so judgmental when you're speaking to people," she said, grumbling under her breath.

"I'm not judging anything other than the party planner who thought this was a reasonable number of people. I've seen markets less busy."

"I'm sure Luke will take that as constructive criticism. Samuel!"

She led me through a heavy wooden door, the swing back clipping my hip as I was tugged in her wake. The kitchen was flashy, cupboards lining the marble surfaces and a substantial island in the centre coated in an impressive selection of bottles.

Alex dropped my hand, going towards a short man who was bent over and busying himself with a wine cupboard. He stood and turned to see her, smiling wide as she enveloped him in an embrace. Oh Jesus, the teeth. They were twice the length they should be and sharp, folding into his mouth some way I didn't want to think about. The rest of him looked normal, ashen brown hair and a slightly ruddy face, a thin long nose and a predatory gaze that was tucked into Alex's neck.

I reached out with my gift and felt the cold shock of his energy which earned me his gaze. He smiled, moving a hand up to pat Alex's back and held a finger up to his lips as he did so.

"Samuel, this is Carter. He's Sarah's brother, and he's here to see if anyone is acting unusual," she said as they parted, waving to me.

"Yes, Luke mentioned you. I'm sure we can assist," Samuel said. His accent was something southern, maybe Kent or Oxford a long while ago.

"We'd be so grateful, if you don't mind us using the party?" She practically pouted the question.

"Quite fine, Alex. Quite fine. I do like Sarah."

"You're a saint." Alex grinned and hugged him again. "Do you want to discuss anything with Carter before we go mingle? I'm going to be playing matchmaker tonight."

"I'll have a word, see if he can jog my memory of anything," he said, eyeing me. I could feel the push of his energy and frowned at him. He gave an imperceptible shrug, smiling. It showed his teeth and I looked away, to Alex, as she went back through the door. "Now, just what are you, my boy?" He stepped around the island and moved in front of me.

"Human and not yours. In that order."

"What type of human is so perceptive as to see me when the rest of them don't?" He peered at me over his glasses. He was middle aged looking, a little paunch which he carried well enough. Without those teeth he'd look like a nice librarian, maybe.

"I'm like Sarah, got the gift. I see things different."

"Evidently. What do you see in me?"

"I spotted your teeth. Bit of a giveaway."

"And why should you see that?"

"I'm guessing you glamour the others. That's not so effective with me."

"Evidently. How curious. Do you know what I am?"

"A vampire," I said. Why did I say yes to this?

"And why do you say that?" He cooed the question, those teeth teeming at the edge of his lips.

"The teeth, and your age."

"My age?"

"Well, you're not in your forties," I said, leaning a hip on the counter and folding my arms.

"Not quite, no."

"I met someone similar to you before, though she looked different."

"Better?" He raised one straight brow with a smirk.

"That's a hard no. She looked like an animated corpse. Scared me."

"We have a habit of that," he conceded, smiling. The teeth pushed forward and shone under the bulbs.

"They don't remember when they see?"

"No." He chuckled. "If they see at all. Many don't bother looking."

"And I take it you would rather I kept it that way?"

"Indeed, Carter. I would be quite happy to assist with that," he said, pushing again with his energy.

"Doesn't work," I reminded him, shuffling slightly.

"Why not?" He looked me over again as if I would sprout a tail.

"I've been shielding for a hell of a long time. Didn't like the gift, shut it out."

"A wise choice if you can see us lurking around."

"Worked for me. Are you happy with me being here or shall I leave?"

"I insist you stay. I've no need to feed from you, and I'll enjoy the events that will unfold from your presence."

"Thank you, I think. Why do you even host these things?"

"I find being among the young keeps me connected to the world. Too many of us become like the wizened you mentioned, blurring from one decade to the next. Interaction and intrigue keep my mind entertained where my body has no concern."

"Been doing it a long time?"

"In different places and different ways, yes. I was turned at a time when social gatherings were encouraged and it stuck with me."

"Do I want to ask?"

"Will it disturb you if you knew?" He grinned, open and amused.

"Alright, when was that?"

"In the early 1880s."

"Not in Glasgow," I said.

"No. And further away than you, by that accent. Though I'm sure you're not having any issue with that."

"No, us northerners tend to get everywhere."

"Useful for blending in."

"Hopefully. Do you have any ideas about Sarah?"

"No." He frowned slightly. "Which is troublesome. I'm aware of most circumstances in this group and yet there's a wolf prowling around."

"Someone you've seen?"

"No. I've just heard the chatter. And your good sister vanished."

"Did Sarah know about you?"

"She thought me eccentric. Most do."

"You ever glamour her?" I asked, tilting my head to look at him more. Those teeth still glistened.

"No need. I don't use my talents for enticing attention at these gatherings. I take my leave well before the more eventful matters. I have never had an interest in such things."

"Excuse my bluntness, but if you aren't a fan of orgies, why do you host them?" I asked, lost.

"One does not need to be a gardener to admire the flowers, Carter." His smiled broadened, eyes sparkling.

"That's an interesting perspective."

"One born of time and experience, I assure you."

"I'm gonna take your word on that. And head back to the party."

"Of course. Here." He reached over the counter and passed me two glasses. "One for yourself and one for Alex. She likes the red. Best to keep up appearances." He nodded to the selection of wine and then turned, dismissing me. Okay then.

I left the kitchen with the wine glasses in a tight grip, chewing the inside of my cheek. Alex was mercifully close and I nudged into her, passing the drink.

"How'd you get on?" she asked.

"Fine. He's lovely," I lied, smiling tight. "He couldn't think of anything but said he'd keep an eye out. I think I got his approval."

"That's excellent. He's usually very discerning."

"Thanks. I'm sure the suit disguise got me through it," I said, resisting the urge to drink more.

"You know what I mean. He can be sniffy. He likes Sarah though, so that'll have helped."

"I'm glad," I said, leaning closer to her. "Anyone obviously evil lurking in the shadows with a sign saying they're looking to kidnap young, powerful women?"

"Given the nature of the party, a sign wouldn't be worrying," she whispered back, smirking at me.

"Good point. It's the obviously comfortable and not evil looking ones we need to watch for?"

"Exactly. The weirdos are all accounted for."

"You know that makes it much harder, right?" I nudged my hip into hers to make her smile.

"There's a lot of people outside the group, so we'll have to keep checking in. You happy to split up and cover more ground?"

"I thought you were my opening act?" I asked, a thrill of panic nipping my chest. I was not drunk enough to mingle.

"Luke's taken care of that for most people. You'll be fine!"

Fuck. "Alright, let's try that. You can find me by the wall, drinking heavily."

"You meant every word of that," she said with a giggle.

"Undoubtedly. But let's try it."

She nodded and set off into the crowd, smile flashing as easy embraces came forward. Forget that. The energy of the place was overwhelming, and I didn't want to attempt to disentangle individual people from the feel of the crowd.

I started on the side rooms instead, seeing what was on the menu. Some of them were designed for specialist use, plastic wrapping on the floor of one, what I took to be a sex swing in another, a selection of blindfolds and gags in third. Interesting.

I paused in one of the larger ones, lit with a photographers' box light. It housed some unusual furniture: the frame of a chair missing its seat, a St. Andrews Cross, and something I didn't know the name for. It looked like a two-tiered table with padding on the tops. Arms jutted out of the higher tier, including fasteners at the ends. Walking round it, I could see other fastening points dotted around the frame.

"A spanking bench." I looked up to see Marc watching me with an unreadable smile.

"I should've guessed."

"You're not really used to these things, are you?"

"Not at all." I laughed, shrugging.

"Why'd you lie?" he asked, sucking air through his teeth.

"I didn't know if you could be trusted, and I'm looking for someone who might have hurt my sister."

"You think that might be me?" The smirk really nullified any effect at sounding hurt. He stepped into the room, circling around the bench.

"I didn't know. You were the first person I met besides Alex, and Sarah hadn't mentioned you. Or any of this."

"She didn't tell us about you, and she didn't tell you about us. And she didn't tell Luke about that little book, or Alex about her investigations. Lots of secrets for Sarah." His eyes flashed at the last part.

"Lots from everyone."

"Do you have a lot of secrets, Carter?" He looked me over, hand lingering on one of the cuff fasteners.

"Fair few, yeah." I nodded, tilting my chin despite myself. I was on the wrong side of the bench, the door behind Marc.

"Feel a need to confess?" he asked, fingers stroking the leather of the padding.

"Not one to be struck by that too often." I smiled, my best debonair grin pulling forward. I started to move, circling around to the other side of the bench. There was something he wasn't saying, and I didn't know where Marc was leading this.

"No, I suppose not. I find myself the same way. Are you going to tell Alex about Dex?" He paralleled my steps, moving towards the head of the bench as I reached the end.

"Not if I can help it. She didn't like the fallen angel, never mind something like Dex."

"Literal fallen angel?" His brows furrowed, hand falling away.

"Yeah, dances at the Golden Globes."

"You are so fucked, dude." He chuckled, shaking his head. "I'm gonna split. I've done my supply run." He sucked in his cheeks for a minute, looking me over again. "I don't know if I can trust you," he said, eventually.

"You can trust I'm looking for Sarah and that I'll keep an eye out for Alex. If I think someone's making moves to hurt her, I'll step in."

"That's fair," he said with a nod. "You should stick to Luke tonight, see what happens after his duties."

"Duties?"

"Luke always finds some pretty young thing to take to bed. There are rumours about what happens when he does. You should find out."

"You've gone from warning me off him to me getting in bed with him."

"You're not the only one who has people to look out for. I don't stay around to watch slaughter at the meat market."

"Just supply the knives?" It was out before I could stop it, and I was surprised I got a laugh rather than a fist.

"Something like that. Knives for the willingly butchered."

"Gotta make a crust," I shrugged, "No judgement."

"I wouldn't care if you did," he said with his nicest smile. "Though I like you, so try to keep away from the sharp edges."

"I'm going to go find more wine," I said, raising my now empty glass.

"Good plan. You'll need it."

"Can you stop sounding so fucking ominous without telling me what the issue is?"

"No." He shrugged. "But then I never stick around long enough to prove myself right."

"Wise man." I made for the door.

"Carter?" he called before I was free of him.

"Yes?" I turned to face him again. The light struck his hair, haloing him with the reflection, and he looked statuesque.

"If Dex is offering you a good deal, I'd think about taking it. The guys I know about, they're not so nice as this crowd. Sarah's probably hiding for a good reason."

"Thanks, Marc." I nodded, letting that little detail settle in. Not. Drunk. Enough.

"Welcome. Let me know if there's anything fun you need."

"No doubt," I said, stepping through the door before I could get caught in some other terrifying titbit. Fuck this.

I aimed for the kitchen, intent on finding more wine or tequila. The crowd had thinned a little, bodies clustering in groups with larger gaps. Alex was somewhere up at the other end of the room, gesticulating at the man across from her with a laugh.

I glanced around for Luke and caught his eye, a warm smile lighting his face as he spoke to someone facing away from me. I raised my brows and shrugged a little, glancing around. He nodded, raising his glass in a small toast then went back to his conversation. I had no idea what we'd communicated but he'd been watching for me.

That played into my hands if I wanted to follow Marc's advice. It was tempting. Luke had made no secret that he was interested, and my curiosity was itching. Maybe he could find out who left that little present for me, too. I turned and went back into the kitchen, glancing around to find Samuel looking at a selection of bottles.

"Do you always run the drinks or is this just to let you see who's about?" I asked.

"I enjoy seeing who can recognise something good when it lands in front of them," he said, placing a plain bottle amongst the red wine selection.

"You play 'spot the expensive wine' at a sex party?"

"I'd describe it more subtly."

"You're not worried it'll get knocked over?" I asked, thinking about the counter height.

"I'd never allow it. I retire before such activities. What can I do for you?" He turned to face me, smiling with his mouth mercifully closed.

"Two things. What do you know of a being called Dex?"

"As little as possible." He sniffed, frowning. "It pays to steer clear of such things."

"And if you didn't have any choice?"

"Then I would go bearing gifts and hope for a gentle visit. There are some quite veracious in their pursuit of that particular being, and they don't lend themselves to subtle discussion."

"Sounds peachy. Say you were directly approached?"

"Are we talking about you?"

"No."

"Then why are we discussing this?"

"Sarah may have had inadvertent contact with it, and I'm trying to fix that."

"My goodness," he said, taking his glasses off to polish them briefly. "That would explain a few things. You honestly feel that is the case?"

"Got it confirmed."

"How?"

"You know The Collector?" I asked.

"Yes, he's a good fellow."

"Him."

"Accurate then. A shame. I'd advise abandoning such enquiries and making your peace, but I suppose that's unlikely?"

"Entirely," I said.

"Then I suggest a bargain if one can be had, and if not then subtlety in every measure."

"Make a deal or hope not to get noticed?"

"Indeed. Here." He passed me a glass of something amber tinged with pink. I took a sip and shook my head because of the sweetness, not cloying but unexpected.

"I thought the cliché was vampires drinking red wine?"

"A sweet tooth doesn't vanish upon death." Samuel smiled, patting his stomach. "It appears you have more of a need of it than I. A Sauternes Château Suduiraut, should you care to know."

"Thanks, it's nice."

"Rather. Why did you ask me about Dex?"

"Everyone else knows about it, and I'm new to the table."

"You are of course trusting my word," he said with a level look.

"Can't see you having a reason to lie, and if you did, I can't be at much more of a disadvantage."

"A fatalistic view."

"Thanks. Do you happen to have anything I could trade The Collector?" I asked, drinking another swig of the wine.

"Was that your second line of enquiry?"

"No. Chancing it."

"What an appropriate phrase. What did you wish to trade for?"

"Sarah was speaking to him and he won't tell me what she got without something to trade."

"Ever a stickler for the order of things. I have two items you could use. Trivial things, but they will entertain him. Come with me."

He took me through a side door revealing a windowless set of stairs. The sounds of the party above quietened to a whisper as we descended, the scent of damp soil and old paper blooming up around us.

"There any lights down here, Samuel?" I asked as the last from the door way vanished.

"No. I have no need."

"Mind if I use my phone to help me see?"

"Of course," he said.

I pulled it out, lighting up the screen. The steps were wide and low, worn with use and spotted with odd stains I didn't fancy thinking about. We came to a long, low space I took to be a wine cellar.

"Carve it yourself?" I asked, shining my screen around.

"Not quite, though I can appreciate the investment. Of course, I could have lured you down here to dispose of you given our earlier conversation." The push of his powers came against me again.

"Still doesn't work. And I doubt you'd want to drag my body up all those steps."

"You think manual labour would dissuade me?"

"I think it'd be inconvenient and you enjoy the party too much for that."

"I could leave your body here and deal with it tomorrow."

"You could, but Alex would ask questions and you like her."

"Do you understand how much of a threat I am to you?" He sighed, exasperated.

"No question. You could tear my throat open and leave me to bleed out on the floor. My nonchalance is from necessity rather than ignorance."

"Necessity?"

"I think about this lot too long and I'll go crazy. Easier to make a joke and refuse to look into the void." Or the ancient evil thing lurking in the void waving at me.

"A curious approach. I can understand its merits," he said with a nod.

"Glad to hear it. Do you actually have items or did you just lure me down here to remind me you're the apex predator?"

"One moment."

He walked off into the dark, and I flashed my phone around. The anticipated racks and vats sat to one side, almost full. I crept along a wall with my light, exploring what I could see. The remains of deep red wallpaper shone with gold threading, like the folds of curtains. I traced along it and found a mural of a young woman hunting in a forest clearing, her bow drawn against a squat imp.

"Artemis, taking aim," came Samuel's voice. Far too close.

"You like her?" I asked, trying not to flinch.

"She was one of the dual goddesses, the hunt and death."

"A natural combination for a vampire to admire," I said, moving my phone over the painting. "She was well known before the Greeks."

"Never so beautifully represented until then. Or so widely worshipped for both aspects."

"That why you have her here?"

"I admire things of beauty and she is one of them," he conceded, smiling. "Here, for your discussions with The Collector." He passed me a necklace and a ring, heavy and cool in my palm.

"Do I want to ask why he wants these?" I slipped them into my jacket pocket.

"No. They aren't worth a vast amount, but enough to allow you discussions about Sarah, I'd venture."

"Thank you very much. That's a huge help."

"It is for Sarah's benefit, but you're welcome. We should go back. You'll be missed."

"What will I tell them when I'm missed?" I asked, following him.

"Touring my wine collection, an honour reserved for a select few."

"Duly noted. I'll sound impressed."

"Don't forget your bottle. It wouldn't do for you to be caught coming from a wine cellar without a good drink."

We made our way back up the steps and into the refreshing light. The hum of the crowd had lessened in our absence which was fine by me.

"Looks like we missed the start of the fun," I said, picking up the sweet wine.

"I am sure you won't be left out. You're the talk of the party."

"How'd you know that?"

"People will tell you a lot in exchange for a nice glass of wine." He smiled, tapping his nose.

"Great." I forced a smile, looking out to the swirl of people. "I suppose I should go join in."

"You didn't pursue your second query," Samuel prompted.

"That was more delicate," I said. "How long have you known Luke?"

"Since his enquiry into using this property as a venue for the parties, so around ten years."

"You've been renting your place out for ten years?"

"This property isn't mine. I simply care for it. The owner has matters overseas that required their attention."

"Alright then. Ten years. Have you ever had any unsavoury instances?"

"Luke and I've never had cause to quarrel, though our association does not extend past here. Why do you ask?"

"Just a comment someone made."

"What was said?" he asked with a hiked brow, all old gossip.

"That he picks up the pretty young things for his own fun."

"That's accurate. The evenings he spends here have little to do with his spirituality and more to do with his carnal enjoyment. He's very fond of that."

"Fair enough, thanks."

"You fear Luke had such entanglements with Sarah?" he asked.

"Not my business if they did. It's at odds with the image presented, is all."

"The wise leader, unsuited to such base pursuits?"

"Something like that, yeah."

"Luke has a vast power at his disposal and the charisma to lead people. It is not uncommon for such combinations to lead to indulgence."

"That's not really a glowing reference. Charlie Manson had that, and people ended up dead."

"Cults often lead to bloodshed," Samuel said with a shrug.

"Cults do, but this group wouldn't be one of those."

"Possibly, but the sharing of energy could be considered a trait of a cult. I'm an old man who has seen many unsavoury things; age may cloud my view. I trust Luke as far as our limited interactions have given me cause to, and have encountered no reason for that trust to be broken."

"Do they know it's a cult?" I asked after a beat, drinking my glass down.

"Do they ever?" he asked back.

I poured myself another glass and thought about that for a long minute. "Not often. Usually they're just special. Everyone wants to be special."

"Indeed. I shall be taking my leave soon. I hope your evening is enjoyable."

"Yours too." I nodded, taking the bottle with me as I left. Looking over the party I saw the clear intention of the night, people touching a bit more than necessary and smiling more than needed.

I made for a loveseat set to the side of the crowd and placed the bottle down, crossing one ankle to a knee and sipping from my glass. Samuel's words knocked around in my head, snagging with Marc's. A cult? Sarah couldn't be stupid enough to get into a cult. Unless she didn't know it was one. Unless she only realised later.

Still, she'd have reached out to us. We were always at the end of the phone. That's why I was here now. The thought sat heavy on me, and I kicked it around a few more times, testing it. The few people I'd spoken too about Luke were glowing in their adoration of him, but Alex was young, and I couldn't speak to Sarah to find out what she really thought. There was Marc, the only voice of dissent in the mix, but he didn't practice or have the gift. And Samuel admitted bias.

I shook my head, taking a deep sip from my glass and topping myself up. There was a temptation to get hammered and see what happened. I settled for drinking the glass a little too quickly and nursing the next one instead. I caught glances from people and returned them with a small smile, batting my lashes and not lingering too long.

Luke was watching me from across the room. Not all the time, but his glance kept coming back to me, and he didn't mind my noticing. Got to give the guy credit for owning his choices. Interesting.

I still couldn't decide if Luke liked the look of me or my power. It made Luke as fair a suspect as the rest of them. His particular brand of practice maybe made it more likely, all sorts of coercion and rubbish went on with that. Though, he didn't seem the type to enjoy forcing someone. Which was bullshit, of course. Rapists didn't wear bloody nametags. He seemed like a guy who would get off on being wanted, rather than forcing it.

This was becoming fucking circular. Get a grip, Carter.

I got up and wandered to one of the side rooms, joining a small crowd watching the occupants. A woman stood bound to the St. Andrews Cross, her wrists and ankles secured and her black dress pulled up to bare her buttocks. It was quite the image, the backless number like a corset at her waist. Her partner was whispering to her, one hand caressing the back of her neck. His other hand held a small flogger.

"It's always nice to get a demonstration, isn't it?" I heard beside me and spotted Alex.

"I was wondering where you'd gotten to," I said, leaning in to speak close to her ear.

"I could ask the same. I thought you'd run off."

"Samuel was showing me his wine collection."

"You got to go down to his basement?" she hissed, turning to face me.

"Yes. Is that not the usual?"

"No. I've never been down there. Neither's Luke. What did you say to him to get such generosity?"

"My dad has a collection as well. We were discussing the practicalities of ventilation and cooling systems in older houses."

"Sarah never mentioned that."

"She thinks it's boring. I know a bit about the tech." I shrugged. It was a lie, but one I could bluff my way through. "Doesn't mean I know anything about wine, just how to store it."

"She is more of a whisky girl." Alex nodded, turning back to the room.

The gent had begun to swing the flogger, small arcs that swished through the ambient noise of the crowd. He crossed the back of her legs with light swipes then moved to quick, harder hits on her cheeks. The interest of the room sharpened, the quiet hunger of the crowd narrowing on the scene. I took a gulp of wine, the energy like a vice.

"Will you count for me, or would you prefer I keep you guessing?" the man asked.

"Counting, sir," she responded, glancing over her shoulder to him. She was pretty, lips painted a deep red and wide eyes framed with false lashes.

"Good girl." He smiled, stepping closer. "Remember your words?"

"Green is good, yellow for time, red to stop," she intoned by rote, glowing under his approving smile.

"I'm gonna go find another drink," I said to Alex, weaving my way out of the crowd. I had no particular dislike of this but the power imbalance sat poorly. I knew they were doing the right stuff with communication and safe words were important, but I couldn't stay there while my mind was working on ideas of abuse and cults.

I plucked my bottle up and went back into the kitchen, pouring another glass. Cupping it to my chest, I settled against a counter, rolling my head back. The energy of the place was like a livewire in the back of my skull now, and the current of desire threading about was making me heady.

I knew what I was going to do. I knew it was a bad idea. I knew I'd already made the decision and I was trying to justify it by the time I was having this conversation with myself. I was going to see if I could bed Luke and test my suspicions. Alex might hate me for it a little; I still hadn't figured out if her adoration came from loyalty or lust, but it would give me more information. That had to help with finding Sarah.

I pushed myself off the counter and plucked up the bottle, refilling it as I went. There was only about a glass left inside, but I could drink slow to make it last while I plotted.

# Chapter 17

*2 November, 1885*

*There is a coven of witches practicing at the necropolis beside the larger cathedral. They are rather brazen in their methods, attending the graves in black and joining together in the scrub land after legitimate mourners have left for the night.*

*These are not the Black Mass hags that King James would have us warned about but a smattering of women and men working together in spiritual and elemental magics. I am fascinated to see their sharing of energy; there are certain practitioners within who clearly are more skilled than others. It would be intriguing to share correspondence with them and examine how they have mastered this apportionment without the use of additional tools or familiars. Such an undertaking should come at a cost, be that a sacrifice or a need to seek assistance from another power, but there is nothing like that visible from what I have seen.*

*I have made attempts to observe them, but that damned access road is unsheltered and obvious as a bell. I will have to find another way to reach their secluded meetings.*

*Given what little I have seen, I intend to pursue the investigation. I would envisage this could be significantly beneficial for further development of my skills, should I study their actions without immersion into their ranks.*

I propped myself against a wall, watching the remaining people mill about. It wasn't too different to a networking event, people drinking a bit too quickly and exchanging promises. Nicer dresses, more roving hands. I nodded when someone came past, eyeing me up, raising my glass only to see them scarper. Oh well.

A tipsy Alex bumped up next to me, grinning with her mouth but not her eyes. "You good?" She glanced over the remaining bodies as she turned her head to me. "You got out of that room pretty quick."

"Just too many people. You?" I grinned back. We were evidently keeping up appearances for someone.

"Oh yeah, fine," she said, waving to someone who went past. "Fielding twenty questions about you. Lots of people want to know if you're eligible. Chris over there is keen on you." I stared at her for a second as words failed to come. More wine needed.

"Eligible?" I repeated. "They know I'm looking for my missing sister, right?"

"They do and they're all so keen to help you search. But they're also all horny, and you're fresh meat. What did you expect?"

"Flattering as that is, I'm kind of focused on other things," I said, taking a deep swig of the wine. "I thought you were only on information gathering tonight, anyway?"

"After today, I really need some fun. Don't worry about it, none of them'll do anything with the way Luke keeps drinking you in." She elbowed me as she said it, laughing at my dance not to spill any wine.

"Easy, Alex!" I said, fighting a blush.

"He's been making eyes at you. Though that may be for your benefit more than his, since it's keeping all the helpful volunteers at bay." Her face became serious at my blanche. "Relax. At least try to have a good time. If you're right and one of us is involved, then you won't be able to tell if you're wound up like a clock. Let's go see if Luke's spotted anything."

I knew she was right which did nothing to improve my mood. Little in Glasgow would tonight. I gave her a long look out of the side of my eye and nodded, pushing off the wall.

I followed her lead, progressing through the groups of people studded here and there while they snagged us to speak. Alex made the introductions and fielded most of the questions as I sipped my wine and tried to look alternatively sympathetic or attractive depending on the attention. It wasn't a natural combination.

We reached the table where Luke sat holding parliament. He was excellent at handling the crowd; they were all in rapt attention, and I couldn't feel anything other than his personality. He was recounting the tale of some uncouth client he'd managed to charm through the Sheriff Court and out of a sure prison sentence. He was, of course, innocent, and the whole matter a terrible misunderstanding Luke assured them, preening like a peacock as they all agreed.

I couldn't tell if it was the assurances or how they were eating his story up, but he loved it. Not all that surprising; there had to be an element of ego that went with the job, never mind for the rest. He spotted us as he fended off another compliment and smiled.

"Alex, Carter, how nice of you to come over. How are you enjoying the evening?" The little huddle broke off as his attention turned to us.

"It's wonderful as ever, Luke," Alex said, leaning in to hug him, and I gulped a mouthful of wine to counteract an eyeroll. Picking a spot on the wall, I stood and watched them instead.

"Glad to hear you're having a good time. We've missed you. Especially James and Diane. They were asking after you." He nodded to a broad man who was watching us with some obvious interest. Was that the dude who was eyeing me up earlier? I couldn't tell which of the women around him would be Diane, but from Luke's comment, I took it they came as a pair. Alex bit her lip in a way that confirmed it, and I saw the decision cross over her face.

"It would be nice to catch up with them," she said, glancing at me.

"Go for it. Don't let my wallflower nature stop you." I nodded, raising my glass in blessing. This was a terrible plan, but Luke's distraction of her had been so obvious it caught my curiosity. Where had my bottle gone?

"Thanks. I'll catch up with you later, Carter." And with that she was gone. Luke's full attention fell on me. He was doing a bad job of seeming less predatory.

"And how are you finding it?" he asked, moving to stand beside me.

"It's different. Not what I imagined for a sex party."

"Marcus tends to make them sound sordid. I think he rather likes the idea."

"As opposed to this? It's nice." That was a lie but a palatable one.

"Marcus prefers getting involved in what he considers the seedier side of life. Hence his habits and suppling for the parties."

"How very Shakespearean, Falstaff will be out next." I shook my head and tried to keep my face pleasant.

"You could be said to be the same, no?"

"How? I run my own business and live cheap when it suits me. I don't pretend that it's my whole life. Or make a fetish of it." I wrinkled my nose.

"Renfrew Street suits you?" He arched a brow and took a sip from the amber drink he nursed.

"How do you know where I'm sleeping?" I glanced at him sideways.

"Alex mentioned it. Said she'd offered you Sarah's room, but I didn't think you'd need the pressure of that." He was watching me for a reaction, and I was half tempted to give him it.

"That reminds me, can I show you something?" I asked instead.

"Of course. Do we require privacy?"

"No, it's on my phone," I said, finding the picture I'd taken earlier. "Do you recognise this handwriting by any chance?" I passed him my phone and he double tapped, enlarging the scribble.

"I can't say I do. Why?"

"Someone left me a little present at the guesthouse, a piece of jewellery Sarah was working on for you, with a curse on it."

"A curse?" He repeated, mildly scandalised.

"To confound and 'confuse' me, apparently. If I hadn't had some protection on me, it could have been nasty."

"You recognised it?"

"No. I got it checked out by The Collector," I said, watching his lack of reaction.

"You found the individual?" he asked before another sip.

"Yeah, that's a weird one. Better discussed in private."

"How curious. I'm intrigued. I've some further information to discuss about your nocturnal visitor as well."

"Alex tells me I'm the topic of much gossip," I said. "Should I be concerned?"

"I don't think you can blame people for being curious, Carter." He liked saying my name. He made a show of tasting it.

"Watch me," I said, and he laughed, a short bark of a sound.

"I'd ask if you were always so petulant, but I feel I know the answer."

"I'm hardly petulant; I just shy away from playing freakshow. Turning myself into that for a night is unusual."

"Is that what we are, a freakshow?" he asked, amusement clear on his face.

"Oh no. You'd be the guests, and I would be the exhibit," I corrected, smiling despite myself.

"I don't think that's entirely fair to you. You're blending in remarkably well with the guests." He gave me an appreciative glance over, and I felt something like a blush rise in my cheeks. Blaming the wine for that.

"I'm sure you tell that to all the new attendees." I laughed, scanning the crowd. We'd lost most of guests to the side rooms by now, couples and more choosing the best set ups for their preferences. Alex was gone too.

"As a rule, I don't meet with new attendees." He sniffed, and I could feel him watching for my eyes coming back to him.

I went to take another sip of my drink and cast a look over the edge of my glass, "Really?"

"Certainly. It would be inappropriate. They might be influenced by my reputation. That could lead to blurred boundaries."

"You're concerned you would trick someone into consenting? That's not what they mean by charming the pants of someone." I snickered, my face and head warm. This was more than the wine—I was a bit buzzed, sure, but I knew that feeling.

"It might come across as arrogant," he said with that same small smile, "but it's a real risk given my profession and my abilities."

"You've got to explain that to me. I've never heard of psychic roofies."

"I wouldn't call it that." He turned to face me, his shoulder to the wall. "My will or desires can be picked up on by those around me. Anyone with weaker defences, or who isn't used to this sort of environment, could be unduly influenced. They could agree with me just to please me rather than because they wanted to." He caught my eyes in a long stare, and I suddenly felt the sliver of his power brushing over me, like walking into mist. He was doing it on purpose! He either didn't know I could tell or didn't care, and neither was great. Fuck it. Let's do this, then.

"You're dangerous for the uninitiated? Should I be worried?" I shouldn't have arched my eyebrows with that question, too obvious, but it had a desired effect. Luke's pupils widened as he ran a hand over my arm. When had he gotten close enough for me to notice that? He was practically in front of me now, bracing me against the wall. Careless, Carter.

"I'm sure I wouldn't give you anything to worry about. As I said, I'm happy to help you whatever way I can."

"And, in your knowledge and experience, what would you suggest, to help me?" I couldn't believe the nerve of the man, speaking about influence while trying to manipulate my energy.

"In my professional opinion, water, a pain killer, and some sleep," he said solemnly, his eyes sparking as he inched closer still. He put a hand against the wall, close to my head, bracketing us together.

"And in your unprofessional opinion?" I glanced down to his lips, laying open the invitation.

"In my unprofessional opinion, I think you need to quieten your mind. I know a few ways to do that." He leaned it and kissed me softly, testing. I froze, my brain stalling. I hadn't expected this so quick. He hadn't expected me to be easy either, given the use of his powers. He picked up on my hesitation, pulling away. "Is this okay?" He stroked the knuckles of the hand holding his glass over my cheek. The smell this close told me it was whisky, warm and strong.

To hell with it.

I nodded and pulled him closer, crushing my lips against his and snaking a hand to the back of his neck to keep him there. I'd done this before. Usually in circumstances I was more into and less nervous about. He didn't know that though and smirked against my lips, the hand on the wall moving to my shoulder.

He pulled back and looked at me, a thumb stroking along the line of my neck. I leaned into it and gazed back through my eyelashes. I was aiming for something between debauched and conflicted which came easier than made me comfortable. It had the desired impact, and he hummed, leaning close to my ear.

"Do you want to retire to one of the rooms, or would you rather put on a show?" he asked, leaning in to peck lightly at the dip of my collarbone. That was awful distracting, a shiver thrumming along my body. At least he was intent on us both having a good time? I glanced around the room. There were two or three people sitting there, talking and touching each other, but everyone else had moved off to their own distractions.

"You like being watched?" I asked, lost for a moment.

"I enjoy it as much as anyone else." He grinned, his mouth coming close to my ear again. "Though I do get that through ritual work, so I have no complaint about privacy."

"Privacy could be good for tonight," I managed, inhaling as he dipped his head to lick lightly at the spot his thumb had been tracing.

"Just for tonight?" I felt the push of his energy again and growled low in my chest. I'd consider this insulting if it didn't get what I wanted.

"Surely you'd want to see if we're compatible?" I said, pushing my body into his to get more contact. I could feel a swell to him. He grinned and pushed back, his hips meeting mine roughly.

"I think we're showing that effectively just now, don't you?" He chuckled, nipping at the lobe of my ear. The friction of him against me was sending sparks down my spine. I was caught up in it for a long moment, enjoying the grind. I pushed my thigh forward so it rubbed against him and sought his lips again, catching the lower one between my teeth.

"Private room then," I said as I pulled back.

"Agreed." He nodded, taking my hand and pulling me towards a door to our side. I hadn't noticed it before, too carless.

The room was nicer than I'd expected, the same tasteful paint work and a plush king-sized bed in the centre of the far wall. There was a drinks fridge and various bottles beside a dresser, glasses lined up on top like soldiers. A fire was burning low in the fireplace across from the bed, with two chairs before it, and I spotted a jacket draped over another chair in a corner. His room then.

I made a line for the bedside table, slipping my cufflinks off and placing them within easy reach. I wanted to see Luke's play, so I looked over my shoulder at him with a coy smile. He'd closed the door, though he did not lock it from what I heard, and was looking at me from there. I tried not to blush and instead raised my brows in a silent question.

"Simply admiring the view."

"That's got to be an old line," I said, turning, my hands moving to my pockets automatically.

"A true one. I choose my lovers for a variety of attributes, and you are very beautiful." He moved towards the fridge, reaching for a bottle of something amber.

"So you only want me for my body?" I asked, grinning.

"Not only that, but is there anything wrong in appreciating beauty?" he asked, offering me a tumbler of whisky. I moved forward and pulled a face as I took it from him. He quirked a brow. "You're not a fan?"

"I've been drinking wine. Isn't there some rule about not mixing those?" I lied, smelling the liquid. It was the same as he'd been drinking in the main room, expensive stuff.

"An old superstition, which I've never placed much stock in." He held his glass up in toast and took a sip, so I matched him. The drink was a smooth, peaty blend with a slight sweetness.

"That's nice," I said.

"I believe in having the best of what you enjoy."

"A reasonable approach depending on your vices, I suppose," I said, looking him over.

"Indeed. Isn't that the sticking point for most," Luke said with a ghost of a smile. "On that topic, it would be remiss of me not to ask what you enjoy."

"As in, whether I like whisky?"

"As in your preferences, Carter." I felt a ripple of his power over me. "I intend to make sure you enjoy yourself and knowing what you like is a good way to ensure that."

I blushed and hated myself for it a little, swallowing. "Right. Are we talking generally or specifically?"

"I would hope both." He smiled, indulgent, sitting in one of the chairs before the fire and patting the other. I was more comfortable by the bed, frankly. I did as indicated, sitting across from him and holding the whisky close.

"I've usually been on the receiving side with my male partners, though I like both. I tend to be a bit, um, I tend to bite and scratch a little." I bit my lip as I said the last part, hoping it wasn't overkill.

"You're aggressive in your enjoyment?" he asked, tone innocent and grin wicked.

"You could say that." I glanced down, fidgeting slightly. I sipped my whisky, surprised at how much was gone. Shit.

"I can't say I'd complain, though I'd ask that any marks are below the collar line."

"Of course," I said, watching him enjoy this far too much. "And you're happy with that?"

"Quite happy. We're well suited. I do enjoy being in control."

"Well, that's a surprise," I blurted before I could stop myself.

He chuckled darkly, nodding. "I appreciate it's not a shock. Are you a control freak too, Carter?" he asked as if he already knew the answer.

"I can play switch with that, though I don't usually do power play with people first time," I lied, a little. I liked both as far as I knew, but I didn't do the kink stuff with people at all.

"I'm happy to keep things vanilla if you'd prefer? I want to be sure you're comfortable with what we're doing."

"I could be up for light stuff, a pinned wrist here and a bite there." I shrugged, floundering. It had the desired effect as I could see his enjoyment.

"I don't know if you understand just how tempting you make yourself." He sighed, finishing his drink. I raised an eyebrow at the gesture and received a smirk in return. "Care to join me on the bed?"

I laughed lightly and stood, knocking my own drink back and walking over. I was about to bend to untie my shoes when I felt Luke at my back, pressing close. I straightened up, pushing against him.

"I thought you'd prefer me without those," I said, letting my head loll back to look at him.

"I will," Luke agreed, nuzzling the nape of my neck and peppering it with kisses. "We'll get to that in a minute."

He laid beside me, his head resting next to mine as he caught his breath. I pecked small kisses on the side of his neck and cheek, shivering as the electric feeling left my skin. The room hummed with the spent energy of sex and our panting.

I could hear Luke murmuring, though I couldn't make out what he was saying at all. I had no idea what his sort of sweet nothings would be and was about to ask when I felt a ripple go through the room and the energy left, wiped from the slate. I froze, unsure of what I'd felt happen.

"Carter, are you well?" Luke asked, feeling my tension and pulling his head up.

"Yeah, I've just gone cold, and I didn't want to knock you with shivers," I lied.

"Very considerate." He grinned and pecked a kiss to the bruise I could feel forming on my shoulder from his earlier efforts. "If you stay, I'll return momentarily." He stood and moved to a side door. I heard water running. I was still trying to grasp what had happened when he leaned into the room, wiping his hands with a towel. "I do have a shower in here, but I'd suggest we save that for morning."

"You want me to stay?" I'd expected the opposite.

"It would be rude of me to send you on your way without breakfast," Luke called, disappearing back into the bathroom.

"Won't there be a few others who need your attention?" I called, thinking of the crowded play rooms. "I'm not a great bed guest. Nightmares and things grabbing me in the night."

"The others will have made their own arrangements, and I'm sure I've had worse bedfellows than you."

"Got a thing for a bit of rough?" I asked.

"Not what I would call it." He smirked, shaking his head as he came back towards the bed. "And that's certainly not what I would call you. Would you care for something to drink before sleep?" I felt a push of tiredness and couldn't tell if it was exhaustion or his influence, but I didn't care.

"No, I'm beat. Are you sure you're okay with this?" I asked as he slipped under the sheets, still naked. I did the same. He put out an arm for me to lean on; he was a cuddler. Wonders never ceased.

"I wouldn't be making the offer if I was uncertain. In the morning, this can be whatever we want it to be. For now, you should rest. I'm sure the bed will be much nicer than your current accommodation."

He wasn't wrong.

I worried my lip before moving into the crook of his arm, resting my head on his shoulder and casting one hand over his chest. He was well put together for an older gent, upper body firm. It would've been nice to be led there and think this was all there was to it.

He settled himself and ran a hand along my arm, stroking from elbow to wrist. I felt him tense when he felt my scar, but he continued on without delay. He was told about them, so that was either for my benefit or he'd forgotten.

"You're quite the unusual creature," he whispered, leaning his cheek to my crown.

"Not really. You must've met loads like me."

"None as interesting as you." He laughed lightly to himself.

"Not even Sarah?" I couldn't help the question. I knew Sarah wouldn't have done what I just did, but I was sure he'd tried.

"Sarah is a wonderful soul, but she's different to you. You have an aggressive openness that you're at pains to hide from the world. It makes an unusual mix. And I've never met someone so connected to the other side who rails so against it."

"Interesting way to be special."

"Indeed." He stroked a finger through the edge of my hair and smoothed the covers over us, "You must be tired. Sleep." I could feel the push of his power but made no effort to resist it, the tug of unconsciousness pulling me down.

# Chapter 18

There has been a most fascinating development with The Collector. He has been introducing me to a number of parties, such as Mr. Christie and the Merchants Guild, but today he provided a meeting with a gentleman of business in the city, Mr. Cathcart. I had not made his acquaintance previously which is irregular given my position as secretary for the guild. We were to visit the home of this man during the evening, for a discussion over drinks, and The Collector assured me this would be beneficial.

The house was substantial, either inherited or a significant purchase for the man, and our arrival was welcomed by several servants which incline me towards the latter. The man himself, though it is certain he has not been a man for some time, was secluded within an impressive library and greeted us with aged dignity. Oh, but what age he must have, for he is certainly older than his visage.

His hair is white and his skin is wizened, rendering his rich colouring into a mosaic of lines and fractals that show a history I hesitate to guess at. He tells me he was Spanish when he was first in business, but now his accent is such as you would not know him from another in the city.

He is involved covertly with a mass of industry, from the docks, to engineering, to the exports out to the continent. Even to Liverpool and the cotton mills. His wealth is held in various matters so his position is not betrayed too readily, for I can only imagine many tradesmen do not realise they are bargaining with a creature of the undead.

I cannot fathom how my friend came to know of a vampire, unless something he procured led to their paths having crossed, but I am delighted he has allowed me to share this fortuitous connection. I am uncertain if Mr. Cathcart will expect to feed upon me. I would not be *opposed to the principle provided there was no lasting damage done. It could be very interesting to see what matters of folklore are true and what are simply superstition grown wild.*

30 October 2017

I woke without having spoken to Dex, which was a welcome surprise. It was still dark and I felt Luke next to me, breathing even and slow in his sleep.

"He won't wake up."

The voice came from beside the fireplace. I sat upright, eyes wide to see who was in the room. A petite woman perched neatly on one chair, knees crossed and face turned towards the fire. There was still light from the embers which meant I couldn't have slept that long. Of course not.

"As in 'call an ambulance' he won't wake up or as in you're making sure of that?"

"I have no intention of him being aware of our conversation."

"Should I be worried about that?" I moved to get out of the bed but paused, looking closer. She was an attractive woman, dark golden hair and her skin shone in the fire light. She was in thigh high boots and little else, which was impractical. Not human from what I could feel coming from her.

"You done checking me over?" She sounded amused, hopefully a good sign. She had an airy voice, not one I'd be able to place in a crowd. She kept watching the embers.

"No, but we'd best get on with this, hadn't we?" I slipped from the bed and padded over to the chair. I'd forgotten my own nakedness until I sat down, the heat of the leather stinging the back of my thighs. Flinching, I crossed my legs and looked over woman.

She was classically beautiful, a strong nose and almost hollow cheeks, a cupid's bow lip I wasn't certain was natural. Her breasts were attractive too, but I tried not to look at those too long given the situation. I failed miserably at that, but she was unconcerned.

"Do you know what I am?" she asked, slipping a finger under my chin and tilting it so I met her gaze. I got a rush of feelings from the touch, sex and lust, hunger and amusement. There was a carnal thrum to the energy she gave off. I looked at her boots again, trying to push the parts together in my head.

"Succubus?" I asked, hoping I wasn't hallucinating.

"Clever boy." She grinned. "Do you want to see my feet?"

"Isn't that kind of rude?" I asked, floundering. I knew the old warnings.

"It would be rude to ask, but I'm offering." She shrugged, unzipping a boot in one long flourish and lifting the leather clear of her leg. I could see her thigh leading down to a knee leading down to a sudden coating of dark blonde fur and a thin, hoofed leg. It was the same size as a human leg but shaped like a goat's. The boots were designed to fit the hoof from what I could see, padding all along the inside.

"That is… I'm sorry, I don't know what to say. This is not what I expected. Can I ask your name?" Smooth Carter, revert to being a fucking idiot if all else fails.

"Aren't you precious. Last one I did that to ran away screaming, so I had to eat him." She shook her head, and I made a mental note to never leave the house again once I got back to Manchester. "I can't give you my real name—names have power—but most people call me Jenna."

"Nice to make your acquaintance, Jenna. I'm Carter. And I have no intention of doing something that would make you need to eat me."

"I know who you are." She smiled, indulgent, teeth flashing in a way that made my nerves stretch.

"I'm going to regret asking but how do you know who I am? And can I ask why you're here, if that's not rude? I'm in over my head."

She giggled at that, patting my knee and then settling to look at me. "You're Sarah's brother, and you're in bed with the leader of her group. I dislike her group. They make things difficult for my kind." She leaned down to zip her boot back up and brushed a hand up my leg.

"Sorry if this is stupid, but wouldn't sex parties make it easier for you? Open season."

"That's not how we function. We enjoy general sexual energy, but the one on one connection is what we need to feed. Desire is important. These gatherings are like walking through a restaurant but never being able to order."

"That doesn't sound pleasant," I said.

"And why's the boy who's looking sleeping on the job?"

"You know my name's quicker, right?" I asked, cocking an eyebrow at her.

"I know, but not everyone likes to use your name in case someone is listening." A soft snore from Luke punctuated her point. "I want to know if you're aware of what you're getting into."

"Not at all. Not even close." Her smile faltered, and she frowned at me. "I know Sarah's been dealing with this group. I know the group is linked to the sex parties. I know Luke's in charge of both and isn't as nice as he makes out to be. I'm pretty certain he stole the energy from what we just did. I know Sarah's missing, not dead. I think she went missing because she was getting close to something. I don't know what that something is. I know lots of people know who I am before I know them and that makes me unhappy on many levels. And that's about it, really. The rest, I have no idea about."

She opened her mouth to speak then closed it again. She seemed to settle on her choice of words after a beat. "Sounds like you're up to date then, really. Do you know why Sarah was speaking to us?"

"Curiosity? She had a lot of that."

"A good guess," she said with a smile. "Sarah wanted to get a better understanding of our powers, how we transfer energy. She was looking for someone to help her access other worlds."

"I think she managed that."

"It appears so. She was under threat from a group of human practitioners who wanted to use her powers. She wanted to keep them segregated from her friends."

"This doesn't look segregated," I said and earned a chuckle from her.

"That's because I'm here speaking to you. Would you have noticed me at the party? You were too busy making eyes at that one to see anything else."

"I'm just as good at hiding when I want to," I said, more ruffled that I should be.

"I didn't say it was a bad thing. Sarah's doing it, now that she has to. She got too close to the source of this group's power and they don't take well to that."

"That sounds like she pissed some people off. You know anything about that?"

"Only what she told me, and that was only shared to ensure I didn't harm anyone unfairly. But, we're on a tangent. I know you're not affected by Luke's usual tricks, it would taste different if you were."

"The taste? I thought you fed off energy, that doesn't have a taste." I wasn't even close to okay with that idea.

"Doesn't it? What if I told you there were flavours you couldn't understand? Would you dispute that too?"

"Okay, that may have been a stupid comment. Apologies. I was surprised. And slightly creeped out."

"Says the boy who can see through the veil. Some would consider that quite creepy, you know?" she said with a level look.

"I can't help it. Only way to stop is if I put my shield up."

"And I can't make my nature go away. So, I suppose that makes us even. What are you doing in his bed if you know he's stealing the energy here?"

"I wanted to see what he was doing and no one knew for sure. Best way to get the information was to get in the middle of it."

"You understand that's a terrible course of action?"

"What else could I do?" I asked, shrugging. "She's been gone for weeks. This is one of the only solid leads I had, outside of demons and Dex. Everyone knows my name, but no one knows where she is. I had to do something."

"Quite something." She nodded, glancing at Luke over her shoulder.

"How'd you make him sleep?" I asked, ignoring the comment and watching the firelight slip over her skin.

"It's something we can do. Saves any awkward questions."

"What, no cuddling?"

"Some of us enjoy that, but it's useful to have an immediate exit." Her eyes sparkled in amusement.

"It sounds similar to what he does," I said.

"You're a manipulative little man sometimes, aren't you?" she countered, head tilting to one side.

"Hey, less of the little." I crossed my legs further.

"Not in that sense. You're perfectly adequate there."

"Adequate, thanks for that."

"I would know," she continued archly. "This magic is different to ours. We feed off energy, but it's far less effective if the person doesn't want it. It must be freely given to us. Tricking them beyond the obvious would be pointless. We couldn't feed."

"Frustrating."

"It lends itself well to various things. Escort work, burlesque and dancing clubs, shot girls."

"Shot girls?"

"Everyone wants to fuck the shot girls, Carter," she said.

I felt certain I would never find another reasonable thing in the world after this. "Why do you dislike him in particular? This isn't the appropriate way to file a grievance. He probably won't even want to see me in the morning."

"I wouldn't wager on that. I don't think he'll let you out of his sight, if he can help it."

"You make him sound besotted," I said, not liking where this was going.

"More like covetous." Well, that was ominous. "We've discussed our concerns with this group before, in round about ways. When they didn't listen, we sought direct action with Luke, but that proved more difficult than expected. Luke's much stronger than he lets the group see. No one's sure why, just whenever direct methods were tried, we experience repercussions."

"Like what?" I asked, curious now.

"Spells rebounding or not working at all. Messages being left. The warnings weren't subtle."

"That sounds a bit mobster."

"That's one name for it. We can't tell if it's because he's been taking the energy here or not, but we didn't wish to pursue the matter. Luke has power stronger than us—it wouldn't befit us to interfere. However, if you were looking for assistance in your enquiries, we'd be willing to help you."

"I'm getting a lot of offers of help."

"I imagine you're unsure which are genuine," she smiled, sympathetic. "If it helps, our interest is self-serving. While I like Sarah, our community is more important."

"My interest is Sarah. Once I have her, I'm done."

Her smile changed at that, grew teeth that looked on the edge of sharp. "I'm sure you believe the truth of that. It may be that both our needs can be satisfied at the same time. We'll have to see how that develops. Now, I've spent enough time chatting with you, so unless you plan on helping me feed, it's time I took my leave."

"I'm going to have to skip that offer. I'm kind of exhausted."

"Quite. I think I've done enough to ensure our meeting will go unnoticed, but should he ask, I'd be obliged just saying how much I miss Sarah."

"I'll do my best." I nodded, standing as she did. She was shorter than me by at least a head, but those heels brought her closer to eye height. This amused me much more than it should. I started to giggle, high-pitched and strained.

"Carter?"

"Just a surreal day catching up with me," I managed to choke out.

"I wondered when that might hit. Have a gift from me then." With that she leaned up on her toes and kissed me, sending me into a dead faint.

I awoke to the feeling of Luke getting up, tugging the covers as he did. I raised my head, still half gone, and squinted at him.

"Good morning." He smiled, pulling on a robe. "I'll bring you coffee, if you wish?"

"Coffee's good," I groaned, sluggish. I didn't know if this was a spiritual hangover or the regular kind, but my head felt like wet sand.

"Rest. I'll get it."

I must have fallen asleep because I woke again to him fully dressed, sitting on the bed with a cup of coffee and a tray.

"It's a little basic." Luke grinned, passing it to me. There was a selection of pastry bites with jam and butter, and a warm croissant.

"It's better than I'd manage." I smiled, reaching for the coffee. "Sorry, I'm so out of it. I'm usually a morning person."

"You have had a wearing few days, Carter. I won't begrudge you. Did you sleep well?"

"No terrifying dreams."

"I'm pleased to hear it. Do you have plans for today?"

"Check out some places in Sarah's notes, catch up with Alex. These look delicious by the way," I said, biting into the croissant.

"Would you think me too forward if I asked you to come to dinner? I'd like to discuss your findings, and I've built up quite the list to review."

"Two meals in one day. Won't you be sick of me?" I asked between bites.

"I doubt that'd be possible from such a brief exchange," he said with a smile. He stroked my face with a thumb, and I felt a gossamer brush of his power over me again. I let it happen, to keep the illusion up, and felt a flood of warmth and arousal go through me. It was nice, except the back of my brain was screaming about undue influence and abuse of power. "I'd very much enjoy seeing you again."

"If you're sure I won't be imposing, that'd be nice." I dropped my eyes, swirling the coffee in the cup for something to do with my hands.

"Are you unused to compliments?" Luke asked, teasing.

"I'm more used to negotiating the next date by text rather than via breakfast."

"I'm happy to text you confirming if that makes you feel more at ease," Luke said with a deadpan voice.

I chuckled into my coffee and shook my head, eyes coming back up to meet his. "I think I can manage. You want to text me an address or will I get it from Alex?"

"I'll send it to you. I can give you a lift if you would like? I'll be leaving shortly."

"I was going to get a taxi. Don't fancy doing a walk of shame in the suit. I'm not entirely sure where Alex is, and she was my ride. It'd be rude to dump her."

"I think you may already have been dumped, so to speak. She'll have left with her companions last night."

"I thought people stayed over?"

"Oh no, I have my private room, but most people scene here then depart for their own fun at home. It's an easy way to continue good chemistry and means the kind soul who owns the building has no risk."

"That makes sense." I nodded, head swimming a bit. The coffee was helping at least. "I suppose I should order my taxi. You'll be wanting to make your escape."

"I hardly think parting ways is an escape, but duties call." Luke sighed, mock weary, standing up from the bed and rolling his neck.

"Sore?"

"Not at all. I'm missing my morning exercise routine is all. I work out for an hour each morning."

"Hence the legs," I said then blushed as I realised he heard it. He smirked but made no further comment, instead reaching for my folded clothing and placing them on the bed beside me.

"I must depart. Feel free to use the bathroom and close the door behind you once you're done. Until this evening, say 7:00 p.m.?" He leaned in and kissed me, a gentle peck of his lips.

"Sounds good to me," I said as we parted.

He moved to the door but stopped, glancing at me. "Carter?"

"Yes, Luke?"

"I do very much look forward to seeing you again."

"As do I."

He left at that. I sat, holding the coffee cup close to my chest and wondering what the hell I was doing.

I let my head fall back onto the headboard and groaned, stacking up the details of last night. Luke was using the power of the parties for something, but for his own ends. I should feel bad about that, but the sex had been good and I needed to know, so it was fine. I wouldn't mind exploring that some more if possible, influence aside.

Jenna's comments about Sarah came back to me; safety. I needed to find this group of Dex worshippers. Marc made them sound like the magic mafia, heavy hitting shit. I shook my head, downing the last of the coffee and slipping into the bathroom. The heat was good. I turned it up as much as I could stand, showering longer than necessary to clear the fog which still sat in my brain.

I ordered a taxi and waited outside, uncomfortable in the echoing house. The day was grey and almost stormy, the wind up enough to ruffle me. It was a decent house from the outside, yellowed sandstone with thin windows and that heavy door.

I hadn't noticed signs of anyone else last night and wondered what the owner was off doing. Overseas business, Samuel had said. It was quite the property to leave behind. Something about it snagged in my mind, but the thought was interrupted as my taxi arrived.

The driver was an enthusiastic conversationalist. I barely had to say anything once I'd given him the address. He spoke about sports and I nodded, answering vaguely about Man United and City and anything that would make his stream of chatter continue. We made it back to guesthouse before I needed to speak much, and I paid with a nice tip, heading up to my room. I got a nod from the gentleman at the front desk which implied he knew why I was only returning now. He wasn't wrong, so I gave him my best sheepish grin and a shrug, then jogged up to the steps.

I was too wired to sleep, so I logged into my laptop, checking for any jobs. An urgent one flagged up, and I fumed at it—a human error issue that would take hours. I made a cup of the awful coffee that came with the room, which was much worse given the taste of Luke's coffee, then I got to it. The client would eat me alive if it wasn't up and working as soon as possible.

# Chapter 19

*7 May, 1886*

*A set of disappearances is being quietly investigated at Glasgow Green. There is little doubt in my mind this is in relation to the more recent activity I have seen reported at the site: dancers in the night, music only children can hear, animals behaving as if directed by unseen masters.*

*I was not of the view that Fair Folk had made their place in the city. Common wisdom said they shunned the industry and iron of the place, but there's little doubt the flowers and mushrooms growing in rings around the grass are a sign of activity by the Fae.*

*This would explain the huge opposition to mining the area. Can you imagine the disaster of disrupting an encampment of the Good People and what it would do to the surrounding areas? I would like to investigate if there have been other instances of missing people, earlier in the life of Glasgow Green, and if a pattern could be found. Of course, some may just have vanished of their own devices. Plenty of humanities ills are evident in the city as well and may account for some of the missing. But for so many people to be gone in the space of a scant few weeks, around the time of the blooms and rings appearing, merits review. I doubt the good constables will be examining matters with the same eye I have, but it will be interesting to see what discussion filters through the pubs and Lodge meetings. I will record more when I have it.*

I powered up Sarah's laptop and logged in to her account. I felt less guilty about it than last time and wondered when my sense of normality would fade. If I was working for Dex, would I get used to his horrors?

It felt unlikely, but Luke's taking advantage of his party guests was horrifying, and it seemed to be normal to him. He was apparently fine with it. He could be a creature of his time, thinking someone who has been drinking was fair game. The thought sat poorly—Luke had spoken of influence and affect and being aware of that. He knew, and he still did it. That'd have to be nipped in the bud.

Staring at the screen, I wondered about trying to sleep, bargaining with Dex for information. It would be worth it if it meant I could get to the cult today. That could give me an idea as to where Sarah might be. I didn't fancy doing a shake down on them—not enough information to know if that was safe —but I could fight if I had no other options.

I remembered the items from Samuel in my pocket, the ring and necklace he had said The Collector would be interested in.

That would be a more savoury option.

I set off for the West End. I didn't know if The Collector kept regular shop hours, but he looked enterprising enough to be there.

Halfway through Kelvingrove Park, I received a text from Luke with a link to his address.

*See you at seven. I hope your morning has gone well*, he signed off. Keen.

The property was in some place called Circus Park, which I hadn't heard of, but I could find later. I grinned to myself at the idea, quick moving as it was. I thought back over Marc. He felt Luke was covetous, and Samuel had agreed by implication. No one except Jenna had mentioned the energy going missing, but I'd felt it.

It was a strange combination of things, mixing sex and power and theft. Just to make himself stronger? I could ask him outright, see what his response to that was. He enjoyed poking at my emotional reactions last night, so it'd be fair to trade some barbs.

Back to the task at hand. I needed to know what she'd gotten from The Collector and where I could find the group who worshipped Dex.

That should let me avoid trading with Dex. The idea of staying with it for fifteen years made me shudder.

I found my way back to the shop, tripped down the steps and through the, naturally, open door. The Collector was wearing his human suit and smiled when he saw me.

"Back so soon, Mr. Brooks?"

"Well, it's you or Dex. Not a huge swathe of choice." I shrugged, looking him over. "You can take the shield off if you want."

"How generous of you." He smirked and shook himself, disguise falling away like smoke.

"Grand. So, how do we do this?"

"As with any other transaction—you give me the item and I tell you the value. This lets you decide what questions to prioritise and allows me to ensure you aren't being traded with unfairly."

"You mean so you're not left short," I snorted.

"What items have you brought?"

"Two. First one's this." I handed him the ring, placing it gingerly on his palm.

His eyes fluttered and he let out a low grumble, closing his fist around it. "Where did you get this?" He turned his amber eyes on me with a hungry curiosity.

"Someone gave it to me, to help Sarah."

"Who?"

"That would be telling."

"Do not toy with me, Mr. Brooks."

"I'm not. The supplier didn't say if they were okay with me disclosing their name. They knew you, though. Spoke highly of you, in fact."

"Human?" The Collector asked.

"No."

"That is acceptable. The ring will give you access to three significant questions."

"Alright Can you tell me where to find Sarah?"

"She is between worlds, in a space that is not yet accessible. It will be available once the barriers are weaker. I do not know where the access point will be, but all of them come forward at the same time."

"Of course. Why half arse it?"

"Indeed. Your next question?"

"Can you tell me where to find the group who worships Dex?"

"Which one?"

Oh, crap. "The one Sarah was hiding from."

"Which one?"

"There's more than one of those?" I sighed, exasperated. Course there was; evil old fucking thing had fans all over the place.

"Yes, there are two. I suppose strictly speaking, one is an offshoot of the other, but they practice separately. Except for one member, who moves between them."

"Like a negotiator?"

"I think the better term would be a spy."

"I really am not enamoured with this place," I muttered.

"I'm sure it finds you fascinating," he replied dryly.

"Apologies. That was petulant. Can you tell me where to find the group Sarah was afraid of?"

"You are running dangerously close to forming another question by minor enquiry."

"Can you tell me if she went into hiding to get away from one of these groups in particular?"

"One of the groups is more aggressive than the other. She is hiding from that one. They're sometimes known as the Open Door, though that name is old. They frequent the underground system in the city and meet at one of the disused stations. They are fond of the one in botanical gardens, but there are a number around the city."

"That's a surprise."

"It often is." He smiled, all teeth like the Cheshire Cat. It turned something in my stomach, and I swallowed hard.

"How many questions would this get me?" I asked, holding up the necklace.

"That should not be in your hands, Mr. Brooks." The Collector bristled, eyes narrowing.

"Where should it be?"

"In my cases. How did you come about it?"

"Same as that ring. Donation on Sarah's behalf."

"And what is Samuel doing these days?" There was a smile there, but it was more of a warning.

"Making vague threats, talking about the duality of death and the hunt."

"He was fond of such things. Give it back to me and I shall answer a further three questions."

"Why is it special?"

"You have not given me something for that answer."

"I know, just asking."

He hummed, looking over my face. "It is part of a set, and I dislike having things incomplete. That is all the answer I will give you."

"Fair's fair." I nodded, passing the jewellery over. "Can you tell me why Sarah was more concerned about the Open Door?"

"They barter with Dex in the old terms, sacrifice and ritual. The newer group is less forthright."

"And how did Sarah find that out?"

"She was their intended offering." I felt his words go over me with a shudder, the coiling in my stomach from earlier returning with a violent lurch.

"They were going to feed her to Dex?"

"That is the principle." The thought rang through my head for a moment, white hot anger and sheer fear for Sarah warring. Those motherfuckers thought they were handing my sister to that thing? They thought they could dare? "Caution, Mr. Brooks. Anger tends to cloud the mind."

"I'll kill them if they think they're doing that to her," I snarled, pacing away from him so I didn't do something stupid.

"I suppose you would, but that brings its own difficulties. They would be missed. Bodies can be traced."

"And I'm evidence that she would be too." I shouted, turning to glare the demon down. It didn't work, but he inclined his head.

"Unexpected evidence. She did not tell many of you." That thought punched the wind out of me, the implications shuffling forward. I looked over to him, the power of him rolling around his body like a rising mist.

"She was counting on me coming."

"It appears to be the case."

"Best make sure I do the job then. Do you know the consequences of trading with Dex?"

"I'm afraid you will have to be more specific. Each deal is different."

"If you trade with it are there any ramifications outside of the deal you strike? Can it influence you, taint your soul, read your mind?"

"The closer you get to such beings the easier it is to be tempted, but that is due to their knowing your weaknesses. They are ancient and have been dealing with humanity a long time; desires are not that different in the end."

"Anything else?"

"Certain ones can keep a connection open to observe through humans, though not to intervene."

"It could see what I'm doing but not do anything about it?"

"No direct intervention."

"Good to know."

"What is your last question?" he asked with a smile, running his fingers over the necklace. I sucked air through my teeth, the anger and spite still clouding my mind.

"A preface, if I may?"

"By all means."

"If I ask you a question you can't answer does that use up the opportunity?"

"Yes. Certain exceptions apply, as with your first question today."

I nodded, walking back to him so I could look him in the eyes. "Can you tell me who the member who goes between the groups is?"

"Certainly—John Mercer."

"Say again?"

"John Mercer," The Collector repeated.

"The guy that wrote the guide?"

"The same."

"He goes between the two groups."

"Yes."

"Is he alive?" I asked, my brain struggling to process.

"Yes, though we are in danger of this being another question."

"Can you give me more detail without me giving you another item?"

"I can confirm he is living and practicing within the city and works both with the Open Door and the other group who worships Dex. Anything further would require a trade."

"I'll have to come back for that," I said.

"I anticipated such. I'm happy to continue to trade, should you bring further items of interest."

"Thank you for your time," I said with a short bow of my head.

"Mr. Brooks?" he called as I went past the cabinets and their glowing hoard.

"Yes?" I asked, turning back to him.

"I'd advise that trading yourself with Dex is not the only option."

"I didn't ask that."

"Indeed. I hope to see you again."

I left the shop and made a line for one of the benches by the river, my mind swirling away with the water. They wanted to kill Sarah. It might not involve them doing it directly, but that's what it meant. Anger coiled low in my gut and I itched to use it, to inflict it on someone. They thought they could do that to her? I made myself stare at the water and breathe myself calm, desperate for a plan.

I had a name and a place for this group, the Open Door. I had a name for who it was that moved between the two groups. I had an idea of what Sarah had done, leaving her trail of breadcrumbs. Now to find the witches house.

Pulling my phone out, I started tossing it between my hands as I weighed my choices. I could tell Luke about this, but he probably wouldn't love news that there two groups following Dex. Or that there was subterfuge between them. Marc knew about one group but would he even want to get into what I was talking about? Alex was a no go for all of this. I didn't want her neck on the line because of my fumbling. I settled on Marc and dialled his number.

"Carter. An unexpected pleasure." He chuckled, the smirk evident down the line.

"Hi Marc. You free to meet up? I could do to chat."

"Sure. The workshop in a half hour?"

"Sounds good. See you then."

I stood and wandered back along the river, winding my way towards the university. It felt longer than a day since I'd met Alex there yesterday. The Collector's words echoed after me. I'd considered trading with Dex if needed. If it meant that she lived, in every sense, then it might be worth it. She could come visit, take me for sushi, and pretend we weren't trapped by the things we wouldn't talk about. That could be a life. Perhaps. Or I could give Dex someone else, someone equal to Sarah. That would mean leaving someone else to be devoured while we ran from the mess.

Letting myself into the workshop, I slumped onto the work bench, halfheartedly moving parts around. I was wrapped up in the process when Marc came in, his pale hair down and shaggy today.

"You look awful," he said, an eyebrow raising.

"Sorry. Bad news," I said, turning to face him.

"You and Luke?"

"That happened. He's abusing his position and taking the energy from his trysts."

"Taking the energy?"

"Yeah. I don't know what for. Maybe to make himself more powerful."

"Are you going to ask him?"

"Not sure yet. That's not the bad news though. You know the Open Door?"

He nearly flinched at the question. "How do you know that name?"

"Traded for it."

"Who with?"

"The Collector."

"Don't know him." He looked like he was lying.

"He's an interesting gent," I said, starting to jog my leg to get some of the nervous energy out. "Can you hook me up with the Open Door?"

"Why the fuck would you want to do that?" he asked, shaking his head.

"Sarah's hiding from them. They're my best bet of finding her."

"They're not good guys. Proper hard shit happens around them. They're not these hippies fucking about."

"People going missing, full moon parties, ritual sacrifice?"

"Yeah. That." He looked perturbed at my casual listing off.

"They offer to let you join?" I asked, cocking a brow.

"Not my scene, pal."

"I figured. Might not stop them asking, though."

"True enough." He barked out a laugh, shrugging. "Not what I want to do. I need to be seen too much to join a cult and hide in the dark."

"Fair point. Can you get me with them?"

He scowled, chewing his lower lip. "They might kill you. They don't fuck about."

"I know. But I have a plan for that."

"What?"

"Run like fuck and maybe sell my soul a little bit," I said.

"A little bit?"

"A fifteen-year little bit."

"Fuck man! That's a long time." He shook his head.

"It's not that bad."

"You're making a deal."

"It's not my preferred idea, but it might work. Would rather get Sarah and get the hell out of Dodge, to be honest."

"You told Alex about any of this?" he asked.

"No. I didn't want to scare her with it, and I was worried what it might do to her."

"Knowing what you're planning to do?"

"No, the thing I might do a deal with."

"I can see if they're willing to meet up. What are you going to do?"

"I'm going to speak to it about a deal then see what I can offer them. Best case scenario, they let me in. Worst case scenario, I have to run," I said with a shrug.

"That's a lot of risk for no pay off."

"She's not got long left. I've got to do it."

"For real?" he asked, locking eyes with me.

"Days at best, getting lower as we go."

"Fuck." He turned away, running his hands through his hair. "You talked this through with Luke?" He turned back, pacing over to one of the work benches.

"Not yet. Planned to this evening."

"There's no meeting with the group tonight."

"I've been invited for dinner with him."

"Nice. Not heard of any other partners being invited up to his place," he said with an appreciative nod.

"Consider me unusual."

"That's already covered. You have to tell Alex." He sighed, leaning against the work bench and shaking his head. His lips were pressed into a thin line, pale on his face.

"Marc, she'll freak out. She could barely handle those angels."

"She isn't being unreasonable there. The idea of them is terrifying. This is worse. If you're sure it's the Open Door Sarah's hiding from, there's a real chance of someone getting hurt. Alex could be helpful."

"Let me run it past Luke first. I don't want to put her at risk."

"Alright, if Luke's on board then you let her know. I'll see what I can do for a meeting with the Open Door. They might have something happening tonight if they're on their usual schedule."

"Thanks. That's a huge help."

"I'm not so sure about that. It's your neck," he said grimly, hefting his bag back onto his shoulder.

"Give me a text when you know."

"Alright, speak later."

He was out the door like a shot. I couldn't blame him. It wasn't a stellar plan. I wasn't even sure if it was a plan. All I could think of was my desire to tear these guys apart for thinking they could do that to Sarah.

I needed to speak to Dex. I didn't know if I could sleep with how wired I felt, but I rolled my jacket into a pillow and laid down underneath a bench, counting sheep and breathing deeply.

I was back at the campfire, within the circle of light. Sitting up, I saw the cliffs stretch out beside me, the always wrong stars twinkling out over the sea.

"You came looking for me," came the elemental hum of Dex from over the fire. It stood at the edge of the firelight, the flicker strobing it in and out of visibility. It was the size of a tall human now, wearing what looked like a black suit draping down it's body. Its skin was the waxy hue of a corpse and its face a torn copy of Luke's, split from chin to nose to leave an oozing blackness between the pale sections.

"What the shit?" I yelped, jumping up. "Any reason you chose that face? Is Luke...?"

"I thought it appropriate you saw some of the things I can do. Your Luke is fine. You came looking for me."

"Yes. You've been omitting an important fact in our chats."

"Multiple. What has caused you such outrage? Your anger is charming." It smiled and the split in the skin flapped, showing more of the oily gap below.

"You were getting Sarah as a sacrifice."

"That was the intention of some. Your sister was never going to allow that."

"You're so sure?"

"I ensured it. She may not have known she was talking to me, but I made sure she had the best information."

"And why would you do that?"

"Because it suited me."

"Why?" I shouted, pacing in the circle. Something in my body was shouting that staying inside the circle was essential, that the darkness pressing in on the side wasn't just the absence of moonlight.

"Because I enjoy the trauma of those left behind far more than the shedding of blood. It all gets routine after a few centuries." I stopped dead, looking over at the mask of a face it wore. Somewhere behind the eyeholes there was a soft red glow, the colour of dried blood in sunlight.

"You feed on emotional energy as well as literal then?" I asked, shaking my head. "Stupid, Carter. Should have seen that one coming. The emotional manipulation wasn't to encourage a deal, it was to get a taste."

"A rather lovely taste. You are delicious in your anguish."

"Pretty when I cry. How nice," I said sourly, bitter at this thing playing me for so long.

"If it is any solace, no one else outside those I control have realised that particular method of mine."

"I'm so glad to be special," I spat, bristling at its tone.

"You are, indeed. You would have been dealt with much differently if you were not."

"You'd have the Open Door ensure I vanished?"

"Or simply had you on a platter."

"Nice to know. I'm going to meet your group."

"They may not be welcoming," it said.

"I don't count on them being welcoming. I do expect them to tell me where she is."

"You think they know that?" it asked, surging at the edge of the dark.

"You know it. Why wouldn't they?"

"I may not have told them."

"They're your cult. Why would you keep that back?"

"I enjoy it. They fear being unable to fulfil their contract with me, and I satisfy my desire whichever way they fall."

"You make yourself sound awful untrustworthy for someone who wants me to trade fifteen years."

"You would not be foolish enough to warrant such treatment, Carter." It shifted what I took to be shoulders, twisting its head to an unnatural angle and observing me. "You understand what I can do; they have been comfortable for too long."

"Motivating the workforce then?" I breathed out a laugh, panic and fear shooting through me again.

"Something along those lines."

"And what about your second group?"

"I do not have one."

"The Collector thinks you do," I said.

"He is being too literal." A shrug those maybe shoulders.

"What do you mean?"

"What will you give me?"

"What do you want?" I sighed, my head slumping. "To answer these questions, what do you want? I know what you really want."

"An answer for an answer."

I looked over at it, trying to read anything I could. It hungered. "Alright. You ask first."

"Why did you sleep with the man whose face I wear?"

"Why do you know or care who I'm fucking?" I shot back.

"That is not an answer."

"I thought he was abusing his power. I wanted to check."

"That is all?" There was a taunt to its voice I didn't like.

"That was the deciding factor. Any others were incidental."

"But there were others?"

"Yes. Do you want them too?"

"We may return to that."

"What did The Collector mean?"

"One of the Open Door members works with another group on my behalf, but they do not know they serve me. All too self-interested to look beyond the benefit they are getting."

"Right. How is John Mercer still alive?"

"You know of John?" Dex sounded delighted, surging into the light for a moment. I was glad when it went back.

"I know he goes between the two groups now and was writing a diary in the 1880s. He should be dead. How is he not?"

"By trading."

"What?"

"That would be another answer."

"Ask your fucking question then," I growled.

"What will you miss most when you have to stay with me in the city?"

"Assuming that I do."

"You will," it promised.

"Assuming that I do, I'll miss the feel of Manchester. Glasgow isn't the same. It's friendly and historical and beautiful, but it's not my home."

"John trades me souls for his own benefit."

"How does that even work?"

"He sacrifices something to me, I take the soul, he retains the life energy. What would have been lived, had he not intervened, becomes his."

"He gets what is left on their life span?"

"Precisely." It was enjoying this far too much. I could see Luke's face stretched into a sick grin.

"That's so fucked up." I clattered to the floor, sitting hard on my arse and staring into the fire. "He was planning to do good. Now he's killing people."

"That is an accurate summary."

"Does it make him young again?"

"Sometimes. He gets as many years as were left. He was awfully upset when one such morsel had an undiagnosed tumour. That only gave him a few years. He had been expecting thirty or forty."

"An easy mistake, I'm sure," I said, my hopes for any sensible way out of this falling away from my chest.

"You are distressed," it said, sounding displeased.

"I'd taken it he was dead, from his book. He didn't keep writing after he planned a ritual to speak with ancient beings. You, I take it?"

"Indeed. You felt better thinking him dead?"

"He was smart and had good intentions. Wanted to change the world."

"Everyone wants to. Some would say he still does. I can make many things happen."

"He got you building orphanages in Darfur, has he? Setting out to solve corruption in politics?" The anger flashed hot in my chest.

Dex laughed, and I could feel the smile before I saw it. "No. He has me assisting with his business and ensuring his secrets are kept. He controls a lot of things in the city. I afford him much influence."

"A bit low level for a being of your power."

"It suits me to help him in this. It ensures his loyalty. I would not have to ensure loyalty with you, but I would enjoy doing so."

"What do you mean?"

"You are insistent that I am some terrible thing. I admit my sense of morality is different to those of mortals, but I am not so far removed. I can make a situation mutually beneficial."

"Now you're sounding like Luke as well as wearing his face," I said, anxiety spiking and ebbing over me.

"Is it so surprising?"

"Why would you be helping me if John's in your care?" The question was out of my mouth as it crossed my mind. "Wouldn't getting Sarah as a sacrifice suit you?"

"Getting you may suit me better."

"You didn't know about me until I arrived here. If I succeed, you don't get either of us."

"And I am still left with John. I see no loss."

"You're helping as it suits you?"

"I have my preferences. But I am empowered whichever result comes."

"Why should I trust you?"

"Because I would not lie in a trade. It would make the terms unenforceable."

It was said so matter-of-factly that I paused, looking at Dex hard. "Even the chaos of the universe has rules?" I managed to say, the words cloying in my throat.

"Naturally."

"Alright. I have other questions. Do you?"

"Why are you fighting so hard for your sister?"

"Because I love her and she's my blood."

"She told no one of you. She denied your power."

"And it's served her well since I'm here looking for her," I said.

"A fair response. Your question."

"If I were to trade with you for help with Sarah, how would I do it?"

"A conversation."

"Suppose I wasn't unconscious."

"I can be contacted through meditation, or blood. Spill some for my name and I will come to you."

"I thought you couldn't do that, hence the bonfire?"

"Blood helps lubricate the process." Well that was a combination of words I had not planned on hearing any time soon.

"Duly noted."

"Why do you ask?" It sounded curious.

"I might have a trade for you at short notice."

"I do not enjoy being rushed. What are you planning, Carter?"

"That would be giving the game away. Next question."

"How comfortable are you with killing?"

"I can't say I've tried it."

"You've thought about it."

"Mostly because a group was planning on feeding my sister to you and I don't take kindly to that."

"Either way, how pleasant," it said.

"I'd rather not. Say I gave you fifteen years. I reckon your Open Door gents would be after me pretty quickly. Either way, we're all looking for Sarah. We're likely to end up in the same place. I could do with the help."

"You would expect me to assist?"

"I want to know if you'd help me over them. Since I'd be your shiny new toy."

"They have been useful to me."

"And now you're using me as a threat against them. I assume it was them who left me that little present?"

"That was John. I was displeased."

"If I wanted you to help, what would it take?"

"If you had already given me the fifteen years then I would consider it. If you had not then I would need a good reason."

"Say I offered someone else. Another sacrifice."

"You would trade someone for Sarah?"

"I could."

"Not yourself. I would prefer to have you living."

"Someone equal to Sarah instead of her."

"You would be happy doing so?" It peered at me over the flames, the red in those eyes glowing.

"Would you take the trade?"

"I would consider it. Though I want you."

"Because you can't have me?" I asked, laughing.

"I am always patient, Carter," it said, the rumble grinding down my spine.

"Will you tell me where to find John Mercer?"

"No." I wasn't even surprised at the answer.

"Why not?"

"Because it is much more entertaining for me to watch the way you interact."

"We've not met."

"That you know of." Ah, fuck.

"I know he was responsible for the gift at my guesthouse, what else?"

"That would be a lot of information. What will you give me?"

"What do you want?"

"A taste of your blood?" It asked, pushing into the light of the fire again. The split mask of Luke's face was degrading, flaking and starting to slough off.

I looked back to the fire, suppressing a shudder. "Nope. If we trade for those fifteen then sure. Before then I'll keep all that within my veins, thanks."

"A reasonable concern. In that case, if you are looking for my assistance then spill some of your own blood for me and I will appear immediately."

"That's awfully reasonable of you."

"You sound to be making reasonable plans. I am eager to assist."

"I bet you are," I said. "The second group, can you tell me who they are?"

"You have met them already. Do you really require further introduction?"

"The sex group?" I asked, a coil of dread peeking between my ribs.

"Indeed."

"There was someone at that party," I said, up on my feet again. "How the fuck did I miss that?"

"They were ensuring their own narrative. I would not criticise yourself."

"Is John a vampire now?"

"That would still require your blood, Carter."

"Shit! Fine. I'll have to come back to you on that one."

"I look forward to it, as ever."

"I'm not able to say the same."

"I appreciate that, in every sense," it said, slipping into the deeper shadows and vanishing.

# Chapter 20

_29 June, 1886_

_I've made a slight miscalculation in relation to one of my investigations._

_There has been a level of activity in the necropolis, missing bodies and disturbed graves that are nothing in relation to the coven which practices within the walls. It is causing no end of scandal in polite society, as the great and the good worry about which dead relative may be next dug up._

_I had wondered if this may be the work of a ghoul, an incomer to the city or a member of Mr. Christie's tribe who had become desperate enough to disturb public graves. This would be quite at odds with what I was told by the gentleman himself, but one must examine all sides of an argument and making direct contact would allow this. As such, I ensconced myself within the necropolis for an evening and kept watch._

_In all truthfulness, I would have preferred it were a ghoul, for what I witnessed instead was a desecration of the corpses by someone with enthusiastic proclivities for the dead. I was so startled that I watched for longer than was decent or savoury. I made my escape over the boundary wall and intend to avoid matters within the area for some time. With any luck, a ghoul will eat the scoundrel before I return._

I woke with a start and the taste of bile in the back of my throat, causing me to jolt up and smack my head against the work bench. Fuck. I managed to swallow down the curse and more, checking my watch. Just into the afternoon. I ran a hand through my hair and sat up, hugging my knees.

Dex's promise chimed round my head along with the throbbing. I didn't know if the roads I'd set up would pay off, but I needed it hungry. I could promise it Alex. That would be condemning her to death, if Dex wanted her. But the thought of it sat badly with me. I didn't want to do that to her, but she was so much like Sarah, passionate and sure of herself. It was an option.

Shaking my head to disperse some of the melancholy that had crept in, I sat and tried to focus. I had dinner at Luke's later, and Marc was going to set up the meeting with the Open Door as soon as he could. I was tempted to go see The Collector again. I could probably wrangle another question or three out of him between the guide and the people I'd met. I was really stalling for what I needed to do though.

I needed to speak to Alex.

*You up yet Mrs.?* I texted her.

Crawling out from under the bench, I pushed up, hefting myself onto it and rubbing my face. I pulled the guide out and began flicking through it, hoping for inspiration. I snagged some leather scraps off the workbench to mark pages but nothing leapt out at me, the words blurring into a smear of ink.

Cursing, I plopped the book down and looked around instead. There was a sketch peeking out from under a workbook. Tugging it free, I could see a sketch of a church, the steeple and windows painstakingly recreated. Trees lined the perimeter of the plot it sat in, with grass leading back to the larger building. The tower reached up to dwarf the squatter wings. It was odd, instead of the usual cross shape there were two large branches coming out of the main body at either end, giving the impression of a mansion or public hall. The cross at the top was unmistakable though, and I saw '*Anderson Free Church, Blantyre*' in Sarah's handwriting on the back. There was a signature, but it was some terrible squiggle I couldn't hope to make out. Not hers, certainly. I dropped it back down, then took a photo. Might be worth a look.

I jumped as a text came through on my phone, slipping my arse off the bench with a yelp.

*Awake, and I need food. Union?* Alex asked, and I laughed despite myself.

*Sounds good. I'm nearby, I'll get us a table.*

I grabbed a spot by the window and waited, checking the guide against my list again. Alex slumped down across from me, lazily grinning and eyeing me up.

"You've been awful quiet today," she said, flicking through the menu.

"Wasn't sure when you'd be up. Didn't want to interrupt a hangover." I shrugged, putting the guide away and picking up a menu.

"I'm sure it was all that," she smirked.

"Oh, spit it out!" I rolled my eyes, smiling at her.

"You and Luke?"

"Yes?"

"And his private room?"

"Yes?"

"Come on, Carter, don't hold out on me. I want the gossip!"

"What do you want to know? Did I spend the night? You know I did."

"No, I didn't," she said, looking over the menu again.

"Oh please, I don't believe Marc didn't tell you."

"He may have."

"And how did you get on with your lovely couple?"

"That's not the current line of questioning. However, we got on marvellously, as always." She preened over the comment, grinning to herself.

"You know them well?"

"Yes. I did an enjoyable amount of experimentation with them when I was working out some stuff. You ready to order yet?"

"Sure. Let me get this one," I said, welcoming a break from the questions.

"Okay, get me a mushroom omelet and orange juice."

"Sounds good." I ordered up at the counter and came back with drinks, seeing Alex grin into her phone. "Arranging the next meet up?"

"I'm surprised you haven't done the same." Her brow arched in question.

"I'm going to his place for dinner tonight."

"You're keen." She giggled.

"He invited me, and I want to discuss some ideas about Sarah. I found out a bit more last night. I know why she's hiding; I just don't know where. It has to be on one of the connected planes the angel spoke about, but I don't know how to get there."

"Why not wait for tomorrow?" she asked.

"What?"

"Halloween? That's the traditional thinning of the veil, so it makes sense it'd be when you could get between places. That'd be why that ghost kept saying it was happening soon."

"Are you serious?"

"Ask Luke. I don't know, just makes sense."

"That is not a whole lot of time," I said, grateful for the food appearing. "Do you know anything about the areas around Glasgow?"

"The basics. Why?"

"I found a sketch in Sarah's workshop, here." I pulled my phone out to show her. "It's in a place called Blantyre, a bit outside the main city?"

"Yeah, it's like a village, about a half hour out. I recognise this." She frowned at the screen, tapping it to zoom in.

"Did Sarah bring it home?"

"No. I've seen it somewhere else. Let me have another look after I've eaten. That might help."

"Fair enough," I nodded, digging into the meal. I was suddenly ravenous and barely let a word out as we ate, satisfied in devouring my food.

"Hungry?" she asked with a grin.

"Yeah. I didn't realise how much." I drank some of my glass to hide my shame.

"Did you see anything at the party?" she asked as she finished up her plate.

"I met someone—can't name names—who gave me information about some misused energy. It's being sent somewhere surreptitiously. They were most displeased."

"And you can't say who they are because of why?" she asked.

"Sworn to secrecy and could possibly be eaten."

"Well, that would be quite the undertaking." She snorted, giggling at her own joke.

"I'm so glad you find levity in my life being threatened," I exclaimed in mock outrage, throwing my napkin at her.

"If you mean literally being eaten, it would take a while. You're tall, dude."

"I can pray they start at my head then." She was soft and happy and I felt like an absolute bastard. Sat here laughing with her with the offer of swapping her for Sarah gnawing away in the back of my head. I pushed the guilt to the side and forced myself to grin, glancing back up to her. "This person seemed equipped to follow through with the threat, so I plan to stick to my side of the deal."

"Alright—human person or non-human person?"

"Distinctly non-human."

"Like the other ones I've seen with you?"

"A bit different. Succubus."

"A sex demon?"

"It was a sex party. Is it that much of a surprise?" I asked.

"The demon part is!"

"That's fair."

"How gracious of you to concede." She rolled her eyes at me. "You think they were a regular or did they make a special trip for you?"

"I doubt it was for me," I scoffed.

"I wouldn't bet on it. You keep going around, kicking over bins, the foxes get your scent."

"That is a weirdly ominous saying."

"You get the idea. Seriously though, a regular?" she asked, twisting a napkin in her hands.

"Looks like."

"I wonder why Luke never said anything."

"He might not know. They're pretty harmless. Not like they want to kill people. Dead bodies are an inconvenience."

"Yes, the inconvenience is the main issue here," Alex agreed, deadpan.

"A girl's gotta eat." I shrugged, busying myself with my drink again.

"You're not worried?"

"Not really." I tried to find the right words. "They've been there for a while from what I can tell, and they've not done anything so far. Something would need to change for them to want to mess with that."

"That's a way to look at it." Alex looked unconvinced but nodded. "That reminds me, the picture! It's a sketch of Luke's. He does a lot of pencil work."

"Why would Sarah have it?"

"For some jewellery? I know she does pieces for him."

"Yeah, that. Funny."

"What?"

"The piece she was working on turned up at my lodgings, cursed."

"Cursed?" Her brows went up.

I was struck by the reaction. "Yeah, if I hadn't had a protection charm, it would have screwed with me."

"Where did you get a protection charm?" The brows came back down in a frown.

"Someone wanted to help Sarah. I've sort of been feeling my way through the supernatural world on that basis."

"And you didn't think to mention that someone tried to curse you?"

"We had other things to worry about."

"Carter, if someone's trying to interfere with your search, that's a huge deal. They could be targeting people other than you." Oh, maybe not so much then.

"Gee, thanks. I'm touched."

"Oh, stop it. You're tough enough to survive most things, apparently. You're a lost cause. What about Luke? Or Marc?"

"Do you think Luke needs much help?" I snorted into my drink.

"He will if he doesn't know about a threat!"

"That's fair," I said, my mouth twisting down in a moue. "I did tell him yesterday."

"At least he knows. I can keep an eye out for Marc."

"He's taken with you," I said, fiddling with the table settings.

"Yeah, he's been crushing on me since my first year here."

"And?"

"No. I know he likes me; he knows I'm not interested. We work at being friends."

"And you're not interested because? If you don't mind my asking."

"Because he's a fucking drug dealer who laughs at my religion. I like him as a person, but that shit isn't what you want in a life partner."

"Never fancied having him on the side?"

"Whose side are you on?" she tutted.

"Just saying, you could tap that if you wanted."

"I prefer more clearly defined relationships."

"Fair enough." I nodded, dropping it while the going was good. "You got any classes?"

"None that I'm attending."

"Good life choice."

"Now that I've got the idea about Halloween in my head, I couldn't do anything, anyway. What do we do?"

"Well, The Collector suggested I speak to an aggressive cult, which sounds peachy. I've got someone arranging that. Not sure how it'll go, but there's not many other options left."

"You're meeting a cult?"

"Not all of them at once, but yes."

"That's unreasonably dangerous," she said, frowning.

"It's the only link we've got to the thing Sarah's hiding from."

"She's not hiding from the cult?" Shit. Shit shit shit shit.

"She is, but cults always have something they're after. Makes sense to find out what that is."

"And you're planning to what, go in there and ask them?"

"Yeah. Maybe we can trade."

"Or maybe they stab you."

"I do try to keep my initial meetings mutilation free."

"This isn't funny. What if they do something to you because you're her brother?"

"That's not the main issue. We need to know where she is. She could be hurt, could be in shock. We can't have her stumbling out of where she is unprotected. If she can even do that. I mean, we might need to find a way to physically get her out."

"This is impossible." Alex sighed, chin sinking to rest on her hands.

"No, improbable and terrifying, but not impossible."

"You know just what to say to make me feel better."

"We could go visit The Collector if you have anything to trade? I didn't want to take you there 'cause he's creepy as hell. Literally. But he's a reliable source of information."

"Assuming he's honest," she said with a sideways look.

"It's a trade. Pays for him to be honest."

"You been doing a lot of that?"

"More than I care to think about. It works."

"What've you been trading?"

"I found a couple of pieces from the guide," I not-quite-lied and hoped she let me get away with it.

"I'd rather speak to the fallen angel. I feel like they'd know about cults," she said, wrinkling her nose.

"We could. We could hit up some more parts of the guide as well. We must have seen most of the nearby ones, may as well finish it off."

"Do you think we should ask Marc to help?"

"Not yet. He might still be dealing with last night," I said.

"I suppose. He'll help if I ask, though."

"I'm sure he will," I said, suppressing my eye roll. "How about we speak to the angels first and then ask Marc to join up with us later?"

"Sounds good. I don't know how he'd take to them."

"You've come around to them."

"I'm not going anywhere near them. You're doing the talking. I'll wait outside."

"Really?" I asked, watching her uncurl from resting on her elbows.

"Really. I'm not getting in on that."

"Alright," I said with a shrug. Couldn't be worse than last time.

We headed out and slipped onto the subway, listening to the crackling of the train along the tracks. My idea churned away in the back of my head, an ember burning where it should be stamped out. I couldn't think too much about it, couldn't have it broadcasting through my mind, so I turned to Alex instead.

"Tell me more about Luke?" I asked, nudging my shoulder into hers.

"You didn't get enough last night?"

"Last night wasn't a lot of talking," I said, feigning sheepishness.

"Oh my god! You guys went at it and didn't even cuddle?" She arched her brow at me.

I faked a swipe at her. "Leave it. We spoke in the morning, but it's not exactly pillow talk stuff. Why's he in Glasgow? He's not from here if his accent is anything to go by."

"No. He's from Stirling, but he's been practicing in Glasgow for ages. I think he said he got the job through a friend and liked it, so he stayed. He's been in a big firm for as long as I've known him. I've never heard him complain. Good money and great holidays."

"Nice. Job stability is such a turn on these days."

"I honestly can't tell if that's sarcasm," she said.

"Neither can I. Being self-employed makes it a real possibility that I'm not joking."

"It's not like us students have it much better. Have you seen the job market?" she asked with a snort.

"Not if I can help it." I laughed, standing with her as the train came to our stop.

"Anything else you want to know?" she asked as we shuffled up the steps.

"What's he like food wise?"

"How do you mean?"

"Is he a fancy eater? He looks like he would be, but that might be a lawyer cliché. He doesn't seem to be a functioning alcoholic, maybe he's breaking the mould."

"I think you're right on that one. He likes his food and wine. No alcoholism that I've spotted."

"Reassuring."

"He'll make you something nice for dinner. His food's always delicious."

"That's a plus. Anything else? I feel like I've been thrown in at the deep end with the search for Sarah. All my chats with him have been about her."

"I know he likes poetry, and he's a big reader," she said, chewing her lip as she thought. "Other than that, we're going to get into stuff about the group."

"That's cool. I don't need to know about that if you don't want to share."

"I'm okay to share about me, but maybe not the rest of the people in the group. Speaking of, I checked in with some them and no one could spot anyone suspicious there last night."

"There was someone."

"What?" Her head swivelled to glare at me.

"I didn't notice, but according to The Collector there was. I don't know how we missed it, but I was pretty lit by the end of the night."

"You were hugging that wine bottle pretty tight. Me too. How would The Collector know?"

"He knows stuff," I said with a shrug.

"Yes, but how?"

"He's a demon, Alex. I'm not asking how he gets his information."

"He might be playing you." She sniffed, looking away.

"He might be, but we traded. The old rules say if you cheat a trade you get a kick back."

"What rules?"

"All the old stories. The idea's the same—cheat the deal and you get the nasty ending."

"You're basing your belief in a demon off of old fairy tales?" she asked, voice going up a touch.

"Pretty much. It's the same throughout almost every mythology, so there's a theme." I shrugged, not willing to mention my other sources.

"I suppose you're right. It is in every moral story. Even Disney uses it. That's the best we've got, isn't it?" she asked as we walked along, weaving between people.

"It is."

"So heartening."

"I know. It sucks." I put an arm around her shoulder, hugging her into me. "Let's go see what we can find."

Alex lurked at the end of the block while I stepped inside the dance studio, basked in the afternoon light. Tobias sat at the front desk, his head in a book. Maya Angelou, good choice.

"Thank you. I enjoy her work," came the bright response. His powers were tucked away again, just his eyes glimmering underneath.

"Can you not do that mind reading thing?"

"I can, but I choose to do it anyway," he said with a soft smile.

"It's really creepy, dude."

"Of all the things you see, that's what you define as creepy?" he asked with a warm chuckle.

"I see things. I don't listen to peoples' thoughts."

"Yet."

"That's not my skill set," I said, trying to keep my mind blank.

"Do some work and it might be."

"I'm nowhere near okay for this conversation right now. Is Elisha about?" I asked.

"Faith's out, I'm afraid. I can let her know you were looking for her?"

"Why do you call her by her dancing name?"

"It's the closest to what her actual name is."

"Humans not good at pronouncing it?" I asked with a quirked brow.

"Something like that."

"Sorry. Take it yours is the same?"

"Correct. Though I do rather like my current given name."

"Yeah, you look like a Tobias." I nodded.

"Can I assist you or is it essential that you speak to Faith?"

"Do you know much about cults?" I asked, sitting in one of the waiting room chairs.

"Rather a lot. They're useful," he said with a tilt of his head.

"You didn't have a hand in Jonestown, right?" It was unlikely, but I felt the need for confirmation.

"No, I'm removed from the physical groups."

"You know about one called the Open Door?"

"Why do you want to know about them, Carter?" He rose up in his seat, leaning forward over his desk.

"Sarah's hiding from them. I want to get some information on the group before I meet up with them."

"You plan to meet with them on your own?" he asked, slipping a bookmark in his page.

"A friend'll be there, but I reckon he'll bail pretty quick."

"That's a foolish choice. They're traditionalists. You'll be at risk."

"Worse than Dex talking to me?"

"Not far off."

"I'll take the chance."

"Why?" he asked, shaking his head.

"They might know where she is. I might be able to trade something to distract them. Or warn them off."

"I would advise against that. You'd do better to find her and run far away."

"I can't find her without trading with Dex or getting a clue from them."

"An unpleasant bind," he conceded, sitting back. "A suggestion, if I may? It would be better for them to think you an ally. The cruellest blade is the bite from behind, and the surest too."

"Present myself as a friend then betray them?" I asked with a bitter laugh.

"They'd certainly do the same."

"I'm sure you're right. Know any more about them?"

"It's a group of men, mostly older, who use ritual magic to gain favours with Dex."

"Isn't there a kick back from that?" I asked, chewing the inside my lip.

"Yes, but the consequences are taken as part of the agreement. Dex can be generous."

"That's reassuring," I said, dropping my head into my hands.

"There are worse beings to owe, should that occur. You also have a less savoury option."

"Alex?" I asked, looking up at him.

"Would you be willing to trade her?"

"I'm willing to help Sarah."

"That's not an answer, Carter. You're probably capable of killing, but do you want to?"

"Any weak points I can use against this cult?" I asked brightly.

"There's the old practicing ground."

"The train stations?"

"They used somewhere else before those. Having your meeting there would be useful; old blood and promises hanging in the air."

"That sounds good. Where's that?" I asked, heart soaring.

"It's a church outside of the city. It's in ruin now, was burned down twice, each for one of their rituals."

"Do you know what it looks like?"

"Yes."

"Is it this one?" I asked, pulling up the sketch on my phone.

"Yes. Did you know about it already?" He frowned, passing the phone back to me.

"No, Sarah has a picture of it."

"Has she been there?" Tobias asked, sucking his cheeks in as he thought.

"I think so. It's listed in the guide. You aren't, by the way."

"No. I joined Faith after her meeting with good John."

"Good?" I asked, giving him a look.

"A personal joke. John was always sure his intentions were good, even when doing wicked things."

"Wicked things like joining Dex?"

"Yes. If Sarah knows about the church, she may have used it to her advantage. There's a lot of history there. The place has soaked up the horror they bring."

"The sacrifices?"

"That and others, yes." He nodded, expression dark.

"Do I want to know what those other things are?" I asked after a heavy beat.

"You're going to find out much worse, either by your own actions or Dex's."

"Fair point," I said, shaking my head. "What are they?"

"Torture, rape, violence. Bringing creatures from other planes through that shouldn't be here."

"Overachievers, aren't they?"

"That's one phrase, yes." He looked me over, a sort of sympathy playing over his features.

"You said the place has soaked it up. You mean ghosts, or is the energy out of whack with all their work?"

"The latter. I don't think there is usually enough left for ghosts to form."

"Oh goody," I said, my head falling back to rest against the wall.

"You're considering a deal with them. It's important you know."

"If I trade. If I give them Alex, then we're out of here."

"Do you think you could?"

"I think I'll see what happens when we get there."

"Go careful. If I were you, I'd meet with the cult sooner rather than later, as the solstice grows closer so do the planes. Wherever Sarah is, she'll be found soon."

"That's the point," I said, standing up. "Thanks, Tobias."

"You're welcome. Good luck."

I found Alex propped up against a wall, chewing on her thumb nail.

"Good news, we might have a new lead. Bad news, turns out that cult is more super evil than we thought. There's an old church they use for sacrifices. The angel says I should meet them there."

"Okay. What now?" she asked, tugging her hoody sleeves down over her wrists.

"Call Marc, see if he can help us look. If Tobias is right, we need to find it today. We'll cover more ground if we all look. I'd like to speak to Luke too."

"That a bit clingy?"

"If he doesn't know about the person at the party there's a chance he's at risk too."

"That's fair," Alex grumbled, face forlorn. "You call Luke, I'll call Marc." We stepped apart and I grabbed my phone, dialling Luke's number.

"Carter, an unexpected pleasure," he said as he picked up. "Calling to cancel our dinner?"

"Not at all. Is now a good time?"

"Yes, I have a moment between cases."

"I spoke to The Collector today. He told me someone from the Open Door was at your party. Sounds like they've been attending them for a while now, but he wasn't clear about that. Just that they were there last night."

"You're confident this creature told you the truth?"

"I'd say so. Everything else has been above board."

"We'll have to discuss this further tonight. I'm concerned about the risk this exposes us all to," he said, the sound of tapping keys in the background.

"Me too. Hence the call. Wanted to warn you. I have to go. Alex is trying to reach Marc. We're going looking for spots for Sarah. I'll see you later tonight."

"I look forward to it," he said, voice rich with a smile. "Until later."

I turned to see Alex still on the phone, gesticulating and pacing up and down the pavement.

"You okay?" I mouthed to her on a pass by and she frowned, shaking her head. She hung up with a grunt and shoved her phone into her pocket.

"Marc can't come yet. He has to finish a deal for a big meet up. Like that's more important."

"He's maybe thinking if he gets it finished, he'll be free tomorrow?" I bluffed.

"I guess, but it's nearly two now. It's going to get dark soon. We can't go around under the city when it's dark."

"We can check some spots this afternoon and pick up again in the morning. Or we can check the weirder places now and look for people in the evening. We can start early tomorrow too. Let me discuss things with Luke tonight and come up with a plan from his info too."

"That makes sense," she said, rubbing her temples. "It feels like we're not doing enough."

"We could see The Collector."

"What would we ask him?"

"He couldn't tell me exactly where she was, so that's out the window. He told me she was looking for ways to move between the worlds, but not where to."

"What use is he if he can't tell us where?"

"He doesn't know which way she went, just that she was looking for the routes," I said, joining her in leaning against one of the old buildings.

"What else?"

"That she was hiding from the cult. That there was someone at the party last night. That they told the cult about the party, which makes me think they've been at it a while."

"That's not good. Everyone gets checked. Who'd get past that?"

"Someone serious about what they're doing. Cult's pretty bad news."

"And yet you're still going to see them. And might get stabbed."

"Hopefully not though," I said, dropping my head forward to look at her.

"Do you have any actual plan?" she asked, worry tightening her face.

"I can offer them things Sarah can't, and I could be a threat. That makes me useful and dangerous. Got to keep on the right side of that line."

"That's a terrible plan." She sighed, slumping back. "I need coffee and then we need to see what we can find. I want to do something substantive before you go off on your date."

"It's dinner," I muttered, looking for a coffee shop to drag her into.

"I know Luke. It's a date." She grinned, nudging me in the shoulder and pulling me forward. We found a table and ordered, both staring into our cups as the steam rose up.

"You know something you're not telling me," she said, blowing on her cup.

"What makes you think I'm not telling you something?"

"This cult. Cults have a point, like you said. I know Luke's talked about one before, a voracious little group that targets the young and the beautiful and corrupts them. Is that who you're going to see?"

"I don't know much—Luke has more information for me to look over. I know they scared Sarah. I'm pretty sure they were planning something bad to happen to her, but I don't know what."

"Liar," she said after she stared at me over the coffee.

"I strongly suspect something and it's a big thing to say if I don't know I'm right."

"Alright. So why are you going off alone?"

"If they get me, you guys still have a chance of finding her."

"Fuck, man. You can't keep saying shit like that." She leaned back in her seat, shaking her head. "What do we say to her if that's what happens?"

"You'd manage something. I'm more worried about her. I might ask Marc to come along with me. Or Luke. He's more likely to be noticed missing."

"That's depressingly accurate," Alex said, sipping her coffee, "You and Luke go and see this cult and they don't kill you, what next?"

"We find Sarah and get the hell out of the city."

"So that's it. You just steal her off?" She said it light, but I could see the stiffness in her posture.

"This isn't about me. It's about getting her somewhere safe. I don't think she'd feel safe in the city after this. Which is heart breaking. She'll miss it." I had my hands wrapped around my cup and focused on the heat there, the steam rising. Anything but what was screaming in the back of my head about switching places and sacrifice and if Alex would miss things.

Or have the chance to.

"We go up and down the city and expose ourselves to all this, and we still don't know where she is. How do we fix that?" she asked.

"We find her. We go see people and get what we can from them, and we hope tomorrow pays off. She left her trail of breadcrumbs, so she'll be ready for us."

"You think she planned this out?"

"Yeah." I nodded, forcing myself to take a too hot swig.

"Why not run back to Manchester?"

"She didn't think she could, for some reason. I don't know why but maybe meeting these guys'll tell me."

"That's some big reach she's worried about." Alex frowned, glaring down at her cup.

"It is, but she may be right. Everyone says these guys are the worst. If she thought she wouldn't be able to make it back then hiding here would be safer. We just need to figure out where *here* is."

"Your angel thought meeting them at the church would be good. Why?" she asked.

"It's stained by what they've done there. Should favour us over them."

"Can a place do that?"

"I don't know. Can you build up so much bad that there's a push back? I suppose so." I took another sip. "It might make them confident, but we could use that."

"Blind side them? You think they'll fall for it?"

"I'm not sure, but I have an idea of what I could use to help with that."

"That doesn't sound good."

"It's something The Collector has, a knife designed to make people fight."

"You want to get a magic murder knife and take it to meet an aggressive cult?" she asked, her cup going down with a clunk. "You're fucking insane."

"It's to cause an imbalance. Get them confident then wind up the tension."

"And you think that'll mean they're less likely to kill you?"

"The knife wants blood. It doesn't care who bleeds. It'll amp them up against each other as much as me. Cults always have power imbalances. See what way it swings."

"I don't like that this is the best plan we have."

"Only until the doors open. I'm hoping when that happens tomorrow, you might be able to find her."

"What do you mean?" she asked, swirling the remains of her coffee in the cup.

"Once the worlds are all aligned, so to speak, then you should be able to feel her again. If you look as a group."

"Are you sure?"

"No. But she'll be coming back, if she can, and that'll mean she can be found."

"That's your back up plan?" Alex asked.

"It's not a good plan, but it would do." None of the plans were good, but it was as many as I could think to set up. Something had to work.

"We have three shots at this and all day tomorrow to get this sorted?" she asked, setting her cup on the table and standing.

"Yeah. Loads of time. Plenty of chances," I said, matching her.

"Say it often enough and you might believe it." She smiled wickedly with the comment, and I knew she was feeling it as much as I was. The potential was potent, heavy on both of us as we left the café and went back towards the West End.

"Can you think of two things to give The Collector?"

"Two?"

"One for the knife and one for a question."

"You need to ask him more questions?"

"Just the one."

"And that is?" she asked, digging an elbow to my ribs.

"Complicated. I've not figured out the wording. I'll explain after we've found something to give him. The knife is more important, anyway."

"Alright. What can we give him?"

"I could tell him about Blob."

"She'll be gone soon."

"Exactly. It's a fair trade, and she can get away," I said.

"That could work. I don't want to tell him about our group. That would feel like inviting the Devil to our door."

"It'd be irresponsible. We could tell him about Luke, without naming him. A lawyer that practices must be unusual."

"That feels a bit close to home, but I suppose it would be okay if we don't name him. A lot of people don't know his job, so it shouldn't screw him up," she said, chewing a nail again. "Could we ask him before we do that?"

"I was going for it being better to beg forgiveness than ask permission."

"That's a terrible idea, but I may end up agreeing."

"Okay, we go to The Collector now and see what else we can find from the guide. I meet Luke tonight, see what he can give me on the cult, and we regroup tomorrow and find her through your group or the physical spots we know about. We could ask those women at the bar again, too. I feel like they'd know about places."

"Hard pass. They creep me out, and I can't even see what you do," she said, shaking her head.

"They're pretty wild."

"Can you do them and I'll do something else?"

"Sure. If I speak to them and you speak to your group, we'll have double the progress."

"Okay. I'm good with that." She nodded, shoving her hands into her pockets. The promise of thunder tingled through the air, and I gave her a lopsided grin.

"Could be worse," I offered.

"Yeah right. Do you think we'll find her, really?" she asked, her voice small as we made our way along the street.

"We'll find where she is and the cult will be far too busy fighting amongst themselves to notice us rescuing her. We'll head off to Manchester with no issue, and Sarah will come back next year, once things have settled down."

"Liar." She grinned, knocking into my shoulder.

"We will though," I assured her, almost confident of it.

We stood beside each other on the subway platform, feeling the electric crackle of the tracks and the fug of bodies around us. Alex looked a little lost, eyes distant as she gazed at the tracks.

"Carter," she began, glancing over to me. "You've gotten very enthusiastic about seeing different people despite your gift. Will you keep using it once you've found Sarah?"

"Will you be disappointed if I say no?" I asked, surprised it would matter.

"Not disappointed, but it'd be sad. You've done a lot of good with it. Seems a shame to lock it away."

"A lot of good? I've been terrifying people."

"A little." She smiled, glancing over again. "But you've helped Marc, and me, and by the sounds of it, Luke, too. You don't want to see if you can take that further?"

"I doubt I'd be able to do much good. Glasgow's been tough enough, never mind all the stuff floating around in Manchester."

"You don't think you could carry on, help people?"

"Alex, I'm a terrible human being. Let's leave it at that." I forced a laugh, shaking my head and silently thanking anything that listened when the train arrived moments later.

# Chapter 21

<u>9 July, 1886</u>

*Glasgow Green continues to surprise me, in the most genuine sense.*

*I was investigating the area yesterday evening to ascertain if my earlier hypothesis in relation to the Fae was correct, and I encountered a spirit different from any I have yet met in Glasgow. Initially, I thought them to be huldra, for their form was beautiful and their disposition pleasant. But after open discussion, I believe them closer in essence to that of a nymph in ancient lore. I must confess I was grateful for this. I can only imagine the scandal if I had been caught pleasing such a creature in a public park, as a hulda may force to occur. My university position and any hope of an apprenticeship would have been ruined for the sport of some spirit! Or she would have eaten me, if unsated.*

*I was told these nymphs are able communicate with those of talent in the city and that there is a network of such spirits, which is amenable to assisting worthy parties. Naturally, there is a price for such intervention, and I am unclear as to what this may be presently. It is uncertain if this would be more beneficial than the agreement I already have with The Collector, but it will be a fascinating point to discuss with him further.*

We emerged into the dying sunlight, the shadows cooling as we passed through.

"What's this guy is like?" Alex asked, breaking through the noise of traffic and bodies.

"Depends how he presents. If he's wearing his human suit, then a bit twitchy but sharp. If he's not wearing his human suit then he looks... Well, he looks like a demon. Not sure how else to say it. I think he'll look human though."

"Do I have to come in for your trade?"

"You mean, you want to stand outside?" I asked with a laugh.

"Kinda."

"I thought you wanted to meet him?" I asked, looking over to her. Her chin was tucked low, and she was chewing a nail.

"I did, but it's not right. A demon knowing about you and Luke is bad enough without him knowing about me too. Someone needs cover should this all go to shit."

"You can lurk. Do you want me to make introductions and then you go out?"

"No. Get me in after the trade. I want to meet him when he's in a good mood."

"I like that you assume he'll be in a good mood post trade."

"He's got to be. Wouldn't be worth it otherwise," she said.

"Okay. You go grab a seat on that bench." I pointed her off towards the riverside and traipsed down the steps then entered.

"Mr. Brooks, I did not expect to see you so soon," I heard as I came through the door.

"I was convinced to come back."

"By your friend outside?"

"She's quite keen to meet you," I said, walking to the counter. I couldn't tell if he was no longer bothering to wear his human suit for me or if he was feeling particularly pleased, but he stood unguarded, yellow eyes glinting.

"You have more to trade?" he asked, looking me over.

"Information. I want the jaw bone knife you have and an answer."

"Why would you want a knife that causes conflict?"

"I want to piss some people off."

"An effective approach. What can you offer me in exchange?"

"Details of a being stuck on this plane when they shouldn't be and details of a sex practitioner who's abusing their position," I said, slipping my hands into my pockets so I didn't fiddle with something.

"You intrigue me. Which do you wish to trade first?"

"The knife for the creature," I offered, watching the air around him swirl.

"That is acceptable. The details?"

"It's a being who should be in water, large and powerful but here out of place. She was isolated in one of the underground tunnels by mistake. She's trying to get back over."

"That is new. If you would, I can take the details from you?" He held his talons up, moving to cup my face.

"Hey, woah—" I began to protest as his hands touched my skin. I felt a jolt of power go down my spine, the shock making me curl forward over the counter. It was like lightning on my nerves, hot, white pain. I shuddered against it, my stomach churning as I bit down against a shout.

"My apologies, Mr. Brooks," he said, scooping me up by the shoulders and looking at least a bit concerned. "I forgot you would be susceptible to the touch given your abilities. I will not be so rude again."

"What was that?" I slurred, rubbing my face to try to shake off the feeling. Pulses of pain lingered through my larger muscles, jolting my leg with a little jerk.

"I bonded with you, momentarily, to see the being you spoke of. Quite a beauty. I had not thought to shield you from my powers. That was remiss of me," he said with a short bow of his head.

Fuck me, that was sore. "Alright, well, I hope we never do that again. Can I get the knife now?"

"A moment, if you will?" It was said as a question but he was already gone, his large frame slipping through the shop and into the side room.

I leaned forward on the counter, head between my crossed arms and breathing deeply. The last twinges were making their way out of my body, my arms jumping against my bones. This was not how I liked to spend my afternoons. This was not how I envisaged my day going. At least I was getting the knife. That was a step forward.

"Do you have any warnings about it?" I called towards the side room as I straightened up again.

"In which ways, Mr. Brooks?"

"Well, genie lamps always tell you to be careful of what you wish for. Ouija boards tell you not to ask for treasure or when you're going to die. What about this?"

"I would only say what you already know." He smiled as he came back, all teeth. "Which is that this knife causes conflict, and it is hungry. It has been some time since it was given blood, so it will increase the tension in a room if you let it."

"How do I do that?" I asked, looking away from his grin.

"Drawing the blade. Do watch out for the teeth, though. They're sharp when they want to be."

He handed me a short knife, the full thing no longer than the span of my hand. The blade sheath was studded with teeth, short sharp things that curved up greedily. The handle was stockier, the bone flat and broad. It was light, and I toyed with the weight in my hand, practicing gripping the underside.

"This a human jawbone," I said, feeling the item with my gift. "A lively one at that." I could pick up the lightest impressions of the person left in the bone: an angry young man, a yearning for aggression, a chance to rip and tear.

"It was. Now it is this blade."

"People tend to notice their jawbones going missing."

"When alive, yes." He nodded, just the once.

Fucking-A. "Noted. If I have this in my pocket, it'll wind up the tension?"

"Having the blade drawn is most effective, though simply having the knife handle out will induce the reaction."

"Thanks very much. Now, my question."

"Indeed. What do you want to know?" he asked, hands folded in front of him like a cat.

"I've been told I should meet the Open Door at a church in Blantyre. Can you tell me more about that?"

"Do you have something particular in mind?" he pushed back.

"The person I spoke to said the place would hold a grudge against the cult, that there'd be things there to use against them."

"I understand your query. And what will you give me in exchange?"

"Details of the practitioner."

"I'll ensure I do not repeat the same intensity of before, if you'd be so kind?" He held his hands up and I nodded, dipping my head forward. It was much nicer this time, like having your brain dipped in warm water. The heat trickled down the length of my spine and I sighed, relaxing. "Thorough research, I see."

"Had to be sure," I smirked, shrugging. The Collector hummed and pulled his hands away, clasping them before him on the counter.

"The church is a wise choice. There has been much bloodshed at that place and the fear of those used by the cult has lasted, even if their spirits have not. That energy has an intent, if given the right opportunity it would seek to harm the group."

"Does the energy have a shape?"

"Not for most, but then you are unusual, Mr. Brooks. I would not be too surprised if you could find a shape in those shadows."

"Well that's fucking ominous," I said, pocketing the knife and shaking my head.

"You are seeking to betray a collection of killers. I would be surprised if ominous was the worst you encounter."

"Valid," I said, nodding. "You want to meet my friend?"

"I think it would be better to save such introductions for after the equinox, when my dealings are not so potent. Your friend is a wise woman. She will see the truth of me too clearly at this moment."

"I can see you. Why would her seeing you be a problem?" I asked.

"Your ability allows you to see me without concern. I do not believe your friend so lucky."

"Alright then, lets skip that trauma. Thank you for your time."

"And you for yours, Mr. Brooks. Good luck is the traditional wish for such endeavours, but you seem to be chasing bad fortune throughout."

Even the demon thought I was screwed. "You could just wish me well?"

"I hope the situation works out the way you desire."

"I'll take it. Bye." I was out the door before some other weird half wish could be given and jogged over to Alex, savouring the cool weight of the afternoon.

"Alex, hey," I called as I approached, disturbing her contemplation. She looked fit to throw herself into the river.

"Time to go in?" she asked, twisting in the seat.

"No, he's got to shut up shop for the day, says to come back next week."

"He's going away for a week?"

"I guess it's busy season," I fluffed, glancing out at the water. "Anyway, that gives us more time to set up for tomorrow."

"You want to go back to the flat and look for ideas?" she asked, standing from the bench and brushing the backs of her legs off.

"Good plan," I said, falling in step with her.

We got into the flat as the last of the light died. I flopped onto one of the large couches, breath going out of me as I landed. I felt bone tired and had no excuse for it besides the weight of my ideas and the demon's touch. Alex brought through tea and set mine on the table, glancing over to me as she sat down.

"You alright there?"

"Just thinking," I said, swiping my hands over my face. "Too many options all at once, no routine. I'm overloading."

"Sarah's outsmarted us all, and she'll be back tomorrow," she offered, holding her mug close to her chest.

"She'll have three exit plans ready. She's had time to think, wherever she is, and she'll know exactly where she's going," I agreed, sitting up from my stupor and plucking my cup. "Right, you grab a notepad and go through the book. I'm going to go through the entries on my phone. Let's look for anything about a door or a portal or things like them." I passed her the guide and pulled up the list, the chronology of Sarah's visits.

"Carter, something's been bothering me," Alex said, flicking through the pages with no real intent.

"Go on." I watched her not look at me.

"Blob recognised Sarah, yes?"

"Yeah."

"How'd Sarah know about the tunnels?" she asked, glancing at me then back to the guide like she was afraid what she'd see.

"How'd you know about them?"

"I told you, I dated a guy who was into that kind of thing," she said with an irritated nose wrinkle.

"Who says Sarah didn't? She was seeing multiple guys." I said, scrolling along the list.

"I don't see her going after that type. And this guide can't talk about the tunnels, they're too new."

"Either she found out about them as part of her research into the cult or someone told her," I said, weighing the options.

"The cult?"

"Yeah, The Collector said they like using them for meetings and rituals. Guess it's unlikely to get disturbed."

"That's weird."

"It's a cult. Working in abandoned places is kinda standard."

"But they're new for the city. And there's loads of old places that are empty or nearly empty," she said, chewing her lip.

"They're less likely to be noticed? Houses might have security systems. That padlock we tackled was pretty easy." It didn't taste right as I said it.

"That's true. But it's weird for Sarah to know about the tunnels without any input."

"You think she had another source of information?"

"Feels like it," she said. "I don't know why for sure, but I think she did."

"That's got to be a known unknown for now. We need to track down ideas for the portals first. I'll ask Luke about it tonight. I need to speak to him about the cult anyway. It's reasonable those could be connected."

"Yeah, that makes sense." She nodded, unconvinced by the look on her face. "But he didn't know Sarah was involved with the cult."

"She wasn't involved with them; they wanted her," I said, too quickly.

"What do you mean?"

"They wanted her power. Like I told her would happen if people knew about her gift."

"Don't be like that. She'd found a good group with us. Maybe she thought the same would happen with them," Alex said, frowning at me.

"I hate being proved right."

"How do you know that, anyway?"

"The Collector." I wondered if he offered frequent buyer perks at the rate I was in with him.

"Shit. Can he tell you more?"

"Not without a trade." I smiled, bitter. "Talking about trades, I need to go speak to those women at the bar."

"What have you got to trade them?"

"My charming good looks?" I offered as I got up, slipping back into my jacket. "I don't know what they'll want, but it's as good a chance as any. I'll come back once we're done, I need to be at Luke's by seven, but we should manage to get through some places before then." She stood as well, hovering beside the table.

"I'll call around the group and see what we can get arranged for tomorrow."

"That's great. Thank you, Alex," I said, giving her a quick hug before I stepped away.

"What aren't you telling me?" she asked, staring me down before I could make it to the door.

"Gonna have to be more specific. That could cover a whole bunch of sins," I said, hands slipping into my pockets again.

"What about the search for Sarah aren't you telling me?"

"If there was something I wasn't telling you, don't you think there might be a reason?" I countered, ruffled.

"And who would you be to make that decision for me?" she asked, eyes narrowing.

"Maybe it's not about you. Did that occur to you?"

"No need to go back to being a dick. What is it?"

"They were going to kill her. The cult," I spat, letting my anger flare up. "You feel better knowing that? Happy knowing the reason she hid was because someone was going to slit her fucking throat?"

"You can't be serious. People don't do that." Her hands went up as if to grip her hair and then dropped back away.

"Sure, the same way there aren't sex parties amongst the upper middle class and students don't practice magic rituals in their spare time."

"That's hardly the same, though." She began but stopped, looking away. "You're not lying?"

"No."

"Why didn't she tell me?"

"I don't know. You're surrounded by people trying to keep you out of danger. No idea why they might want to keep you safe."

"Fuck you," she said, but there was no heat to it.

"They'll be wanting to make good on that plan, tomorrow when she's back, so I'm keen not to waste any time."

"Right," she said, wrapping her arms around herself.

"Hence the knife. Longer we can keep them unstable, the better it'll be."

"Can I blame the knife for your being a dick?" She half smiled.

"Yeah." I nodded, matching her. It was a lie. I was thrumming with nervous energy over the half-formed plans bargained between the different influencers all more powerful than I was. It was easy to blame on the mixture of blade and bone I carried with me. "I'm gonna head over to the bar before they're busy. Be right back."

I half sprinted down the stairs, desperate for distance. I patted the knife in my pocket and felt no response from it. Just my own guilt then. I stopped at the building door, fishing my phone out.

*We good for tonight, mate?* I sent Marc in a rush, heading off towards the pub.

It was quiet, the regulars still propping up the bar, but not many others were around. The same younger woman was behind the bar and her visage was still haunting, straggling hair catching the light in a bloody halo. At least I expected it now.

"No shield today, pretty lad?" she asked when she saw me.

"None. I was wondering if I could speak to Alala?"

"Why should she want to talk to you?"

"She might not. But if she can, I'd appreciate it."

"Sit," she commanded, pointing to a stool. I did as told, and she stepped away from the bar.

I fiddled with my phone, checking for a response from Marc. Fretting over him wouldn't make things go any quicker. He knew what he was doing. I was halfway through convincing myself of this when a hand landed on my shoulder, turning my body with ease.

"Come upstairs," said Alala. The shield had been a good idea last time. She was the same height as before, but her skin was a deep tan like a bog mummy, with the dull sheen of leather. Her eyes were wild though, sparking with promise and threat. The hair I could see had ivy and what looked like snake skin through it, wild and matted. I nodded and followed her through a door marked private.

"Thanks for seeing me," I said as we went into her office.

"What do you want?"

"I want to ask you some questions about portals between the worlds. I know tomorrow is when all the barriers are weak, and some of the portals will be open."

"Your girl gone and hidden behind a door?" she asked, looking me over again, her eyes going hungrier.

"Something like that. I've still got to find her."

"Why not wait for tomorrow?"

"I'm not the only one looking for her," I said, watching the darkness in her gaze swirl.

"You think someone else will be at the door waiting."

"They might be. Don't want to take the chance."

"You could avoid the need for all this," she said, all reasonable like.

"I could but doing that would make things complicated."

"More complicated than trying to second guess the people who are after your sister? Vicious bunch, that."

"Yes."

"You want to know where I think she'd be." She shifted in her seat to lean forward.

"That's why I'm here. I don't expect it for free. I understand I might have to pay or trade."

"What do you think you can offer us? We run our own worship, source our own needs."

"I come before you humble and willing. If I can give, I'm ready to. If I can't then I beg your pardon."

"Flowery words." She sniffed but her smile stretched the skin around her mouth wide and dripping. The same dark stains were on the teeth as the girl downstairs.

"Seemed proper to be respectful given we're in a house of worship," I said.

"Sensible lad. I can tell you the churches in this city are strong, but there are stronger places. The river, the city of the dead, the shells of places left behind. These spots hold onto energy from the elements they have ties to. Cities grow by their destruction as much as development."

"Thank you. What may I give?"

"We don't need anything from you now. We'll call on you in the future."

"I might not be in the city."

"You think we're the only wild women?"

"I hadn't thought of their being contact between different groups. My apologies." I bowed my head, hoping for the right mix of deference and respect.

"Head up, boy. I don't need my feet kissed. It'll suit us to have a favour due by someone like you."

"Thank you kindly. May I go?"

"Yes, trot on."

I nodded again and left, mulling over her comments; strong elemental areas and religious buildings. That ruled out a few places, like the tunnels or the former execution sites. That could cut a swathe out of the guide as well. I felt cheered a bit with that. At least it was good news to give Alex. I felt a twinge in my chest at that and pushed it down, picturing Sarah. I buzzed at the flat door and jogged up the stairs with something like a grin.

"Good news?" Alex asked, seeing my face.

"Sort of. I now owe a favour to them, but they said we should look for churches or religious buildings and places with a lot of elemental energy."

"As in parks and the river?"

"Something like that, yeah."

"Weird mix." She frowned, lips pursing.

"In places that have spare energy. It's saturated into them," I said as we went back through to the living room.

"That's going to cover a lot of places."

"It will, but I think it'll be somewhere in the guide, so that should cut it down. Loads of the churches and parks will be younger than that book."

"Alright, yeah. Let's work to that."

"You spot anything while I was gone?" I asked as I retook my place on the sofa with renewed optimism.

"I was tied up phoning people. We don't usually meet until the day after tomorrow."

"Not Halloween?"

"The night is the start of the proper festival for us, so Halloween night and the day after it. There's always so much crap going on during Halloween night that it's easier to meet up the next day."

"That's cool. I hadn't realised that's how it worked."

"Not everyone agrees with us," she said with a grin. "But we do. Everyone I've spoken to is willing to get together to hold a circle for Sarah."

"That's amazing. Thank you so much, Alex," I smiled, honestly, and put a hand over hers. "You've been a huge help for me. I'm so grateful."

She gave a non-committal noise then buried her head back into the book. I followed suit, trying to settle back into looking through the list. I found three mentions of the river, a few burned down churches, and several mentions of Glasgow Green. I noted them on an email, and leaned my head back against the couch.

"What've you got?" Alex asked, glancing up.

"About eight. The Green comes up a lot."

"Not surprising. Glasgow Green has been around a long time. So far I've two, but I don't want us to be doubling up."

"I listed mine in an email. I'll pop it over to you."

"Thanks. I think I'll have to spend the evening going over this book. It's pretty dense."

"Yeah, his way of writing's a bit weird. He's concise. When he's not busy saying how amazing The Collector is." Or how he's going to join up with unholy forces from another dimension.

"You talk like you like him." She huffed a laugh.

"I did. He's got a lot of ideological stuff that's easy to sympathise with."

"I'll look forward to it. You really think we'll find it in here?"

"Sarah's been using the guide for about a year. I think it's the best we've got," I said, tilting my head to look at her.

"Hardly gold standard, but we'll have to take it."

"We'll make it work. Maybe the cult meeting will narrow it down. I'm hoping they give something."

"I'm still not convinced about that."

"You guys are here in case it's too much risk," I said, breaking eye contact.

"I don't like it. You've got to scoot, though. I want make dinner and grab a shower before I settle in for this. I need to get into the right headspace."

"No problem. I'm gone." I smiled, hefting myself up again. "Have you heard anything else from Marc?"

"No, I'll give him another call later on if he doesn't show up."

"That's cool. Let me know if you don't have any luck."

"Will do. Give me a call after your dinner date, and we can plan for tomorrow? I'll still be reading this thing." She held the slim book up, curling a lip at it.

"Sure thing. Good luck with the book."

# Chapter 22

*12 December, 1885*

*One of The Collector's books discusses a creature I find unusual. I have come across no such being in my other studies, no grimoire or diary provides notes of the same.*

*It is a sentience attached to particular forms of energy, with a focus in relation to emotions of distress and pain. They can manifest in any places with a high concentration of these resources; I imagine places like poorhouses, hospitals, prisons, churches, battlegrounds. Under the right circumstances, this collection of misery can blossom into a living thing, able to interact with those with the sight to see it.*

*Such a creature would be unpalatable in the extreme, but what a source of power that could offer, a collection of energy enough to sustain and fuel a new life. It is unclear how intelligent it would be, though the notes I have read detail conversation and intent that is equal to that of a man or woman. Could it tell us stories of those who have given it form? Would it remember the agony that bled it into creation?*

*The implications are unpleasant for many infamous areas in recent history. I wonder if Waterloo is haunted by a garrison of such forms. However, the opportunity they would present, the access to history and power. Those are points worthy of note.*

I left the flat with my gut churning, gulping the cool air. Alex was as worried as I was, though for different reasons. I should clear my head before meeting Luke. I wanted his view on the cursed bracelet, to see if he could trace anything on it.

I wandered over to the subway and made my way back to the guesthouse, nerves rattling. It felt like a hangover from The Collector first touching me, electric under my skin. My feelings about Alex nagged low in my chest, competing with the impending energy of Halloween and concerns about seeing Luke. I'd be lying if I said I wasn't a bit excited; he was nice if problematic. That could be worked on though.

Plodding up the steps of the guesthouse, I slipped up to my room, grateful to avoid chatter with the front desk. No stomach for more lying today. Opening the door, I was met by the screaming urge that something was wrong, darkness deeper than the night.

"Hello?" I said, moving to put on the lights.

"I would not recommend you do that," purred a familiar voice, and my stomach dropped.

"Dex? How are you in my room?" I asked, keeping my voice as level as I could manage around the tightening of my chest.

"I'm not, truly, but it would be unwise of you to see how I have chosen to manifest without due warning."

"Why, you wearing someone else's face? 'Cause I hate to break it to you but last time it really didn't suit you." My heart was thumping loud in my head, the kick against my ribs hard enough to make me sweat. It wasn't meant to get through unless I gave it blood. It wasn't meant to physically find me. It wasn't meant to fucking speak to me about whether I should look at it or not.

"I like your humour, Carter. It reminds me of others who have served me."

"That's nice. I'm going to turn the light on now. Should I be worried?"

"I am sure it is no more unsettling than your last view of me," it smirked. I could hear the bloody smirk in its voice.

I flicked the light and saw the looming silhouette of a man, a solid body coated in viscous blackness that radiated out over the frame, making it half as large again. The body was broad and tall, naturally imposing, and made horrific in its adaptation by Dex. It stood on the other side of my bed, leaned against the wall. Nonchalant. The only hint of whose body was under there came from a tuft of off-white hair leaking through the darkness.

"You have Marc?" I growled, surging towards the bed.

"Careful, I might disentangle too quickly and cause a ruckus."

"Fuck you," I spat, snarling at it. The face it wore was still like Luke, up high on the false head this possession created. The skin had fragmented now, islands of shapes ebbing over the void and melting at the edges.

"Manners, Carter. I appreciate it may have been a touch underhanded to use him to walk into your room, but the owners already recognised him. It was too tempting."

"Why are you here? I thought we'd agreed I'd give you a blood call if I wanted to bargain?" I asked, staying by the bed.

"We did. Someone else wanted me to ensure you could not do that. I must say, for someone scrambling around in the darkness, you have disturbed so many people."

"Someone wanted you to kill me? That's a bit menial. I thought your followers did the bloodshed themselves."

"You are correct, and that is in part why I am here speaking to you rather than to simply stop your heart or melt your brain through your eyes. I could do so, but I would much rather keep you alive."

"I'm touched." I laughed, breathless from the edge of fear pressing through me. "Honestly, I'm very glad you prefer me to live."

"I know. I can feel how grateful you are." I felt the ghost of a pressure creep down my chest, over my heart, then lower.

"Hey, no! I've had more than enough uninvited touching today, thank you very much."

"I could make it pleasurable. I'm sure this body would be willing to do so as well." It stepped Marc's body closer to the bed, and I took a matching step back.

"Okay, can we not get any creepier? I'm not raping a friend. That's wrong on about fifteen different levels. Why else are you here?"

"You seek to speak to one of my groups."

"We discussed that this morning."

"You did not mention that trinket in your pocket this morning." It pointed with Marc's arm, a finger towards my pocket.

"Didn't know I had to. There's more of them than me. I need some assistance."

"I approve. How did you get it?"

"You don't know already? You're usually stalking me," I said, crossing my arms.

"You managed to evade my usual methods."

"I traded for it," I said. No point lying.

"And who did you deem worthy of trading with, when you have withheld such enjoyment from me?"

"Less worth and more necessity. They didn't want a chunk of my life, just information."

"Who?"

"Are you jealous?" I asked.

"I do not wish another like me to be in contact with you, if that is what you mean." What was left of Luke's eyebrows lifted in challenge, and I felt bile creeping up my throat. I wasn't expecting the dead looking skin to move.

"Dex, I wouldn't dare speak to another being like you. If you recall, I didn't even start speaking to you. I woke up surrounded by you."

"A situation I would enjoy maintaining."

"Can you be less creepy? You're possessing one of my friends. This is way too much."

"I did wonder if this would distress you. He was willing to harm you."

"He doesn't owe me anything. He's looking out for his own," I said, forcing myself to breathe deep and meet its gaze.

"A foolish thing to forgive. He could have promised you to my followers in exchange for those he cares for."

"You wouldn't be here wearing him if he had. Someone wouldn't have asked you to kill me if he had."

"All true. Do you know who it was that asked?"

"John?" I asked, a stab in the dark. I didn't know the man from toffee. He could be trying to cut me off at the pass.

"No, John wants you all to himself. It was the second in command, a gentleman known as Nigel. He is a hungry little man. Never satisfied."

"Is he an ambitious man as well as a greedy one?" I asked, wondering if that could be an in.

"Ambitious in the covetous way. He would never earn his desires." It emphasized the last word with relish.

"A good man to show my new toy to?" I asked, rolling the idea around in my head.

"Certainly."

"Why are you helping me against your cult?"

"I do not lose anything weeding out those weak enough to fall for such base methods," it sniffed.

"Glad to be of service."

"You will be."

"And we're back to being creepy. Since you've hijacked Marc, I don't suppose you know when he's set up this meeting for?"

"They expect to see him again this evening, eleven o'clock. They intend to meet with you tomorrow, when the barriers are weakest."

"They expect me to be dead?"

"Nigel does. The others expect Marc to prepare you."

"Like a turkey," I said, a line of anger chasing the fear in my chest.

"A lamb would be more appropriate."

"You do like your imagery, huh?"

"You grow to appreciate it when you see it used well. I have had time enough around you humans to see that."

"I'll make a note of that. Is there a nice way for me to ask you to get out of Marc? Is he going to be okay?"

"There are complications, but these pass after a short while. He will feel unpleasant."

"Hangover from hell," I said, watching the rippling of the shadows that made up Dex. "Why are you still wearing Luke's face?"

"Because I knew it would affect you," it said with a quirk of the lips spread over its face.

"It's so mashed up, it's hard to tell what it is."

"You still managed to though. How much are you willing to sacrifice before you come to me? Who are you willing to see hurt? Killed even."

"I've done a lot of thinking," I said, moving around the bed to stand in front of it. It pulled itself up, smiling back at me. This close I could see the shape of Marc properly, his features slack and eyes closed. "You know that or you wouldn't keep pushing me away from my plan."

"On the contrary, I am exceedingly excited about your plan. I cannot wait to see what bloodshed and pain you bring. And if you manage to find Sarah."

"I will. And if I don't and your group kills me, the others will. She'll be safe."

"I am certain you will do everything you can to ensure that." It leaned down, and I felt a puff of breath on my neck, an echo of its intent from the body it hijacked. "I am certain I will enjoy watching you rip and rend through them like you wanted to do this morning. I can almost feel it." It floated a hand over my arm and up, over my shoulder, never quite touching but leaching the warmth from my skin.

"Did no one ever have the personal boundaries talk with you as a young...being?" I asked, unsure which face to watch.

"I am an expert in getting people to relinquish such things. We will be intimate once I have your blood. More than intimate once you serve me. How am I meant to resist such temptation when I have a body here that could soothe you?" The hand did touch me this time, clammy skin stripped from the blackness, resting on my neck.

"This is the opposite of soothing. Literal opposite. This is so not okay," I said in disbelief, trying my best not to shake the hand off. I had Marc, or at least part of him, as he should be. I didn't want to let that go.

"Are you sure you wish me to leave so soon?" The question was whispered as an invitation, the hand at my neck gently kneading the muscles there.

"Certain. I'm sure Marc would like himself back too. And will have lasting psychological trauma from being possessed."

"It never lasts unless I want it to."

"Please could you not want it to?" I asked with as much respect as I could muster.

"How could I not indulge you when you ask so nicely? Until later, Carter."

"Bye," I said, ready to catch Marc if he dropped. The lights of Dex's eyes blinked out like doused embers and the black shell fell apart like ashes. The energy drained from the room in a downpour, the sudden difference chilling. Marc arched up, his spine stretching tall. He gasped a breath then doubled over onto the bed, coughing and spluttering.

"Easy, mate," I said, patting his back while he hacked.

"What the fuck just happened? Why am I on a bed with you?"

"Only you're on the bed, to be fair," I said then dodged the open-handed slap that was coming for me.

"Carter, what the fuck did I just do?" he shouted, looking stricken.

"Seems you helped someone trying to curse me and were setting me up to be jumped by that cult."

"What?" His face went blank, the professional mask an emotional void.

"You left that bracelet for me. That's how you could come up to my room. The front desk knew you."

"It was only meant to confuse you. No real harm," he said, starting to shake like he was in withdrawal.

"You an expert in that?" I asked and regretted it the minute it was out of my mouth. "It doesn't matter. You got commandeered by the entity I keep talking to in my sleep. It liked you."

"Then why do I feel like I've had the shit kicked out of me and my head pissed in?" he asked, glaring at me as he perched on the mattress. That was a mental image I never needed.

"Because a god thing was wearing you as a human suit," I said with a shrug.

"I told you you were fucked," he said after a long silence.

"And I told you I didn't mind so long as I find Sarah. You need a rest?"

"Why?"

"I have a dinner date to discuss this fascinating cult and you're meeting them at eleven, I hear."

"How'd you find that out?" he asked, tapping his body for his phone.

"Dex knew about it. Either from your head or from the cult. Not sure."

"I need a lot of alcohol to prevent the memory of this ever forming."

"I don't think that'll work. Save it for after we find Sarah. I'll even buy you a bottle of that nice tequila."

"You really know the way to a man's heart," he said, folding in on himself and holding his head between his hands.

"You can sleep here if you want. I have to go in like twenty minutes. I'm happy for you to use the bed. Or go see Alex. She's researching places to find Sarah."

"Sleep would be good. I could get an hour then go see Alex. You could come to the meeting at eleven, scope them out before tomorrow." He tried to sound casual, but I could hear the strain in his voice.

"This you feeling guilty?" I asked with a raised brow.

"Man, I don't owe you shit."

"I know," I replied with a shrug.

"You did right keeping Alex safe though. I feel a bit shitty about that cursed trinket, but I had my reasons. Seeing these guys ahead of time'd help you, let you see what you're dealing with."

"Sounds good. Sleep, and give me a message when you're going to meet the group. I'm going to get ready for Luke's."

"You aren't mad?" he asked, glancing up to me.

"I don't know you well enough to be too pissed. You probably thought you were doing right. Or had to do it. Or you didn't give a shit for anyone but you and the person you're protecting. Anyway, I can't say I've not done similar. Or wouldn't."

"Dark shit," he said, deadpan.

"Hopefully not. Sleep, I'm grabbing a shower."

I closed the bathroom door, pushing myself back into the solidness of the wood. Dex had been in my room. It wasn't really Dex, it was some projected shadow puppet coming from a possessed Marc. But it had been in my room, talking to me. And offering to do more than talk. I shuddered at the idea and moved to turning the water on, hoping it would shift the sickly feeling clinging to my skin. I stripped and stepped under the stream, trying to rationalise the conversation.

Nigel, second in command, had tried to circumvent things by having me killed. He was short sighted if he thought asking Dex was enough for that, but maybe he didn't have the same direct line I had. They were expecting Marc but not me. I could shield myself and have a root about the place. If I found anything new, it would be worth it. I wondered how I'd explain the late-night excursion to Luke. It wasn't exactly date material. I'd tell him the truth and see what he wanted to do. He could decide himself.

I finished my shower and towelled off, wrapping myself up before padding back into the bedroom. Marc was lying on his stomach, staring over to the far wall like it might explain something.

"You alright?" I asked, gathering my clothes.

"Just trying to put my memory back together," he said, sounding far away.

"Not had that happen before, I take it?"

"What do you think?"

"Dex was very blasé about it. I didn't know if that was because it happens often or if it's just like that. It's always like that with me at least."

"Why do you keep calling it an *it*? Felt male," he said, wiping his hands over his face.

"It's never told me what it would be, and I don't have enough knowledge to attach a gender."

"Fair enough. Still felt like a he. A horrifying he."

"Could you see what was going on? It looked like you were pretty vacant."

"It was like being frozen. I don't know how I got here, but I was aware of things once you arrived. It was like they were taking forever to happen though. I could feel your skin when he put my hand on your neck. I didn't move to massage your neck, but I couldn't stop it from happening. It was worse when it was like that, with that bubble or whatever stripped away. Makes me want to be sick."

"Sounds like shit, too," I said, buttoning up my shirt. "I'd recommend not dwelling on it. Your head's messed up enough without trying to unscramble things. Sleep and have a drink when you go see Alex. You'll feel better being around her. She's chill."

"That sounds about right, yeah," he said. He shrugged off his top and bundled himself under the cover. "This is weird."

"Dude, you being in my bed is nothing like the weirdest thing that's happened to you in the last hour."

"You might have a point there," he said, head going under the covers too. I shut the curtains and logged out of Sarah's laptop then ordered a taxi. I was going to know the drivers like friends by the end of this search.

"Give me a message when you're heading out," I reminded him. "Where are we meeting them?"

"That church. They want to get it ready, so they're spending as much time there as they can."

"Awesome. See you later," I said, closing the door. I went down the steps and stopped at the front desk. "Sorry if there was any disturbance earlier. My friend was watching football and got a bit animated."

"No problem, Mr. Brooks. We didn't have any complaints," the man said with a nod and I left, lurking outside for my taxi.

It was a swift trip to Luke's house, and I was early. Not a great look.

I walked up the short steps and glanced to either side of me. Identical houses ran each way, all neat and well cared for. A long fenced-in garden ran down the middle of the area, thick with hedges on one side. Who didn't love a private garden?

Standing in front of the door, my stomach twisted itself into a knot. I tried to look normal, waited until it turned seven, then knocked on the door, cursing at being overeager. It opened to reveal Luke in an almost casual ensemble, work trousers and a heavy cotton shirt that tapered to his form.

"Carter, I'm pleased you're punctual." He grinned, spreading an arm to encourage me through the door.

"Sorry about that. Too keen," I said, stepping into the house.

"Not at all. I value people showing up just when I want them to."

I glanced around for coat hooks and took in the hallway. The house was spacious as a gallery, all high ceilings and statement art pieces. The walls were deep green, almost like the ocean, with bold sculptures and intricate hangings disturbing the colour.

"I hadn't realised you liked art so much," I said as he took my jacket and hooked it over a tall rack, crooked in behind the door. Clever.

"I think it's good for the soul to see emotions represented in the physical world."

"That extend to books, too? Alex said you liked poetry."

"I adore poetry. It is both serious and fun. Come, I'll take you through to the sitting room. Dinner is in the oven."

"Should I ask?"

"And spoil the surprise?"

"Would hate to do that." I nodded, following him through to an imposing sitting room. The colours were subtler, autumn tones accented with orange and mustard yellow. A deep-set leviathan of a couch dominated the room, with a large rug that reminded me of the old markets in Manchester splayed before a fire which crackled away in the tiled fireplace.

"Would you care for a drink?" Luke asked, gesturing for me to sit. I opted for a corner seat and nodded.

"What are you having?" I asked in turn.

"I prefer red wine, but I have beer or whisky."

"No gin? I thought that was a lawyer's staple."

"For the ladies of my profession, I tend to go for the smokier option," he said with a conspirator's wink. I laughed lightly, his enthusiasm infectious.

"Wine would be lovely, thanks."

"As you wish." He vanished down the hallway, and I checked over the room again. There were a lot of books. One of the longer walls was lined with bookshelves which brimmed over. I couldn't spot a TV or computer though, nothing for studying or working. A room for entertainment then.

"Here you are." His voice brought me out of my musings. I took the glass from him with a tight smile. He leaned in to peck his lips to mine before scooping my bag from my lap and over the side of the couch. "I'm sure this can wait beside us rather than between us."

"It can, but I need to have a word with you about that," I said, sheepish and tired from the breakneck speed of the day.

"Are you alright?" he asked, his brows drawing down.

"Yes. Well, no. Marc showed up in my room possessed by Dex. He's kinda freaking out about it, and I wasn't over the moon with it either. And I have to go spy on a cult at eleven tonight. Things got really complicated this afternoon." I stopped for breath.

He put a hand over mine, staring at me. "Carter, stop. Tell me from the beginning."

"Right. I need that." I pointed to the bag. Luke passed it to me, a quizzical look following as he sat down. "Someone left this for me a day or so ago," I said, pulling out the envelope with my name on it and passed it over, flap open. "Try not to touch it."

"Why not?"

"This is the one I told you about at the party. It's cursed."

"Excuse me?" his head snapped up to meet my eyes.

"Watch." I grabbed Lou's gift and picked the jewellery up, the material flaring up like magnesium. "It was worse before. The first time I touched the bracelet, I thought this stuff was on fire."

"When you mentioned this, I assumed you meant ill intent, not an actual curse. And you have a fairy protection charm. What have you been doing?"

"Looking for Sarah." It was true.

"In all the worst places."

Ha! "I got a fairy charm. Seems pretty good to me."

"This isn't funny. The curse on this is a sophisticated bit of work," he said as he passed a hand over it.

"I figured with the whole burning up thing, it might be bad."

"You're awfully calm about this."

"Dex was in my room on top of Marc like a puppet. Most other things are pretty far removed from that," I said dully.

"Can you explain that to me?" Luke asked, face baffled.

"I went back to my room after working with Alex this afternoon. We'd been busy, getting stuff set up for tomorrow."

"What about tomorrow?" he asked, sipping his drink and tucking the bracelet under a cushion.

"That should be when Sarah comes back. Alex has arranged your group to get together to search for Sarah, and I asked Marc to set me up with the cult he knows."

"Marcus is foolish for agreeing. They're dangerous."

"Yeah, Sarah's hiding from them."

"You're sure?" he asked, sitting forward to keep my gaze.

"They were going to hurt her."

"I don't see why they'd do that." Luke frowned again, moving back so he was angled to face me on the cushion.

"Because they want to sacrifice her to Dex," I replied.

"Excuse me?"

"You heard," I said, taking a sip of my drink.

"I know this group is considered dangerous, but do you really think…" He trailed off, face grim.

"Dex confirmed it."

"You've been speaking to this entity a lot, are you sure it's not simply manipulating you?"

"Pretty certain. I got it from a good source."

"Who?"

"The Collector. Turns out he's a demon who trades stuff. Still around. Very nice, if a little nerve frying."

"How do you know he's a demon?" Luke asked, glass frozen part way to his mouth.

"I could see it."

"I'm sorry, what? That would surely kill you."

"Thought he would when he touched me. Anyway, he's not the point. I asked Marc to get this meeting set up while Alex and I did other stuff. We got what we could, I went back to the guesthouse to get changed for coming to see you." I paused, running through the afternoon in my head.

"Go on," Luke pushed, placing a hand on my knee.

"I got to my room, and I could feel Dex. It started talking. Marc was there, but Dex was possessing him. It was like Marc had another person set on top of him, extended out. Dex was wearing your face, but it looked different."

"My face?"

"It started doing that after we slept together. It's a bit weird."

"Certainly," he said, paling.

"And it taunted me for a bit. Made Marc stroke my neck. I didn't like that. Then it left, and Marc freaked out. Now he's sleeping it off in my bed. He's meeting the cult at eleven, thinks I should go too, do some recon ahead of meeting them tomorrow."

"Did Dex say why it had visited you like that?"

"Yeah. Someone in the cult had asked it to kill me."

"Excuse me?"

"You're excused."

"This is not the time to joke, Carter." Luke bristled, anger spiking off him. "Someone has invoked a very strong and dangerous creature to kill you."

"And it said no."

"It said no?"

"Repeating me doesn't get you more information," I said, sipping more wine. "It talked to me about that and agreed that killing me was far too a menial task."

"You had a conversation with Dex about it killing you, and it did not do so."

"Not unless I'm a really insistent ghost."

"Do you understand how much danger you're in? You're far too flippant about this," Luke said, moving his hand to my chin and tilting my head so I met his gaze.

"I'm more worried about Marc. He got made into a meat puppet," I said, liking the warmth of his fingers against my skin. He let his hand fall away as he swirled his glass, humming.

"That is unfortunate. Did he say how this came about?"

"Marc got used because he could come into my room."

"He could?"

I felt a bristle of something other than anger at that. "The front desk thought he worked with me. He dropped off the cursed bracelet."

"But why?"

"Because he got asked to. He didn't say who asked and he was too fucked up for me to push him."

"That's kinder than many would be," Luke said, pursing his lips.

"Dude isn't having a good day. But he set up the meeting, so I'm going along to lurk and see if I can get anything useful."

"And you're still attending said meeting after they have tried to have you killed?"

"Only one of them tried to have me killed. Dex even told me which one it was."

"Of course it did. Why wouldn't it do that? It's sharing everything with you." Luke sighed, almost theatrically, glancing over to the fireplace.

"It's weird," I said, nodding a little.

"I'll be attending with you."

"That's dangerous." I said, twisting to look at him.

"No more dangerous than it will be for you. I'm at least used to the city."

"It's a bit out of the city, at an old church. I think you know it. Blantyre? Sarah had a sketch of it from you."

"Fitting," Luke sniffed, unimpressed. "That's no matter. We can take my car. We have plenty of time to have dinner and attend to other matters."

"Other matters?" I was surprised to find him leaning in, his lips brushing against my neck.

"Indeed," he said, planting little kisses along my jugular. "I think you'll need something to help shift such gruesome events from your mind."

"You're back to offering your unprofessional opinion?" I asked, leaning into the contact. It flooded me with sensation, and I felt the languid heat pooling low in my gut. He plucked the wine glass from my hand and set it down beside the couch.

"It sounds like you have had a simply exhausting day." Luke grinned, mouthing lower towards the marks he'd left the night before. "It only seems fair you get some goodness in as well."

He straddled my legs, continuing to nip and suck at my neck as he rested his hands on my chest. I let my head fall to the side as he reworked the marks, teasing an edge of teeth against the bruises.

"This's unfair to you," I said, arching my back as he moved one hand lower, stroking firmly against my stomach and resting at my hip. "Wouldn't you prefer some reciprocity?"

"I'm sure we can catch up with that after this ill-advised meeting," he whispered in my ear, his hand moving to open my zipper and grip my hardening cock. I moaned low as he pulled it free of my underwear and squeezed, moving his hand slowly upwards.

"That'll be awful late if we're seeing them at eleven," I said, my hips gently rocking into his grip.

"That is no trouble. My bed is large enough to share."

"Two nights in a row?"

"Unless you'd prefer to return to the guesthouse. I promise, my breakfasts are better." He punctuated the promise with a nip of my earlobe, and I groaned. Luke took advantage and moved to kiss me, slipping his tongue into my mouth and stealing a lick along my lower lip.

"If it's not weird for you, I'd be okay with that," I said when we parted. He twisted his wrist at my tip and I whimpered, my hips stuttering as it sent a shot of pleasure deep into me.

"You make the nicest noises for me, Carter," he purred, moving back to peck kisses along my jaw line.

"You keep doing what you're doing and I'm going to keep making those noises," I said, panting as he sped up against me.

"I have every intention of making sure of it." He chuckled, pushing his own hardness against me as he continued his pace. My hands came up to his shoulders, moving along to the nape of his neck to grip his hair.

"Luke, you're going to push me over the edge," I gasped, arching into his touch. I could feel the skirting of his power against me and was confused but infinitely too distracted to question it, my eyes closing as he kept moving. I was wound up to burst and felt my body tense before I came hard, gasping against Luke. He hummed his approval, leaning back enough to pluck a handkerchief from somewhere and wipe himself off.

"There's a bathroom at the top of the stairs to freshen up. It'll be around fifteen minutes 'til our meal, if you'd like to look over the documents I mentioned?"

"That would be good," I confirmed, my heart rate thudding back to normal. My head still rested against his shoulder, and I felt him running his fingers through my hair. "That's nice," I murmured, hazy and tired from his ministrations.

"I'd be happy to do it longer, but you might object to wasting what little time there is. We'll have to take our jaunt to spy on strange and violent men."

"You make a good point," I conceded, content and boneless.

"I'll fill up your wine and have the papers ready for your return," he promised, disentangling from me and moving off into the hallway.

# Chapter 23

<u>6 November, 1887</u>

*My choices confound me. I have before me the opportunity to approach a being greater than I in every sense I can conceive, and which must without doubt hold the key to achieving my desires. To set the world to order, to ensure the wheels of power turn in such a way as to benefit those around me, and not only when it favours the landed, or financiers, or business holders. Such an endeavour must be worthy.*

*Yet the cost is such that I balk, turned away from my training with nerves that befit some weeping child rather than a student of law. What an example I present, ashen and sweating as I consider whether I should take action that would grant me the abilities I claim to aspire towards.*

*I have no way to verify that which I have been able to parse out from my limited contact with the being. After my investigation with St. Mungo's Well, I am certain the contact was true. My friend was entirely accurate when he warned me of the greater powers, their ability to slip between the cracks once they know of you. I have not visited him in some days, distracted as I was with my consternations. I must go to him and ascertain if he has any dealings with this creature. His counsel is heartening even in troubled times. I should not have reacted so poorly.*

*The name of this being strikes me as false. I cannot find a Dex or similar discussed in any of the more recent correspondence as to the presences within the city. I do not believe matters will have developed so quickly as for a god to manifest purely around the maelstrom of cultures we now see in the area. This one strikes me as more ancient than that.*

*I will endeavour to visit my friend swiftly. Matters may be more discernible after his assistance.*

I padded up the stairs, spotting the bathroom. A high-sided tub glistened under the window with a corner shower stood beside it. The colours were darker than I expected, the floor raw slate and the walls a deep teal. The sink was in front of a large mirror, well-lit like a vanity.

I was still lazy and warm from my orgasm as I washed, using the soap I'd found. I finished up and came back downstairs to find Luke placing bits and pieces on a table in the room.

"These your findings?" I asked, moving to stand beside him.

"Yes. I've got what I can from the records I can access. There's been one iteration or another of this group for at least the last hundred and fifty years. They were known for human sacrifice but moved more into exploitation and extortion in the early twentieth century."

"A bunch of swell chaps."

"Indeed. They were thought to be dying out, but with this recent activity and what you've revealed about their intentions for Sarah, I suspect they simply got better at hiding."

"Yeah, I think they just blended in more," I said, flicking through the papers.

"Is there a particular reason we're going to that church?"

"They do their rituals there. The guide mentions something about them using the fire to prepare the place, flood it with energy."

"An old-fashioned method, unlikely to still be used. Arson investigation is much more sophisticated now."

"That's a good point." I pursed my lips and thought of Jenna's comments. "What would you use energy like that to do?"

"If it were a matter of simply taking advantage of a large amount of energy, that's easy. It can be redirected into healing rituals, sent out into the universe, poured towards someone who needs the spiritual boost, reinforce psychic barriers. Our group often does that with energy after works. It's allocated out as needed. Using destruction or a large volume of elemental energy is different. It's raw and base."

"Mopping up scraps versus trying to direct a river?"

"Something like that, yes." Luke smiled, pleased with my understanding. "It feels unwise to meet them on their home ground, but I am sure there is a reason." He raised his eyes to meet mine.

"The place hates them. Too much blood and fear," I replied, my mind going back to Tobias.

"An interesting approach. Who recommended that?" His tone was light, but I saw tension creep into his posture I hadn't noticed earlier. Was he jealous?

"A fallen angel who felt like chatting."

"At the risk of sounding deaf, please repeat that."

"A fallen angel who felt like chatting."

"You were speaking to a fallen one and didn't have your eyes melted out?"

"Dex offered to do that. As well as sexually assault me. It's been a weird day."

"Undoubtedly. How did you find a fallen one?"

"That book has all sorts of information. Me and Alex have been looking through it for spots to find Sarah. Turns out one of them included the location of a fallen angel." It was mostly true. I didn't get the impression Faith or Tobias would appreciate a name check.

"You must be exhausted," he said, cupping my cheek.

"I hadn't noticed it until I got here, but yes," I conceded, smiling at him.

"Read these and I'll check on our meal. I should be serving shortly, then we can relax over the food."

"That sounds good," I said, moving to let him past.

I looked at the papers he had spread out, copies from handwritten books and newspaper clippings, interspaced with his own notes. The oldest were from the early 1870s, comments about dock workers going missing, market stall helpers vanishing on the way home. There were gaps, sometimes close to two decades and sometimes only a couple of years. Luke's notes made mention of gang wars and bloodshed, a reduction in sacrifice due to natural violence. This was mirrored in the world wars though people still went missing even then.

These changed into stories about families progressing in the city, fortunate land acquisitions, unexpected voting results, business start-ups flying when they should have sunk. He called it a legitimisation of assets, a way to use Dex to get power and attention without question.

"Enjoying the reading?" I heard behind me and turned to see Luke leaned against the door frame. It was an oddly relaxed stance for him, one foot cocked up behind the other and his arms crossed. It reminded me of a tarot card, one I'd seen a lot at fairs and carnivals.

"Pretty ominous."

"Human sacrifice is such a tricky business. Ancient beings like Dex don't really benefit from the life that is lost."

"No. They get the spirit."

"Indeed," Luke said with an upset frown. "Dex shared this with you, too?"

"Felt I should know what would happen to Sarah if the cult found her before me." Again, not quite true, but close enough.

"Carter, I do wish you'd told me this earlier. It must have been so difficult for you."

"At this point it's all starting to blur together." I shrugged, blinking back the hotness creeping at the edges of my eyes.

"But to have such a creature become so intimate with you, it must be wearing."

"We're not intimate yet. I said no to the offers." I laughed, trying to break some of the tension. "It's nothing compared to what Sarah's going through."

"You shouldn't dismiss your own suffering because they're less than someone else's," Luke said, moving in front of me. "I worry this matter will have unforeseen effects on you."

"What's a little PTSD among siblings?" I joked, not able force a laugh this time.

"I have two siblings and wouldn't suffer such things for either of them." He sniffed, stroking his hands along my shoulders and down my arms. "I worry you devalue yourself."

"Don't worry. I know I'm worth it." I grinned, gripping his hands as they moved to join with mine. I'd been left with no doubt as to how much I was worth in this whole fucking endeavour.

"Good. If you go through to the dining room, I'll serve." He pointed to one of the doors off the hallway, and I went into the dimly lit space.

It was all mismatched lamps and fat cream candles that flickered with multiple wicks. A large pair of windows illuminated the far end, a thin, almost sheer curtain over them and the orange light of streetlamps diffused by blue drapes. The walls were a forest green, not dark enough to be gloomy but almost changing in the light. It felt like a cross between a parlour and a theatre, the same muffling of the world outside.

I saw two place settings laid out across from one another and dithered, unsure where I should sit. I was about to turn around and collect my wine when Luke came in with two large plates.

"If you'd like to sit on the left-hand side?" Luke asked, setting the plates down.

"Of course, thank you." I grinned, trying to discern what we were eating.

"Mushroom and spinach stuffed ox heart with carrot batons and a potato puree with fresh pea and mint."

"That's a lot of effort," I said, eyes wide.

"I take great pride in my cooking."

"I don't think I've ever had ox heart before," I said, examining the large parcel of meat in front of me. It was one half of the heart, the corresponding part on Luke's plate, and the stuffing spilled out.

"A shared heart is quite an undertaking," Luke said with a raised brow.

"I imagine so. Look how much there is to get through," I replied, watching the man's face. It was far too early for such obvious allegories, so I wasn't going to imagine this was him declaring love.

"Hearts carry much symbolism, but I've more of an interest in them anatomically. They're the hardest working muscle in the body but so often discarded as offal," Luke said.

"They bear the same fate physically as emotionally." I sliced off a part of the dark meat. It revealed a warm pink interior, the texture like steak. "This is delicious."

"Thank you. I hoped you would enjoy. Many people turn their nose up given the associations, but it was popular historically."

"I think there's a snobbery in turning your nose up at heart," I said, savouring the taste. "Are we sharing a heart because oxen are so large or is this a different type of undertaking?"

"I'll admit there's a temptation in saying it's to cement an intention at further courtship, but I think that would be a bit schoolboy. How about an invitation for future discussion?"

"I'm happy with that, on the proviso that I'm not likely to be staying in Glasgow. Once I find Sarah, I'm out of here."

"I'm sure Sarah will need time to recuperate. That's better done elsewhere." His expression was unreadable, almost as blank as Marc's had been.

"Can't blame her," I said with a nod. "There's no other symbolism in eating a broken heart the day before Halloween?"

"Does it count as broken when it's deliberately severed?" Luke asked with an amused smile.

"Does intent change the result? The heart's still in half. Is it important how it came to be on separate plates?"

"An interesting debate—would it matter to the ox? Perhaps not. The heart is still in two, as you say. The ox is still dead. Would it feel better to know its heart was sliced apart rather than torn? I suppose it depends on when the heart is taken." He smiled as he took another section into his mouth, chewing thoughtfully.

"An appropriate consideration for Halloween when everything is obscured with masks and tricks. Intent verses result, which matters more?"

"Which matters more to you, Carter?" There was a sparkle to Luke's eyes now, a teasing amusement that begged to be pushed.

"I'm results focused. I'm usually more concerned with getting what I need done rather than how I'm going to do it."

"An ambitious young man with a willingness to get what he needs?"

"That's a flattering way of saying I'm an asshole." I laughed, shaking my head.

"Possibly, but then it is good to see someone who's honest about their outlook. Many people are the opposite." An almost innocent arch of the eyebrow again.

"Lies and smiles your usual fare?" I asked, cocking my head.

"Something like that. People hide behind masks and complicate matters. It's so much easier when you can get to the point of a thing."

"That can be dangerous though. It puts people on edge. Edges are awful sharp," I said, finishing the meat on my plate.

"Alas, true. Do you wish to talk about the meeting, or would you rather continue our philosophical discussion? I have dessert prepared, but we may have to save that for after we return."

"Do I get to know what dessert is?" I asked, setting my cutlery down.

"Chocolate and rose tart. I would offer an evening brandy, but that'll have to wait too."

"You still want me to come back after going spying?"

"Of course. It'll be exhilarating if nothing else, and it's a shame to abandon the whole evening when I may not be seeing you for a while."

"I'm pleased you think we're going to find Sarah tomorrow as well," I said, following him into the kitchen as he took the plates away. Like the rest of the house it was impressive with bright lighting showing off the space. It reminded me of a hotel, industrial steel and sleek counter tops.

"I've no doubt of it," Luke said, setting the plates into the sink. "You and Alex have worked incredibly hard."

"I'm annoyed we didn't realise it sooner. We could have spent longer looking for where she is."

"I don't think anyone had expected Sarah to take such extreme steps. I do wish she had spoken to me about it."

"She was worried about someone in the group. She probably didn't want to say anything to you until she got confirmation. I mean, we don't even know who it is, just that someone was at the party."

"It is troubling." Luke said. "We should set off now. We don't want to be late."

I shouldn't have been surprised Luke's car was as fancy as his cooking, but it was impressive to see. It was a Rolls, a Phantom he informed me in passing.

"Company car?" I asked as we buckled in.

"No, my personal preference."

"Your preference is a Rolls-Royce?"

"I believe in having the best of what I want," he said with a grin.

"And leading a spiritual class ties into that how?"

"It lets me give back, assist others in their growth and discovery. It's a pleasant way to help the world."

"An altruistic educator."

"Aren't most?" he asked, glancing over.

"Can't speak for them all but most of mine were only altruistic to their pensions."

"It's sad to see such cynicism in one so young."

"I'm not that young. Late twenties," I said, batting his shoulder.

"My apologies. One younger than me."

"It's the generational thing. We're doomed."

"Surely you're not so acceptant of that?"

We were moving smoothly through the city, the lights bright enough to show the passengers of any passing cars. It was a false sun colour, the saturation of the light all wrong. There weren't many others on the road except delivery cars and taxis.

"I've never thought of myself as that, no. I suppose it's a natural protective mechanism, fatalism to prevent becoming uninspired."

"Better to be cynical and proved right than positive and proved wrong?"

"Something like that," I said.

"Do you feel Sarah shares that view?"

"She hid in an interdimensional space, Luke. I'd say that's pretty deep in line with it."

"I suppose that's a fair assessment," he said with a snort.

"Do you know who it is, in your group?" I asked, hoping to change the subject. The inside of the car was plush and warm and lulling me into relaxation despite the thrum of adrenaline in my veins.

"I've precious few ideas. The group's been established for many years. Members come and go, but we're careful with whom we invite. It would be upsetting if it were someone who was with us from the beginning. I'd feel better if it was a sign of my judgement flagging rather than someone so good that they've fooled us all along."

"I wonder what tipped Sarah off about them."

"A good point. And where she found that guide. Where is that, by the way?"

"With Alex. She's looking for other spots we can search tomorrow."

"Dedicated as ever." He smiled at that, almost seeming like he was enjoying himself. I suppose that was what you got when you drove a Rolls.

"How'd you learn about the cult?" I asked, glancing over at him.

"It's hard not to hear of them. They're secretive, but they have to look for new talent. Much has been written about them tempting talented practitioners"

"Like vultures," I said.

"More aggressive. They use people up, unless there's someone unusual. Interesting individuals might be invited to join the cult. Dex is not alone. There are other beings that wish to be served. My understanding is that Dex is geographically fixed. He can't go far beyond Glasgow."

"I wonder why that is?"

"It could be the spiritual nature of the city making it easier for him to push through here. It could be he's bound here."

"Can the others move?"

"It appears so, though I must confess I've never attempted to find out."

"Can't blame you if it's anything like talking to Dex," I said, shaking my head.

"It takes a toll?"

"It's been getting easier. Less vomiting afterwards at least."

"How do you feel about that?"

"I've been trying not to think about it too much," I said, setting my head back against the seat.

"It may be helpful to discuss it."

"I can do that after things are finished." I shrugged.

"I suppose so." Luke said, and I could hear the smile. Tendrils of anticipation were creeping up my back at the thought of seeing the cult, despite the comfort of the car. I thought of the knife in my pocket, the promise of aggression and instability. That had to help, right?

"Can you think of anything I should keep an eye out for with these guys?" I asked, trying to refocus my mind.

"This is recognisance, so I'd suggest keeping ourselves quiet and watching them."

"I hope we find out which one is Nigel," I said, spite curling in my chest.

"Why?"

"He's the one who asked Dex to kill me. A bit of a poor request. It's like asking the cat to open the tin."

"What a curious analogy. Do you picture Dex without thumbs?"

"More like the type of creature to push things off countertops and stare at you while it happens."

"Try not to worry too much, Carter. The meeting tomorrow will be more important. This is to see if we can garner anything helpful."

"You're right. I just feel like we're ill prepared for a cult. A few random psychos, yes. But cults are trickier. Though at least I know there are a bunch of beings in the city who would help Sarah."

"Just for Sarah?"

"What do you mean?" I asked, glancing over to him as he watched the road.

"You've made a few friends despite your blunt manner. Maybe some of them would be willing to assist you, rather than Sarah?"

"They've only known me a few days. I'm pretty sure it's for Sarah's benefit rather than mine."

"Would you be surprised if they wished to help you?"

"They don't owe me anything. Rather the opposite."

"That sounds unfortunate."

"Most of what I've done has been trades. One's me owing someone a favour. That'll probably come back to bite me, maybe literally. But not too soon."

"What did you do?"

"I owe a favour to a bar owner."

"Which bar owner?"

"A woman in the West End. Nice Greek lady."

"You made a deal with the maenads?" He turned to look at me, a mix of disbelief and admiration on his face.

"Watch the damn road. And yes, them."

"You understand that they eat people?" he asked, face back to where it should be.

"Traditionally."

"Have you volunteered a limb or are they going to choose a muscle later?"

"I don't think they're going to eat me in that sense—they have plenty of pickings in the city. My other talents are more useful." I hope.

"That's either brave or foolish."

"So's going to spy on a cult."

"At least the cult meeting is somewhat organised. Do you expect the wild women to be the same?"

"It's pretty organised in the bar."

"I suppose so," he said, nodding. "You've gotten yourself quite involved in the city for someone so opposed to it."

"I'm not opposed to the city. It's nice. More than nice."

"I thought you hated it?"

"I did when I first got here. It reminded me too much of Manchester without being there. It was like walking around in the dream of a city. That on top of no routine, the constant noise, it was too much. But the beings I've met are interesting. Some of them make me concerned for my continued sanity or what I'm attracted to, but that's normal I reckon."

"Question what you find attractive?"

"Met a succubus—she was hot but had hoof feet. That's a weird boner for anyone."

"I've never met one. I can see how that would be a cause for concern, though."

"Never met one?" I asked, my head turning to him now.

"No, I've never had the company. At least not that they've let me be aware of."

"I would have expected you'd encounter some with the nature of your practice." And the fact they know who you are and what you do.

"They may have met me, but I've not known it. That would upset me, as I'd like to discuss things with them."

"Compare notes?"

"Something like that, yes." He chuckled, moving his hand from the gear stick to stroke along my knee and thigh. "How are you feeling?"

"I'm alright," I said, raising the best smile I could.

"Good. We're almost there. I know the area from work. If things are still as they were, we should be able to park a little way off and approach the church by coming around the back of a funeral parlour then over the rear fence."

"A funeral parlour?"

"Not the most inspirational location, I suppose. Sorry," he said.

"I shouldn't be surprised." I shrugged. I couldn't find it in myself to be upset.

"Here we are."

Luke pulled us into a deserted Asda car park. There was patchy lighting from the over head lampposts, but the sea of tarmac was shadowed. I wouldn't have been surprised to see some phantom figure lurking under the sodium bulbs.

"It doesn't look a bit conspicuous leaving this in an empty car park?" I asked as we got out.

"No more suspicious than parking close to the funeral parlour," Luke said. He moved around the car and took me by the shoulders, staring hard at me. "Carter, I want you to be careful with this. You'll want to take advantage of the element of surprise, or help Marcus should something happen, but it's imperative you don't let them know you're here. I'll have to do the same, and I appreciate this might be hard for us. Please be safe."

"No problem," I said, nodding.

"I'm serious. You cannot help Sarah if you get killed tonight."

"I hear you," I said, putting a hand to his arm.

"Right. Follow me."

# Chapter 24

<u>5 September, 1886</u>

*There is to be a hanging today. My tutor believes we should attend to see it, so we know the cost of the justice we intend to practice. He wishes us to see the length of our knowledge is no better than the length of the hangman's noose. As if we do not know the cost after our studies and living in the boroughs we belong to. As if hangings and worse are not following us when we journey home or to our apprenticeships.*

*It is pathetic showmanship and below an educator to encourage such ghoulish tourism. I find my view of my tutor tarnished by it, though maybe it is for the benefit of others in the group more than myself. I have no shortage of knowledge they do not yet possess.*

*It is open for me to attend with them. I may visit it to watch the crowd. Death is such a curious challenge to those of us with plans and power, an inevitability to the termination of our intentions. Not so for them. It is simply a bit of entertainment. I do not begrudge the hangman his work. Even the executioner must eat.*

*Maybe there will be a member of Mr. Christie's family there, ready to whisk the body off to be shared as a meal. A poor soul for a meal, whoever our condemned man is. The goal does not tend to fatten one, in the usual circumstances.*

*Yes, a trip to see the people and observe what reaction my fellow students give to the drop. That would be worthy of the effort.*

He strode off into the darkness. I started after him, matching his pace. We probably looked like an odd pair, Luke in a winter coat that cost more than I really wanted to think about, and me in my old jacket. I glanced over to him, his profile highlighted as we passed under streetlights.

"What are you thinking?" he asked.

"I'm thinking we look a little weird walking along here at night."

"Because we're walking at night or because we're walking together?"

"A bit of both."

"Do you think we make a nice couple?"

"That's hardly a conversation for now."

"Indeed, we should focus on looking for Sarah. We're not far."

We paced through a domestic area, council houses with well-tended gardens in a well-kept neighbourhood. It was an odd area to be walking through to meet a cult. I would've been happier in the cramped darkness of the subway tunnels.

The houses were falling away, spaces between the red bricked semi-detached getting larger. Up ahead I could see a substantial sandstone building and, next to that, a grove of trees shrouded in darkness.

"Weird spot for a park," I said.

"That's not a park. That's our destination."

"What?"

"That building is the funeral parlour, and behind that is our destination."

"Why's it surrounded by trees?" I asked.

"I suppose to hide the unpleasantness of a burned-out shell?"

"They could rebuild it."

"For it to be burned down again?" he asked with an arched brow.

"Good point," I said after a beat. "So how do we get in?"

"We hop the fence at the back."

"Have you done this before?" I asked, looking at him.

"I have, to get references for my sketch. And other things similar," he said, smirking in the glare of the streetlight.

"I'm not even going to ask."

"Best," he said. Turning up his coat collar and glancing about us, he put a hand to the base of my back and ushered me forward, close to the tree line. Tall railings, black in the evening light, lined the edge. We reached the far corner and found a thinning area between the trees, the bare branches offering an archway.

"How long since you've climbed over railings?"

"Not as long as you'd expect," I said.

"Give me a boost then, if you're in practice," he said with a wink. I knelt and offered my knee for him to step up on, his hand on me for purchase. He clambered over, and I followed suit, landing amongst the dead leaves.

"You're taking to all this rather well," I commented, watching his grin.

"It's invigorating, doing a bit of field work," he replied, eyes lingering over me. "And who doesn't like the idea of being caught on a dark evening with an attractive younger man?"

"A run in with the police might be better than a run in with this lot."

"And that's why we're using the back door. Or whatever there may be."

"Fair point. Let's go."

We moved forward quiet as we could, the undergrowth giving us cover. Beyond the trees I could feel a looming space, the promise of cool air and darkness. We breached the edge and came into an open clearing, filled with high grass and the bones of the church lit by the streetlights filtered through the trees. The walls still stood, and I could see the shape still matched the drawing.

I stretched my gift out and was met with a confusing mass of information. The flood of energy soaking the area was overwhelming enough to make me flinch. Luke glanced to me, and I shrugged an apology, reigning my sense back in. Hazy lights moved inside and these became clearer as we crept forward, approaching what would have been one of the large windows at the end of a wing.

"This way," Luke whispered, guiding me to a door underneath the hollow of the window.

"Good eyes," I breathed back and he smiled, preening. He put his shoulder and hip to the door and shoved, the door springing inwards. I scrambled forward, grabbing it before it could slam. I didn't fancy our chances with the building, never mind the cult, and loud noises.

"We're late. Keep to the walls," he said, voice low and close to my ear. "I'll go on the opposite side; less likely to trip each other or fall into a common trap." I nodded, moving ahead into the welcoming shadows.

I felt my way in the half light, steps hesitant as I clung to the left-hand wall. I could hear voices milling around up ahead and slipped the knife from my jacket to the back pocket of my jeans, the top of the handle sticking out.

The gathering reminded me of my meeting with Dex at the camp fire, the flickering of a host of candles washing the ruin with a warmth that was long gone from this place. About fifteen men sat on old crates and up turned cargo boxes. Rubbish was scattered around, chairs half broken and what looked like benches in a haphazard circle. I couldn't see Marc yet so I held back in the shadows, counting my breaths and willing my heart to stay in my chest.

The men were all white, all in their late forties or early fifties, all thick set and muscled. They looked like they could move a body if required. I was working out a way to play those numbers when I felt a tug on my hand.

I froze, looking down to see a small hand pulling on mine. It was human sized, like an eight or nine-year-old's, and attached to the dark shape of a similar sized body. Its skin had the waxy smoothness of burnt flesh and rippled with a deep red shimmer, the promise of flames underneath. I tracked up to where there should have been a face and saw just a gaping, grinning crescent moon of mouth, licks of the same crimson energy spilling out. I flinched and felt it tighten the grip, surging forward to wrap its arm around me.

The fear hit me first, people screaming and weeping and railing and fighting until an inevitable end loomed, crashed, and devoured. I felt the cold, ancient hunger I assumed was Dex. Then the bright, covetous desire that could have been the infamous John or just the cult, wheeling and turning on the primeval current. I felt the heat and voracious wildness of the fire that had been here more than once, the fatal certainty of its end. And I felt a glimmer, just a touch, of the hope and honesty and devotion of the place, the prayer and penitence and faith long departed.

The fire child stepped back and looked at me with its face without eyes. I stood stock still, trying not to pass out from the aftershocks of the overwhelming creature in front of me. This was worse than the fallen angel. It still held my hand and tugged again, pulling me back into the darker shadows.

"This way," it said in a voice that was fire and destruction.

"What the shit are you?" I managed in a choked whisper, helpless to do anything but follow it.

"I'm what is left. I hate them." The voice was all wrong, too deep to come from such a small body, a mix of popping wood and screaming flames.

"Can't they hear you?" I asked, glancing back towards the light I'd now abandoned.

"No. Only you."

"Oh. Great," I mouthed, creeping along after it.

"Here." It pointed to a door in the wall I'd crept past, the wood warped and blackened.

"The door?" My head was going to explode with this.

"Her door." I heard what was recognisable as pride in that cacophony of a voice this time.

"What?"

"Your door to her. Go, now. They will see soon."

"See you or the door?"

"The door. They never see me." Pride was there again in that voice, and I was too scared to figure out why. I looked the door over. This could all be a trap. This little fire child could be Dex, or one of his minions. It could be a waste of time, and I was missing Marc and his meeting with the cult. "Now," the fire child insisted.

I cupped the handle and found it burning to the touch, biting my lip to stifle a yelp as I yanked my hand away. I shucked my jacket over my palm and took it again, gripping hard and pushing into it, my shoulder to the warm wood. It opened, to my surprise, and I half toppled into a huge stone walled corridor. Heat and light poured out like the stones were molten, oppressive and brighter than my eyes could handle. I jumped back, closing the door, and felt the fire child by my side, its grin wider than should be possible, hands reaching for the door.

"You need to get her, quick," it said, hovering at the edge of the threshold and basking in the residual heat. "She knew you would come."

"I swear to anything listening, if my sister isn't in here, I will come back and find a way to tear you apart," I said through gritted teeth, steeling myself.

"I would appreciate your attempts. I am the suffering of a hundred and fifty years. To be torn apart would be peace."

"Oh fuck this whole place," I sighed, squaring my shoulders.

I opened the door and stepped through, pushing it closed behind me. The hallway was hideously bright, like standing in the desert, and I had to heft my jacket over my head to protect my eyes.

It was just taller than I was and long, the thick stones stretching off beyond what I could trace. They looked like sandstone maybe, the glare of them blinding. I stepped forward, panting in the heat as I went. I glanced behind me, irrationally terrified of what I might see. The door remained in place, the same blackened and warped wood smearing the bright corridor. The handle glowed red hot, but other than that, it was identical to in the church. I nodded and looked forward, taking a deep breath that burned.

"Sarah!" I bellowed, turning my head both ways along the corridor. Hopefully nothing here was hostile. The fire child didn't mention anything.

I heard a hollow clang in response, along the way I was walking. I broke into a jog, the same clang ringing twice as I moved forward, until the door was a black speck in the inferno of this place. I was worrying my legs would cut out from under me when I found a black tent pitched in the middle of the corridor, the clang coming from inside it. It was a sturdy thing, the thick black material spread far enough back to let someone stretch out.

"Sarah?" I called and heard the zipper being scratched at, the long pull of it opening. A hand pushed out of it, a metal bowl in its white-knuckled grip. The bowl dropped; the clang of it echoing off the walls and trilling as it circled to a stop.

The hand planted beside it and carefully, agonisingly, the flap was pulled back. Sarah sat inside, her hair straggly and thick with grease, clothes stained with sweat and dirt. She wore loose trousers rolled up to her knees and a tank top, looped through to expose her stomach. Her face was haggard, dirt stained and pinched against her movements.

"Carter?" she asked, squinting out at me.

"Holy fuck! It's you!" I ran towards her, knocking the bowl out of the way, dropping to my knees and lunging into the tent. We clung onto each other, and I was panicked by how much thinner she felt but grateful to have her again, to feel her tremble and shake against me. "I knew you'd be somewhere clever."

"I don't know how clever hiding here was," she choked, sobbing a little. "I was so scared you wouldn't make it. I was so scared they'd find you instead."

"The cult? They're here, but they don't know you are. We're going to get you out, and we're going to go back to the flat so you can get what you need. Then we're going to Manchester and killing anyone that follows us."

"Promise?"

"You know I'm smart enough to hide a body." I laughed, tears in my eyes as I gripped onto her.

"Do you know what they want?"

"They want to feed you to Dex. It doesn't particularly want you, turns out."

"What?" she flinched back, shoulders bunching round.

"Seriously, it's philosophical about this. Impressed with your skills."

"How do you know that?" she asked, voice wavering.

"I've been talking to it. It wanted me. Offered to swap me for your safe passage out of here."

She frowned, coming forward and out of the tent. "I didn't need it. I had my plan. We need to go."

"I'm with you one hundred percent on that, girly." I smiled, not caring about the heat or oppressive light now that I could see her. She was thin and half wild in the eyes, but she was certainly Sarah. "You okay?"

"No," she said, rolling her neck and shoulders.

"That's fair. It's dark and cold outside the door. Do you want my jacket?"

"Open my pack. There's a jacket in there."

I leaned into the tent and pulled out a biker jacket, the leather tacky with the heat. I passed it to her, and she shook it out, holding it up to shield herself.

"Come on." I grinned, joy bubbling up at being able to touch her arm and guide her along the torturous corridor.

"I wasn't sure how the way out would form. In some places it's a door. In others it's a tear in the world. With some it's almost like a person."

"Like at the church."

"You're using your powers?" she asked, head twitching over to me.

"That's how I found you. Met the dancer and the shop keeper and even The Collector."

"And you saw them?"

"Yeah. Had a massive freak out at the poor shop keeper. His wife was very disapproving. He liked you though. Alex wasn't very impressed."

"She's been helping?" Sarah's voice was tight.

"Yes. She knows about my stuff. Didn't like me to begin with. I think we're cool now."

"I wanted to keep her away from it."

"She knows about the cult but not about this. Or about me meeting them."

"You didn't know I was here," she said, shaking her head a little.

"No. I think Tobias maybe did."

"Tobias?"

"The other angel. The male one."

"I only met Faith. I like it that way. There's so much wrong that happened, Carter. We were so blind about it. All the time I've been here, he's been at the group. No one suspected."

"It's okay. We're getting you out of here. You can come back to Glasgow if you want to, but right now we need to get you as much distance as possible. Dex can't get you if you're outside Glasgow."

"Really?"

"Yeah. He's restricted to the area. Not sure why. Didn't ask."

"God, that's a relief." She smiled, actually smiled, and I pulled her to me, hugging her tight.

"I was so scared for you," I said into to the top of her head, tears slipping out past my closed eyes.

"Me too," she said, shaking a little but squaring herself down.

We were almost at the door now, and I shrugged my jacket back down. Sarah slipped hers over her arms, raking a hand over her face and back over her hair. She gathered it up into a ponytail, twisting a bobble off her wrists, then glanced over to me.

"We good?" I asked, putting a hand on her shoulder.

"As good as you can be in this place." She glanced around.

"Yeah, we need to talk about why you're doing the world's worst form of camping."

"Later, sure."

"Right. After three, we go low and quiet. One."

"Two."

"Three." I grabbed the handle of the door, breathing against the burn, wrenching it open and ushering her through before following. I closed the door as quietly as I could and shaded my eyes, trying to adjust to the darkness of the church. I glanced around, blinking through my confusion, the darkness flooding over me. The fire child was still there, glowing away with its smirk.

"You found her." Sarah froze, looking over at it and glancing up to me.

"Fire kid," I whispered, wrapping my arm around her.

"They have your friend," the impossible voice said.

"What?" Shit, had Luke been spotted? Or come looking for me?

"They have your friend. In their circle."

"Sarah, what do you want to do? We can get out. Marc can take care of himself."

"They'll kill him if they think he helped you," she said, shaking her head.

"Fuck. You're coming with me. I'm not leaving you again."

"Course I am, like fuck am I being alone with that." She glared at the fire child.

"Rude," it tutted. "I helped him find you."

"You look like you'd eat me," she hissed back.

"I would," it agreed.

"That's not okay. Let's go!" she said, grabbing my arm. We inched forward, closer to the bodies and light. I could hear voices raising and to my absolute horror, recognised one of them not just as Marc but Alex too.

"Fuck," I spat, my head dropping. We got within sight of the group, and I saw Marc and Alex standing there arguing with one of the cult members, a short man with white hair and a matching bushy moustache. He was glowering between the two of them, gesturing at Alex. Marc moved in front of her, glaring back. I slipped the knife higher in my pocket, the edge of the teeth gripping the hem, and pushed forward.

"You brought her here without warning or explanation!" the short man shouted, eyes wild as he scowled at Marc.

"She's my fucking squeeze. So what if I brought her? She doesn't know shit about this, and she's useful. Drop it." Marc's face was a blend of calm and icy anger, his full height drawn up and his chest out. Alex was busy making herself smaller, shoulders down and gaze flicking between the cultists around them.

"Useful? What use would she be other than a fuck and a cut?"

"Don't start that with me, Nigel. You know I don't truck with your shit!" Marc yelled back, stepping up into the man's space and looming over him, his shaggy coat appearing to bristle.

"You know we could kill you both and no one would ask questions," Nigel said, low and menacing, but he stepped back first, Marcs' physical presence overwhelming. So this was the bastard who asked Dex to kill me. Prick. I could see one of the other cultists was gliding forward, creeping closer to Alex while Nigel was agitating Marc.

This would not end well.

"Shall we?" I glanced to Sarah, and she nodded, a grim set to her mouth.

"Let's go."

We surged forward, Sarah shrieking like a banshee while I shouted a string of curses. I barrelled an elbow into the back of one of them while Sarah kicked the back of another's knees out, toppling him over. We stopped in front of Marc, Sarah snarling at the man skulking towards Alex. He flinched back.

"Sarah?" Alex shrieked, grabbing and hugging her close.

"Catch up once we're not about to get stabbed," I said. Sarah grinned, hugging Alex and standing back to back with her. "What the shit is Alex doing here?" I asked Marc as I looped his arm around mine. I groped behind me and found Alex's, grabbing that too and linking hands with her.

"She wouldn't leave me alone. She wanted to scope out the cult too. I figured they'd ignore her like they have previous ones."

"He means he hadn't anticipated them being racist," Alex said, louder than was really necessary, gripping onto me.

"Racism is not the main issue right now," Marc bit back, glancing over his shoulder.

"We need a plan," Sarah said, matching me and linking arms with Marc and Alex, our square of hate glaring out at the assembled men. It wasn't a great numbers game, but we were young and vicious. We could get a few of them down, hurt them bad enough to scare the others off. And that would have been absolutely enough for me to think we could make it, if I hadn't heard the clapping start.

# Chapter 25

<u>8 March, 1887</u>

*I have encountered someone similar to myself, exploring the city to develop his powers. This is not a practitioner such as those within the necropolis whom I enjoy a healthy interaction with. This person seems studious and determined, acting alone every time I have seen him. His curiosity seems to be developed for a selection of areas for I have seen him in many of the same haunts I frequent.*

*He displays an unusual habit of seeking to close or constrict points of access, portals and weak areas between the veils. I have seen him carving patterns of seals and bindings in places, chalk used in the harder areas where the rock will not give. One wonders what he has studied to know such magics for they are powerful and sure, not some trifling in the dark. No other practitioner I have met does this, restricts their own potential in such a way by closing off areas of power. I am intrigued as to why he does this.*

*I may ask Natalie if she knows of him. Very little gets past a succubus, and if there is a new person of power in the city, either she or her sisters would be aware. News never takes long to reach the Other.*

"A very good show," crowed a voice from in the shadows, the owner meandering towards the circle of light. "Quite the heroics. Are you going to share your plan for getting out of here, Carter?"

"Luke?" Alex's voice was smaller than it should have been, the tremble there a sign I didn't like.

"Fuck you!" Sarah howled, lunging forward with the venom of it. Her eyes were wild, lips curled in a snarl of fear I hadn't even seen in the hot place. I pulled her back, passing her to Marc so there was a wall of us in front of her. Alex inched closer, pressed against me.

"What's going on here?" I asked, watching Luke's relaxed amble towards the circle with a plummeting in my stomach.

"What's going on here is that I just knew you'd find dear Sarah, and I wanted to ensure you succeeded. Something you seemed determined to avoid at all costs, running off to pester demons and fallen filth." He laughed, shaking his head like a sardonic professor. "I was worried you'd get yourself killed before you managed it."

"Shut up, shut up, shut up!" Sarah shouted, shaking. "You abusive, manipulative bastard!"

"Sarah, what's going on?" Alex said, voice thick.

"He's John! He's the one who wrote the book." She stopped shouting, her breath becoming ragged and gulping. Marc wrapped an arm around her, hugging her to him while glancing at me in confusion. I looked between the cult and Luke, who was now within the circle of light.

"You're John?" I asked, calm as I could. My voice sounded strange, separate from me, and the dual torrents of fury and fear warring through my head were as loud as waves on the shore.

"I prefer Luke now, but yes, that was my old name."

"That's why you were so keen on getting the book back."

"I missed it. I was so disappointed when I found Sarah had stolen it."

"Couldn't have traded without it," she said. "Wouldn't have been able to get away from you."

"Yet you did, so cleverly. You're both such exemplar students. And so responsive." The emphasis on the last word made me want to vomit.

I shook my head, trying to make the information make sense. "You were alive in the 1800s?" My brain rattled through the implications.

"Yes." He smiled, his face that same predatory grin as the night of the party. "Pretty spry for an old man, no?"

"Luke, stop playing with your food. We've still time to do the ritual now that we have her again," Nigel said, sweeping a hand back towards Sarah.

Marc jutted his chin forward, his arm tightening around her.

I mirrored the move, pulling Alex close to me, my arm curling around her shoulders. "Touch her and I'll kill you," I promised Nigel, a smile I didn't know I could make flashing on my face.

Luke was John. Luke was the person who Dex was baiting, using me. Luke had written the guide and was the person Sarah was hiding from. Luke who was in front of me, smirking with a grin that I wanted to punch off his face.

"He means that, Nigel," Luke said. "I think he'd manage it as well. He's powerful, even when he's just fumbling."

"I'm sure we can handle it," came a grumble from the men behind us. I glowered around at them, Marc mimicking me, then back to Luke.

"I don't need you to," Luke said with a lazy chuckle, starting to move his hands in front of him. "I'll just call on some assistance."

"Don't!" Sarah shouted, flinching closer to Marc and grabbing for me and Alex.

"There's no need for fuss, Sarah. It'll be painless for them," Luke assured, his arm movements wider, a glimmer forming in the air around him.

"It's a creature of hunger. It takes people away, off to somewhere else. I don't know if they die or if they're eaten or if they're abandoned in one of the other places," Sarah muttered, starting to shake.

"What's she talking about?" Alex asked, panic spiking her voice.

"That," Marc said, nodding to Luke.

The shape of a body was forming in front of him. It was still insubstantial, but I could see it writhing and twitching, a mass of tendrils and teeth. The thing was hulking, a good head over Marc, and its mouth took up almost all the face, a mashing throng of teeth and a flickering tongue. It stepped forward, the shuffling gait of something in pain, filling out as it moved.

"That will kill you," came the crackling voice of the fire child, appearing beside me.

Alex squeaked and flinched away from it.

"I got that," I said, glancing at the wide smile it wore. "Why does that make you happy?"

"It could eat them too if he didn't control it."

"Thanks for the advice," I said, pulling out the bone knife and holding it high.

"Do you think a dagger will give you any hope against what Luke can bring forth?" Nigel sneered, pulling his shoulders back and puffing his chest out like a cockerel. "This place is soaked with the energy he's been stealing up from you idiots for years. Anything he wants to happen will."

"Not if I slit her throat and give her to your god," I said, my grip round Alex tightening, the knife coming up to her throat.

"What the fuck?" Marc shouted, whirling around to face me and bringing Sarah with him.

"Carter?" Alex asked, going rigid in my grip.

"Trust me, Alex," I lied, keeping my grip tight on her.

"You don't want to do that, Carter," Luke shouted, his movements wavering. The creature of hunger was fully fledged now, it's shuddering body a tangle of swirling power.

"No? I kill her and Dex likes me better. You know he'll favour whoever offers the best trade, and I don't need to suck the soul out of her to stay young!"

"You don't even know what Dex can do," Luke laughed, nodding to the creature to carry on.

"I know enough to make a trade," I shouted back, bearing my teeth in a grin. "I know Alex was the back-up, so don't think I won't fucking usurp your plan and make it my own."

"Don't!" Luke began, pushing forward against his creation.

I raised the knife up and felt the world slow down, the dull thud of my blood hammering through my temples. I felt rather than saw Marc's outrage, his hand reaching out to me, Sarah's insistent tug down and away from us. I felt Alex tense to swing for me, felt that she would be too late to stop me if I buried the knife in her neck like I had threatened to. I felt the frank disbelief in Luke's face turn to panic. And I felt the furious realisation that I couldn't do this to her, not for Sarah or for me, not to doom her to be another part of the fire child that stood gleeful in the disaster unfolding around us. I couldn't be the same as Luke.

I shoved Alex down to the floor, twisting the arm that held her and sliced into my flesh with the hungry blade. I screamed for Dex as my blood spilled out, the spark of pain overwhelming the thundering in my ears.

The slowness solidified; the others frozen. The rumbling cackle that was Dex appeared, his presence rising out of the shadows beside Luke. He was the same oversized dark impression of a human but too much, too blurry at the edges. He wore my face, the jagged edges dripping red beads that sizzled and curdled when they dropped into the darkness of his form.

"Why the shit are you dressed up like me?" I asked, my head cocking to one side.

"I wear whoever sought me," it replied with a grin. Should I call it a he now? It was a he in my head, the surge of his presence pressing close, so that was a yes.

"Are you male aligned?" I asked, too far gone.

"For your purposes, yes."

"Those last two times, it wasn't that I was fucking Luke, it was Luke who sent you after me. Or John. Whatever you call him. Bitch ass murderer."

"Language, Carter!" Dex chuckled, the glee in his voice bubbling over. "You are correct that I wore his face because he summoned me. However, you did not call me to trade insults about the desperate creature behind me. Speak freely, we are quite private in this discussion. No one will know unless I allow it."

"I found Sarah without you. I can't get us out of here though. That thing Luke called up is going to kill me, Alex, and Marc, and then they're going to feed Sarah to you."

"That is their intention."

"I spilled my blood and offer you my service. The deal we agreed before, fifteen years, I stay in this city and assist you, you get us out of here. All four of us, Marc, Alex, Sarah, and me, safe and alive."

"And if I don't wish to trade on those terms anymore?"

"Then I'll kill as many of them as I can before that thing gets me, and I'll slash my own throat before it can take me anywhere, so you can't get me either." I held the knife up, red with my efforts, and waggled it. "You know I can overpower some of them, and I'm sure Marc would love an excuse to get a bit of blood on his teeth."

"They could simply give me your sister, anyway."

"She'll do herself in before they can. We're a decisive family."

"It would be a shame to lose you both. You will do as I direct you?"

"No slavery, no children, as little murder as I can get away with."

"You make a conditional offer?" His face, my bleeding face stretched over his form, schooled itself into mock surprise.

"You asked, I answered. Do you want me or not?"

"You will stay in the city for the fifteen years." It was said as a statement, but I could feel the curiosity.

"Well, if someone dies, I'll ask permission to go to the funeral, but other than that, yes. I'll stay here."

"I want twenty years."

"You said fifteen."

"Fifteen was because the worlds do not align again for that period. Your clever sister found her way between them once, but she would have burned up in there if you did not find her. You did, but now you need my help. Twenty years," he said, grinning.

"Fine. But if I'm here twenty years then I'll need to emphasise the no kids and as little murder as possible rule."

"I will make you more than you dreamed of being. I will give you power you could not hope to achieve on your own." I could feel the slick desire of his energy creeping forward, crackling with potential.

"Right now I want an out. Transport us, or smite down the cult, or whatever you do."

"I need your blood."

"I'm already bleeding pretty heavily here, dude!" I waved my arm up, blood spattering over the dirty floor.

"Come to me."

"Still so fucking creepy." I sighed, stepping over Alex, who was prone on the floor, to move towards the creature's rippling reality around itself. This was all wrong. Part of my brain was screaming, screaming over and over how terrible this was, that talking to an ancient being wearing my face was an appalling life choice. I pushed past it, forcing my feet to keep walking.

All wrong.

I reached him, offering my arm. A long tongue, thick and black, slipped out, snaking into the sticky liquid. It burned cold, and I flinched but kept myself steady, the tongue coming out over and over to lap the blood. The slash healed as he licked, the skin patching over with thick red scar tissue.

"That a usual part of the offer?" I asked, my stomach lurching at the mark.

"No, but your enthusiasm may have left you at risk. I would be a poor trader if I took your offering and let you die."

"It'd be a bad investment," I agreed, numb. I could feel a wave of emotion cresting over me, but I was pulled away from it, grounded in the feeling of tongue rasping against skin.

"I will ask you to do many things for me, Carter," he promised, still licking my arm. "But I will make it worth the effort. You will have a fine house, a following to worship you, and your powers will be made much more."

"What?" I asked, my focus snapping back.

"John has served me in many ways, but his dedication is lacking now. He is greedy, petty, does not seek to serve for anything more than his continued youth. This tires me. You will have what has been his, and in return, you will bring me what I require. I will be fair." The idea of what Dex felt was fair astounded me, but I pushed that from my head, focusing on his words. "Go back to your friends and stand as you were. I will allow your removal."

"Alright," I said, walking back over to my spot. The conversation felt like it had been hours, but the people around me had barely shifted, anger and fear clear on their faces. "Knife up?"

"It will only serve for theatrics, but there can be pleasure in that."

"Okay then," I said, holding my knife out.

"You may enjoy this." Dex hummed, raising my eyebrows, and my stomach flipped over itself. With the whistling of a storm the world came back to full speed. The glower of the fire child washed over me as it turned, hot anger spiking.

"You chose it," the fire child pouted, voice pitching up into a wail. "You sided with it!"

"I sided with getting out alive rather than joining you, so sue me." I shrugged, shaking my head at it. "At least I'm here. You might get your release yet."

"Carter?" Sarah shouted, grabbing onto my arm. "What have you done?" The angry swirls of Dex's ministrations shone in the light.

"We're about to find out," I said, smiling weakly at her.

Dex's form was gone, but I could still see the distortion he'd created, the ripple of his presence polluting the air. I frowned at the gap he had left, watching it grow larger. I was distracted by Alex screaming as the creature of hunger lurched at her.

"Get here," I shouted, grabbing her under the armpits and hoisting her to stand.

"What the fuck are you doing?" she barked, glaring at me.

"Moving you out of the way of whatever your esteemed leader has summoned to fucking murder us. Now get your ass next to me and we'll figure out what we're going to do," I said, twitching my head to my side.

"We're having a talk about this once we're out of here," she spat, standing beside me.

"If we get out of here," Marc offered, hugging Sarah close.

"We will," I promised, looking around to figure out how we were going to manage it. The cult was crowding us again, avoiding the creature of hunger but hemming us in. The ripple where Dex had been continued to raise, stretching up towards the sky and shimmering like oil on water.

The how presented itself with a mournful note emitting from the growing undulation, the sound echoing around us. I grabbed Alex, fear spiking in my chest as the noise grew louder.

"I know that," Sarah said, turning from Marc's chest to look for the noise.

A figure emerged from the place Dex had been, the large shape pushing into our world with a plaintive call. It took me a beat to realise the familiarity of the shape as it shook itself off. It hung in the air, twisting and stretching as if in water as it glanced around.

"Holy shit," Alex whispered, "Blob."

The twirling shape turned, the blinking black eyes finding us. I laughed a little, pushing out to feel for the previous connection she'd given. I was rewarded with a chirrup and her swimming over to Alex and me, sniffling around us. She floated over to Sarah who stared at her, reaching a hand out to touch the skin of the Blob's face. A happy ripple went through the slab of muscle, the same chirrup pealing out.

"What the fuck is that?" I heard from behind me. I glanced over to see a very worried looking Nigel stepping back.

"It's Blob," I said, looking again to Sarah and Blob sharing their connection. "I'd suggest you get out of the way."

"That thing is useless against my minion," Luke called out, waving a hand towards the creature of hunger.

"No, she's not," Sarah said, coming nose to nose with Blob, their feral grins matching. "She's amazing. And you couldn't see it because you were looking at the wrong thing."

"What would you know about looking for power?" Luke laughed, the cult members echoing him like jackals.

"I traded with demons to find a way between worlds. I hid myself where none of you could touch me, and I found the fallen angel you had lost to the city, Luke. I know more about looking for power than you've managed to scrabble together here."

"We'll still fuck you and feed your soul to our god!" came a shout behind her.

"Too late for that," said Dex, materialising back from the void.

"My lord," Luke gasped, dropping to one knee.

"There is little point in such showmanship, Luke," Dex drawled, a cruel amusement on his version of my face.

"Carter, why does it look like you?" Marc growled, looking between us.

"Long story. Catch you up on it when we're out of here."

"And how's that going to work?" he asked, passing a hand over his hair.

"Something like this," Dex provided, snapping two tendrils of what stood for fingers.

Blob stiffened, twisting around to look at Dex. There was a short whistling exchange, and then Blob drew up to her full height. Blob's muscles flowed, stretching and smoothing, and her claws flexed in anticipation.

Dex inclined his head and Blob looked over to Sarah, Alex, and me before shooting through the air, coming to rest in front of Luke. She hovered there for a moment, sniffing over him and smiling wide. Her teeth glistened, a stubby tongue flicking forward to taste the air, before she twirled over herself and pounced onto his summoning. There was a wet, shrieking sound from the creature, and it reared up, but Blob easily overpowered it. Pinning it down with her claws, she sank those teeth into its torso and the twitching, long muscles of its limbs, tearing chunks from it.

"Why isn't she killing it?" Alex whispered.

"She doesn't need to. This is to send a message," I supplied, understanding it as soon as I saw Dex smirking.

"I might throw up," Marc said, looking away from the death spasms of the creature of hunger. Blob sat up, chirruped, then blinked out of sight.

"Aim for one of them if you do," I said.

"Fuck you, man. We need to have so many conversations after this."

"Sure thing. Let's just escape the cult first," I said, looking at where Blob had been.

"You will have no issue with that," Dex said, swinging to look at the man beside him. "Luke, by your own failings you are undone. You have neglected me in service, and I no longer seek you out in the darkness. You will age as a normal human. You will feel the fear and cold of my absence."

"My Lord, this can't be. I've served you faithfully for over a century. I have brought you sacrifices and organised your worship. I've ensured your honouring each solstice."

"You knew the gifts borne by this one and sought to hide him from me." Dex pointed to me, and I felt the cult turn to look. Awkward.

"I had designs on bringing him into the fold. You know of the actions I took," Luke blustered.

"I know you took your own enjoyment and threw me scraps, hoping I would not notice. I know you," Dex swivelled, pointing to Nigel, "sent me off like a servant to kill someone with more power than you. Which you would have known if any of you had thought to look further. If any of you had thought to consider how and why this girl hid him from you, and from her own group, and then he appeared with presence and power."

"What power? He sees through the veil, nothing useful if you can't influence beyond that."

"Shut up, Graham," barked Luke.

"It's true. What can the whelp do?" shouted another.

"His power is unused, you insolent and ignorant worms." Dex swelled, his form absorbing the shadows around him and the remains of the creature, a snarl splitting his version of my mouth. "Not that you would pay enough attention to find that, evident as it may be. He sees but has not practiced. You all recognised his sister and despite your lusts, you could feel her potential. His is equal, at least, and his talents more appealing. You are all complacent and blinded by your comfort."

"My Lord!" Luke shouted, his face fallen, going to both his knees. "You can't forsake me this way. I've served you better than any other."

"You have always served yourself, Luke, and kept your end of the bargain begrudgingly. This was acceptable until you began to seek your own gratification without due consideration to me. Your pact is finished."

"Carter, what is going on here?" Alex asked, inching closer.

"Luke is getting the boot, and the cult are getting battered."

"Why does that thing keep talking about you?" she pushed.

"I may have made a bit of a pact with it. Twenty years or so. Little details, not important right now," I said, panic bubbling up my throat.

"What the fuck?" she shouted, whirling on me.

I held my arm up, revealing the scars Dex had licked.

"Would you prefer to have become a part of that?" I nodded to the fire child, still sulking at the edge of our group.

"Why's there a fucking kid here?" Marc barked, going to reach for it, then yanked his hand back as the head turned to face him.

"Fire child. Leave it be," Sarah said, hugging Marc close and crying.

I felt the impact of Alex's hand on my face and spun with it, grabbing my cheek as I turned to look at her. "What the fuck did you go and do?" she shouted, making to swing at me again. A thin black tendril reached out, encircling her wrist and holding it still.

"I would suggest you do not do that again," rumbled Dex, the wide grin tracked by rivulets of blood on his version of my face.

"Easy!" I hissed, tugging her close. The blackness let go, leaving an indent on her arm like rope marks.

"You are lucky he chose not to simply kill you, woman. I would have taken your blood in place of his sisters, and you would have never left these stones. You raise your hand to him again, and I will tear your soul from your bones, slowly."

"Okay, we're going to have to have a boundaries talk, aren't we?" I asked, hugging Alex against my chest and turning her away from Dex.

"I don't need you to protect me," she spat.

"I know you don't. He might though." I shushed her, my back to Dex as I looked over my shoulder to him. "Can we leave?"

"Not yet. It is my decree that this group is disbanded. You may worship me under Carter, but should any of you seek me out under Luke, I will ensure your pain is long lasting and entertaining. All that was Luke's now falls to Carter."

"What does that mean?" Sarah piped up, peering over.

"Carter is the new leader of my worship. My house is his. My wealth and the group both of you practice under all fall to his domain."

"Your house as in the church? He gets that fire thing?" Marc asked, eyeing the flickering to the pouting being.

"No, the house I provide for Luke. I required him to be in the city, so I bought the property."

"How does something like you own property?" I asked half-heartedly, resigned to the weirdness of what was going on. At least I got a perks package.

"I arranged it for him. The deeds are all transferable. I'll ensure it's done," Luke said, rising back up. "Carter, we'll have to discuss the practicalities."

"Like hell you're getting him on his own again," Sarah spat.

"Luke will not do anything to harm Carter. He knows the price," Dex intoned, looking between the two of us. I glanced to Luke and saw a desolation there, the usual calculating warmth gone.

"Okay. Can we go now? Please?" I asked with as level a voice as I could manage.

"Luke, I trust you will assist?" Dex said, enjoying himself.

"Naturally," Luke confirmed, inclining his head. "Gentleman, good night. Carter, if you would come with me."

"How did you guys get here?" I asked Alex.

"Marc drove. I'm insured on his car," she answered, still watching the cult.

"Marc, feel like a ride in a Rolls-Royce?" I asked, voice tight.

"Sure."

"You don't need to suspect I will do something untoward, Carter," Luke admonished with a ghost of his old smile.

"I'm sure you wouldn't, but I'm having a bit of a day. I'm sure you've noticed."

"Quite," he agreed.

"We'll be on our way then, Dex," I nodded, head going low in a slight bow.

# Chapter 26

*2 September, 1887*

*An unexpected benefit has befallen me. The group I have been informally involved with, for their behaviour is too unabashed for my tastes, has invited me to become not only a full member but to assist with the management of their business.*

*I hesitate somewhat to accept the proposal, given the stage of my studies and the associated risk should there be any investigation to their activities. This guide is sufficiently undetailed about my identity to be of little concern, but their conduct is a touch too public for safety.*

*If they were to accept my concerns and could be moved to a sufficiently private method of practice, then this would be vastly beneficial for my future plans. The ability to offer worship and the devotion of others as part of bartering with something more powerful than me is certainly a better position than simply my own efforts.*

*Habit and devotion pay well in this esoteric system, but multiplying that through a group in your thrall is almost equivalent of a congregation. Almost. What being doesn't want to be worshiped?*

Our group left, shuffling out through the ruined church and into the crisp evening. I walked between Luke and Sarah, with Alex and Marc leading us towards the trees.

"There's a front gate?" I asked.

"It would have seemed a touch too coincidental, no?" Luke asked with a shrug.

"You're an ass," I said, shaking my head.

"How can you talk to him like that?" Alex asked, fizzing. "How can you act normal?"

"I can freak out later, preferably with tequila," I said, running a hand along Sarah's arm.

"You sold part of your soul, and you're acting like this was a bad date," Alex said, hands clenching at her sides.

"I didn't sell part of my soul. I gave time. Twenty years of service, not my life energy and not my soul," I said, tired and aching and running out of adrenaline as we walked away from that disaster.

"Oh, Carter, no," Sarah moaned, slumping into me.

"Shush you. It's not so bad. Less than the prison sentence if I'd stabbed one of 'em."

"I doubt you'll be given time off for good behaviour," commented Luke, and I shot him a glare.

"You're taking all this rather well," Marc said.

"Me or him?" I asked.

"Both of you. I thought you were going to go for Alex back there."

"I knew he wouldn't," Alex said, shoving her hands into her pockets.

"And you didn't even have to look him in the eye. You've come so far Alex." Luke smiled, an honest one from the looks of it.

"Fuck you," she spat back.

"Why are you so calm?" I asked Luke.

"I've served Dex a long time. I know how to remain useful. His favour will return."

"I'm changing the locks on the house," I told him, knowing it was petulant.

"I would expect nothing less. Alex, are you sure you're safe to drive? You and Sarah have both had a trying night."

"How can you keep talking like I didn't have to go through hell to avoid death at your hands?" Sarah hissed, curving an arm around my waist.

"It was unfortunate. I would have much preferred you hadn't realised."

"I bet you would," I laughed, a hollow in my chest.

"I'm being sincere. Living between the worlds must have been horrendously difficult. I wouldn't wish suffering on such beauty."

"Just ritual murder." Her smile was brittle, acid.

"You would have been beautiful in death as in life, and I would have felt honoured to feel your spirit in mine."

"You feel them?" I asked, balking.

"I carry their essences within me while their youth is spent."

"I think I might be sick," I said, the implication of him and the fire child surging forward. He was a serial killer who could feel his victims through the life they would have had. He fitted it to suit him, but that's what he meant.

"No point in being coy, Carter." Luke jostled my shoulder.

I glowered at him. "I thought using your influence to fuck people was poor, but that's a step beyond."

"You knew about that?" he asked, surprised.

"It wasn't exactly subtle."

"Sarah never noticed," he said with a shrug.

"Oh my god, really? You said you'd never done that." I groaned, my gut dropping.

"Is that an issue now?" He raised a brow at me.

"You are a terrible person in every sense," I said, wiping a hand over my face as if to erase the knowledge. God, I needed a drink. Several, in fact.

We arrived at a car park near a large administrative building, a lone car hunkered in the dark.

"That's our ride. You're coming back to the flat, right?" Alex asked us.

"Once this is sorted. I don't fancy being in that house longer than I need to be," Marc said, voice low.

"Don't feel forced. I won't be seeking to harm Carter. It wouldn't matter if I did. I'm sure Dex would simply repair such damage."

"Nice to know that's why I'm safe," I said.

"I wouldn't hurt you. I'm simply pointing out the practicalities for Alex."

"It would be a massive help if you could take Sarah to the flat. We'll come back as soon as we can," I said, turning to Alex and imploring her.

"Marc goes with you. We'll see you when you're back," she said, taking Sarah from me and helping her into the car.

"Shall we?" Luke asked after the doors were shut.

"Sure, back to your car," I said. "Why'd you feel the need to tell me you'd fucked my sister, anyway? It's a bit petty."

"The evening's events have left me in such a humour. If you'd continued to be as eager and open as your previous efforts, we'd have Sarah, and I could have initiated you into worshipping Dex."

"You thought you'd fuck me so good I'd join your cult?" I asked, tilting my head to watch him as we walked.

"Rude, Carter. I'd planned to convince you in other ways."

"Not influencing me through sex?"

"I do have other methods of persuasion," he said with a smirk.

"This is so fucking creepy. I thought the sex parties were bad." Marc sighed, pulling a cigarette out and lighting up.

"I've never seen you smoke," I said, frowning.

"I'd quit. This is my emergency stash. This is the emergency. What exactly did you pull back there, getting the cult signed over to you?"

"Just traded, nothing more." I shrugged, non-committal.

"Carter's good at that," Luke said.

"Don't you fucking start. I told you what I was being offered. I didn't even know what it meant to you, and I still told you." I huffed, hating myself for my earlier ignorance.

"I hadn't imagined you'd be so enterprising as to trade your youth for power."

"For my sister, you prick. In case it escaped your long memory, she's why I'm here. If you hadn't summoned whatever that thing was, I wouldn't have had to."

"I would have ensured it didn't eat you," he sniffed.

"Thanks, pal," Marc said, puffing smoke out.

"I would've been sad to see you gone, Marcus, but my hand was forced."

"And now it isn't?" I barked a laugh.

"Now I find myself in an unusual situation. Traditionally, the previous leader is killed. Dex has merely banished me."

"Lucky for some. You kill your predecessor?" I asked. I still couldn't pair the image of him with John.

"Oh yes. Quickly. I didn't have followers to impress with theatrics then. That was my first sacrifice to Dex."

"Hell of a promotion. Should I have killed you?" I asked.

"I much prefer you didn't." He grinned, almost flirting.

"Why are you special enough to keep around?" Marc interrupted, dragging on his cig.

"I'm uncertain if it's my specialness or Carter's. Dex had his blood, less than usually given, but he accepted it. And he marvels at your potential." Luke glanced to me, a detached sort of curiosity blooming. "Which is, of course, untapped."

"I liked it that way," I said, rolling my neck to unhunch my shoulders. My arm was still numb and thick feeling, the skin heavier than it should be.

"Yet you took so well to it while searching for Sarah. Most people would have run screaming from the spirit at the church."

"It was fucking creepy," Marc said, defensive.

"Undoubtedly," Luke said, opening the car door and sliding in. "But it touched Carter. Most would be harmed by that."

"I think I built up some resistance with The Collector frying me earlier." I shrugged as I settled into the passenger seat.

"That is an amalgamation of souls and suffering that has been building for some significant time. I've avoided it for the better part of a century."

"Wasn't keen on you guys. I suppose it was all the murder," I replied, my anger flaring up again.

"I make no apologies. My actions served me as I wished. You'll have to do the same," he promised.

"I don't have a cult, remember? It's disbanded."

"They'll come to you and ask to reform. Nigel couldn't imagine his life without his little schemes. He'll seek you out." Luke hummed, thumbs drumming the steering wheel while he started the car.

"I think it's more about you than me, anyway," I said, looking out at the passing scenery. It was still dark, the streetlight flicking by like luminous rain.

"Why do you say that?" Marc asked, frowning at me in the mirror.

"If the previous leader is usually killed, it's Dex's choice that Luke lives. He talked about him aging. That's a personal insult to Luke, I'd say."

"You notice a lot, don't you, Carter?" Luke asked, mouth pulling down at one side.

"Why'd you start stealing their youth?" I shot back.

"I stole nothing. It was a simple trade. More time to do what I wished in the world."

"More time to defend jakies and the neds at the court, sending drunks and thugs back out into the world?" Marc interrupted from the back, one eyebrow hiked.

"I've done much more than that, Marcus, and as you recall, you've benefited from my connections in that regard."

"You helped me not get charged. It's hardly setting the world on fire," Marc scoffed.

"I've no desire to set the world alight, just to ensure things were better. I've worked in parliamentary planning committees and legislative bodies that have assisted many poor and disadvantaged. I had to relocate every few decades to avoid people noticing my unusual proclivities. The law is a small community, so I had to alter my professional occasionally, but I achieved my aims."

"And the people you killed?" I asked, pushing at buttons I knew I shouldn't.

"A means to an end. I didn't get too attached. Sarah was an unfortunate deviation and look how that served me."

"Oh, don't tell me you liked her. That why you fucked me, 'cause I reminded you of her?" I said, swallowing the bitterness on my tongue.

"Sleeping with her was necessary for my influence. Sleeping with you was enjoyable as well as useful," he replied, sounding almost hurt.

"Glad to know I'm special," I said, shaking my head. "I get your house and your practice group; does that mean I have to deal with the orgies as well?"

"Yes." Luke chuckled.

"I bet Samuel isn't going to take well to that."

"How come?" Marc asked.

"Vampires are creatures of habit and Carter doesn't fall under their influence. It's most inconvenient," Luke said.

"He's a vampire? Jesus Christ!" Marc came close to crossing himself.

"You didn't need to do that. Poor bastard's had enough of a shock tonight," I admonished Luke.

"He'll have to get used to it being around you," Luke said, clicking his tongue. "And he'll continue pining after Alex, so he will be."

"I don't know how long she's going to stick about. She didn't like the fallen angels never mind 'sold some of your soul' friends," I said.

"She'll stay. You saved her best friend. Alex owes you. And in time, I'm sure she'll forgive your foolishness." That was one word for it.

"Why are you giving us a lift back, anyway?" Marc grumbled from the back, tapping his cigarette packet and lighting another.

"There are arrangements to be made, and I see no point in making it more difficult than needs be." Luke shrugged, glancing back to Marc.

"And?" I asked.

"And perhaps I wish to speak with you before I make my way elsewhere. I've no intention of giving up my goals, but we don't have to make this unpleasant."

"I don't believe you," I said, watching him.

"One for the road? Really?" Marc laughed.

"A crude way to put it, Marcus. I was rather fond of you, Carter. I'd planned to bring you into the group and let your power flourish. Dex has beaten me to it, but I don't wish to leave things cold."

"You wanted to kill my sister. How nice can we make it?"

"I preferred to offer Alex, but the group wanted Sarah."

"They would have raped her, too?" Marc spat, choking on the smoke.

"Yes," Luke said, frowning. "I didn't agree with that aspect of the ritual, so I would have removed her soul by then."

"I don't know if that makes it better, and I resent having to think about it," Marc groaned.

"Just wait for the tequila," I said, giving him half a grin. We pulled up to the house and Luke turned the car off, letting the engine cool.

"Marcus, you're welcome to attend the drinks cabinet," Luke said and smiled, almost sympathetic.

"Hardly fair to start before the deserving," he said, gently punching my shoulder as we walked up the steps.

"Carter is welcome to them as well," Luke said, entering the house.

"What do we need to arrange?" I asked as we walked through to the living room.

"There's the basics of the shop, the dungeon, the parties, and the house," Luke listed off, shedding his jacket and throwing it over the sofa. "Marcus, you may not wish to imbibe yet, but I certainly need a drink. Would you be so kind?"

"Carter?"

"I'll take a beer," I said.

"Okay, orders are in." Marc headed to the kitchen.

Luke went for me immediately, forcing me into the back of the door and pushing his weight against me. He snaked a hand over my mouth, gripping tight.

"I want to take you here, without him being able to stop me," he growled close to my ear. I resisted the urge to bite his hand and instead raised a brow at him. He must have known I could force him off if I wanted to. I still had the knife in my pocket. I could probably ask to have him killed with some mental screaming at this point. The hand moved off my mouth, Luke watching my face. "I would have done so much with you."

"I was quite liking the idea of a relationship with you, but, well... I'd have preferred it without your influence." I shrugged, as much as I could with him pressed up close. I could feel his hardness against my thigh. I had an unfortunate twitch of arousal, and I cursed my body for it.

"We must try at some future point and see if we could make it work," he said.

"I don't know how good I'd feel about that, given I should have killed you and all. And the sexual assault. The murder."

"You're not pushing me away. Do you want me as well?"

"A bit of me does, but that bit will be getting dealt with through a lot of alcohol."

"Petty, Carter. You know I could help you. Or hurt you in a way you'd like." He punctuated the offer with a sharp bite to my collar bone, and I swallowed my response.

I couldn't feel any attempt at influence, no trace of his energy. "No tricks?" I asked, trying to refocus my mind. "Last time we did this you were pushing your intent."

"It was necessary. I had to drain you before the church meeting. But I enjoy it much more when your mind's clear. Your deliberation's intriguing."

"And you're back to sounding creepy again. Marc'll be back in a moment."

"He won't. I've a distraction in place."

"That's a red light again. Do you even hear yourself?" I asked.

"I'd like it if we could revisit this. Would you object?" He dipped his head down to the join at my shoulder, mouthing at the hickeys fading away there. This was an absolutely terrible idea. I couldn't trust him, but he was proving distracting.

"I think we'd need to have a proper talk that didn't involve me pinned to a door. Or couch," I said.

"How about a bed?"

"If you don't listen to my serious objections, I might just punch you," I warned, resting my forehead against his.

"Objections noted. A conversation for another time. I suppose requesting your company this evening would be too much?"

"I need to take care of Sarah."

"I think you've done more than enough of that tonight," Luke said, pecking a kiss to my lips before stepping away. "Let me see your arm."

I pulled my sleeve up and showed him the angry red scars, the flame like pattern licking up the muscle. "It doesn't feel sore. A bit stiff, or rubbery maybe, but not painful."

"That was a mercy on his part. He could have made it much worse."

"I have no doubt," I said, rubbing the marks. "I don't get why he thinks I'm something special."

"You have potential. That is something Dex has not had access to for a significant time."

"I also have agency— I can make my own decisions."

"I'm sure you'll enjoy it while you can. Twenty years is a long time."

"Not for you," I said.

"Even for me, it could feel like a long time. I have not disliked my service with Dex, but I am aware I compromised many of my previous standards."

"Idealism replaced with practicality?" I asked with a shake of my head.

"Something along those lines, yes. On that note, we should return to business."

"Yeah. You mentioned a dungeon?"

"Underneath the house. Could be used as a wine cellar if one wished. It's currently fitted with various items for the parties."

"Those were yours? I suppose you've had time to work your kinks out." I nodded, silently vowing I would find a way to outsource as much of the party stuff as I could.

"The shop is operated by Lou, but you will be asked to assist with running it when she is otherwise engaged. And the group will look to you for guidance."

"The house, the group, the, uh, dungeon, and the shop. What else?"

"There's a sum of money in the safe, the code to which I'll text you, and the house is otherwise yours. There is a space in the dungeon for worship should you wish to use it, though you may be content to keep conversing in your sleep."

"That's up to Dex."

"Indeed." Luke smirked, running a hand over my new scars. "You're very brave."

"Anyone else would've done the same."

"I've witnessed many do the opposite. Siblings offering each other in sacrifice, parents providing children. You knew the dangers. This wasn't an impulsive choice. Brave or foolish, it's impressive."

"Thanks, I guess. We'll have to see how it works out. I'll stay away from the house for a day or so if you need time to get stuff cleared out."

"That would be gracious of you." Luke smiled, inclining his head.

"I have the guesthouse booked for like a month, anyway. And I'll have to start explaining to customers that I'm not coming back. That's going to be an awkward conversation."

"You can't work remotely?"

"For some of them, yeah. For others, I'm on-site support. Can't do that long distance."

"A shame, I'm sure they've enjoyed having you there," he said.

"I would hope. I'm going to go. Let me know if you want to talk about handing over keys and all that." I stepped away from the wall I'd been clinging to, moving towards the door.

"Carter," Luke called as I crossed the threshold, "was that your way of saying you'd appreciate me calling?"

"It's an offer to talk in a few days when my head isn't screaming."

"Not beyond doing deals with the Devil?" It was a teasing question, and I looked around to see a challenging smile.

"You're not the Devil, Luke. You're many interesting things, but not that."

"No, you already have your Devil, I suppose," he said, following me into the kitchen.

Marc was frozen by the fridge, one hand on the door.

"What did you do?" I sighed.

"Just a simple enchantment, over in a snap." Luke grinned, clicking his fingers.

"Come on, mate," I said, slinging an arm round Marc's shoulder and directing him away from the fridge. "We need to go see the others."

"You're done already?" Marc asked, looking between me and Luke.

"Yes, just the formalities. Best run off before Halloween creeps in." Luke smiled.

"Taxi?" Marc asked.

"You order one, and I'll grab my bag," I said, slipping back into the living room to pluck it from beside the couch.

"Do you suppose you would've considered killing yourself for Sarah?" Luke asked from behind me.

"Dex didn't want me to."

"But you'd offered?" He stepped closer, grasping my hand in his.

"We had the conversation."

"So eager to throw your life away?" he asked, running his fingers over the new scars.

"As someone who's been riding on other people's lives for a century, I can see why that would be confusing," I shot back.

"No need to be bitchy."

"I'd have done it if necessary, but I couldn't have given Alex to him any more than I could Sarah. This means we're all alive, Sarah's safe and I have a new business. There are worse lives."

"They don't all involve murder. Dex doesn't need a yearly sacrifice, but he's demanding."

"All gods are if you listen to the scriptures. Are you asking me these questions out of curiosity or to keep me here?"

"A touch of both. I'm loathe to let you leave." He tilted his head, looking me over.

"But you're going to."

"Of course. It would be unseemly to do otherwise."

"Goodnight, Luke." I smiled as I walked past him and found Marc at the front door.

"We good?" Marc asked, eyeing the corridor.

"For a couple of days, yeah. I need a drink."

"Right there with you, pal."

The taxi arrived and we piled into the back, Marc giving the address. We arrived at the flat and walked in on Alex and Sarah packing.

"You had a chance to call home yet?" I asked Sarah, hugging her. Alex and Marc grouped in, surrounding us in a tight embrace.

"Not yet. Focused on getting everything in a suitcase," she mumbled into my chest.

"Don't stress it. I can ship stuff down. So can Alex. How you doing, Mrs.?" I asked Alex over Sarah's head.

She stepped away to cross her arms. "How long have you known about that creature you did the deal with? How long did you plan on keeping me in the dark?"

"I wasn't going to tell you at all, but you ended up at the meeting."

"How dare you?" she spat.

"I didn't want you to show up in case the cult killed you. You were their plan B." Almost the truth. Close enough.

"You think I couldn't defend myself?"

"There were sixteen of them and a creature from somewhere I don't want to think about, Alex. The maths wasn't good."

"He did tell me not to say, in case it was dangerous," Marc said.

"You're lucky I'm happy she's back," Alex said, stroking Sarah's arm.

"I'm also nowhere near drunk enough to continue having this discussion," Marc said, retreating to the kitchen.

"We've got to do something about this. You can't stay here twenty years. What about Mum and Dad? What about your life?" Sarah said, running a hand over my scarred arm.

"It'll be okay," I said, kissing the top of her hair. "I can work up here like I worked at home, but I'll have to find some new clients. I get that ridiculous house to live in. Mum and Dad'll have to come visit. They did often enough to see your shows."

"You talk a lot of shit sometimes, man," Alex muttered, eyes lighting up when Marc came back in with a tray loaded with booze. He passed a bottle of wine and glass to Alex, a cider to Sarah, and cracked open the tequila.

"I'm serious—I'll figure something out. First being to get some housemates. That place is fucking huge. I'm not rattling around in it like a pea in a pod."

"I'm glad you can be so practical," Sarah said dryly, popping open the cider and taking a seat beside Alex.

"You know me." I forced a grin, trying to keep a lid on the undercurrent of fear left over from the night.

"Speaking of practical, Sarah, tell me how the fuck you ended up in that church," Marc said, passing me a glass of clear fluid and sipping from his own.

"I took a shit tonne of water and old army supplies with me and went camping." She laughed, an honest giggle escaping her as she tipped the bottle back for a long pull. "The shop owner thought I was off to a trip in Israel. He helped me plan for how much water I'd need, food and clothing, how to make travelling between places less brutal."

"You backpacked between different worlds?" Marc said, slack jawed.

"It was weird. I had to plan how to get between them when the links were weak, so I could slip through. I could go to sleep camping in one place and wake up in a different world. Or wake up with a portal outside the tent."

"You talk like it was a mountain hike," Alex said with a shake of her head.

"Kinda was," Sarah shrugged. "Just with a lot more bears. I knew about the grinning mouths. The ones you called Blob," she answered to my confused look.

"Blob's awesome, but I'm terrified at the idea of there being more of her," Alex said.

I nodded, drinking a sip.

"They're a whole species, but their world works different than ours. That's how she moves through the air. And those teeth. Up close they're furled with little hooks on each, perfect for shredding ice or frozen flesh."

"Why'd she help Dex?" I asked, frowning at the thought.

"Dex has a lot to do with water. He maybe has influence over her world. I don't know for sure. I've never dealt with him directly," she answered, sipping again.

"You did. You just didn't know about it. He bragged about it," I muttered, matching her drink.

"I'm not even surprised," she said, shaking her head. "That whole tangled mess is so fucked up. I'm glad their cult is disbanded."

"Luke reckons they'll come back and ask Carter to start up," Marc said.

"Doubt they'd stomach an Englishman leading them." Sarah scoffed, finishing her bottle. Marc provided another, and she nodded her thanks. "They might go to Luke. You should be careful with him, Carter. He'll use you for what he can get and make it sound fair."

"I'd noticed that, yeah." I rubbed the bruises on my neck.

"I mean it. He'll bring something to you and make like it's an opportunity, but he'll only wring out what he can get," Sarah pressed.

"He felt he was doing good. Says he's done a lot of good in the world. The sacrifices were a part of the cost," I said.

"And what was your trade?" Sarah asked.

"Just the twenty years. Dex likes the idea of having someone who can see like me. I'm going to be taught magic."

"Who's going to teach you?" Alex asked, perking up.

"I don't know," I said, holding my glass out to Marc for a refill. He obliged, topping up his own at the same time.

"What are you going to tell Mum?" Sarah asked, leaning her weight onto Alex's shoulder.

"Not much 'til she's here and sees this." I held up my scarred arm. "She can't freak out too much if she knows it saved us both."

"That's emotionally manipulative," Alex said.

"It is," I said, "but you've not met our mother."

"There's a reason for that. He's not entirely wrong" Sarah said.

"Your whole family's fucked up girl," Alex muttered, drinking her wine.

"What's the plan for getting you back?" I asked Sarah.

"Booked a flight for tomorrow morning. Taxi booked from the airport too."

Alex grinned, wrapping her arm around Sarah.

"Dad would have picked you up," I said, quirking a brow at her.

"I'd have to speak to him tonight, and all I want to do is be with you guys and drink," Sarah said, leaning into Alex.

"I can get behind that." I grinned at her. I was so relieved to see her, to look at Alex sit with her and see the soft smile Marc had watching them together. This was good.

# Chapter 27—Epilogue

<u>15 December, 1887</u>

I have been discussing the ritual with The Collector, and he has provided me with as much material as he possesses. His gift is extensive, and he details the ingredients needed to complete sufficiently high workings to allow the contact I seek.

I have prepared a sacrifice sufficient to curry favour and devoted my focus for the past two weeks to ensuring the area is sufficiently saturated with power. It will hold stable during the act. It is a sad way to spend one's recreational time, surely, but devotion is a powerful currency with these powers.

If the writings I have read hold true, I will no longer be constricted by our base limits. Was this what Plato spoke of when escaping our ignorance? Will I want to bring my fellow cave dwellers out of the dark tunnel and into the sunlight? I do not know. I imagine his Republic would not have survived the academic process if it were.

I do not know what success I will have. I have no reason to doubt what The Collector has given me. He has often spoken of his own dealings in ritual. If I am truly to enact the change, I wish to see if this will let me access the powers I need. If I can wield these powers then I can encourage the development and improvements necessary to bring better quality to those in the borough. This has to be for the good. Though the means are somewhat unanticipated, this will allow me the influence needed. I will narrate my discoveries after completion.

<u>31 October 2017</u>

I awoke on the sofa, a blanket slung over me. I groped around for my phone and saw it was before six in the morning. The glare from the screen made my eyes hurt. I grumbled to myself and turned over, hunching over the back of the cushions.

I noticed the message light was winking at me and opened it, seeing a short text from Luke.

*I would like to see you once arrangements have been made for Sarah. Please let me know when is suitable x*

My blossoming hangover reminded me now was not the time to think about this. I ignored it, flipping the phone over and closing my eyes.

"Are you sure that is a good idea?" rumbled the voice of Dex, backed by the sound of waves. I was at the cliffs, the campfire flickering away.

"What do you mean?" I asked, hazy. I stood up and padded towards the fire. It wasn't cold in this wrong-starred place, but the light was comforting.

"Engaging in further discussions with Luke." Dex was just outside the firelight, the same too big shape lurking black in the darkness.

"Why didn't you have him killed? He said he had to remove the previous leader himself."

"I enjoy the idea of him aging. His betrayal was slow and his punishment will match."

"Death'd be too easy," I said, seeing the twisted logic.

"Exactly. He is still interested in you."

"I imagine he's either planning to kill me or glean enough information to barter with you. Or hey, he might just want a good hate fuck."

"Such cynicism, I marvel," Dex purred, chuckling.

"Are you surprised? You've had my energy as well as my blood. It's got to taste as bitter as I am. I thought you might be keeping him around to teach me, some sick 'train your replacement' type of thing."

"While that is a delicious idea, I suspect it would be too risky. Such danger would be unreasonable. If you wish to continue associating with Luke, that is your decision. You will surpass him by far in terms of your powers once you are educated. He may seek to stifle that."

"I'm not under the illusion that Luke will be interested in anything other than what he could get from me. He might justify it to himself as something else, he might believe it too, but I know what it'd be. I don't think it'd be beneficial long term. Are you going to give me dating advice on every partner I choose?" I asked, looking over the shadow shape of him.

"If I feel they will affect your ability to serve me, yes."

"That's fair. Will I always be talking to you like this?"

"In some form or another. You can reach me through meditation now we share a link. You will not always come here in your sleep, though you are free to do so if you wish."

"You're being very gentle," I said.

"I would hate to damage the chrysalis of your change. What emerges must be your own creation. I can influence and provide, but your own outcome is essential."

"How encouraging. You have someone in mind for teaching me?"

"Yes, Faith. You have met her already."

"The fallen angel? The one who melts my brain when I speak to her?"

"You will grow past that stage."

"She's like looking into the fucking sun with a telescope. At least you do whatever this is. Makes it easier to speak."

"You will overcome it. I have made the arrangements. You will begin in a week or so, once you have had an opportunity to make your own schedule."

I could have cried. Faith was wonderful in her own mordant way, but the idea of training under her was terrifying. I couldn't even look at the woman. But it was better than Luke.

"Okay," I said, voice low. I would have to see what I could do. Maybe Tobias would help.

"I do not need blood often, but I expect many forms of service. There will be things I expect you to do, places to attend. You are the leader of the human aspect of this city now, but there are other creatures I deal with and will expect you to encounter."

"Lions and tigers and bears, oh my?"

"Some of them you have already met, some are more organised. There is a warlock I will need you to work with, and the wild women."

"Sounds good. Also, I'm planning on getting roommates in that house. Anything about it I should know?"

"There are various protection wards in place to remove anyone who would threaten you, or my interest in you. These should ensure that no one unsavoury is granted entry."

"Hell of a security system."

"It has been very effective for Luke. I am sure it will serve you well."

"When does it start?"

"It is already in place. The wards aligned to you when I appointed you."

Huh. Interesting. "Thank you for that. Can we talk about not killing my friends?"

"I will kill whomever I find necessary. I would not have killed the girl last night, merely marked her."

"Okay. We'll revisit that in the future then." I nodded, watching the fire crackle and crumble in the space between us. "One other question, if I may?"

"By all means."

"Why does that fire child exist at the church? Seems sloppy."

"I enjoy it. The raw emotional spark of those killed was always distinct and decadent. I did not need such theatrics, but they enjoyed them. It fed their ego."

"The gang rape and murder was set dressing?"

"I will always desire blood of some form. A sacrifice must be given. You have given yours, but I will require other types throughout your service. The rest, that was always for their benefit rather than mine."

"People are such pricks."

"People are as good as they need to be and seldom better," Dex said, an amused smirk to his words.

"No one's the villain in their own story."

"Except you, Carter." Dex smiled, pushing towards the edge of the light and looming tall. "You know your own worth as an asset and a monster. You were willing to give me that girl in trade. You were willing to let Luke believe you were fooled in order to manipulate him. You know your own darkness."

"Nothing new about that, mate. My monsters sleep in my head. I know what I can do when I'm pushed."

"Which makes you unusual, and valuable. I will leave you now. See your sister off and make your peace here."

"Thanks for that, boss," I nodded, flopping back onto the grass beside the fire and closing my eyes to the garbled stars.

I awoke to the sound of someone in the kitchen and padded through to seek human company. Marc stood at the fridge scowling into its interior.

"Looking for breakfast?" I asked.

"Something to stave off the hangover," he said.

"Either drink more or have an omelette, they do wonders. Or order in pizza, but it might be a bit early for that."

"Omelette sounds good. You cook?"

"I'll make you one if want."

"That would be good. We need a chat while that happens," he said, sitting down at the table with a cup of tea.

"Do we?"

"Last night, at that church. I hadn't planned to bring Alex along."

"Good. I said it'd be risky."

"Would you have given her to that thing?"

"Dex," I supplied, setting the ingredients out on the counter.

"Yeah, that. What is it?"

"It's like a little god. Maybe not even little, just old. Cruel in its abstraction. He's so big and so old he doesn't really understand the human things. Understands emotions and manipulation and greed. Doesn't rate people highly but finds us useful. Literal boss from Hell."

"Would you have given it Alex?" he asked again. His voice was quiet and low, and I could feel it was a dangerous subject for him.

"No," I replied, mostly honest. "I knew she was their plan B, as did you. It was a distraction. I couldn't have let her be part of that thing at the church. Couldn't have left her to what I couldn't abandon Sarah to."

"That's decent of you. That deal with Dex, is it going to cause you problems?"

"Oh, undoubtedly." I laughed as I poured the egg mixture into the hot pan. "But it was necessary."

"And if hurting one of us was necessary?"

"You involved in something you think'll become my business?" I looked over my shoulder with a cocked eyebrow.

"I know a person or two." He shrugged.

"I'm going to be busy training on how to use this shit, anyway. I'll be too busy with that to check you over for anything."

"You'd do it if you needed to."

"I don't plan to find out. Help me make sure that's the case and we're all good."

"Sounds fair," Marc nodded, taking the plate from my hands as I passed it over.

I set about making my own omelette and cut up enough vegetables for Sarah and Alex too. Once plated up, I joined Marc at the table.

"You giving them a lift out to the airport?" I asked between bites.

"God, no. Too hungover for that," Marc said, shaking his head. "We'll get a taxi. It won't be much if we all chip in."

"Sounds good. Want to wake them up, and I'll make more?"

"Good plan, Masterchef," Marc said, rinsing his plate in the sink and heading upstairs. I set the pan back on the heat, humming to myself before the threat of the hangover reminded me that was a bad idea. I had one omelette ready in the oven and the other almost prepared when both women piled in, worse for wear but settled.

"Food and rehydration," I said, putting the plates in front of them with a jug of water on the table.

"Thanks," said Alex, digging in.

"Sarah, do you want me in the taxi out to the airport?" I asked as I started washing up.

"Yeah, I'd like that," she said, chopping the omelette up into small pieces. "It'll be weird, but it'd be worse not seeing you."

"Alright then. Taxi fare is split four ways, cheaper for everyone," Marc said, putting the kettle on for more tea.

We pottered around the flat until it was time to head off, the expectation of the morning heavy. It was the crackle of lightning before a storm, the anticipation of the upset at the departures, emotion and stress.

The taxi ride was quiet and the airport was a scrum of people, mad as wasps. It reminded me of the bus station, the bustle of folk around and about, all milling to the same point. I hugged Sarah outside check in, kissing the top of her head and trying not to cry. She failed miserably at that, tears streaming down her face.

"It'll be okay," I whispered to her. "Nothing is good just now and it'll all hurt for a while, but it'll get better. Promise."

"Liar," she said with a miserable laugh, squeezing me tight. "I don't want to leave you here."

"You're not leaving me here. You'll be coming back to visit," I said with more confidence than I had. "And you've got to give these two hugs yet, don't cry all over them."

She laughed again and disentangled, moving to each of them in turn. Alex was a mess already, her tears almost a match for Sarah's. Little shaky sobs hiccuped out of her.

"You look after yourself, and call me, and email," she said sternly before tugging Sarah into a massive hug, clinging like she would vanish. "I only just got you back, girly. You got to make sure you keep in touch."

"I will, I will," Sarah soothed, hugging back and pulling on a wobbling smile.

Marc came up and enveloped her in his shaggy coat, the form of her body half vanishing within.

"You have to head through now," I said, watching the departure sign change from a lounge number to boarding notice.

"I'll be in touch as soon as I'm home safe. And once Mum and Dad finish fretting. What am I telling them about you?"

"Say I like the city and that Mum should give me a call."

"She's going to hit the roof," Sarah said, toying with her bag straps.

"We're alive. That's the victory." I shrugged. "We'll work it out from there."

We watched her move through to departures and made our way outside to the taxi rank, flagging someone down to take us back to the city.

"What's the plan for the rest of the day?" I asked Alex as we watched the rain fall.

"Go back to bed and check in with reality when I feel less like shit."

"Sounds good. Can I use your sofa to do the same?"

"Of course. Marc, you need one too?"

"Sleep would be nice." He nodded, head to the glass and eyes unfocused.

"Alright then, sleep and then we face the world again. Together. Onwards and upwards." I smiled despite myself, terrified and satisfied all the same.

# About the Author

**Charlotte Platt** is a young professional who writes horror and dark urban fantasy. She spent her teens on the Orkney Islands and studied in Glasgow before moving to the north Highlands. She lives off sarcasm and tea and can often be found walking near cliffs and rivers, looking for sea glass. Her short stories have been featured in *Dig Two Graves: Vol. 2*, *The Monsters We Forgot Vol. 2*, and *The Stuff of Nightmares*. She can be found on Twitter at @Chazzaroo.

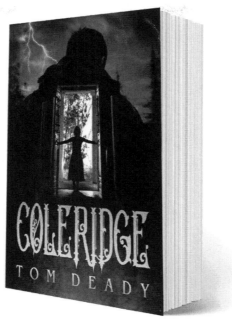

Coleridge was the start of everything for Zadie and Dalia. Their love of the old house began as a restoration project and blossomed into a love story. Until the tragedy.

Coleridge was all Dalia Cromwell had left. It served as both a tribute to their love and a harsh reminder to her loss. Until the visitor arrived.

Coleridge was his obsession. Slade knew more about the house than Dalia did. And he knew of its past. By the end of their long night together in the house, Dalia would know all of Coleridge's secrets, and Zadie's.

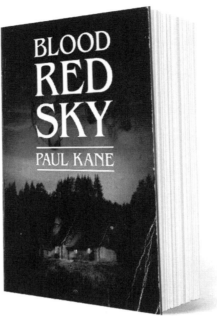

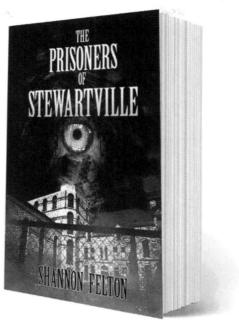

For the idyllic mountain town of Jerome, Arizona, a blizzard is coming. A storm of such magnitude, the likes of which the town hasn't seen in thirty years. Nestled at the top of the mountain is the Jerome Grand Hotel, a historic inn rumored to be haunted. The perfect setting for both a Romance writer's convention and ghost hunter enthusiasts, alike. James Landes is neither, but his wife Victoria is a writer, and he's hoping for a weekend away at her convention filled with sex, food, and fun.

But in this blizzard, there is more than snow and ice. There is an evil born from rituals of long ago, and only Jerome's lifelong residents know how to stop it. James never believed in the supernatural, but if he wants to make it out of this weekend alive, he will have to embrace it.

Printed in Great Britain
by Amazon